DEXTER IS DEAD

Center Point
Large Print

Also by Jeff Lindsay and available from
Center Point Large Print:

Double Dexter
Dexter's Final Cut

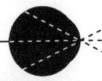

**This Large Print Book carries the
Seal of Approval of N.A.V.H.**

DEXTER
IS DEAD

JEFF LINDSAY

CENTER POINT LARGE PRINT
THORNDIKE, MAINE

This Center Point Large Print edition is published
in the year 2015 by arrangement with Doubleday,
an imprint of The Knopf Doubleday Publishing Group,
a division of Penguin Random House LLC.

This book is a work of fiction.
Names, characters, places, and incidents either are
the product of the author's imagination or are used
fictitiously. Any resemblance to actual persons,
living or dead, events, or locales is entirely coincidental.

The text of this Large Print edition is unabridged.
In other aspects, this book may vary
from the original edition.
Printed in the United States of America on permanent paper.
Set in 16-point Times New Roman type.

ISBN: 978-1-62899-645-6

Library of Congress Cataloging-in-Publication Data

Lindsay, Jeffry P.
  Dexter is dead / Jeff Lindsay. — Center Point Large Print edition.
    pages cm
  Summary: "Dexter faces a murder charge for a crime he did not
commit. His only chance for freedom lies with his brother, Brian, who
has a dark plan to prove Dexter's innocence. But the stakes are deadly,
and the epic showdown that lies in Dexter's path may lead, once and for
all, to his demise"—Provided by publisher.
  ISBN 978-1-62899-645-5 (library binding : alk. paper)
  1. Morgan, Dexter (Fictitious character)—Fiction.
    2. Forensic scientists—Fiction. 3. Serial murderers—Fiction.
    4. Large type books. I. Title.
PS3562.I51175D475 2015b
  813'.54—dc23
                                                    2015015441

This book is dedicated to the Dex-heads—all the people, all around the world, who made a place in their hearts for My Little Monster, and by doing so, made me feel special for a few years. It would never have happened without you. Thank you.

It is also dedicated to three special spirits— Bear, Pookie, and Tink—who are my reason for living (and for getting old).

And above all, to Hilary, who is everything to me.

ACKNOWLEDGMENTS

I would like to thank Samantha Steinberg for her continued help. She provided valuable background, and some real-life inspiration for a few of the plot points in this book. She also got me inside Turner Guilford Knight Correctional Center—in a *good* way.

At TGK, I am indebted to Captain Richardson, who took time out of her hectic schedule to talk to me, answer my questions, and suggest things I should see. Sergeant Faure, too, was generous with his time and knowledge. And to Officer Rondon, who led me around the center, my special thanks. He was incredibly helpful, thoughtful, and thoroughly professional. Without the help of these people, I could not have written what I did. They are very good people doing a very hard job—and doing it well.

My thanks also to Alexander J. Perkins, of Perkins Law Offices in Miami, who advised me on some of the legal matters in this book, and to Julius, for his advice on music, war, and Zen.

My gratitude also goes to my editor, Jason Kaufman, for kicking the whole thing off—

—and to my agent and friend, Nick Ellison, who made it happen. Thank you, St. Nick.

ONE

I T WASN'T SUPPOSED TO END THIS WAY.
In a flash of steel, yes; a flurry of gunshots, a chorus of strangled moans and anguished sighs, blending with the distant wail of sirens, certainly. A properly dramatic ending with a good body count, a futile struggle against impending doom, even a dash of treachery, absolutely. And then the fatal blow, a few moments of anguish, a last sigh filled with regret for things undone, and fade to black: a fitting end for a life of wicked pleasure.

But not like this.

Not with Dexter in Durance, horribly wronged, slandered, unjustly accused of doing terrible things that he did not even get to do. Not *this* time, that is. *This* time, this one catastrophic multi-homicidal time, Dexter is as innocent as the driven snow—or perhaps the sand on South Beach would be more apt. Although truth be told, nothing on South Beach is really innocent, any more than Dexter, whose catalog of wicked whimsical works is, to be fair, quite lengthy. It just doesn't include anything from current events, more's the pity. Not *this* time.

And not like this. Not locked away in the tiny chill ill-smelling cell in Turner Guilford Knight Correctional Center—and on the top floor, at that, the special purgatory reserved for the most heinous and unrepentant monsters. Every basic freedom ripped away. Every moment, waking and sleeping, subject to scrutiny. Dexter's entire world reduced to this tiny cell, no more than a thick steel door and even thicker concrete block walls, broken only by a slim slit that lets in light but does not let out sight. A narrow metal shelf with a thin and battered thing on it, laughingly referred to as a "mattress." A sink, a toilet, a shelf. Dexter's World.

And no more than this, no connection at all to the outside, beyond the narrow slot in the door that delivers the Officially Nutritious meals. No Internet, no television, no radio, nothing that might distract me from contemplation of my many uncommitted sins. Of course, I may request reading matter—but I have found through bitter experience that the two most popular titles in the library are "Not Allowed" and "Don't Have It."

Regrettable, lamentable, even pitiable. Poor Sad-Sack Dexter, tossed on the sterile institutional scrap heap.

But, of course, who could have sympathy for a monster like me? Or as we must all say in these days of conscience fueled by lawsuits, *alleged* monster. And they do allege it. The cops, the courts, the correctional system itself, and my dear sister, Deborah—even I, if pressed, will allege that I am, in fact, a monster. And I truly did, without allegement of any kind, flee the scene wherein lay the murdered body of Jackie Forrest, famous actress, and coincidentally known to be my paramour. I was then discovered *in flagrante sangre*, with the bodies of my wife, Rita, and Robert the famous actor, not to mention the very much alive but scantily clad Astor, my twelve-year-old adoptive daughter. She it was who killed Robert "Famous Actor" Chase, who had dressed her in a negligee and then killed Rita. Poor bumbler that I am, I stumbled in to Set Things Right and instead tumbled it all into deep, dark, endless, and possibly permanent Wrong—and very nearly became Robert's next victim.

My story is simple, straightforward, and unassailable. I learned Robert was a pedophile and had taken Astor. While I looked for him, he killed Jackie. And as one final irony in our King of Fools Crown Derby, Rita—helpless, hapless, hopeless Rita, Queen of the Scatterbrained Monologue Dear Ditzy Rita, who could not find her own car keys if they were welded to her fist—*Rita* found him before I did. Robert thumped her on the head, from which blow she died while Robert was busy thumping me and planning a romantic escape with his True Love, Astor. While I lay bound and helpless, Astor stuck a knife in Robert, set me free, and so ended this zany, madcap adventure of Doofus Dexter, Bumbler Extraordinaire. If there really is a God, which is, at very best, extremely debatable, he has a terrible sense of humor. Because the detective in charge of deciphering the carnage is Detective Anderson, a man who has lived his life without making a friend of intelligence, wit, or competence. And possibly because I am so very liberally endowed with all three, and additionally because he knew me to be intimate with Miss Forrest, a thing he could only drool and dream of, Detective Anderson abso-lutely, without compromise, hates me. Loathes, despises, detests, and abhors the very air I breathe. And so my simple story quickly became an Alibi, which is never a good thing. Even quicker, I moved from Person of Interest to Suspect, and then . . . Detective Anderson took one quick glance at the crime scenes and formed a simple conclusion, undoubtedly the only kind he *can* form. Aha, quoth he, Dexter Done It. Justice is served. Or words to that effect, probably a great deal simpler and less elegant, but in any case resulting in my promotion from Suspect to Perpetrator.

And I, still reeling from the death of Jackie, my ticket to a new and better life, plus the death of Rita and her entire book of delightful recipes, and the sight of Astor in a white silk negligee—still reeling, I say, from the utter destruction of All the Order and Certainty that was Dexter's World, past, present, and future—I find myself hauled roughly to my feet, handcuffed with hands behind my back, and chained to the floor of a squad car, which drives me to Turner Guilford Knight Correctional Facility.

Without a kind word or sympathetic glance from anyone, I am led, still draped with cold steel chains, inside the huge concrete, barbed wire–bedecked building, and into a room that looks like the waiting room of the Greyhound station in Hell. The room is full to overflowing with desperate characters—killers and rapists and thugs and gangsters all, my kind of people! But I am given no time at all to sit and consort with my fellow alleged monsters, no chance for a Hail Felon, Well Met. Instead, I am hustled straight through to the next room, where I am photographed, fingerprinted, stripped, and issued a lovely orange jumpsuit. It is fashionably baggy, and the bright colors say *spring!* The aroma, however, has a less cheery message, blooming somewhere between insecticide and lemon candies made from old Chinese drywall. But I am given no choice of color, nor of odor, and so I proudly wear the orange, which after all is one of the trademark colors of my alma mater, the University of Miami.

And then, still festooned with restraints, I am brought here, to my new home, the ninth floor, and deposited without ceremony in my present tidy nook.

And here I sit in TGK. The joint, the slammer,

the Big House. One small cog in the gigantic correctional wheel, which itself is only a little piece of the massive and coldly incompetent machine that is Justice. Dexter is now being Corrected. What is it, I wonder, that they hope to Correct? I am what I am, irredeemably, irretrievably, implacably—as are most of my fellow desperadoes here on nine. We are monsters, stamped from birth with forbidden hungers, and these can no more be Corrected than can the need to breathe. Bird gotta whistle, fish gotta swim, and Dexter gotta find and flense the slippery wicked predators. However InCorrect that may be, it irreversibly Is.

But I am in the Correctional System now, subject to its clockwork whims and institutional hardness. I am no more than an unCorrectable error waiting to be Corrected while the proper forms are filled out and filed and forgotten, however long that may take. Parenthetically, it *does* seem to be taking quite a while. There is some small tidbit of arcane Constitutional Trivia rattling around in my poor withered brain that mumbles something about a speedy trial—and I have not even been arraigned. Surely this is somewhat irregular? But I am offered no company other than my guards, and they are not terribly chatty, and I have no opportunity to make the acquaintance of anyone else who might answer my polite questions about due process.

So I am forced into the ludicrous position of trusting in the system—a system that I know far too well is far from trustworthy.

And in the meantime? I wait.

Life is, at least, simple and regular. I am awakened at four-thirty a.m. by a cheerful bell. Shortly after, the slot in my cell's door, sealed over by a steel flap that is held shut by a very strong spring, reluctantly opens and my breakfast tray comes through on the metal tongue of the cart made for that purpose. Ah, delectable viands! Institutional cereal, toast, coffee, juice. Almost edible, and there is nearly enough! What bliss.

Lunch is similarly delivered, at ten-thirty. It is an even greater flight of gourmet abandon—a sandwich containing a cheeselike substance, carefully hidden under a piece of soft and fluffy green stuff that is clearly synthetic recycled iceberg lettuce. Beside it on the tray, some lemonade, an apple, and a cookie.

In the afternoon, under the watchful eyes of my shepherd, Lazlo, I am permitted an hour of solitary exercise in the Yard. It is not really a yard at all; there are no trees, no grass, no lawn chairs or toys. It is in fact a wedge-shaped concrete floor whose only virtues are that it is open to the sky and contains a netless basketball hoop. Of course, this time of year it is usually raining in the afternoon, and so even this small virtue is somewhat double-edged. I also discover that once

I am In The Yard, I must stay there for the full hour, or go back to my cell. I learn to enjoy the rain. And soaking wet, I return to my cell. Dinner at five. Lights-out at ten. A simple life of modest comforts. So far the great rewards one reaps from solitude and simplicity, as promised by Thoreau, have not been forthcoming, but perhaps they will emerge in time. And Time is the one thing I have plenty of.

Ten days in jail. I wait. To a lesser man, the endless spell of oppressive nothingness might seem stifling, even soul-destroying. But, of course, Dexter has no soul, if such things even exist. And so I find a great deal to do. I count the concrete blocks in my wall. I arrange my toothbrush. I attempt mental games of chess, and when I can't remember where the pieces are, I switch to checkers and then, when that fails, to Go Fish. I always win.

I pace my cell. It's large enough to permit me almost two full steps. When I tire of this, I do push-ups. I do a little tai chi, bumping my fists on the walls with nearly every move.

And I wait. From my wide reading, I know that the greatest danger of solitary incarceration is the temptation to succumb to the dreadful weight of tedium, sink into the stress-free bliss of insanity. I know that if I do, I will never get out, never resume my safe and sane normal life of happy wage slave by day, even happier Knight of the Knife by night. I must hold on, keep a tight grip on what passes for sanity in this vale of tears, hold on white-knuckled to the absurd and baseless belief that innocence still counts for something and I Am Truly Innocent . . . relatively speaking. In *this* case, at least.

I have certain knowledge, based on vast experience with That Old Whore Justice, that Actual Innocence has nearly as much influence on my fate as the starting lineup for the Marlins. But I cling to hope anyway, because anything else is unthinkable. How can I face even one more hour of this if I don't believe that eventually it will end—with me on the outside? Even the thought of endless cheeselike sandwiches is no comfort. I must believe, blindly, unreasonably, even stupidly, that someday Truth will out, Justice will prevail, and Dexter will be free to run laughing into the sunlight. And, of course, smirking into the moon-light, sliding softly through the velvet dark with a knife and a need—

I shiver. Mustn't get ahead of myself. Must avoid such thoughts, fantasies of freedom that steal focus from right now and what to do about it. I must remain here mentally, as well as physically, right here in my snug little cell, and concentrate on getting out.

Once more I flip through my mental ledger and add up the blurred and uncertain figures. On the plus side, I really and truly am innocent. I didn't do it. Not even some of it. Not me.

On the minus side, it sure looks like I did.

And worse, the entire Miami police force would like to see someone like me convicted for these crimes. They very publicly promised to protect our two Famous Actors, and more publicly failed to do so. And if the killer was some plausible insider—me again—they are off the hook. So if the officer in charge is willing to bend things a little bit, he almost certainly will.

Even more minus: Detective Anderson is in charge. He will not merely bend things; he will mangle them, hammer them into the shape he wants, and serve them up in sworn testimony. He has, in fact, already done so, and it must be said that the legion of Wonderful Haircuts that constitutes the media has been eating it up, for the very simple reason that it is *simple,* as simple as they are, which is possibly even simpler than Anderson, a shudder-inducing thought. They have lunged to grab my guilt with both greedy fists, and the photo of Dexter Arrested, according to Lazlo, has festooned the front pages and adorned the evening news for over a week now. The picture shows me draped in chains, head bowed, face set in a mask of stunned indifference, and I must say I look extremely guilty, even to me. And I do not need to point out that, moral clichés to the contrary, Appearances do not Deceive, not in our age of Instant Summarized Sound-Bite Certainty. I am guilty because I look guilty. And I look guilty because Detective Anderson wishes it.

Anderson wants me dead, enough so that he will cheerfully perjure himself to get me halfway there. Even if he didn't loathe me, he would do it because he has a professional hatred for my sister, Sergeant Deborah, who he quite rightly sees as a rival, and one who must eventually surpass him by a considerable margin. But if her brother—*c'est moi!*—is a convicted murderer, this would almost certainly derail the mighty choo-choo of Deb's career track, and consequently advance his.

I do the math. On one side: Anderson, the entire police force, the media, and most likely the pope himself.

On the other side, my innocence.

This does not add up to a terribly encouraging bottom line.

But surely there is more. Certainly it could never end like this. Somewhere, somehow, isn't it absolutely essential to the immutable principals of Balance, Righteousness, and a healthy GNP that some small but powerful hole card exists? Shouldn't it be true that some unknown but potent force will emerge and set things right? Somehow, somewhere, isn't there *something?*

There is.

Unknown to the forces of evil and indifference that grind so ponderously powerfully slow, there is an equal and opposing force that even now must be gathering its irresistible strength for one mighty, liberating blast of Truth that will topple the whole rotten mess and set Dexter Free.

Deborah. My sister.

She will come and save me. She *must*.

This, I must confess, is my one Happy Thought. Deborah is my Forlorn Hope, the tiny ray of sunshine trickling into the dark and dreary night of Dexter's Detention. Deborah will come. She must, she will. And she will help me, her only living relative, the last of the Morgans. Together we will find a way to prove my innocence and spring me from this, my soul-crushing confinement. She will breeze in like the winds of April, and the doors will spring open at her touch. Deborah will come and end Dexter's Durance Vile. Put aside for the moment the memory of Deborah's last words to me. These words were far from supportive, and some might even say they were rather Final. They were spoken in the heat of an unpleasant moment, and not to be taken at face value in any permanent sense. Remember instead the deep and abiding bonds of family that lock us unchangeably together. Deborah will come.

The fact that she has not come yet, has not in any way communicated with me, should not really trouble me. It is almost certainly a strategic move, creating the appearance of indifference to lull our enemies into complacency. When the time is right, she will come, I must not doubt it. Of course she will come; she's my sister. This implies quite strongly that I am her brother, and it's exactly the sort of thing one does for Family. I would do it for her, willingly and even cheerfully, and so I know for a stone-cold fact that she will do it for me. Without even a moment of doubt, I know it. Deborah will come.

Eventually. Sooner or later. I mean, where *is* she?

The days pass, and inevitably they turn into weeks—two of them now—and she has not come. She has not called; she has not written. No secret note written in butter and pressed into my sandwich. Nothing at all, and I am still here, in my ultrasecure cell, my little kingdom of solitude. I read, I ponder, and I exercise. And what I exercise most is my healthy sense of very justified bitterness. Where is Deborah? Where is Justice? Both are as elusive as Diogenes' Honest Man. I ponder the thought that I, above all, should be reduced to hoping for real justice—a justice that, if it frees me as it should, has clearly done an outrageous *In*justice by turning me loose to resume my beloved pastime. It is ironic, like so much of my present circumstance.

But out of the many ironies in my current unhappy contretemps, perhaps the worst of all is that I, Dexter the Monster, Dexter the Ultimate Outsider, Dexter the Nonhuman—I, too, am reduced in extremis to that ultimate human lament: Why Me?

TWO

THE DAYS PASS INDISTINGUISHABLY. Dull routine plods along in the wake of dull routine. Nothing, in short, Happens that has not already happened yesterday and the day before, and will almost certainly happen again the next day, and the next, and the next, ad infinitum. No visitors, no mail, no calls, no sign at all that Dexter still has any sort of existence outside of this unchanging unending unpleasant one.

And yet, I hope. This cannot continue eternally, can it? Something must someday happen. It is not possible that I should be a permanent fixture here, on the ninth floor of TGK, perpetually repeating the same small and meaningless rituals by rote. Someone will realize a monstrous injustice has been done, and the machine will spit me out. Or perhaps Anderson himself, overcome with shame, will perform a public mea culpa and set me free in person. Of course, it is more likely that I should burrow through the concrete block walls with my toothbrush—but surely there will be *something*. And if nothing else, sooner or later, some bright day, Deborah will come.

Of course she will. I hold on to that certainty, raising it in my mind to the status of Immutable Eternal Truth, something as certain as the law of gravity. Deborah will come. In the meantime, I know that at the very least, TGK is not a prison. It is merely a detention center, intended for temporarily housing the provisionally wicked until such time as their promotion to Enemy of Society is made permanent. They can't keep me here forever.

I mention this in passing to my shepherd, Lazlo, as he escorts me to my daily stint of sitting in the yard and enjoying the rain. They can't, I say, keep me here forever.

Lazlo laughs—not cruelly, it must be said, but with a certain wry, institutional amusement. "The guy in the cell next to you?" he says. "Know who he is?"

"We haven't met," I admit. In fact, I haven't seen any occupant of the other cells.

"You remember, I think it was 1983?" Lazlo says.

"Not very well," I say.

"There was a guy drove his car into the mall and opened up with an automatic weapon? Killed fourteen people?" he says.

I do remember that. Everyone in Miami, whatever their age, remembers. "I remember."

Lazlo nods at the cell next to mine. "That's him," he says. "Still awaiting trial."

I blink.

"Oh," I say. "Can they do that to me?"

He shrugs. "Sure looks like it."

"But how?"

"It's all politics," he says. "The right people squeeze the right place and . . ." He makes a whaddaya-gonna-do gesture that I am sure I saw on *The Sopranos*.

"I think I need to see a lawyer," I tell him.

He shakes his head sadly. "I retire in a year and a half," he says. And with this apparent non sequitur our conversation is over and I am buttoned securely into my cell once more.

And as I arrange my toothbrush yet again I reconsider: Perhaps they actually *can* keep me here forever. That would avoid all the fuss, bother, and expense of a trial, with its accompanying risk of Freedom for Dexter. That would certainly be the tidiest solution for Anderson and the depart-ment. And later, as I sit down in the afternoon rain once more, I ponder that. Forever seems like a very long time.

But everything must end, even Eternity. And one fine gray institutional day, indistinguishable from all the others, my unending routine ends, too.

As I sit in my cell, alphabetizing my bar of soap, I hear the metallic sounds of my cell door opening. I look up; it is eleven-thirty-four a.m., too soon for my au naturel shower in the Yard. That makes this a unique event, and my eager little heart goes pitter-pat with anticipation. What can it be? Surely it must be a reprieve, a last-minute stay of tedium from the governor—or perhaps even Deborah at last, triumphantly clutching my release papers.

Time slows; the door swings inward at a slothful pace that defies possibility—until finally it comes to rest in the full open position to reveal Lazlo. "Your lawyer's here," he says.

It gives me pause. I did not know I had a lawyer—which is to his benefit, since I would otherwise have sued him for neglect. And I have certainly not had the chance to get one, either. Could it be that my one small comment to Lazlo has caused him enough uneasiness with the vast injustice of Justice that *he* arranged this?

Lazlo gives no indication, and no chance for me to ask. "Come on," he says, and I need no further urging. I leap to my feet and let Lazlo lead me on a long and wondrous journey across ten full feet of floor. It seems a nearly endless expedition after the tiny cell—and also because I have become convinced that Freedom Awaits. And so I trudge forever across the floor and arrive at last at the large, thick slab of bulletproof glass that is my window on the world. On the opposite side sits a man in a very cheap-looking dark gray suit. He is thirtyish, balding, bespectacled, and he looks weary, harried, and hassled beyond measure. He is gazing down at a stack of official-seeming papers, flipping hurriedly through them and frowning, as if this is the first time he has seen them and he does not like what he sees. He is, in short, the very picture of an overworked public defender, a man who is engaged in principle but having trouble maintaining interest in specifics. And since I actually *am* the specifics in this case, his appearance does not fill me with confidence.

"Siddown," Lazlo says, not unkindly.

I sit in the chair provided, and eagerly lift the old-fashioned telephone receiver that hangs to one side of the window.

My lawyer does not look up. He continues to flip through the papers until, at last, he comes to a page that seems to surprise him. His frown deepens, and he looks up at me and speaks. Of course, I do not hear what he says, since he has not picked up the phone, but at least I can see his lips moving.

I hold up my phone and raise my eyebrows politely. *See? Electric communication. It's wonderful! You should try it sometime—perhaps now?*

My lawyer looks slightly startled. He drops the wad of paper and picks up the phone, and almost immediately I hear his voice.

"Uh, Dieter," he says.

"Dexter," I tell him. "With an 'X.'"

"My name is Bernie Feldman; I'm your court-appointed attorney."

"Pleased to meet you," I tell him.

"Okay, listen," he says—unnecessarily, since I am doing nothing but. "Let's go over what will happen at your arraignment."

"When is that?" I ask with keen interest. I find that I am suddenly, stupidly eager for arraignment. It will at least get me out of my cell for a few hours.

"The law says within forty-eight hours of your arrest," he says impatiently.

"I've been here two and a half weeks," I tell him.

He frowns, tucks the phone between ear and shoulder, and looks at the papers. He shakes his head. "That's not possible," he says, digging deeper into the paperwork. Or I assume from the motion of his mouth that he says that. I do not hear him say it, since the act of shaking his head causes the phone to lurch off his shoulder and swing down to the end of its cord, smashing into the concrete wall with a thunderous crash that leaves me half-deaf in one ear.

I switch ears. My lawyer picks up the phone.

"According to this," Bernie says, "you were arrested last night."

"Bernie," I say. The use of his name appears to offend him, and he frowns, but flips a page and continues to look at the papers. "Bernie. Look at me," I say, and I admit I am pleased with the vaguely sinister sound of it. Bernie looks up at last. "Have you seen my face before?" I ask. "In the paper, on TV?"

Bernie stares. "Yes, of course," he says. "But . . . that was a couple of weeks ago, wasn't it?"

"Two and a *half* weeks," I say again. "And I have been here ever since."

"But that's . . . I don't see how . . ." Once again he flutters through the assembled pages, and once again the phone leaps off his shoulder and smashes into the wall. Now I am half-deaf in both ears. By the time Bernie has the phone wedged between his shoulder and ear again, the ringing sound has subsided to slightly less than symphonic levels, enough so that I can hear him.

"I'm sorry," he says. "There's some problem with the paperwork. It's completely . . . Did you have a psych evaluation?"

"I don't think so," I admit.

"Ah," he says. He looks relieved. "Okay, well—I think we should set that up in any case, right? Because to kill all those people like that—"

"I didn't kill them, Bernie," I tell him. "I'm innocent."

He waves that off. "And the pedophile thing, you know. That's being reclassified as a mental illness? So we can work that, too."

I open my mouth to protest that I am innocent of pedophilia, too—but Bernie drops the receiver again, and I choose to save my hearing instead, yanking the phone away from my ear and waiting patiently until he picks it up.

"So anyway, the arraignment has to be within forty-eight hours. The law. So it should have. . . ." He frowns again, and pulls out one stapled stack

26

of papers. "Except—shit, I didn't see this before." His lips move as he reads, flips quickly through three pages to the end, frowns heavily. "Didn't see this," he repeats. "Shit."

"What is it?" I ask.

He shakes his head but miraculously keeps his grip on the phone. "I don't get it," he mutters. "This doesn't make any—" Bernie flips through the entire stack once more, apparently without finding anything he likes. "Well, shit, this changes everything," he says briskly.

"In a good way?" I ask hopefully.

"This whole . . . The paperwork is . . ." He shakes his head.

This time I am ready, and with the lightning reflexes for which I am justly famous, I hold the phone away from my ear as, once again, Bernie drops his end. Even from a safe distance, I hear the crash.

I put the phone back to my ear and watch as Bernie juggles the stack of papers, vainly trying to shove it into some state that resembles neatness.

"All right," he says. "I'm going to look into this. I'll be back," he promises, without sounding even vaguely sinister.

"Thank you," I say, since good manners must prevail even in the darkest circumstance. But Bernie is already gone.

I hang up the phone and turn around. My faithful companion, Lazlo, is right there, and he nods at me to stand. "Let's go, Dex," he says. I rise, still in something of a fog, and Lazlo takes me back to my snug little alcove. I sit down on my bunk, and for once I don't feel the hardness underneath the pitifully thin "mattress." There is much to ponder: arraignment within forty-eight hours of arrest, for starters. It rings a dim bell, summoning up some faint memory from a criminal justice class long ago at UM. I believe I recall that it is one of my most basic rights, along with Presumption of Innocence, and the fact that Anderson has managed to avoid both is very troubling. Clearly things are much worse than even I could anticipate.

I think of my next-door neighbor, here since 1983. I wonder if Detective Anderson's father arrested him. I wonder whether some gray-bearded version of Dexter will still be sitting here in thirty years, listening to some future version of Lazlo, perhaps even a robotic one, telling some new hopeless ninny that poor feeble-witted old Dexter has been here all along, still awaiting arraignment. I wonder if I will have any teeth left by then. Not that I need them for the cheese-substance sandwiches. But teeth are good things to have in any case. They improve your smile, no matter how fake it is. And without teeth, all the money I have spent on toothpaste over the years would be a complete waste.

I vow to keep my teeth. In any case, I am more

worried at this point about keeping my mind. The reality of my situation is not in any way encouraging. I am trapped in a true nightmare, confined to a small and inescapable space, with absolutely no control of anything at all, except possibly my breathing. Even this, I am quite sure, would be out of my control if I decide to stop it. Suicide is actively discouraged here for some reason, in spite of the fact that it would help reduce overcrowding, save money, and lighten the workload for Lazlo and his comrades.

No way out, no power over my own fate, no end to it all—and now, with a surreal flourish of bureaucratic cruelty, my court-appointed attorney has informed me that my papers are not in order, without informing me what that means. Naturally I assume the implications are ominous. I know very well that things can always get worse—the kitchen might run out of cheeselike substance— but really, isn't there a point where even a hypothetical god has heaped on enough? No matter how furious he is at Dexter for violating some basic Rules of the Playground, haven't we piled on sufficient fecal matter?

Apparently not.

The very next day, Things do indeed get worse.

Once again I am sitting in my cell, busily engaged in productive and industrious activity—a nap, to be honest. I have begun to feel the need for naps, and my luncheon has encouraged the feeling. Today's delightful viands included a sandwich of Probable Chicken, Jell-O, and a red liquid whose taste might have been intended to evoke some sort of association with an unspecified fruit. The experience was exhausting, and I had to stretch out on my bed almost immediately to recover.

After far too brief a time, I hear once more the heavy metallic sounds of my door opening. I sit up; Lazlo is there. But this time his hands are full of chains. "On your feet," he says.

"My arraignment?" I ask hopefully.

He shakes his head. "Detective to see you," he says. "Turn around."

I follow his brisk instructions and in a few moments I am securely bound. Once more I allow the small white bird that is hope to flutter from its perch and begin to wing away across the exceeding dark of Dexter's Inner Sky. "Detective" could mean many things—but one of them is Deborah, and I cannot stop myself from thinking she has come at last.

Lazlo leads me out of the cell—but this time not to the thick window where Bernie shattered my eardrums. We walk on past the window, all the way over to the door that leads out, off the cell block. Lazlo must use his radio and his ID card, and then wave at the female guard who controls the doors. She sits in the center of the cell block in a glass-walled booth. There is a row of thick windows around the cells and then a deep, two-story well of space before the second row of windows that surrounds her booth. The booth is like an indoor airport's control tower, standing in the middle in isolation, completely inaccessible from here, unless one has a bazooka and a good ladder, and possessing such things is generally discouraged here.

The woman in the booth looks up at Lazlo's wave, checks her computer screen and monitors, and a moment later the door clicks open. We step through into a room the size of a large closet and the door closes behind us. Two steps forward and we face another door. Lazlo nods at the camera above the door, and a moment later it opens and we are in the hall. Five more steps to the elevator—and crossing such vast space is dizzying after the tight confinement of my cell. But somehow I manage, and in only a moment or two we are in the elevator. The door closes and I am back within four snug walls, relaxing in the comfort of a space more like the one I am used to now, something the size of my cell. I take a deep breath, enjoying the security.

The door slides open. Lazlo leads me out—to my surprise, we are on the ground floor. Ahead of me I can see what must be the lobby. Beyond a brace of armed guards there is a crowd of people milling around. They are unchained and wearing normal clothing, clearly waiting for something—

to get in? I feel privileged—I didn't know I lived in such desirable housing. We even have a waiting list.

But I don't get a chance to tell them all about the wonderful accommodations and gourmet meals. Lazlo takes me away from the lobby and down a corridor, past several guards and a few orange-suited inmates busily sweeping and mopping. They move hurriedly out of our way, as though afraid I might infect them with Felony Fever.

It seems like quite a voyage to Dexter the Dedicated Homebody. Such a long way to travel, and all to see a detective—a detective who must, I am sure, be my sister. My heart flutters with expectation; I can't help it. I have been waiting far too long for Deborah to arrive and strike the vile fetters from my lily-white limbs. And here she is at last; it can only have taken so long because she has banished the ludicrous charges against me and arranged everything. I will be not merely bailed out, but set free at last.

And so I fight to keep my hopes from rising up and drowning me, but I do not succeed very well. I am very nearly singing when we come at last to our destination, and it is not a place that speaks in any way of freedom. It is a small room deep within the bowels of the building, with windows on three sides. A table and chairs are visible inside; it is clearly an interrogation room, just the place for a detective to meet with a suspect, and not at all the kind of place where an Avenging Fury might stand to strike off my fetters.

Visible through the windows is a more-or-less human form that has no resemblance at all to a Fury, although it does look somewhat grumpy. It has even less resemblance to Deborah, Freedom, and especially Hope. It is, in fact, the very embodiment of the exact opposite of all these things.

In short, it is Detective Anderson. He looks up and sees me through the glass, and he smiles. It is not a smile that encourages in me any of the finer feelings. It is instead a smile that says to me, quite clearly, it is time for all Hope to die.

Hope obliges.

THREE

LAZLO HOLDS MY ARM AS HE OPENS THE door, perhaps afraid that the sight of Anderson will turn my knees to jelly and render me incapable of maintaining an upright posture. He pauses in the doorway, and of necessity, so do I.

"Wait outside," Anderson says, still smiling at me.

Lazlo doesn't move. "You alone?" he asks.

"You see anybody else?" Anderson sneers.

"Supposed to be two of you," Lazlo says, stubbornly refusing to move.

"I'm not afraid of this fuckhead," Anderson says.

"It's regulations," Lazlo says. "*Two* of you."

"Listen, chump," Anderson says. "My regulations say I'm a cop and you're a fucking corrections clown. Wait outside."

Lazlo shakes his head, looks at me. "Seventeen months and I retire," he says. He looks at Anderson and shakes his head again, then turns to go, closing the door behind him.

"Well, fuckhead," Detective Anderson says in cheerful greeting when we are finally alone. "How d'you like it here?"

"It's very nice," I tell him. "You should try it sometime."

His smile morphs into a sneer, an expression that is much more natural for him. "I don't think so," he says.

"Suit yourself," I say. I move to a chair, and Anderson scowls.

"I didn't tell you to sit," he says.

"That's true," I say, "which is unusual for you." I sit. For a moment he thinks he might stand up and smack me out of my chair. I smile patiently at him and glance at the window, where Lazlo stands. He's watching us and talking into his radio. Anderson decides against smacking me and slumps back into his chair.

"What did your lawyer say?" he asks me.

It's a surprisingly illegal question, even from a malignant pimple like Anderson. "Why do you want to know?" I say.

"Just answer, fuckhead," he says with massive authority.

"I don't think so. That's privileged information," I tell him.

"Not to me," he says.

"Especially to you," I say. "But maybe you were absent the day they went over that in middle school." I smile. "Or more likely you never got as far as middle school. That would explain a lot."

"Wiseass," he says.

"Is dumb ass better? I mean, in your experience?"

He has at least lost his annoying smirk, but it

has been replaced by a rather alarming flush of color and an angry frown. This is clearly not going the way he had fantasized. As someone with recent professional acting experience, I wonder briefly whether I should grovel and plead, just to play out his script, but I decide against it; my character just wouldn't *do* that. "You're in a lot of fucking trouble," he snarls. "If you're so fucking smart, you'll cooperate a little."

"Detective, I *am* cooperating," I say. "But you have to give me something to cooperate *with*. Hopefully something legal, and not too stupid. Unlikely as that might be, coming from you."

Anderson takes a deep breath and shakes his head. "Fucking wiseass," he says. "You know why I'm here?"

I did know; he was here to gloat. But since he probably didn't know that word, I decided to avoid it. "You're here because you know I'm innocent," I say instead. "And you're hoping I have found the *real* killer, because you know that even locked up in here, I have a better chance of solving a crime than you do."

"I solved it," he says. He lifts a huge, meaty finger and jabs it at me. "You're it."

I looked at Anderson. His face was full of anger, venom, dislike for me, and above all, impenetrable stupidity. It was possible that he actually thought I was guilty, or had talked himself into believing it. I didn't think so. "If you say it enough times, you might actually believe it," I say.

"I don't have to believe it," he snarls. "I just have to make a judge believe it."

"Good luck with that," I say, even though he is apparently having quite good luck so far even without my wishes.

Anderson takes another deep breath, letting his face relax into its more natural uncomprehending scowl. "I need to know what your lawyer said," he says again.

"Better ask him," I say, helpfully adding, "his name is Bernie."

Before Anderson can do any more than drum his fingers on the tabletop, the door opens. "Time's up," Lazlo says. "Prisoner has to go."

"I'm not done with him," Anderson says without looking up.

"Yes, you are," Lazlo says firmly.

"Who says?"

"I do," says a new voice, and now Anderson looks up.

A woman steps out from behind Lazlo. She is tall, African American, and good-looking in a severe way. She is also wearing a uniform, and her uniform spells trouble for Anderson, because it quite clearly says she is a captain, and she is looking directly at Detective Anderson with an expression that falls far short of friendly cooperation. "I don't know what you think you're pulling here, Detective," she says, "but you're done. Get out." Anderson opens his mouth to say something, and the captain steps closer. "Now," she says quietly, and Anderson closes his mouth so fast I can hear his teeth click. He stands up, looks at me, and I smile. Anderson very obligingly turns red again, and then turns away and stalks out through the door that Lazlo is holding so politely open for him.

I am on the verge of thanking the captain, perhaps offering her a hearty handshake—even a hug—when she turns steely brown eyes on me, her expression leaving no doubt at all that no profession of gratitude on my part, however sincere, would be welcome, and a hug is quite clearly out of the picture.

The captain turns away, facing Lazlo. "I don't need any paperwork this time," she says, and Lazlo heaves a sigh of relief. "But if that dickhead comes back, I want to know about it."

"Okay, Captain," Lazlo says. She nods and stalks out the door, which Lazlo holds even more politely for her.

When she has vanished around a turn in the corridor, Lazlo looks at me and says, "Let's go, Dex."

I stand up. "I think I should say thank-you . . . ?" I say, rather tentatively.

Lazlo shakes his head. "Forget it," he says. "I didn't do it for you. Can't fucking *stand* an

38

asshole cop. Come on," he finishes seamlessly, and with his hand on my elbow, I totter along: down the hall, into the elevator, up to nine, through the airlock, and back once more to the tiny world of my cell. The door closes behind me with absolute certainty and I am Dexter the Chrononaut again, spinning silently through endless empty time in my little steel-and-concrete capsule.

I stretch out on my bunk, but this time I do not nap. This time I have Things to ponder. And ponder I do.

First and most interesting: Thanks to the captain, I now knew that Anderson was "up to something." This was highly significant. I had known, of course, that he was cutting corners—many of them quite savagely. And I had been sure he was shading the truth, shaping the evidence, coloring events. All these things are Standard Issue, part and parcel of regular Shoddy Police Work, which was, after all, the only kind Anderson could do.

But if he was "up to something" in any official way—and the captain had hinted that he was—then perhaps there was some small and exploitable opening for Dexter to wiggle at, expand, turn into a doorway to freedom.

I added that to what dear Bernie, my lawyer, had said: The paperwork wasn't right. Instead of viewing that with alarm, as evidence that they could keep me here forever, I began to look at it as more ammunition in my anti-Anderson salvo. He had committed hanky-panky with *paperwork,* and if something in the System is committed to paper, it becomes transubstantiated into a Sacred Relic. To violate any official and therefore consecrated paperwork was a Cardinal Sin, and it could well result in Anderson's utter ruin. *If* I could prove it—and get the right person to see it. A big "if," but a vital one. Because Anderson wasn't keeping me here: *paperwork* was. And if that paperwork was desecrated . . . ?

We read every day of some vile perpetrator of dark deeds, turned loose on an undeserving world because Proper Procedure had been neglected. Just this once, why couldn't the vile perpetrator be me?

And if Procedure was not merely neglected but willfully falsified, and if I could prove it . . . It was at least possible that the consequences for Anderson might go far beyond administrative scolding, suspension, even loss of pay. He might actually be sent here, perhaps even to the very cell I walked out of. The sheer poetic, balanced beauty of that possibility was dizzying, and I contemplated it for a long time. Switch places with Anderson. Why not?

Of course, first I had to find out a few relevant details. And then find a way to bring them to the attention of a proper authority of some kind—a judge? Perhaps the judge at my arraignment, when it someday came along—if ever? If Anderson kept me here permanently without arraignment, as it seemed he was doing so far, I couldn't wait. Forever was much too long. I had to find someone on the outside to get the information to a judge, or even to Captain Matthews. Someone, yes—and who? It could only be Deborah, of course. No one else had the skill, the cojones, and the sheer force of will to pursue this to its happiest conclusion. Deborah it was, and at last I had something helpful to give her when she came.

. . . which she would. Soon. I mean, eventually she had to.

Didn't she?

Yes. She did.

Eventually.

It was a full two days after my lighthearted chat with Anderson when once again I heard the massive metallic sounds that meant my door was opening. Again it was an inappropriate time for door opening, eleven-oh-seven, and it was close enough to the time Bernie had previously visited me that I assumed it was he, returning with satisfactorily ordered papers and maybe even a date in court. I refused to think it might be something more than that, like a pardon from the governor, or the pope coming to wash my feet. I had allowed that little Pigeon of Hope far too much leeway, and each time I let it soar it had circled the room and come back to poop on my head. I was not going to let it fly again.

So with a face set in Prisoner's Ennui, an expression I was getting quite good at, I allowed Lazlo to lead me over to the thick bulletproof window, with its phone receiver on each side, its chairs facing each other through the glass, and Deborah sitting in the seat on the far side.

Deborah. At last.

I fell into the chair and lurched for the phone with pathetic eagerness, and on her side of the glass, Deborah watched my pitiful performance with a face that might have been carved from stone, and then, with slow and deliberate calmness, she picked up the phone.

"Deborah!" I said with a bright and hopeful smile on my face—a smile that I actually *felt* for once.

Deborah simply nodded at me. Her expression did not change, not even a twitch.

"I thought you weren't coming," I said, still all puppy-dog happy and overflowing with good cheer.

"So did I," she said, and although I would not have thought it was possible for her stone face to harden, it did.

I began to feel some small dark thoughts clouding over my sunny-day happiness. "But," I said, hoping to put things back on an optimistic footing, "you're here. You came."

Deborah didn't say anything. She sat and looked at me, and her face did not soften noticeably.

"I mean, you are here, aren't you?" I said, not at all sure what I was saying, nor what I meant.

Deborah moved at last. She nodded her head, one small nod of no more than half an inch up, and then down again. "I'm here," she said. She didn't make it sound like she was thrilled at being in her present location.

But she was, in fact, *here,* and that was really all that mattered. I launched right into telling her about my discoveries, suppositions, and conjectures regarding the All-Important Case of Dexter Detained. "I think I have a major lead," I said. "Anyway, it's at least something to investigate. Anderson was here—and from what he said, and then what my lawyer said, too, it seems like a good bet that . . ."

I trickled to a stop. Deborah was not merely paying no attention to my excited rambling. With her face still set in its mask of granite indifference, she had actually put the phone down and turned sideways, away from the window, away from any possible glimpse of offensive little old me.

"Deborah . . . ?" I said, quite stupidly, since I could see the phone lying there, several feet away from her ear.

She turned back to face me, almost as if she'd heard, and waited a moment—an interval filled with no more than an unblinking stare from that hard face that had become so monotonously unfriendly. Then she picked up the phone again.

"I'm not here to listen to your bullshit," she said.

"But that's . . . But then . . . But why?" I said, and in my defense I have to say that her comment had rendered me even stupider than I sounded. It was a true miracle of wit, in fact, that I could speak at all.

"I need you to sign some papers," she said. She held up a sheaf of official-looking documents, and in spite of all the massive evidence to the contrary, I actually felt a small surge of relief. After all, what official documents could she possibly bother to bring down here, other than something dealing with my case? And since the true and hidden meaning of "my case" actually meant "my release," a little ray of sunshine peeped out from behind the newly formed dark clouds.

"Of course," I said. "I'll be happy to . . . You know that I . . . What are they?" I said, all pathetic eagerness to please once again.

"Custody," she said, grinding the word out as if one more syllable would have broken her jaw.

I could only blink in surprise. Custody? Was she really going to take me into her house, assume the role of legal guardian to Dexter in Disgrace, until such time as my good name was re-untarnished? It went far beyond what I hoped for—it sounded very much like a full pardon, if only a nonlegal one from Deborah. "Custody," I repeated inanely, "well, of course, that's—I mean, thank you! I didn't think you would—"

"Custody for your *kids,*" she said, nearly spitting the words. "So they don't go to a foster home." And she looked at me as if it had been my plan, my entire purpose in life, to send children to orphanages.

Whether from the look or from her words, I felt so completely deflated that I had to wonder whether I would ever hold air again. "Oh," I said. "Of course."

Deborah's look changed at last, which was all to the good. On the downside, however, what it changed to was a sneer. "You haven't given those kids one fucking thought, have you?"

It may not stand as absolutely the best character reference for me, but in truth, I had not thought about the kids. Cody, Astor, and, of course, Lily Anne—they must have been scooped up somehow when I was arrested. And naturally, Deborah, as their closest relative—because of course my brother, Brian, would be totally out of the question, and . . . Honestly, I had not devoted even one gray cell to thinking about the kids, and I am quite sure that anyone with actual feelings would have a rather large lump of shame in their lap. I did not. In my defense, however, I would like to point out that I did have other things to think about—for instance, I was actually incarcerated.

45

For multiple murders, remember? And unjustly. "Well," I said, "I have been kind of, um . . . in jail?"

"That's what I thought," she said. "Not one fucking thought."

For a moment I was too stunned to respond. Here I was in quite literal chains, with reason to think it would soon be my permanent condition, and she was blaming me for not thinking of the children. Who, it must be said, were perfectly free to wander around and sit on the swings and eat pizza or whatever they wanted. It was a monstrous injustice approaching even the unfairness of my imprisonment, but there it was, and at last my wits returned and brought with them a large helping of indignation.

"Deborah, that's completely unfair," I said. "I have been in here without any kind of . . ." And I trickled to a truly feeble halt, because once again, Deborah was holding the phone away from her head and waiting for me to stop talking.

When I did, she let it hang for another minute before she finally picked up the phone. "The papers give me full custody of the kids," she said. "I'm leaving them with the guard." She waved the papers. "Sign them." She began to stand up, and panic flooded into me, from the basement up. My last, my only hope, and she was leaving.

"Deborah, wait!" I called.

Deborah paused in an awkward position, a kind of squat between standing and sitting, and it seemed to my fevered brain that she stayed like that for an awfully long time, as though she couldn't wait to leave, but some stupid obligation had frozen her in place and kept her from fleeing something distasteful. We both thought she was going to leave anyway. But then, to my idiotic relief, she sat down and picked up the phone again. "What," she said, in a voice as dead as it could be and still come from a living human mouth.

Once more I could only blink stupidly. The "what" of it seemed painfully obvious, so patently clear that I couldn't think of any way to say it that wasn't insulting her intelligence. I said it anyway. "I need your help," I said.

And just to prove that she could insult my intelligence right back, she said, "For what?"

"To get out of here," I said. "To find a way to prove that . . . that—"

"That you're innocent?" she snarled. "Bullshit."

"But—I *am* innocent!"

"The hell you are," she said, looking and sounding angry for the first time, but at last she was finally showing a little emotion. "*You* left Jackie alone, *you* abandoned Rita and let her get killed, and *you* handed Astor over to a homicidal *pedophile!*" I could see the knuckles of her hand clutching the phone turning white. She took a deep breath, and her face settled back into cold indifference. "Show me the innocent part, Dexter. Because I don't see it."

"But . . . but, Debs," I whimpered. "I didn't kill anybody."

"*This* time!" she snapped.

"Well, but . . . but," I stammered, "but that's what I'm in here for. *This* time. And I didn't . . ."

"*This* time," she repeated softly. But even though her voice had softened, her eyes were still hard and bright. She leaned in close to the window. "How many other times *did* you kill somebody, Dexter? How many more times *would* you if you got out?" It was a fair question, and the answer would certainly compromise my innocent plea, so I wisely said nothing, and Deborah went on.

"I've been thinking about that," she said. "I can't help it. I know you *say* Dad set the whole thing up so you—" She looked away again. "I can't do it anymore. I thought I could live with it, close one eye and just . . ." She looked back at me, and there was no softness in her anywhere. "But now this, and I don't have any idea who the fuck you are anymore. Maybe I never did—and you could've been lying all along about Daddy, and . . . I mean, he was a cop, and a *Marine* vet! What would *he* have said, Dexter? What would Daddy say about the shit you just pulled?"

She glared at me, and I realized she really

wanted an answer, but all I could think of to say was, "*Semper fi . . .*"

Deborah looked at me a little longer. Then she leaned back in her chair. "I wake up at night, and I think about all the people you killed. And I think about all the people you'll kill if you get out again. And if I help you get out, I am as good as killing them myself," she said.

"I thought you were okay with—I mean, Dad really did set it up, and . . ."

Once more her expression was enough to make me trickle to a stop.

"I can't do it anymore," she said. "It's wrong. It goes against everything I ever—" Her voice was rising, and she caught herself, stopped, and went on calmly. "You belong here," she said matter-of-factly. "The world is a better and safer place with you locked up."

It was difficult to argue with her logic, but it would have been rather counterproductive not to try. "Debs," I said. "I'm in here for something you *know* I didn't do. You can't let them hang it on me—you're better than that."

"Save it," she said. "I'm not the fucking Innocence Project. And if I was, I'd pick somebody who *deserved* to be saved."

"I've got nobody else," I said, trying very hard not to sound whiny.

"No, you don't," she said. "You let them all get killed."

"That's not—"

"And you don't have me, either," she said. "You're on your own."

"You can't mean that."

"You're goddamned right I mean it," she said. "I help you get out, I do nothing but turn a killer loose—and just incidentally kill my career, too."

"Oh, well," I said. And I was so unhinged at her attitude that I sank into sarcasm. "Of course, if it's a question of your *career*—I mean, what does my life matter compared to your *career?*"

She ground her teeth audibly, and her nostrils flared out and turned white, which I knew from our childhood meant she was about to lose it. "If I can save my career, keep a killer in jail, and help the department at the same time—"

"You're not helping the department," I said, and I was peevish now, too. "You're not helping anyone but Anderson. And you're doing it by abandoning your own brother!"

"Adopted," she spat. "Not my real brother."

For a very long moment those words just hung between us. For my part, I felt as if I had been poleaxed. For her to think that, let alone say it, was so far beyond any possible propriety that I couldn't believe she'd really said it. Surely I had imagined it? Deborah would never . . . I mean, *would* she?

And for her part, Deborah spent a long stretch

of that eternity grinding her teeth at me. There was one small, quick flash of something in her eyes: a frail and fleeting thought I could almost see that said she knew she should never say such a thing, and she couldn't believe she'd said it, either. But that thought was gone, faster than a speeding bullet, and she settled back into her chair and got comfortable, nodding slightly, as though she was actually quite glad she'd finally said something that had been troubling her for a while. And then, just to be sure I was completely and utterly crushed, she said it again.

"Adopted," she said with matter-of-fact venom. "You were never really my brother."

She glared at me for another eternity or two, and then she stood up, gathered her papers, and walked away.

FOUR

I DON'T KNOW HOW LONG I SAT THERE. IT seemed like a very long time. But at some point I became aware that Lazlo's hand was on my shoulder and he was urging me to my feet. I let him lead me back to my cell and button me in, but I didn't actually see or hear anything that happened along the way. There was room in my poor battered brain for only one thing, and it played in an endless loop: *You were never really my brother.*

She'd said that. Deborah had actually said those words, and then looked perfectly satisfied with herself for saying them—and then, on top of that mind-melting sequence, she had repeated them, just in case I didn't hear her the first time. But I heard her. I heard her over and over and I could not hear or think anything else but that.

You were never really my brother.

I know a great deal about Me. I know that I am not, for instance, ever going to change. I will always be Dexter the Monster, human-appearing, but walking through life with one foot always in perpetual Darkness. And I am also not able to feel Real Human Emotions. This is a fact, and it cannot change either. I do not feel. I am not capable.

So what were these terrible *things* surging through me, smashing at the tight slick walls that held Me in perfect cold indifference? This stomach-twisting dread, the sensation of everything around me and in me being diseased, dead, rotten, and empty? What could they possibly be? They certainly *felt* like Feelings.

You were never really my brother.

Barely, only just almost, I could understand Deborah's decision not to help me. Her career was everything to her, and I really was, after all, all she said I was and feared I would be again. I was and I would be, undeniably, unchangeably, and eagerly. It made a certain sense for her to think that way, and while I could never endorse it as a plan of action, I could at least comprehend the mental process that had led her there.

But this, the other, the utter rejection of our entire jointly led life, the complete denial of family ties, stretching back through the years to Mom and the house in the Grove and even including Saint Harry and His Plan—to take thirty-some years of actual existence and fling it away like roadkill—

—and then to throw it in my face, not once but *twice,* in a cold, uncompromising, and, it must be said, a *cruel* manner . . . this I could not understand. This went so far beyond mere self-preservation, so deeply into the surreal realm of Human Emotional Wickedness, a kingdom that was forever closed to someone like me—the Emotion part, I mean—that I could not begin to fathom it. I could not even imagine a set of circumstances that would lead me to deny Deborah in such a complete, absolute, and unbending way. It was unthinkable, no matter how I thought of it.

You were never really my brother.

That sentence of death still rang in my ears at lights-out that night.

It was still there the next morning at four-thirty when my loud, bright, and unnecessary wake-up call sounded. I did not need to be awakened. I had not slept. I had not performed any other higher functions of any kind, either. I had, in fact, done no more than lie on my bunk and listen to the endlessly repeating loop of Deborah's voice casting me out of my entire life and into eternal all-alone darkness.

Breakfast came, delivered with cheerful invisible competence through the slot in my door. I am almost sure I ate it, since the tray was empty when I put it back through the slot. But I could not say what I had eaten. It might have been anything: baked frog vomit, deep-fried possum nostrils, human fingers, anything at all. I would not have noticed.

But things change. No matter how hard we fight it, nothing stays as it is. All things, as you may have noticed, must change, and even end. At some point, even the greatest misery begins to fade. Life, or what passes for life, plods on in its own unending weary footsteps, and somehow we plod along with it, if we stay lucky. Eventually, other little thoughts began to trickle into the Pit of Despair where I lay and, it must be said, where I wallowed. It was this very act of wallowing, of starting to enjoy my suffering a little too much, that finally brought me back to something resembling awareness. I became aware that I had started my own repeating loop, in perfect harmony to Deborah's hard words. It was a simple melody, a sprightly version of the well-known old tune "Pity Me." And when I was at last alert to the fact that I was doing that, I became self-conscious and, from there, conscious.

And so at last, just before a delightful lunch of Strange Brown Meat Sandwich was delivered, Dexter arose from the dead. I sat up, stood, and performed a few stretching motions. Then, still aware of the utterly miserable and friendless wretch that I was, I began to think. My justly famous brain was the very last asset I had; using it to play back one small cruel song over and over was not really the optimum function of this rare and valuable piece of machinery.

So I thought. *Very well,* I thought, *I am in jail. Anderson has schemed to keep me here without due process. Deborah has abandoned me. My court-appointed attorney appears to be an overworked underengaged Twinkie. But is all that really the end of the world? Certainly not! I still have Me, and there is a great deal one can do with a finely tuned resource like that.* And thinking that, I felt a little better—even though I did not, in fact, think of any specific things Me might accomplish that would help Me get out of TGK. But I would think on that, too, and sooner or later I would arrive at some fiendishly clever course of action.

I did not, however, arrive at any such destination for the next few days, no matter how much I put my cerebral racehorse through its paces. If I could only get hold of the forensic evidence from the assorted killings I was charged with, I knew I could assemble a compelling case for my innocence. A significant part of my job had been testifying in court, and hard experience had taught me how to make dry facts come to life for a judge and jury. It was usually fun, since it was in truth no more than dramatizing things a bit. Over the years I had become quite good at taking an array of somewhat gooey facts and teaching them to sing and dance in a courtroom. Of course, it was probable that Anderson had been sticking his huge and grimy fingers into the forensic evidence, too. But it was just as likely that he had missed some-thing important—or left such huge fingerprints on everything that I could hoist him with the petard of his own evidence tampering. Whatever the case, I was absolutely certain I could find something to work with—if I could just get back to my lab. . . .

That is, if it was even *mine* anymore. It was another thing I hadn't thought about yet. Was I fired, suspended, provisionally forgotten, or what? I didn't know, and that might make a big difference.

But then there was Vince Masuoka, the closest thing I had to a friend. He would still be there on the job—and he would surely help me, wouldn't he? I thought over what I knew about him, which was surprisingly little, considering we had worked together in perfect amity for so many years. I knew where he lived—he had thrown me my bachelor party at his little house. I knew he wore a Carmen Miranda costume on Halloween. I knew he liked to go clubbing, and he had invited me to join him more than once. I had always begged off, pleading family obligations. And I knew his laugh was as completely fake as mine, though not nearly as convincing. It was one of the things that made me comfortable with Vince: He was quite obviously just as unclear about how to fit in with the rest of the world as I was.

But other than that, what did I really know about Vince Masuoka? It didn't seem like much when I trotted it out and lined it all up like that, a few little factoids that I might as well have read somewhere, and yet *he* was my closest friend. Is it like this for humans, too? Does anybody ever really *know* anybody else, no matter how well they "know" them? It seemed impossible.

It also seemed like a stupid distraction. It didn't matter how well I knew Vince. It only mattered that he would help me. He *had* to. He was all I had left. He was, officially, my friend—and when family leaves you so dramatically in the lurch, friends are all you have. My friend Vince would help me.

And so my next gigantic mental public works project became trying to think of how I could get a message to him. I had to assume that Anderson was keeping a tight lid on any attempts I might make to communicate with anyone. So I could not come right out and tell Vince what I needed him to do. Anderson would just quash it, and if he didn't, he would in any case know what I was trying to do, and prevent it. Among his many charms, Anderson was a bully, and he would certainly lean on Vince, and lean a lot harder and heavier than poor little Vince could tolerate. So I had to find a way to let Vince know I needed help, and yet keep Anderson off the scent.

I really don't like to boast, but I have so much supporting testimony that I would be less than truthful if I did not admit that I am fiendishly clever. I take no credit for it; I was born this way. Something as basic as a message that Vince would understand and Anderson wouldn't should have been absolute simplicity for me. I pondered it with confidence, certain that some bright and devious ploy would pop into my busy brain. It should have been the work of a few comfortable minutes.

And yet a day later I was still pondering. It may be that the TGK diet, however nutritious and wholesome, did not contain enough fish to keep my brain functioning at the highest levels. But I had thought of nothing, and I was still empty of inspiration when once again, a little while after my delightful midday meal, I heard the gears clicking in my door. Once again it swung open, and Lazlo beckoned, saying, "Your lawyer's here." It was almost certainly my imagination, but he seemed to put a bit more respect into those words than he had done previously.

I trudged out of my cell and over to the large, thick window to face once more Bernie and his fabulous flying documents—and I stopped dead only halfway there. Because Bernie was nowhere to be seen. Instead, another man sat in his place in the chair on the far side of the glass. He was a man unlike any I have ever seen, outside of the movies. Everything about him seemed to radiate calm assurance, power, and money. He was tanned where Bernie was pale, relaxed and confident instead of hassled, harried, and exhausted, and he was dressed in a suit that was so unlike the poor ill-fitting grubby thing Bernie wore that it cannot really be thought of as the same kind of garment.

This man's suit has a life of its own. It sparkles with vitality and wit, and seems to glow with the same perfect health as the man wearing it. This suit is the kind of thing ambitious tailors dream of making when they hear that royalty is in town.

I feel Lazlo's hand on my shoulder, and I turn to look at him quizzically. He just nods and pushes me toward the window.

And so I sit, quite certain that some large and comical mistake is unfolding, but willing to play it through, if only because it breaks the tedium. I look at the man through the glass; he nods and gives me a brief, professional smile. He is holding a beautiful Italian-leather folder filled with neatly aligned papers. With his other hand he picks up the phone, holds it for me to see, and raises an eyebrow at me.

I pick up the phone on my side.

"Mr. Morgan," he says briskly—and without even looking at the papers. Perhaps he didn't want to soil the leather folder.

"Yes. I mean, that's me, but . . . ?"

He nods again, and gives me a smile that seems friendly, but I can tell it is every bit as cold and phony as my own. "I am Frank Kraunauer."

I blink. This is a name I have only read in the papers. It is a name that is spoken, if at all, only in reverent whispers. Celebrity lawyer Frank Kraunauer springs another horribly guilty client while sipping champagne on his yacht. Of course the inhuman fiend was guilty, but he had *Frank Kraunauer* defending him. Killers and cartel kingpins rejoice in his presence, for Kraunauer has but to speak and the chains of their bondage wither and die. He is the Home Run King of our courts; every swing sends another felon over the walls.

And he is now, for some reason, here to see little old me?

Kraunauer gives me several seconds to absorb the incredible cachet of his name, and then he goes on. "I have been retained to represent you. Of course, if you prefer to keep your present court-appointed attorney, Mr. Feldman . . . ?" He lets his smile widen as he says it, clearly amused at the thought that anyone would be naive enough to prefer Bernie to Himself.

Personally, I am not amused. I am startled, confused—and, it must be said, I am also somewhat suspicious. "I don't know," I say carefully. "Who retained you?"

He nods patiently, giving the impression of a man who appreciates caution in prospective clients. "The arrangement is a little unusual," he admits—this from a man who defended wholesale drug dealers, and was probably accustomed to being paid in suitcases full of blood-soaked Krugerands. "But I am instructed to tell you that I have been engaged by a Mr. Herman O.

Atwater." He cocked his head to one side, looking simultaneously amused and yet breathtakingly self-assured and competent. Of course, his suit helped a lot. "You are familiar with Mr. Atwater?" he said, raising a perfectly trimmed eyebrow.

It was a performance well worth taking in and even applauding. But Dexter is not Dazzled; Dexter's brain is, at last, whirling at its favored rate of nine million revolutions per minute. In the first and most obvious place, I do not know anyone named Herman O. Atwater, and I never have. Second, it defies believability to think that a complete stranger would hire the most brilliant, and consequently *expensive* attorney in Miami for me. Therefore, the name must be made up for some reason.

But why? The only possible motive for a fake name is to preserve anonymity, which means that Mr. Atwater didn't want anyone to know he was involved with me—

But wait: He would certainly want *me* to know who he was. Or, to be fair, *she*. Only someone close to me would go to the expense of hiring Kraunauer, whose fees were legendary. But nobody actually *is* close to me, at least among the living. It couldn't be my friends, since aside from Vince I don't really have any. And I know only too bitterly well that Deborah didn't do it. She'd made her position abundantly clear, and I could not believe it had changed so dramatically.

If I eliminate friends, and eliminate family, then who was left? In all the world, there is no one else who really gives a rodent's rectum whether I lived or died—although it did seem like the list of those who preferred me dead was getting a bit lengthy lately. So, not a stranger, not a friend, not family, which left—

I blink again. A tiny little ray of light peeks into the dark and stormy maelstrom of Dexter's brain.

I had been trying very hard to come up with something clever. Somebody had just outdone me, neatly and completely. They had, in fact, run several laps around me while I still stood in the blocks, cringing from the starter's pistol. And in a surge of warm and wonderful relief, I felt my mental powers return to me at last, and I knew who it was. It was all right there in the name.

Herman O. Atwater.

The "O" did not stand for Oscar, nor Oliver, nor even Oliphant. It did not, in fact, stand at all. It *connected*. With *Herman*. As in *herman-o*. *Hermano*. Which any resident of My Fair City could tell you is the Spanish word for *brother*.

Atwater was simply the clincher, the final clue, the one hint so completely private and personal that no one else in the world could possibly know what it meant. Not a name either, but a location: *at the water,* the most significant place of my life. *At the water,* in a shipping container, where I had been ripped out of normal life and reborn into blood. At the water, where poor, traumatized four-year-old Dexter had been found, after three days of sitting in a pool of his mother's blood, all alone in the world, except for Mommy's severed head—and one other, relatively living thing, though just as thoroughly dead inside as I was.

A small, cold shipping container *at the water,* all snug and abandoned in the dreadful sticky red mess, just the three of us: Mommy, Me, and my *hermano.* My Blood Relations.

My brother, born anew like me at the water's edge. *Hermano* Atwater.

Brian.

I had not been flung onto the dung heap by *all* my family after all. My True Family had come through. My brother, Brian, had hired the best lawyer in town for me.

If it had taken as long for all these thoughts to whip through my brain as it took to lay them out, I am sure Kraunauer would have had to leave for an important appointment with his mani-pedi practitioner. But when Dexter's brain is in high gear, such a dazzling train of wit is quicker than the blink of an eye, and in almost no elapsed time at all, I was smiling and nodding at Kraunauer. "Of course," I said into the phone. "Dear Herman. How thoughtful of him."

"You are familiar with Mr. Atwater?" he repeated.

"Naturally," I said.

"And is it your wish to have me represent you

in this matter? Rather than Mr. Feldman?" he said with his small, slightly superior smile.

The smile I gave him back was much larger, and a great deal more real. "Absolutely," I said.

He nodded his head, twice, and opened the beautiful leather folder, all in a way that said, *Of course, what else, and now let's get down to business.* He looked down at the pages and shook his head. "I'm afraid there have been some rather . . . *singular* . . ." He paused and looked up at me. "Irregularities?"

I wasn't sure what he meant, but recent experience told me it probably wasn't positive. "Irregular how?" I asked, not altogether sure I wanted to hear the answer. "I mean, in a *good* way?"

"Good," he said, as if it was a dirty word. "Not if you care about the law." He shook his head disapprovingly, but a single tooth gleamed, like a wolf trying and just barely failing to hide his fangs, and he held up the paperwork. "I'm afraid I can't call any of this *good.*"

"Oh," I said, not quite sure how to feel about that. "So, what does it mean? I mean, for me . . . ?"

Kraunauer smiled, and now the wolf fangs were out for all to see. "Let's just put it this way," he said. "If you're still sitting here in TGK tomorrow at this time, it means I'm dead." He closed the folder and allowed his smile to get much, much broader. "And I don't plan on dying anytime soon, Mr. Morgan."

FIVE

I T MUST BE THAT SOMEWHERE THERE truly is a malevolent deity who watches over the Wicked with tender care. Because Kraunauer did not die, and his word was as good as gold—better, really, when you consider the terrible inflation on the gold market lately. In any case, gold would not have sprung Dexter overnight, and Kraunauer did. Bright and early the next morning, well before I had another chance at the epicurean ecstasy of TGK's lunch, I was blinking in the sunlight of the parking lot at the front of the building and wondering what happened next.

They had given me back my clothing and all else they had taken from me on my arrival—plus a thick folder of paperwork that I assumed gave details of my release and terrible threats dealing with my certain reincarceration. I had bundled it all up and changed gratefully into my own clothes. To be perfectly honest, I had grown a wee bit weary of the cheerful orange jumpsuit, and it was very nice to wear my own, relatively bland clothing again. On the downside, my pants still had some bloodstains on them from the hectic multivictim evening of carnage that had unfolded just prior to my arrest, and the jumpsuit had at least always been a hundred percent bloodstain free. Still, the successful life is a series of trade-offs, and I shed no tears over the loss of my jumpsuit. I'd also gotten back my wallet, my phone, and even my belt. The belt was the real clincher; it was a truly euphoric feeling to know that I could hang myself now if I wanted to. I didn't, of course, but I might consider it soon if I couldn't think of a way to get home. I'd arrived in a police car. Sadly, there were none waiting to give me a ride. And in truth, I'd had quite enough of police for the time being. Walking would be far preferable, and it was good for me, too. A nice, brisk fifteen-mile stroll to my house would get the blood flowing, put a smile on my lips and a song in my heart.

On the other hand, this was Miami—which is to say that it was hot and getting hotter. It would be a terrible shame if I got out of jail only to die of heatstroke. Perhaps if I waited long enough, a cab would turn up. And if I waited only a little longer, they might build a rail line right to the door. It seemed just as likely.

There were few other options that I could see. Although they had given me back my phone, it was of course completely dead after its unhappy incarceration. So I stood just outside the front door, looking stupidly around me. I'd come in through the back, on the opposite side of the building. The view here in front was far more pleasant; towering up behind me was the delightfully ominous gray facade of the building, and wrapped around me, in a thought-provoking design moment, was a high barbed-wire fence. Cars were parked absolutely everywhere and anywhere they might, even in spaces that were not actually spaces. The parked vehicles stretched around three sides of the building and overflowed a large lot in back. They were crammed in two-deep under trees, on top of median strips, and in No Parking Fire Zone spots. Anywhere else in the city such madcap abandonment of vehicles would certainly be rewarded with towing and impoundment. It made one reflect on the irony that here, at the actual *jail,* where the most nefarious repeat meter violators and illegal parking offenders were incarcerated, there was no apparent parking enforcement.

It also made one reflect on a further irony: that with so many vehicles lying about unused, not a single one of them was available to give poor liberated Dexter a lift. It didn't seem fair. But of course, nothing in life ever is fair, outside of a few old-fashioned board games.

Ah, well. Freedom is a two-edged sword, for it carries with it the terrible burden of Self-Reliance. And I now knew, from hard-earned experience, that my spirit yearned to breathe free air, and I should be willing to pay the price.

And I was. But in truth, if paying the price meant walking home, I would rather have put Freedom on a credit card.

So I stood there blinking in the bright sunlight and wishing I had sunglasses. And my car. And what the hell, a Cuban sandwich and an Iron Beer. And I had been standing there for a good three minutes before I became aware of a horn beeping nearby, at regular intervals. The sound came from my right. Out of no more than idle curiosity, I glanced that way.

Some fifty feet away, the car-crammed driveway bent right. Just beyond that, on the far side of the tall chain-link fence, there was a big vacant lot, also overflowing with cars.

Standing half-hidden by the open door of one of those cars, one arm reaching in to sound the horn, stood a man in resort clothing, baseball cap, and large wraparound sunglasses. He raised a hand and waved, beeped the horn once more, and as I realized with a start that he was waving at me, I also realized who he was, in spite of his outlandish Tourist costume. It was my brother, Brian.

The laws of our Universe are not terribly lenient when it comes to unbelievable coincidence. Seeing Brian here, so soon after he had sent me a Get Out of Jail Free card in the person of Mr. Frank Kraunauer, could not possibly be random chance. And so it was with almost no pause at all that I deduced that Brian had come to get me, and that I should take advantage of his presence. I therefore strode briskly over to the fence that separated his car from the detention center.

Brian watched me walk toward him, his terrible fake smile almost too dazzling to bear in the bright daylight. When I was ten feet away he lifted a hand and pointed to my right. "There's a hole in the fence," he said. He jabbed his index finger. "Right over there."

Sure enough, there was indeed a hole in the fence, just a few feet away. It looked well used, and it was large enough to allow me through comfortably. In no time at all I was standing in the mud beside my brother's green Jeep and showing him most of my teeth. "Brian," I said.

"In person," he said. He gestured at the passenger side of his car. "May I offer you a ride, brother?"

"You may," I said. "And I will accept it with thanks."

Brian climbed into the driver's seat as I walked around the car, and he had the motor running, and with it the air conditioner, by the time I climbed in. "I also need to thank you for the splendid gift," I said as I fastened my seat belt. "Frank Kraunauer was a wonderful surprise."

"Oh, well," Brian said modestly. "It was really nothing at all."

"It was a whole lot," I said. "I'm free."

"Yes," Brian said. "But not permanently . . . ?"

I shook my head. "Probably not. That would be too much to expect, wouldn't it?"

"I'm afraid so," he said. "Oh, this wicked world."

"Kraunauer got the judge to release me—the paperwork was a complete mess—but the state attorney will almost certainly try again. He really wants this case."

"And therefore you?" he said.

"And me," I said. "But I'm free for now." I bowed to him, as much as I could while wearing a seat belt. "So thank you."

"Well, after all," Brian said, backing the car away from the fence, "what is family for?"

I thought somewhat unhappily of my other family, with particular reference to Deborah. "I sometimes wonder," I said.

"In any case," Brian said, putting the car into forward and bumping us through the mud of the vacant lot, toward the street, "it seemed little enough to do. You would do the same for me, wouldn't you?"

"Well," I said. "I certainly would *now*. Although I'm not sure if I could afford Kraunauer."

"Oh, that," he said dismissively, waving one hand. "I've had a little windfall. And it's only money."

"Still," I said, "I am awfully grateful. It does get to be a little close in there."

"Yes, doesn't it?" Brian said. He turned out onto the side street, and then right onto NW 72nd Ave. I watched his profile, so much like my own, as he drove us happily away, and I wondered whether he had actually spent time inside TGK. There was a great deal I didn't know about Brian, particularly about his past. We had been separated when very young: me to Harry and Doris and life as a Morgan—or a faux-Morgan, as it now turned out. Brian hadn't had it so easy; he'd grown up in a series of foster homes, reformatories, and possibly jails. He had never offered much detail about this time, and I hadn't asked. But it seemed a good bet to me that he knew very well what life was like on the Inside.

He turned and saw me looking at him, and raised an eyebrow. "Well," he said happily. "What now?"

It may sound stupid—no surprise, considering my recent behavior—but I didn't have an answer. I had been so focused on getting out that I hadn't really thought beyond that. "I don't know," I said.

"As it happens," Brian said, "I thought you might want to lie low for a while?" He turned to me and raised his eyebrows. "Yes? So I took the liberty of getting you a small, quiet hotel room."

I blinked. "That's very kind of you, brother."

"Oh, no trouble at all," he said happily. "I put it on a nice, anonymous credit card."

I thought about it for a moment. Brian was absolutely right that I needed to stay out of sight until I knew which way the wind was blowing. But oddly enough, although I would not go so far as to say that I was actually homesick, I felt the need to see a few familiar places and things, just

72

to wipe away the memory of my cell and feel truly free again.

"Can you take me to my house?" I said. "I'd like to shower, change clothes. And maybe just sit on a real couch for a little while."

"Of course," he said. "And after that?"

I shook my head. "I don't know," I said. "There's too much I don't know."

"About?" he prompted.

I sighed heavily, feeling the full weight of freedom settle onto my shoulders. It had seemed so simple when the world was made up of no more than my cell and the yard and guessing what that stuff was in the sandwich. Now . . . "I guess everything," I said. "All I really know is that Detective Anderson hates me, and he'll do anything to make all this stick to me. And apparently," I said, turning away to look ruefully out the window, "Deborah hates me just as much."

"So I have gathered," he said neutrally. He avoided Deborah with great care, which was really the only smart thing to do, since the one time she had ever seen him was that night a few years back when he had grabbed her, taped her up inside a storage box, and encouraged me to kill her. That type of encounter can make a relationship a bit awkward going forward. Deborah thought Brian was dead, if she thought about him at all. As a sensible monster, Brian preferred not to shatter that illusion.

"Anyway," I said, "I'm not sure of my status at work, but I need to talk to my friend Vince and see what the evidence against me looks like."

"Vince is the Asian fellow?" Brian asked, and I nodded. "Yes, you had mentioned him before." He drove us up the ramp and onto the Palmetto Expressway, headed east.

"Even if I'm suspended or fired, I think Vince will help," I said.

"Ahem," Brian said. It sounded very phony, just the way you'd write it. "As it happens, I have been to visit dear Vince."

I looked at him with surprise. For Brian to go anywhere near so much as a patrol car was a risk. To go down to headquarters was near-toxic insanity. "Really?" I said. "You went inside? To the lab?"

He showed his teeth again. "I did not," he said. "I waited for Vince to leave for lunch. I followed him to a little bistro near Eighth Street, Chez Octavio's?"

I nodded. I knew Octavio's; it was hardly a Chez. It was more like a *basura*, and it served quite possibly the worst Cuban food in the city. But it was extremely cheap, and so was Vince. "What did you learn?" I asked.

"Some very interesting things," Brian said, waving happily to a large tanker truck that swerved in front of him for no reason. "To begin with, Vincent Masuoka really is your friend."

He flashed me his terrible fake smile. "Up to a point."

"Everyone has a point, I think," I said.

"Quite true. Vince's point, however, is well past what you might imagine." He paused to lean on the horn as a pickup truck with three large hounds in the bed meandered across two lanes, apparently for the sole purpose of getting in front of us and slowing down. Brian swerved into the right lane and passed. The hounds watched us with mournful apathy as we went by.

"In any case," Brian went on, "Vince withstood a great deal of pressure from Detective Anderson."

"Pressure to do what?"

Brian smiled at me again. "Oh, practically nothing at all," he said merrily. "A few tiny trifles, like suppressing evidence, falsifying reports, lying under oath—the kind of everyday chore you and I wouldn't even blink at."

"And Vince refused?" I said, marveling a little. Vince was not large, and to call him timid is something of an understatement.

"He refused," Brian said, nodding. "Up to and including a visit from Anderson in the large and angry flesh. He even told your supervisor, who offered to remove Vince from the case if he didn't want to play along. And then," he said, rather dramatically, I thought, "he did the truly unthinkable."

"Really," I said. I tried to think of what might

constitute unthinkable behavior for Vince, and failed. "What?"

"He went to the state attorney's office and Told All," Brian said solemnly. "With documentary evidence, reports and so on, all crudely doctored in Anderson's hand."

"Well," I said. "That is unthinkable." And it was—not that Anderson crudely doctored the documents, of course. I had already assumed as much. But first of all, for anyone in the department to report anyone else in the department to the state attorney was completely outside the Code. Second, for that person to be Vince, a known mouse—it nearly defied imagination. "What happened? Is that why Kraunauer got me out so quickly?"

"Oh, no, dear brother," Brian chirped. "Disabuse yourself of such naive notions. The world is not nearly so simple."

"Neither is getting an answer," I said. "What did the state attorney do?"

"Is there a more modern way to say, 'Go play in the traffic'?" Brian asked thoughtfully. "I'm not sure we say that anymore."

"The state attorney said *that?*"

"Words to that effect," Brian said. We bumped down onto the surface street, and he glanced at me. "Are your illusions shattered, brother?"

"My illusions don't generally involve the state attorney," I said.

"Well, then," Brian said. "It seems unlikely that a mere detective would lean on the state attorney. But I suppose stranger things have happened."

"I'm sure they have," I said. "But I don't think that's what happened." Brian glanced at me and raised an eyebrow. "Not even a unibrowed mental-midget thug like Anderson would try to intimidate the state attorney," I said. "But . . ."

I thought about it: A hardworking and honest whistleblower brings the SA's office a documented report of authentic malfeasance, malpractice, and malingering. And the SA's office does not, as one might expect, give said whistleblower a manly handshake and heartfelt thanks and then leap into indignant action against the heinous perpetrator. Instead, they tell Vince to go away and leave them alone—to play, if you will, in the traffic. On the face of it, it ran somewhat contrary to our general expectations of what a prosecutor's office should do. But, of course, as I knew all too well, nothing at all in our justice system is actually about what it is *supposed* to be about. I suppose the same might be said of most things in life; when is the last time you met a waiter who is actually a *waiter* and not a frustrated actor/writer/dancer killing time until lightning strikes? But, of course, with Justice, where so many shattered lives hang in the balance, the stakes are much higher, and one really does hope for better.

Ah, well. Hope is for people who can't see the Truth. As it happened, in this one instance, I thought I saw Truth. "Aha," I said. "If that doesn't sound too corny?"

"No more corny than 'go play in the traffic,'" Brian said. "So tell me."

"In the first place," I said, "my case is a very public national black eye for the department."

"International," Brian said. "It was all over the news in Mexico, too."

"So they need to have it solved," I said. "And they need to have it done by convicting someone like me."

"Well, then," Brian said. "Who better than you yourself?"

"None other," I said. "But there's more. Imagine you are a lawyer."

"Please," Brian said with a very real shudder. "I have some standards."

"And now imagine that one of your clients—or many of them—have been convicted on evidence supplied by Detective Anderson."

"Oh," Brian said.

"Yes," I said. "When you learn that Anderson has doctored evidence once—"

"Then you can easily persuade a judge he doctored evidence *twice*," Brian said.

I nodded. "Or more. Maybe every time, in every single case. And Detective Anderson has a rather large caseload," I said. "Most of the detectives do."

"And suddenly the streets are flooded with released felons," Brian said.

"Right," I said. "Which many people would prefer to avoid."

"Ah, well," Brian said happily. "We live in wicked times."

"Very busy times, too," I said. "And suddenly every conviction of the last five years is overturned. And?" Now it was my turn to pause dramatically.

"Oh, dear, there's *more?*" Brian said in mock horror.

"Just this," I said. "The state attorney is *elected* in Florida."

"Oh, bravo!" Brian said with real good cheer. "What wonderful stupidity!"

"It is, isn't it?" I said. "The quality of mercy is not strained—but it *is* handed out by someone who got the job by pandering to the lowest possible common denominator."

"And they must present an impressive record of convictions to get *re*elected," Brian said.

"Yup."

"And so the picture is complete," he said. He steered us up the on-ramp and onto I-95 south.

"Very nearly," I said.

"Great heavens, there's *more?*" said Brian with mock horror.

"Quite possibly," I said.

"Do tell."

"Well," I said slowly, "just speculation here, but if it was *me* . . . ?"

"Oh, dear," Brian said. For the first time he frowned. "Poor dear Vince—surely they wouldn't?"

I shrugged. "As I said. Speculation. They might not actually *kill* him."

"But in any case," Brian said, "disgrace, dishonor, discredit, and dismissal."

"Almost certainly," I said.

"And that we cannot allow," Brian said. "Since he is our hole card, and we need him alive, well, and highly credible."

I looked at my brother with some fondness. He had cut right to the very practical chase, without dithering around about friendship, gratitude, or honor. It was nice to be around somebody who thought so much like me. "Precisely," I said.

"If some dreadful accident happened to Anderson . . . ?" he suggested.

"I admit it's tempting," I said. "But it would look a little too convenient for me."

"You would have a wonderful alibi," he said, a little too seductively, I thought. "No one could ever pin it on you."

I shook my head. "Deborah would know," I said. "She has already hinted that she might rat me out someday."

"Mmm," he said, and I knew what he would suggest before he ever said it. "There could be *two* dreadful accidents. . . ."

I opened my mouth to tell him to forget it, drop it, put the thought permanently out of his mind. Not Deborah, never my sister, no matter what might happen. It was out of the question, off the menu, not remotely a possibility—and I paused, closed my mouth, and pondered. It had been pure unthinking reflex to deny the merest thought of Accidenting Deborah, and like so many reflexive denials, it did not truly bear the weight of logical thought. I would never have considered it before, even for a moment; family loyalty and obligation, all drilled into me by Harry and so many years of acceptance and practice, made it impossible. Deborah was unthinkably untouchable. She was Home and Hearth, Kith and Kin, as much a part of me as my arm.

But now?

Now, after she had so thoroughly disdained, dismissed, and disowned me? So very completely rejected Me and all I am? Was it really unthinkable to send Debs away on the Long Dark Journey *now,* when she had already suggested that she did not find it at all unthinkable to do exactly that to Me?

I felt a small, sly, slithering purr from deep inside, where the Passenger napped, nestled in webs and shadows, and I heard it whisper to me what I realized I already knew.

It was not unthinkable, not at all. It was, in fact, suddenly very thinkable.

More: It could even be painted with a light patina of true justice, in a sort of Old Testament way. Debs was willing to see me dead—didn't it make perfect, eye-for-an-eye sense for me to see her dead first?

I remembered her words: *never really my brother*. They still stung, and I felt a slow-burning anger smoldering at the outer edges of my Harry-built propriety. I was never really her brother? Fine. That meant that *she* was never really my sister. We were now and forevermore unsibling, unfamily, unrelated.

And *that* meant . . .

I became aware that Brian was humming happily, so very far off-key that I could not even recognize the melody. He would be just as happy, and perhaps much happier, if I gave him permission to do away with Debs. He didn't understand my past objections, and certainly felt no hesitation himself. After all, he had never thought he was related to Deborah; that had been my tragic fallacy. And even though he was no more capable of human feelings than any other reptile, it was Brian who had come to my aid, after Debs had refused with great self-righteous loathing. The Great Illusion of my bond with Deborah had been exposed, rejected, flung from the fracas at the first real trial. And instead, blood had proved true after all.

And yet . . .

I still found it very hard to picture the world without Debs.

Brian had stopped humming, and I looked at him. He looked back, his terrible fake smile in place. "Well, brother?" he said. "Today's special? Two for the price of one?"

I could not hold his gaze. I looked away out the window. "Not yet," I said.

"All righty, then," he said, and I could hear disappointment in his voice. But he drove on, and I continued to look out the window. I buried myself in dark musings, and didn't really see any of the scenery, even as we approached my house and it got more and more familiar. Neither of us spoke again until, some twenty minutes later, Brian did.

"We're here," he said, slowing the car. And then he said, "Uh-oh," and I looked out the window. He was driving us slowly past my house, the home where I had lived with Rita for such a long time. And right in front of the house, another car was already parked.

A police car.

SIX

A S I MAY HAVE MENTIONED, BRIAN HAD a very real aversion to police in any form at all, and he had no intention of pausing to chat with the two cops we could see in the cruiser. They glanced up at us, just doing their job and checking out the traffic, looking bored but still prepared to spring out of the car and open fire if we should suddenly unlimber a howitzer, or try to sell them drugs. But Brian very coolly smiled and nodded and continued his slow cruise past the house, pointing at a neighboring house in a very good imitation of the House Gawker's Crawl, a South Florida custom that involves driving around at a maddeningly sluggish pace while staring at houses that may someday be for sale. It was a perfect disguise, and the cops gave us no more than a glance before turning back to their conversation, no doubt involving either sports or sex.

But it was, after all, my house, and it contained most of my earthly possessions. I wanted to get inside, if only for a change of clothing. "Circle the block," I said to Brian. "Let me out up at the corner and I'll walk back."

Brian gave me a concerned look. "Is that really a good idea?" he asked.

"I don't know," I said. "But it's my house."

"Apparently it's also a crime scene," Brian said.

"Yes, it is," I said. "Detective Anderson has stolen my house."

"Well," he said lightly, "as I said, there is a hotel room waiting for you."

I shook my head, suddenly feeling stubborn. "It's my house," I said. "I have to try."

Brian sighed theatrically. "Very well," he said. "But it seems like an awful risk, less than an hour out of jail."

"I'll be fine," I said, although in truth I was not nearly as optimistic as I sounded. So far Anderson and the mighty Juggernaut of Justice that he represented had had their way with me, and there was no reason to think things would change now, merely because I was represented by Frank Kraunauer. But one can do no more than try one's best in this Vale of Tears, and so I climbed out of Brian's car absolutely brimming with synthetic hope, a cheery fake smile painted on my lips. I stuck my head back inside and said, "Go up to the strip mall on the corner. I'll walk up when I'm done."

Brian ducked down and looked at me searchingly, as if afraid he might never see me again. "If you're not there in half an hour, I'm calling Kraunauer," he said.

"Forty-five minutes," I said. "If I get in, I want a shower."

He looked at me a little longer, then shook his head. "This is a very bad idea," he said. I closed the door, and he drove slowly away, up toward Dixie Highway.

I understood Brian's worry. It was perfectly natural caution on the part of somebody who preferred the sort of entertainment he liked. He had always seen cops as the Enemy, a rival predator in the food chain to be avoided whenever possible. But even though I shared his distinctive tastes, I had no inbred aversion to blue uniforms. My unique upbringing and career path had made me familiar with cops, and I understood them as much as I understood any human.

So I walked right up to the patrol car, phony smile still on my face, and tapped on the glass.

Two heads swiveled toward me in perfect unison, and two sets of cold eyes, one blue and one brown, looked me over with unblinking readiness.

I mimed rolling down the window, and after another moment of staring, the owner of the brown eyes, closest to me, rolled down the window. "Can I help you, sir," the officer said, making *help* sound as threatening as possible. I let my smile broaden just a little, but the officer didn't seem impressed. He was thin, about forty, with olive skin and short black hair, and his partner, who was much younger and very pale, with blond hair that was Marine Corps short, leaned over to watch me.

"Yes, I hope so," I said. "Um, this is my house here? And I was hoping I could get in and get a few things . . . ?"

Neither one of them offered any encouragement, not even a blink. "What kind of things," Brown Eyes said. It sounded more like an accusation than a question.

"Change of clothes?" I said hopefully. "Maybe a toothbrush?"

At long last, Brown Eyes blinked, but it didn't soften him up noticeably. "The house is sealed," he said. "Nobody in, nobody out."

"Just for a minute?" I pleaded. "You could come and watch me."

"I said *no,*" Brown Eyes said, and he was sliding down the scale now, from cold to positively hostile.

And even though I had absolutely no hope that it would change their minds, I couldn't stop myself from saying, in a kind of desperate, pathetic whine, "But it's my house."

"It *was* your house," Blue Eyes said. "It's evidence now."

"We know who you are," Brown Eyes said, openly angry now. "You're the fucking psycho that killed Jackie Forrest."

"And Robert Chase," Blue Eyes chimed in.

"You made us all look like assholes," Brown Eyes said. "The whole fucking force—you know that?"

A very great number of wonderfully clever replies flitted into my brain, like, *Oh, no, you already did,* or *Maybe, but you sure helped,* or even *It wasn't that hard.* And under normal circumstances I wouldn't have hesitated to let one slip. But looking into the patrol car at Brown Eyes, I realized that there was a very good chance my lighthearted good humor would slide off ears that seemed to be fastened on a little too tightly—Brown Eyes looked altogether too tightly wrapped all over, in fact, to see any fun anywhere in a world that contained me, so I let the bon mot wither unspoken.

"You're supposed to be in lockup," Brown Eyes went on. "What the hell are you doing out?"

"We better call it in," Blue Eyes said.

"I was released this morning," I said quickly. "All perfectly legal." I thought about trying a reassuring smile, but decided it was a bad idea. Blue Eyes was already on the radio, and his partner was opening the door of the car and getting out to face me with the full majesty of the law and barely controlled fury. The effect was spoiled just a bit because Brown Eyes was only about five-foot-four, but he did what he could to make himself taller with his anger.

"Assume the position," he said, jerking his head at the side of the car. I opened my mouth to protest that I had done nothing to give him any cause, and as I did his hand drifted down toward

88

his pistol. I closed my mouth and assumed the position.

I grew up around cops, and spent my whole career among them, and I know perfectly well how to assume the position. I have to say I did it rather well. But Brown Eyes kicked my feet farther apart anyway, hard, and shoved me against the car, clearly hoping that I would bump my head. Considering his mood, it might not have been wise to disappoint him, but it was, after all, my face, and so I risked it and caught myself with my hands.

He frisked me quickly and thoroughly, "accidentally" hurting me wherever possible, and then pulled my hands roughly behind me and snapped on the cuffs. He pulled them much too tight, naturally. I expected it after the rest of his performance, but there wasn't a great deal I could do about it. And then, keeping one hand on me, he opened the back door of the squad car.

I knew what was coming, of course. He was going to push me into the backseat, pausing along the way to "accidentally" slam my forehead into the roof of the car, and I prepared myself to dodge it if I could. But happily for me, before he could shove, his partner called to him.

"Ramirez, hold it," Blue Eyes said.

Ramirez paused, and then grabbed my wrist and yanked my arms upward. It hurt. "Lemme put him in the car," he said.

"Ramirez!" Blue Eyes said. "Dispatch says to let him go."

Ramirez tightened his grip on me. "He's resisting arrest," he said through clenched teeth.

"No, I'm not," I said. And it was true; if I was resisting anything at all, it was circulation. My hands were already turning purple from the tight cuffs.

But Ramirez was locked into Full Bully Mode, and he clearly didn't care. He pushed on me, bumping me into the car. "Your word against mine," he hissed.

"Come on, Julio, he's not arrested," Blue Eyes said. "Come on, you gotta let him go. Julio, for shit's sake, come on."

There was a pause that seemed quite long to me, and then I heard a noise that sounded like steam blasting out of a radiator, which I hoped was Ramirez deciding he really did have to let me go.

It was. He dropped my arms abruptly, and a moment later he unlocked the cuffs. I turned around and looked at him. He was clearly waiting for me to scurry timidly away, and thinking about some ominous parting line to make my heart quail within me, and probably hoping he could stick out his foot and trip me as I went by. He was also standing much too close, a standard ploy of bullies. Maybe he hoped I wouldn't notice at that distance how short he was. But I did notice, just as I had also noticed all his stupid, petty attempts to intimidate me, cause me pain, and otherwise kill the song in my heart. It wasn't necessary—in theory, it also wasn't legal. And I was, after all, innocent. His bullying had irked me. So instead of scurrying, I stepped a little closer to him—not close enough to give him a reason to open fire, but just enough to remind him that I was much taller, and force him to bend his neck a little more to look up at me.

"Julio Ramirez," I said, nodding briefly to show I would remember. "You will be hearing from my attorney." I paused long enough to let him begin a sneer, and then said, "His name is Frank Kraunauer."

I knew, of course, that Kraunauer's name was heap big magic; at its merest mention judges bowed and juries swooned. I had been hoping it might have some small effect on Ramirez, and I was immediately rewarded by a reaction that exceeded my hopes and was very gratifying to watch. He actually turned pale, and then he took a step backward. "I didn't do anything," he said.

"Your word against mine," I said. I let it sink in for a moment, and then I gave him a big smile. "And Frank Kraunauer's."

He blinked rapidly, and then his hand began to drift down toward his gun belt.

"Shit, Julio, would you get in the car?" Blue Eyes called.

Ramirez shook himself. "Psycho asshole," he said. And then he climbed into the car and slammed the door.

It was a small victory, especially compared to the loss of a shower and a change into clothing without dried blood on it. But it was still a victory, and I hadn't had many of those lately. In any case, it was a great deal better than collecting a few facial bruises and a ride down to headquarters in chains. So I put on a confident face, turned around, and headed back up the street, to the strip mall where Brian waited.

I walked briskly: in part because it went with my confident face, but also because I wanted some distance between me and the squad car, just in case Ramirez changed his mind and decided to snap and go medieval on me anyway. Even so, it was a little more than ten minutes before I finally turned the corner and walked the last half block to the parking lot of the strip mall. The day had grown much warmer, and I worked up a nice sweat, which made me regret even more that I hadn't gotten my shower and some fresh clothing. But at least Brian was right there, pulled up in front of a mattress store, with his engine idling. He saw me coming, took in my sweaty face and unchanged clothes, and nodded, a phony sympa-thetic smile on his face.

I walked around his car and climbed in on the passenger side. "Well," he said in greeting, "may I take it that things did not go as you hoped?"

"Indeed you may," I said. I held up my wrists, which were visibly chafed and red from the handcuffs. "Somewhat less than optimal."

"At least you can be grateful," Brian said, "that I am not the type who insists on saying, *told you so.*"

"Didn't you just say it?" I asked him.

"Nobody's perfect," he said, and put the car in gear. "What now?"

I sighed, suddenly feeling very weary of it all. The excitement of my new freedom, and the adrenaline of my encounter with Ramirez had faded. I just felt numb, tired, sick of the monstrous injustice piled at my door—and still angry that my own door was closed to me. I had no idea what to do next. I had thought ahead only as far as a shower in my own snug little shower stall, and some clean, fresh clothing. But now? "I don't know," I said, and the weariness showed in my voice. "I suppose it's time for the hotel. But I don't have any clean clothes, or . . ." I sighed again. "I don't know."

"Well, then," Brian said, suddenly switching to a take-charge voice. "We can get you checked in anytime; that's easy enough. But you should be presentable first." He nodded at the knees of my pants. The dried blood was still there, quite visible. "We can't have you wandering around looking like that." He shook his head with an expression of distaste. "Nasty stuff. It just won't do. People would talk."

"I suppose you're right," I said. "So what do we do?"

Brian smiled and put the car in gear. "There's a very ancient and wise saying of our people," he said. "When in doubt, go shopping."

It didn't seem that wise to me. If I followed it literally, I would be spending all my time at the mall nowadays. But in this case, I supposed he was right. So I held up one weary finger in a valiant attempt at enthusiasm, and said, "Charge."

Brian nodded. "Better than cash," he said.

SEVEN

B RIAN DROVE US A FEW MILES THROUGH
the relatively light morning traffic and then
turned into the lot of a Walmart Supercenter. I
raised an eyebrow at him as I realized where he
was taking us. He smiled that terrible fake smile
and said, "Only the finest for you, brother
dearest."

He parked as close as possible, and I unbuckled
and opened the door, but I paused when I saw that
Brian made no move to get out and accompany
me. "If you don't mind," he said apologetically,
"I would rather wait here." He shrugged. "I
don't like crowds."

"I don't mind," I said.

"Oh!" he said suddenly. "Do you have money?"

I looked at him for just a moment. I had so far
been taking his uncharacteristic generosity
somewhat for granted, and it occurred to me that
perhaps I should not. He was my brother, and he
was more like me than anyone else in the world—
and for that very reason, it suddenly made no
sense that he would be so very attentive and
caring. But for the life of me, I could think of no
possible hidden motive. Perhaps he really was
just trying to be the ideal big brother. It was
hard to believe, but what else was there? So I just

shook it off and showed him what a really *good* fake smile looked like. "I'm covered," I said. "Thank you very much."

I walked into the store, still wondering, in spite of myself. Why would Brian spend so much time, money, and effort on anyone else, even me? I doubted very much that I would have, in his position. Yet he was, and the only explanation at the moment was the very obvious one, that we were brothers, and as a motive for good deeds, that made no sense at all.

It may be wrong of me to assume the worst, to fall reflexively into lizard-brain paranoia, but there it was. That was my world, and a great deal of experience and hard study of humans has done nothing to persuade me that anyone else is terribly different. People do things for selfish reasons. They help other people because they expect to get something in return: sex, money, advancement, or a bigger dessert, it doesn't matter. There's always something, no exceptions. For all the Mary Poppins care he was lavishing on me, Brian had to expect a significant payback. And I couldn't think of one single thing that I could give my brother that he couldn't get easier, and cheaper, by himself.

What did Brian want?

Of course, if I threw that question onto the floor among the larger and more savage questions that were ravaging my life, it would be torn to pieces and eaten in a heartbeat. Brian's motives were almost certainly far from pure, but his being nice to me was not nearly as life-threatening as Detective Anderson, the state attorney, and my likely return to a cell. I truly believed that he was no actual danger to me, and I needed to concentrate on dealing with the very large and real dangers to my life, liberty, and pursuit of vivisection. Plus, I had to find underwear.

So I relaxed as I entered the store and fought my way through the savage crowd, neatly avoiding most of the attempts to ram me with shopping carts. It was actually very pleasant to unwind a little amid the atmosphere of mean-spirited homicidal selfishness. It was soothing, really. I felt right at home, so very much back among My People that for a little while I forgot my troubles and just let the healing waves of psychotic, pinchpenny malice wash over me.

I found some wonderful underwear, exactly like what I always wore, and a new toothbrush, a few shirts, pants—even a bright blue suitcase to keep it all in. And I bought a charger for my phone, and one or two other necessities. I wheeled it all up to the register and waited patiently in the checkout line, smiling as I shoved my cart at the people who tried various ruses to cut in front of me. It was fun, and I was good at it—after all, I grew up here, too. I am brimful of that wonderful Miami Spirit that says, "Up yours! I deserve it!"

And I began to ease back into the old Dexter who really believed he did.

Brian was waiting patiently right where I left him, listening to the radio. I threw my packages into the backseat and then opened the passenger door and slid in. To my mild astonishment, the radio was playing a call-in show, the kind where distracted idiots blather their most intimate secrets to a nationally syndicated audience in the vain hope that a psychologist can convince them they are real, important, and worth more than the chemicals that compose their bodies. Of course, the program's host is never actually a psychologist; she usually has a degree in volleyball from a community college. But she *is* reassuring, and sells a lot of cereal for the network.

I had always found this type of program only slightly more amusing than minor surgery without anesthetic. But Brian was frowning, head cocked to one side, and giving the appearance of listening intently as the host explained that bed-wetting was perfectly normal, even at your age, and the important thing was not to let it affect your self-worth. He glanced up at me as I closed the door, and looked a little embarrassed, as if I had caught him doing something naughty. "Guilty pleasure," he said apologetically. He turned off the radio. "It's just so very hard to believe such people exist."

"They exist," I assured him. "And they out-number us by quite a lot."

"So they do," he said, starting the car. "But still hard to believe."

Brian drove me to a hotel close to the university. Aside from being very near my old home, and my alma mater, it was cheap and clean, and I knew all the restaurants nearby. Once again he waited patiently outside while I checked in. When I had a room key in my hand, I went back out to his car. He rolled down the window and I leaned on the car door. "All set," I said.

"No problems?" he asked—a little too innocently, I thought.

"None at all," I said. "Should there be?"

"One never knows," he said happily.

I held up the little envelope that held the plastic key. "I'm in three twenty-four," I said, and he nodded.

"All righty then," he said.

For a moment we just looked at each other, and once more the wicked, unworthy thought occurred to me that eventually he would expect something in return, and payback was *always* a bitch in my family. But I pushed the spiteful notion away. "Thank you, Brian," I said. "I really do appreciate all your help."

He flashed that awful smile. "Don't mention it," he said. "Always glad to help." I stood up and he called after me, "I'll be in touch!" And then he rolled up the window and drove away.

Room 324 was, as you might expect, on the

third floor of the hotel. It was nestled snugly in between the ice machine on one side and the elevator on the other, and had a breathtaking view of the building next door. But it was neat, comfortable, and completely anonymous, which suited me just fine for now.

I plugged in my phone to charge, and then unpacked my meager but functional wardrobe. And then I was done, out of important tasks, and surprisingly out of steam, too. I sank down on the bed and stared around at my new domain. It was a very small room, but it seemed huge after my super-snug cell at TGK, and all the extra space made me nervous. I would get used to it, of course—and probably just in time to be hauled back to TGK again when they decided to rearrest me.

Which they almost certainly would, and sooner rather than later. So what I really needed to do right now was explode into vigorous and positive action. That was my only hope—find a way to derail their train before it even left the station. Yup, that was the ticket. Charge. Get going. Do something.

And yet somehow I just couldn't. It suddenly seemed futile, hopeless, a complete waste of time and energy. I was just one small bug on the windshield, and there were so many large and mighty wiper blades eager and ready to smear me off the glass. No matter what I tried to do, they were just too big, too powerful. And I was much too all alone, even with my fancy lawyer. I was David, but this time Goliath had a bazooka.

I felt the vitality drain right out of me as quickly and completely as if somebody had pulled a plug, and a dark bleak mist seemed to roll in and cover me. I'd let myself have hope, and I knew better than that. The only thing hope ever does is make the eventual inevitable disappointment hurt even more. I should have learned that by now—learned it for all time when Deborah showed up at last, and slapped me down because I had hoped. I was well and truly alone in a world that wanted nothing from me except to take away my life, and they would win. They had all the guns, they made the rules, and they always won. I was going down, and expecting any other outcome was sheer delusional fantasy. I should just get used to the thought that if I was very lucky, I would spend the rest of my life in a cell. It was going to happen, no matter what. There was no point in pretending, no point in trying to avoid it, no point in anything. Everyone who cared about me was either dead or had changed their minds—and the worst of it was, I couldn't really blame them. I *deserved* to be shunned and locked up with all the other monsters. I was no different; I'd just been luckier. I'd had a wonderful run, longer than most, and now it was over. Accept it, get used to it, give up, and get it over.

I flopped back onto the bed. At least this mattress was thicker than the one in my cell. I lay back, determined to enjoy one last binge of comfort before they took me away forever, trying hard to enjoy the luxury of this huge, soft bed. Unfortunately, this particular mattress favored some new kind of ergonomic design; it was shaped like a soup bowl, with a large depression in the middle, and I rolled right into it as soon as I stretched out. Even so, it was a few notches above the pallet in my cell, so I wiggled around a bit until I got comfy. I did; it was very nice, even though it rolled me into the shape of a hula hoop. What a shame to leave all this behind forever.

I tried very hard to conjure some enthusiasm for fighting back and staying out of jail, where I could enjoy this kind of luxurious freedom whenever I wanted. Isn't liberty worth a little effort? And, of course, there is more to freedom than soft, concave mattresses. There are other things in the world that are far more dear to Dexter's heart—like food! Surely that was worth fighting for. Really good food, and a wonderful variety, any-time I wanted it, day or night!

But that unfortunately gave me an image of Dashing Dexter with cape and sword, valiantly fighting for the honor of a pizza, and that was a little too hard to take seriously as a motive for getting up off the bed. Besides, the food would never again be as good as it had been every night with Rita—and Rita was dead, killed by my very own personal brand of idiotic ineptitude.

The food had been even better with Jackie Forrest, my silver-screen sweetheart, the ticket to a new and shinier life—and the same sheer blind staggering stupidity had welled up out of me and killed her, too. Both of them dead, their bodies laid at my feet, because my monstrous ignorant prideful brainless incompetence had killed them just as surely as if I'd shot them dead. It was all on me and my stupid useless three-thumbed idiocy.

And this was the same great set of skills and smarts that I wanted to raise up against the entire justice system? *How do those odds look, Dexter? One hapless, hopeless clown who has proven that he can't find the floor even by falling face-first onto it? Lined up against him we have the cops, the courts, the penal system, the U.S. marshals, the Marines, and possibly the Taliban. . . . Did you really think you'd do any better this time, Dexter Doofus? Why not face the fact that all you ever were was lucky? And when you let Jackie Forrest die your luck ran out, all of it, for all time. The only good news is that there was nobody left to kill with your incompetence.*

I closed my eyes and let the misery wash over me. I was very glad that I can't feel human emotions. If I could, I would probably start to cry.

But once again, that little spark of self-awareness, that tiny demon that watches Me, started to giggle, and it tweeted me a picture: Dexter in the Dumps, sprawled on a saggy mattress in a cheap hotel and prepared to weep away this life of care that I have lived. I fall upon the thorns of life! Woe is me! And so forth!

And once again the picture was idiotic enough to stir me up from my torpid stew. All right, everything was bleak, black, hopeless, pointless, meaningless, empty of purpose. What had changed? Nothing at all—I had just forgotten, somehow, that life was struggle, and the only reward was to be allowed to live a little longer and struggle harder. Family life had set me up, and then the dazzling illusion of the life I might have had with Jackie had knocked me down. But all that was over, and we were back to basics. And when you came right down to it, the only purpose to life that I have ever been able to find is not to die. You couldn't let them push you out the door to go gentle into that good night. You had to rage, rage, and slam that door on the bastards' fingers. That was the contest—to delay the end of your personal match as long as you could. The point was not to win; you never did. Nobody can win in a game that ends with everybody dying—always, without exception. No, the only real point was to fight back and enjoy the combat. And by gum, I would.

I opened my eyes. "Rah-rah," I said softly. "Yay, Dexter."

All right, I accepted the challenge. Dexter would duel.

I might not win—I almost certainly would not win. But they would know they'd been in a fight.

With that decided, I felt better right away. *Well done, Dexter. Show that good old team spirit. Wave the flag, give 'em hell, and all that.*

Just one small question—how?

It was wonderful to resolve to Do Something, of course, but that meant I had to define "Something," fill in the blanks, dig out a few specific worms and decide where the fish might bite them. And that meant I had some powerful Thinking to do, which, on sober reflection, was not a terribly encouraging prospect.

My once-mighty brain had not really distinguished itself lately, and I was no longer filled with cocky can-do confidence at the prospect of hurling it into the fray. But it was all I had—and really, didn't it deserve one last chance to redeem its honor? Especially since this really was likely to be the last chance.

Of course it did; it was doing the best it could do, poor thing. So I turned it loose on the problem with an encouraging pat on the back. *Go on, Brain. I know you can do it. . . .*

Shyly at first, and then with increasing confidence, my thoughts began to form. First, there were two immediately obvious points of attack. The first was to find proof that somebody else did it. That should have been simple—even elementary, a word my brain suggested to show that it was getting back just a little panache. But after all, somebody else actually *did* do it— Robert Chase. But he was universally beloved, particularly by the cops, who he'd buddied up with. I would have to find very solid proof of his guilt, and that would be tough. Anderson would control all the forensic evidence, and he'd choke off anything that pointed to someone who was not named Dexter.

And that led to the second point, which was Anderson himself. If I could discredit him, the rest would be much easier. And if not discredit, then perhaps something a little more, um . . . permanent? As well as entertaining? Brian was quite correct when he suggested that one small accident would go far toward setting everything right. And Anderson had earned it several times over. It would even be fun. But it wouldn't go quite far enough; someone else would almost certainly pick up the torch and continue the race toward Dexter's Destruction. And sadly enough, it would probably be Deborah. Even sadder, she was almost certainly far too eager to take on the job. She was a lot smarter than Anderson, and she would not make the same stupid mistakes. She would plod grimly ahead until she had enough rope to hang me, and then, if our recent tête-à-tête was any sign, she would even offer to tie the noose herself.

No, if Deborah was suddenly in charge of investigating Dexter's guilt, things would be a lot worse than they were now. She might actually uncover evidence of some of the things I had really done. And then I would probably be back to Option One anyway—a sad accident for Deborah. I wasn't sure I was entirely ready to arrange that, not just yet. It was no longer unthinkable, though, which was certainly a large change. I remembered that night a few paltry years ago when I had stood above her taped, helpless form, knife in hand, every cell in me torn neatly in half between cutting and not cutting, Brian urging me on and the still small voice of Dear Dead Harry telling me it was forbidden.

I wasn't hearing that voice a whole lot lately. I wondered why. Maybe it was a realization that Harry's Plan had holes in it; it wasn't perfect. It had let me down. And maybe it was Deborah's complete rejection of any kinship between us—I was no longer a Morgan, and therefore no longer subject to Harry's posthumous manipulation. I was my own man now, and after all, I had never *really* been her brother. If I suddenly felt an urge to dispose of Deborah, why shouldn't I? And I would, too—if I felt like it. I just didn't, not quite, not yet.

So, casual assassination aside, what were my options at the moment? They seemed rather limited: trust in Kraunauer, trust in Brian, or take a little independent action of my own.

Trust had always been something I had trouble with. Perhaps it's a character flaw. But putting my life into someone else's hands seemed a little rash. To me, even putting my *lunch* in someone else's hands was lunatic irresponsibility. So even though I had every reason to believe that Kraunauer could pull off another miracle, and even though I had no reason to think that Brian would suddenly stab me in the back like Deborah had done, I decided that Option Three, independent action, was my best course.

Either find evidence that Robert was guilty, or reveal to the world that Anderson was playing dirty. Good—I would start with both and see which one paid off first.

I looked at the bedside clock; as hard to believe as it might be, it was still only a little after ten. I had a meeting with Kraunauer at two—and after that, I would begin.

I felt much better once I'd made my choice—so much better, in fact, that I fell asleep almost at once.

When I woke up, I had no idea where I was, or how much time had passed, and I spent several minutes lying on my back and blinking stupidly at the ceiling. It was the wrong ceiling, unfamiliar, and I was sure I'd never seen it before. My back hurt, too; it was bent in a strange half circle, as if I had fallen asleep inside a huge beach ball.

Slowly, memory came back: I was in a soup-bowl bed in a hotel room because I was out of jail and Anderson had sealed my house as evidence. But I was free; I didn't have to stay in a tiny cell and wait for odd sandwiches. It was a nice day outside and I could go out and enjoy it if I wanted to, walk the three blocks to the Italian restaurant and eat something that was actually good. I could do whatever I wanted—for the moment. But my first job was to work at making this giddy freedom a more permanent thing. I thought of Kraunauer—and had a brief moment of panic; I was supposed to meet him at two. Had I slept through it? What time was it? I rolled over and scrabbled out of the crater in the center of the bed with some difficulty and looked at the clock: eleven-twelve. Still plenty of time.

Since I was in no hurry, I didn't rush up off the bed. I kicked my legs over the edge and sat there for another minute or two, trying to organize my thoughts.

It is all very well to decide on independent action. The problem comes when you realize that it is, by its nature, independent. That means that you don't have anybody else to tell you what to do or how to do it, and that generally means that a great deal of deliberation is required before you get to the actual Action part. I pride myself on my vast talent for deliberation, but for some reason the circuits all seemed a bit rusty today. Maybe I had been sidelined for too long. Perhaps sitting in a tiny cell with every decision made for you tended to encourage your mental processes to take early retirement. Whatever the case, it was surprisingly hard to kick-start the mighty turbines of Dexter's Giant Brain, and it was another five solid minutes of stupid blinking before I began to have cogent thoughts.

Finally I got up and staggered to the little bathroom. I splashed cold water on my face, and watched in the mirror as the water dripped off and ideas began to trickle back in. "Independent action"—at the moment I wasn't really even independent. In fact, as I thought about it, I realized that I was stuck here, just as certainly as I'd been stuck in TGK, because Miami is not a city built on the premise that mass transportation is a really good idea. And in spite of the fact that I was only a few blocks from the Metromover, I couldn't really get anywhere and do anything without a car. Kraunauer's office, for example, was miles from the nearest Metromover station. I needed a car.

And I had one—somewhere. With any luck at all it was still mine, and still somewhere within the Metro Dade area.

So my first step was to get my car back. I nodded at my reflection: *Nice work, Dexter. That was real thinking there.*

The last time I'd seen my battered but trusty little car, it had been parked on the street near the house that was supposed to become Our New House, the Dream Home that had a pool and separate rooms for the kids and nearly every modern convenience. Instead, it was now the house where Robert Chase and Rita had died and, not coincidentally, where I had been arrested. I had to assume that it, too, was evidence now. I could also be pretty sure that somebody had found my car nearby—probably not Anderson himself, but somebody a few pegs down on the food chain who had to do some actual grunt work.

It might well be that my car was now evidence, too—but at least I knew how to find out. I pulled off the wire charging my phone and began to call around.

Half an hour later I had found out that my car was, in fact, impounded—but it was not *in* the actual impound lot. In fact, nobody seemed to have any idea where it might be, and I was not successful at getting anybody to see this as their problem. Since losing an impounded vehicle was highly irregular, I had to assume that I was seeing Anderson's fine handiwork again. He had probably donated my car to an artificial-reef program and taken the tax deduction for himself.

I actually admired Anderson's thoroughness; he seemed to have thought of nearly everything. It wasn't at all his usual slapdash knuckleheaded style of doing things—or to be more accurate, his style of Not Doing things. He had clearly taken a special interest in making me as miserable as possible.

Whatever the case, I didn't have a car, and I needed one. And because my Magnificent Mind was functioning at last, it was the work of mere moments for me to find a solution to this vexing problem. I called a nearby rental office. It took two more phone calls, but I found one that agreed to bring the car to me, and within a surprisingly short time the agreeable clerk called me from the lobby. I hung the Do Not Disturb sign on my doorknob and went down, and before I knew it I was behind the wheel of my very own vehicle again, relishing the new-car smell and the security of knowing that I'd bought the supplemental insurance and I could hit something if I really wanted to. Now if only I could find Detective Anderson in a pedestrian crosswalk . . .

I drove the rental clerk back to his office and then turned out onto Dixie Highway. I was free, I was mobile, and truly independent at last.

So what should I do with all this intoxicating freedom? And was it true, after all, that freedom was just another word for nothing left to lose? I had already lost my family, my house, all my clothes, my car—I should have felt *really* free. I didn't—I felt cheated, robbed, and victimized. But at least they'd left me my arms and legs, and my powerful-again brain. That alone put me way ahead of Anderson. Although he probably had more clean socks.

Still, that made me feel a little better—enough to realize that I was hungry. I glanced at the dashboard clock; less than an hour before my meeting with Kraunauer. Not a lot of time. I ran my mind over the list of gourmet dining establishments in Miami that might fit my somewhat narrow needs: sandwich, good, fifteen minutes . . . It was a surprisingly small list. In fact, it was a completely blank list. There was no place that was close and quick that also offered something that was actually good to eat. I would have to do without. I heard a small grumble of protest from my stomach; it seemed to say, *Not really . . . ?* And it was a fair complaint. Maybe I could eliminate one of my three qualifications? It had to be fast, no matter what, since time waits for no man, and neither did Frank Kraunauer. That meant it really had to be close, too. That left only "good," and to eliminate that meant an outright abuse of the values for which I lived.

On the other hand, half a block ahead of me I saw a famous burger logo flashing beside the road. My stomach immediately responded to the sight with a shout of, *Go for it! No,* I said firmly. *I refuse. I will not sink so low.*

My stomach rumbled threateningly. *You'll be sorry. . . .*

I told my stomach that I am more than my hunger. I exceed the sum total of any want that is merely physical. And we have standards, damn it! Would we really settle for anything less than excellence, out of mere convenience?

Apparently we would. Seven minutes later I was wiping the last tendrils of grease from my chin and throwing away the meager detritus of my shameful downfall. Lo, how far the proud Dexter has fallen, I thought, and I heard the burbling echo as my stomach replied, *And loving it.*

EIGHT

FRANK KRAUNAUER'S OFFICE WAS IN A high-rise on South Beach. Most of the absurdly expensive attorneys in Miami have their offices along Brickell Avenue, but as I may have mentioned, Frank Kraunauer was in a class by himself. He could have kept an office in the middle of American Airlines Arena, and the Miami Heat would have cheerfully rescheduled their entire season to fit his office hours. But Frank apparently *liked* South Beach, and so he had taken the entire penthouse of a shiny new tower at the south end of Ocean Drive. He had a spectacular view, of course—the open ocean on one side, Government Cut on another, and, crawling along almost under his feet, the beach and the boulevard with their teeming masses of barely dressed Brazilian models, Italian *contessas*, and Midwestern skater girls.

After working my way through three security guards and a busy but very dignified outer office, I was finally handed off to a gray-haired woman at an enormous desk of steel and walnut. She looked like a member of MENSA who had been a supermodel in her youth before moving on to a career as a Marine Corps drill instructor. She looked me over with a steely, unflinching eye, and then nodded, stood up, and led me to the end of a hall, where a massive door stood open. She waved a hand to indicate that I might have the great boon of passing through the portal and into the Presence. I bowed to her formally and stepped into a large office, and found Frank Kraunauer standing by the window looking down at the beach. The window was actually a floor-to-ceiling wall of thick and tinted glass, but in spite of the huge expanse of window I didn't think he could see very much detail from this high up. Still, the light from the window lit him with what looked like a full-body halo, the perfect effect for the Attorney Messiah. I wondered whether it was on purpose.

His suit today was clearly a first cousin to the one he'd worn to see me at TGK. It was a lighter shade, but the same unearthly fabric: light, supple, and very nearly self-aware. Kraunauer turned to face me as I came in, gave me his polite-shark smile, and waved at a chair that almost certainly cost more than a new Cadillac Escalade. I sat in it carefully, determined to avoid wrinkling it, while at the same time savoring the luxury. There wasn't a lot to savor. It didn't feel much different from the chair I had at home that cost twenty-nine dollars at a thrift shop.

"Mr. Morgan," Frank said. He slid into his own high-backed chair behind a slim and shiny glass desk. "How are you enjoying your freedom?"

"It's very nice," I said. "I don't even miss the room service."

"I wouldn't think so," he said. He opened a folder and frowned at it. "I'm afraid we need to think of this as temporary, however."

I had of course been expecting some such pronouncement, but even so I felt my heart sink a few notches. "Oh," I said. "Um, how long have I got?"

Kraunauer's frown deepened and he drummed his fingers on the glass of his desktop. "I can't say right now," he said slowly, as if he really hated admitting that there was something he didn't know. "That's going to depend on a lot of things. But the state attorney's office has three years to file." He looked up. "I would be very surprised if they take that long. Somebody really wants to see you go down for this," he said.

"Quite a few somebodies," I said.

He nodded. "It's the kind of crime that makes people more than usually upset," he said.

"Including me," I said. "I didn't do it."

Kraunauer gave a quick wave of the hand and one small twitch of a smile, to show that even though he didn't believe me, it didn't matter in the least. "The important thing is," he said, "they've played a little bit fast and loose with legal procedure. In some cases, way over the line. That's how I got you out. But!" He shook his head. "It cuts the other way, too."

"What do you mean?"

"I don't know what other procedural surprises might be waiting for us," he said. "And now that they know I'm onto them, they're much more likely to dot all the i's from here on out. Next time they arrest you . . ." He shrugged. "Anyway, fair warning. The easy part is over."

I had a little trouble thinking of anything that had happened so far as "easy," but maybe he meant easy for *him*. In any case, I took his point. "What can I do to help?" I said.

"Oh, well," he said, looking slightly amused and forbidding at the same time. "You can't really approach any potential witnesses or anything like that. I don't want any amateur sleuthing."

"Actually, it wouldn't be amateur," I said. "I am a trained forensics investigator . . . ?"

"Yes, of course," he said politely. "The point is, we don't want to muddy the water, or give them any more ammunition than they already have." He gave his head a very slight, very elegant shake. "I don't want you to kid yourself. The state attorney is taking this on in person, and he's pretty good." He spread both hands about six inches apart and then let them drop back to the desktop. "I happen to think I'm better—but he will make a good case. You are in very real danger here." He waited for it to sink in for a moment, then let me see three gleaming teeth. "On the plus side," he said, "they *don't* know what I'm doing—or what I know. I can tell you, I've seen the paperwork they've filed already, and I think I know what they're going for. A lot of it having to do with your daughter—ah, *step*daughter?" He waggled a finger at me absent-mindedly. "They're going to hang the whole case around the pedophile angle."

"I'm not a pedophile," I protested.

He waved a hand dismissively. "They'll make you look like one. And they'll assume you threatened your daughter and she'll say what you want her to. Standard scenario, predigested, and the courts eat it up. So whatever you can do with the forensic stuff won't matter." He nodded, as if he approved of the prosecutor taking that approach. "I think that's the plan."

"I see," I said, and to be honest, I almost did. "And do *we* have a, um, counterplan?"

"We do," he said, with the kind of firm, decisive command that added at least one more zero to his fee. "But it's not a sure thing; it never is." This time I got four teeth. "I do have a pretty good batting average," he said modestly. "And I think we have a decent chance of beating this thing. But for the time being, I want you to keep a low profile. You can't leave town, of course. But stay out of sight; don't make trouble." He nodded at his own wisdom, and added, "And keep all your receipts, naturally. We're going to tack all your expenses onto our countersuit."

"Oh," I said, mildly surprised. "There's a countersuit?"

Kraunauer smacked the desktop with both hands, and for the first time he looked genuinely happy. "Absolutely!" he said. "After the bullshit they put you through? They're going to pay for this, believe me. Through the *nose*." I thought for a moment he would rub his hands together and say *mwa-hahaha*—but the moment passed, and all he said was, "Seven figures, certainly. If it's the right judge, eight."

"Eight figures—as in, more than ten million?" I said, almost sure I was misunderstanding him.

"At the very least a healthy seven," he assured me.

"Um—do you mean *dollars?*" I said, which was certainly feeble, but I couldn't really picture that kind of money—in the abstract, no problem, but in my bank account? Three Ferraris, fly-to-Paris-for-breakfast money for little old *moi*?

"Dollars," he said, nodding very seriously.

And I believe he said a few more things, but I'm not quite sure I remember them. Ten minutes later, with my head still spinning, I was back in my rental car. The meeting with Kraunauer had obviously been intended to reassure me and, of course, to keep me from killing anyone else for a while, which was a little more problematic. Other than that, it had seemed like a waste of time. Aside from dazzling me with the picture of

Dexter the Fabulously Rich, I had learned nothing except that I couldn't leave town. And the farther I got from Kraunauer, the more unreal the promised money seemed. Still, at least everything was deductible, if I kept my receipts. Hotel, car rental, even food.

I thought it all through again. The tantalizing tease of a ridiculously large payout was clearly just talk, designed to keep me in line. Even if we won some mythical enormous judgment, it would go into the appeals process for years, and when it finally came out the other end, most of the cash would go to Kraunauer. So aside from pie in the sky, the only thing of substance I could really take from the meeting was the warning: My freedom was temporary, and it was far from certain that I would escape a permanent place in prison. I knew a little about the state penitentiary. It made TGK look like a luxury resort. It would probably make me yearn for my old cell, and wish I could have the Brown Meat Sandwich again.

As that word, *sandwich,* bounced through my head, my stomach rumbled unhappily. The burger was not sitting well, and my finely tuned digestive system was clearly troubled. *Who's sorry now?* I told it. It growled back. Even the taste in my mouth was bad: rancid grease, chemical-tasting sauce, and something that hinted at old and badly abused meat. And even that was luxurious com-pared to what I might be eating soon, and for the rest of my natural life. I was suddenly forlorn. I remembered an old phrase Harry had used: *down in the dumps*. Considering the taste in my mouth, it was very appropriate.

And what could Dexter possibly do to chase away the blues? The answer occurred to me at once, and I accelerated off South Beach, onto the causeway, and away into a slightly brighter afternoon.

By the time I got close to the airport, I was practically drooling again. There was really only one valid way to cheer up Dexter. But since that was out of the question, food is always a satisfactory, though somewhat distant second best. The food that does it better than any other for me has always been Cuban, and for Cuban food there is only one possible destination for me. And so, in spite of my recent Unhappy Meal, I was eager to get there and set things right in the Land of Lunch.

Two generations of Morgans have been going to Café Relampago for their *comidas Cubanas*—three if you count my baby, Lily Anne. She was very partial to the *maduras*. I was, too—and the *medianoches* and *ropa vieja* and *palomilla* and the *batidos de mamey* and of course the black beans. Hundreds of other places in Miami made all these things, but to my prejudiced palate none compared to Relampago. So when I realized that I wanted, *needed,* a Cuban sandwich, it was natural for me to head out to the little strip mall near the airport where the Morgans always went for such things.

But as I pulled into the parking lot it occurred to me to wonder whether I would still be welcome there. Technically I was not a real Morgan any-more—at least according to Deborah. And what if she was having her lunch there right now? Would it be awkward? Violent? Anything could happen—the sight of me might even ruin her digestion. But considering our recent history, I decided I could live with that, so I nosed my new-smelling car into a parking spot and went in.

The decor of Café Relampago had not changed much in twenty years. It was rather basic, running to paper place mats rather than tablecloths, and thick, battered white plates, most of them with a chip or two banged out of the rim. The service was, to be diplomatic, indifferent, and sometimes downright odd. But as I walked in and smelled the aromas coming from the kitchen, I felt like I was coming home. Just to be certain that the homecoming wasn't a little too literal, I looked carefully around; no sign of Deborah. So I just stood for a moment, sniffing, before going to my usual booth toward the back and sliding in, facing the door.

My feeling of homecoming continued through the long and strange ceremony of trying to attract the attention of a waitress, ordering, and then, finally, eating my sandwich and a side of *maduras*. It all seemed to take on the air of a ritual, and when at last my plate was empty and the food was inside me where it belonged, I felt satisfied in a way that went far beyond mere sated appetite. It was very near what I imagine religious bliss must feel like, for those who have souls and can maintain a straight-faced belief in that kind of fairy tale.

In my case, it took the form of a mysterious sense of ungrounded optimism. The sandwich was good, and now it was gone, deep into Dexter; the miracle of transubstantiation had happened again, and now everything would be all right. Even as I recognized this feeling as stupid, I enjoyed it anyway, and I leaned back in the booth, ordered a *café con leche*, and thought about what Kraunauer had said. "Amateur sleuthing." It nettled a bit, though I did see his point. But I had already decided that my only real hope was exactly that, and nothing he'd said changed that. He had no idea what I was really capable of doing—which was probably a good thing. So I considered where I might start with my Independent Action Project. As always, my mind reacted to being well fed by kicking right into high gear and producing a really top-notch analysis.

First: The case against me depended on motive. Kraunauer had confirmed that they would try to make everyone believe I had killed Robert,

Jackie, and Rita because they found out about my pedophiliac interest in Astor. Anderson had probably chosen to go that way because tagging me as a pedophile would automatically trigger the most extreme gag reflexes. I was already guilty just because I was accused of that most heinous of crimes. And just as important, because Astor was a minor, and as Kraunauer had said almost certainly bullied into a fake cover story by me, her brutal slavering stepdad, her testimony would be discounted, if it was presented in evidence at all. That made the whole case a simple matter of my word against a massive amount of circumstantial evidence—and whatever you might have learned to the contrary from watching *Perry Mason* reruns, circumstantial evidence is very convincing. If a prosecutor leads a jury—or even a judge—through a logical, barely credible sequence of events backed up by one or two flimsy pieces of happenstance, he will get a conviction nine times out of ten. When you factor in how badly Anderson, and most of the force, really wanted me to be guilty, it rose to nine and a half.

So that meant that as long as the SA could believably present me as a pedophile, it was ipso facto proof that I was also a murderer. And of course, once I was perceived as a murderer, it was just common sense to believe I was a pedophile, too. Most people find circular logic oddly compelling, even reassuring. I had testified in enough courtrooms; I could see it going that way as clearly as if it was unfolding in front of me.

All right, then: Taking the ipso facto as prima facie, it stood to reason that if I was *not* a pedophile, I was also not a murderer. *Quad erat demonstrandum.*

And that meant that if I could provide reasonable doubt—if I could prove, for example, that Robert Chase was the real pedophile—then I should be in the clear. Robert actually *was* the pedophile in this case. But thinking about things the way I was, reflecting on them as evidence, taking into account legal procedure and precedent, had already pushed my brain into a groove of wily, multifaceted paranoia where nothing was as it seemed. And so I actually had to pause and reflect for just a moment, because the fact that Robert really was a pedophile made it seem like a disadvantage to present him as one. Dealing with our legal system will do that to you. You begin to doubt your own existence unless you have very specific instructions from the judge.

Happily for me, I shook the mood off quickly. Since I knew Robert was guilty, I also knew I could find a way to prove it. I am not being conceited; I am very good at finding things, especially when my precious irreplaceable skin is on the line. If proof existed, I would find it. I tried to cap that thought with another Latin tag, but apparently my teachers had failed to provide me with one I hadn't used yet. Oh, well; there was really no point in being angry at them, even for such an important failure. *Illegitimi non carborundum*, I suppose.

I had been forcibly inflicted with Robert's company for several weeks, while he learned to "be me" for the part he was to play in the pilot, the doomed TV show that had brought all this fecal matter raining down on my undeserving head. In that time, he had almost certainly said a few things that might give me a place to start looking. I thought back over everything I remembered hearing him say, and unfortunately it was a fairly small file. Not what he had said—he'd blathered almost nonstop. The problem was what I *remem-bered* him saying. There had been so much drivel, and it had been so annoying, I had tried very hard to shut him out, to *not* hear what he said, since it was mostly fatuous, vacuous, and even flatulent.

By the time I finished my *café con leche*, I had come up with a grand total of very close to zero significant leading remarks. In fact, it really came down to just one thing: He'd taken a weekend trip to a "private resort" in Mexico. Knowing what I now knew about Robert, I would bet that it was a resort designed especially for someone with his whimsical tastes in romantic

127

partners. But of course, I would have to find the place, based just on his remarks.

. . . Except, wait a minute. He had actually gone there, by airplane. That meant that there would be a paper trail, and even better, a *data* trail. The airline would have kept a record, and so would both U.S. and Mexican customs and the credit card company. Setting aside false modesty for the moment, I have to admit that I am very good at getting into a database where I am not wanted. With that many options, I could almost certainly find a few excellent clues about the location of Robert's Club Ped.

But then I would have to go down there to find absolute proof, which was very dicey indeed. In the first place, such places tend to regard prying in a rather unfavorable light, and also tend to express their unfavorable opinion of the pryer in very vigorous, usually fatal ways.

And in the second and more important place, Mexico was a foreign country with a different language and very different customs. I couldn't simply go down there and flounder around until I saw a gaggle of heavily made-up ten-year-olds marching into a closely guarded compound. And that raised another problem with the whole Mexican Adventure: What kind of proof could I hope to find? The whole thing began to seem more and more tenuous the more I thought about it.

Surely there must be something else? Out of

pure reflex I lifted my little porcelain coffee cup, even though I'd completely drained it several minutes ago. But it may be that there were fumes left in the cup, or that the *café con leche* was particularly strong today. In any case, as I absentmindedly sipped at the empty cup, I had a sudden flash of memory. I remembered the doomed TV show's director—Vic Something?—saying that he'd heard all the rumors about Robert and chose not to believe them. If Vic had heard rumors, others would have heard them, too. In my far too brief stay in the swinging swirling world of show business, I had learned that what we peasants call "Hollywood" is, in reality, a very small and tight-knit town. One drunken remark can echo around that unpleasant little community for years, and I was quite sure that someone else would be able to tell me something helpful about Robert and his wicked ways.

Of course, things being what they were, Hollywood was nearly as inscrutable as Mexico. But at least I knew one or two residents of that bright and brittle world, and I could hope that they would remember me as "poor Jackie's boyfriend," rather than "the pedophile/killer." And if I could confront them face-to-face, I could give one of my justly famous impressions; Grieving Boyfriend should be easy. I'd seen it often enough on the afternoon dramas I used to study.

And perhaps the coffee really wasn't as good as

I'd thought a minute ago, because in the midst of feeling slyly smug about my anticipated acting, I remembered that I was not supposed to leave town, and that made it just a little harder to get face-to-face with somebody on the West Coast. I was back to the legendary Square One.

So I sat for a few more minutes, trying to think, and realizing only that I was still not as good at it as I used to be. Maybe I never really was. I'd probably just been stumbling along wrapped in a cloud of ignorant luck, unaware that there was a huge storm of Retribution trailing along behind me. It had caught up to me at last, and I wasn't going to think myself out of it.

Happily for the tatters of my self-esteem, when I was just about to think up some wonderful new adjectives for Self-Deluded Idiot, I pulled myself back from the bleak landscape that I was suddenly finding far too comfortable. *Misery is a weakness,* I told myself sternly, *and you can't afford it right now.* There were things to do, people to see, and no time at all to sit and mope. I looked at my watch; it was almost four. I could still get back to my hotel room before the worst of the rush-hour traffic turned the roads into a homicidal crawl.

I paid my check and headed out the door.

NINE

RUSH HOUR STARTED ANYWAY WHEN I was only about halfway home. I thought about it that way, "home," out of some kind of strange mental reflex. Of course, the first part of the drive was the same one I used to take going home from work, back in the Golden Days when I actually had a home. And a job. One way or another, I would have a home again someday, either in a nice little house or in the Big House. But the idea of a job was starting to seem odd— especially a job working alongside all the people who were trying to frame me now. I wondered whether I would ever go back to work there.

In any case, the traffic had slowed to a vile-tempered crawl long before I got off the Palmetto Expressway and came down onto South Dixie. I tried, but I couldn't make myself relax and get into the true spirit of it, honking and flipping people off. It just didn't seem worth doing. I'd always enjoyed it in the past, but now . . . I wasn't enjoying anything lately. Not getting out of jail, or Kraunauer's suits—nothing at all. It was very disturbing, but on the list of Dexter's Big Problems—Survival, Freedom, Life Itself—I couldn't rank it very high.

Nevertheless, that was what I was musing about

when I finally got to the hotel: Why couldn't I take pleasure in anything? Had it been too long since I'd had a chance to unwind and enjoy a quiet evening with a Special Friend and a roll of duct tape? I tried to remember the last time and couldn't. Patrick Bergmann, the idiot redneck who'd been stalking Jackie Forrest, didn't really count. Smacking somebody with a boat hook in broad daylight just wasn't the same thing as really taking time to get to *know* a person, really *expressing* myself in a pointed way, getting a New Friend to Open Up and share his feelings— muffled by a gag, of course. Some of those feelings were quite loud and shrill, and it wouldn't do to bother the neighbors.

But how long had it been? It seemed like an awful long time ago. In fact, I couldn't remember the last time. That was even more disturbing. I tried harder, but my memory wouldn't cooperate, no matter how much I furrowed my brow. And finally, I couldn't think about anything else but trying to remember, and as I turned into the hotel parking lot, I was so busy flogging my memory that I almost didn't see the police car parked at the lobby entrance.

Almost—at the last moment I did, in fact, see the patrol car, and I had absolutely no doubt that their presence at this hotel was no coincidence. They were here because they'd discovered that this was Dexter's Secret Hideaway. I didn't know if they were here to observe, to hassle me, or to rearrest me, but I didn't look favorably on any of those choices, so I drove calmly around to the rear of the building and found a parking spot near the Dumpster, where they couldn't see me getting out of the car.

I sat for a moment with the engine off. It was unlikely that they were here to arrest me—there was only one unit, which meant two uniformed officers. If they came for me—*when* they came—there would be several of those, plus a couple of motor-pool cars filled with detectives, and probably a satellite truck or two from the TV stations. So they were probably here just to watch, or to prod me a bit. But the smart thing to do was still to avoid the cops altogether; my morning chat with the two gendarmes in front of my house had proved that amply. So I got out of the rental car, locked it carefully—I knew well that Anderson was not above planting something incriminating—and used my room key to slip in the back door of the hotel.

I took the stairs up to the third floor, not really a hardship for me—although I found that I was actually breathing a little heavily by the time I passed the second floor. It reminded me forcibly that I had been sitting in a cell without my evening jog for much too long a spell. I would have to start again soon, or risk losing all my hard-won fitness.

Still, I did make it all the way up to the third floor without fainting. I peeked through the fire door to make sure nobody in a blue suit was watching. Nobody was. I stepped through and strolled down the hall to my room, thinking that the really clever move here was to grab my stuff, slide back down the stairs, and find a new hotel. I didn't actually have anything to hide, of course. But if They knew where I was, They would hound me. The fact that They were here now was proof of that. I didn't want a repeat of my encounter with the pair outside my house, and I didn't want a cop sneering at me every time I stepped out of the shower. Far easier just to ease on down the road. It would only take a minute to pack, one of the few benefits of having almost nothing. I could go south and inland a bit, find another cheap and anonymous hotel, and then call Brian to let him know.

Wonderful—I had a plan. I stuck the plastic key into the slot on Room 324 and waited for the light to blink green. It didn't. I tried again, jiggling the handle, wiggling the key. Nothing. Out of nothing more than frustration and spite, I kicked the door. The light blinked green. I left the Do Not Disturb sign in place and strode confidently through the door and into my tiny but free domain. I managed two very nice strides before I looked at the bed and jerked to a halt as abruptly as if I'd been yanked backward by a rope. Not because I'd run out of striding room, and not because there was a cop on the bed.

There *was* somebody on the bed, but he didn't look like a cop. He was short and stocky and dressed in dirty work clothes. His skin and hair were dark, and his face was scarred and pockmarked, almost as if it had caught fire and somebody put it out with a golf shoe. It was the look of a day laborer hoping for a green card, not a cop. And I really, truly, devoutly hoped he was *not* a cop in disguise.

Because he was also dead.

He lay on the right edge of my bed, one arm crossed peacefully over his chest, and the other dangling over the side. He looked just like he had been sitting on the edge of the bed and then suddenly fell asleep and flopped over. On the floor right under his dangling hand was a wicked-looking folding knife, the kind they call a tactical knife. It had a six-inch blade, and it had been used quite recently, judging by the color of the blood that decorated it.

For what seemed like a very long time I just stood and stared, stupid with shock. I am certainly not a stranger to violent death. I have been around dead bodies in both my personal life and my professional career, and I am not shocked, horrified, revolted, frightened, or dismayed by the sight of an obviously murdered body. Under different conditions, I might even enjoy one from time to time. But to find one here and now, in my room and in my present circumstances, was so calamitous, appalling, and perilous that I could not even think.

I finally became aware that my mouth was dry—I had been gaping, with my mouth hanging open. I closed it hard enough that my teeth made an audible click. I took a deep breath and tried to concentrate; this was no time to dither and gawk. I was a murder suspect, and there was a lobby filled with eager cops below, and here I stood consorting with a dead body in a room registered to me. No explanation I could possibly invent would get me out of this, not even if it was presented by Frank Kraunauer.

Action was required, decisive, effective, and immediate action. First step: Determine who had the audacity to be dead on my bed. I summoned all the shards of my cool analysis and stepped in for a closer look at my new roommate.

The bed around him was still relatively clean and blood-free, which was wonderful news. But the front of his shirt was soaked with the stuff, and it appeared to be coming from a wound in his chest, just left of center, right where the heart is located.

For a moment a little voice nagged at me that something was wrong, and I didn't get it. Then, quite suddenly, the nickel dropped. This picture didn't make sense, and not merely because it was in my room. The wound that must have killed him should have spouted a fountain of blood and colored the whole room; it hadn't. That meant he had died rather quickly. Otherwise the wound would have pumped out a great nasty geyser, enough to soak the mattress and ruin the carpet. The heart stops gushing out blood when it stops pumping. So he had taken the wound, and enough time had passed for the blood to soak his shirt—ten seconds? Maybe a little more, but not much. Then he sat down on the bed and flopped over, dead, heart stopped before it could pump out any more. And that left me with a very interesting question:

How had he died?

I mean, obviously from a wound in the chest, yes—but was I supposed to believe he had stabbed himself? Because I didn't. And that meant that somebody else had done it.

I looked around the room, hoping for some clue—a matchbook from a strip club, perhaps, or a monogrammed glove. No such luck. But I did notice something else: My closet door was ajar.

I admit that I have my foibles. They are almost all harmless, most of the time. One of these is that, when I check into a hotel room, I always look in the bathroom, then in the closet, and then I close both doors securely. I do this out of mere paranoia, just to satisfy my inner child that nothing is lurking, but I always do it.

But my closet door was now ajar, which meant that somebody had opened it. It wasn't house-keeping—the Do Not Disturb sign would keep them away. So it was almost certainly my new and silent friend. It was possible he had searched the room. It was not possible that he had searched the room and then stabbed himself.

And that meant there had been *two* people in my room.

And one of them was in my closet.

I felt my heart leap instantly into high gear and I looked around me for some kind of weapon. Nothing. Perhaps the chair—but wait. *Calm down, dear Dexter, and spend one more moment in beautiful thought.*

I did. I took a deep breath—keeping my eyes on the closet door, just in case—and I thought.

If somebody was waiting in the closet to leap out and cause me grievous bodily harm, possibly resulting in death, it would be stupid to wait this long. They would have done it almost imme-diately after I came in the door, well before I saw the other body and pulled my own weapon—not that I had one. But in principle, you jump the other guy before he figures out you're there and takes countermeasures. No such thing had happened, and therefore . . .

Either there was no second stranger in my room—which meant that Stranger One really had stabbed himself—or Stranger Two was still there in the closet. And if he was, in fact, there in the closet, then either he meant me no harm, or he was no longer capable of doing any harm.

Slowly, and with all the caution I could muster, I stepped over to the closet. I listened for a moment and heard nothing. I stepped to one side, reached back, slid the door open, and waited. Ten seconds, twenty, thirty. No shots fired, no charging mastiffs, no flashing blades and cries of, *Kali!* Nothing.

Just as slowly, I peeked around and into the closet, and sure enough, there was Stranger Two.

He lay on one side in an impossibly uncomfortable position, slumped against the back wall of the closet with one arm pinned awkwardly under him and the other tucked behind him, between his back and the wall. His left eye socket was a nasty mess; something very sharp had clearly been shoved into it, far and hard enough to cause his present apparent lack of life. I knelt beside him in the doorway of the closet and looked closer.

Stranger Two was hatched from roughly the same gene pool as Stranger One. He was younger, and perhaps an inch taller, but he had the same olive complexion, stocky build, dark hair—even the same crappy skin. I didn't need to feel for a pulse to be sure. He was indeed quite dead.

I stood, hitting my head on a coat hanger on the way up. I took a step back and tried to put together what had happened. The closet was next to the room's door, on the left as you entered. It was the perfect place to wait; anyone entering would step into the room and be a step past the closet before they knew someone was there.

From the closet it was three good steps to the edge of my bed, where Stranger One had so thoughtlessly chosen to die. So: One comes into the room. Two steps out and stabs him—but no. Then the fatal wound would be in the back, not the chest. And One would have had no time to react and draw his knife.

This way, then: One has his knife out already. In fact, he uses it to jimmy the door, which also explained why I'd had trouble opening it with my key. He steps into the room, knife at the ready, every sense quivering and alert—and he sees or hears something in the closet. He pauses, ready for trouble.

In the meantime, Two is waiting in the closet. He assumes that whoever comes through the door will walk past, allowing him to leap out and dispatch them easily. But One has paused just inside the door; Two can't see who it is or what he's doing. Freeze frame; nobody moves. Tension mounts. Finally, unable to stand the strain any longer—and perhaps confident of his ability with a knife—One flips open the closet door.

But Two is waiting for him, with *his* knife ready. One sees this and raises his arm instinctively, leaving a clear target for Two's knife, which plunges into One's chest. At almost the same moment, One strikes back. With his arm held high, he stabs down from above, directly into Two's eye, and his blade enters Two's brain and kills him almost instantly.

As Two collapses onto the closet floor, One staggers on into the room, three steps to the bed, perhaps unaware that the wound he has taken is also fatal. He sits, and moments later, he joins his adversary in the dark and toasty-warm afterlife—dead so quickly there's not even time for much blood flow.

Problem solved. *Very nice work, Dexter.* I now had a good idea of what had happened. It proved once again that my brain was returning to its natural lofty roost. But as satisfying as that was, there was one remaining question:

So what?

What did it matter how this happened? The only really vital piece of knowledge was *why* it had happened to *me,* and that might as well be written in Aramaic and sealed in a cave. With only two dead bodies to go by, there was no way I could know why these two had come to *my* room to die—and that meant that I was just as ignorant about whether they had living friends, who might be on their way up here right now to see what was taking so long.

There was only one piece of that important

question that I could unravel, because in general terms there were only two possible explanations for why it happened here, in my room. First, it was entirely coincidental. This was Miami, after all. Random murders happen all the time, and they have to happen somewhere. The killers had simply chosen the handiest room, and that just happened to be mine. I thought about that for nearly a full second before concluding that it was nearly as likely that the sun would come up in the west, and just stay there for a few weeks.

All right, coincidence was laughable, and that led inevitably to the second possibility: The two strangers had deliberately come to *my* room, *knowing* it was my room, in order to (a) snoop, (b) kill me, or (c) something I didn't have enough data to guess. That was more likely—but it also meant that there were two sides in the struggle, and apparently neither side looked on poor mistreated Me with anything approaching Loving Compassion.

I am quite comfortable with the notion that someday, somewhere, I may meet some benighted, unenlightened individual who decides they just don't like me. Different strokes for different folks, and so on.

Carrying this thought to its logical conclusion, I can even accept that in some distant time and place, one of these people may decide he dislikes me enough to kill me.

But two *teams* of people? In the same time and place? And both teams finding my existence so distasteful that they break into my room carrying sharp instruments?

Who would want to kill me that much? And what had I done to deserve two separate squads of haters?

Of course, Anderson, or someone lurking in his shadow, was the most obvious suspect. But I could not believe he would approve something that was a major felony. His faults were so numerous they left almost no room for virtues, and he would certainly fool around with misdemeanors, if it served the end of Dishing Dexter. But murder was a bit much, even for him. Even if his victim was somebody who richly deserved to die, what kind of law enforcement officer could possibly countenance murder, even of another killer? It was unimaginable. Besides, he was clearly having too much fun keeping me alive and miserable.

So who did that leave? Who else really had it in for me enough to try to kill me? Could it be some random vigilante? Somebody who was so enraged to see me released that he decided to take things into his own hands? It was possible, but it seemed just a trifle far-fetched. And then to imagine two of them competing to be first to take my scalp . . . No. It just wouldn't do.

But there wasn't anybody else who hated me

this much—at least, not among the living. If you could choose from among those I had helped over the edge and into death, you could easily make up two teams—even an entire league. Other than that, though, it seemed impossible. In truth, aside from my recent unwelcome burst of publicity, nobody even knew I existed. I had worked very hard my whole life to keep a low profile. I had worked even harder to be certain that no surviving friends, relatives, or business associates of my Playmates knew who and what I was. Who did that leave?

Without thinking, I sat on the edge of the bed to ponder. My weight caused the body to roll toward the crater in the middle of the mattress, and one of its arms flopped over toward me. If nothing else, it confirmed that the body was freshly killed. It also confirmed that I was still stupid. I got up quickly and moved over to the desk and pulled out the chair.

I sat, and unconsciously assumed an erect upright position. My second-grade teacher, Mrs. Parker, had always insisted that we sit up straight. She said it encouraged a good flow of blood up the spine and into the brain, which would help us think and learn better. We had always laughed at her for this lunatic idea—behind her back, of course; Mrs. Parker had a temper. After all these years, though, it now seemed that she might be right. Because after only a few seconds of sitting up straight in the wooden desk chair, I had an Actual Thought.

I couldn't possibly figure out who these dead strangers were, not just from looking at them. And if I didn't know *who,* I couldn't tell *why.* Beyond the fact that it's always nice to know who hates you enough to kill you, I needed to know *who* before I could decide what to do about it. And that's when my Actual Thought spoke to me.

All right, Dexter, it said. *Then try to figure out who knew that this was your room.*

The list of people who knew I had checked in here was much smaller. I had to assume that Anderson and other interested cops might know. And anybody else who could sneak in the back door of a database could find out, if they wanted to know badly enough. I could have done it myself in under ten minutes, simply by checking for a credit card. The moment I used a card with my name on it my location became public knowledge. And the record would state quite clearly the name and address of the hotel, and then—

I blinked. I had just had *another* thought, something very significant; I was quite sure of it. I didn't know what it was, but I knew it was there. I rewound my thoughts, marching them by again at a slower speed. I sat up even straighter in my chair as I scanned—and there it was. I don't know if I found it because I had such excellent posture, but just in case, I sent a little mental thank-you card back through time to Mrs. Parker.

It was indeed quite true that anybody with a computer and half a brain could track me by following what I did with my credit card. But there was a tiny factoid that was even truer.

I hadn't used my credit card.

Brian had used *his* credit card.

What had he called it? A "nice anonymous" card. I'd thought nothing of it at the time, so I tried to make up for that lapse now. Brian could not possibly have a credit rating of any kind; he had no fixed address—for that matter, I wasn't sure he even had a fixed identity. That obviously meant that the card was either fake or stolen. Most financial companies would look on this with very strong disapproval. But as evil and mercenary as they are, most credit card companies stop just a wee bit short of actually killing people who abuse them, even if unwillingly.

Could it be the hypothetical person Brian had possibly stolen the card from? That was a little more likely—but then why were there two of him?

I thought deeper. Aside from this faux card, Brian had a sudden excess of cash, enough to hire Kraunauer. Where do sudden large chunks of money come from, and what connection could they have to the corpses in my room? I stood and looked at them again, first on the bed, then in the closet, and then I went back and stood over One, where he lay so peacefully on my bed.

All of us who work in law enforcement are taught to shun racial profiling, so I tried not to leap to any conclusions that might offend anyone, no matter their ethnic background. But it was not possible to avoid the observation that the dead men looked very much like they might be Mexican or Central American. And having said that, one could not help adding, with all possible political correctness, that if indeed they *were* Mexican or Central American, and since they had actually been violently murdered, and it had happened right here in Miami—and if, additionally, there truly were significant amounts of money lurking in the background, then it was at least possible—*possible,* mind you, no more than a chance that had very little to do with the men's ethnic identity—it was, as I say, *possible* that drugs might be involved somewhere along the line.

Brian would certainly have no moral scruples about the drug trade. In truth, he had no actual morals at all. He had all the advantages I enjoyed of being heartless, soulless, empty inside, and devoid of human feelings—but he was not burdened with any of my disadvantages of artificially grafted-on standards. The business of buying and selling drugs would seem like a perfect opportunity for profit, and even self-expression, considering the nature of the competition. He might well have gotten involved in some way. And knowing Brian, he could just as easily have done something that made someone in this ultraviolent world just a trifle peeved.

That didn't explain who my new friends were. But it did offer the first clear explanation of how and why, and it had the added virtue of being very easy to check.

I picked up my phone and called.

After only three rings, Brian answered. "Brother," he said with low-quality artificial bonhomie. "How art thou?"

"Not bad," I said. "A great deal better than my uninvited company."

"Company?" he said. "Is this wise in your present circumstance?"

"Terribly *un*wise," I said. "Especially since they are both exceptionally dead."

For a long moment Brian said nothing.

"Should I add that I have no idea who they are?" I said at last. "And that I also didn't do it?"

"Good additions," Brian said softly, and there was a dangerous edge to his voice I hadn't heard before. "Describe them."

"Both about five-foot-six and stocky," I said. "The nearer one is mid-thirties, dark hair, olive skin, pockmarked face."

Brian hissed. "The left wrist," he said. "Please examine it."

I stepped over to the bed and flipped the left arm off the chest. There was a tattoo, about four inches long. It showed a bleeding Jesus wrapped in the coils of a cobra. "Interesting tattoo," I said into the phone.

"Jesus with a snake?" Brian said.

"Yes," I said. "You know this guy?"

"Stay put," he said. "I'm on my way."

"Brian, there are cops in the lobby," I said. But he had already hung up.

I looked at my phone and wondered whether I should call Brian back. I decided not to. He probably wouldn't answer, and anyway, I felt that somehow the phone had let me down. I didn't trust it anymore.

But I had to do something. "On my way" could mean a few minutes—but it also might mean half an hour or more. I still had no idea what was going on here, but whatever it was, I didn't think I could simply stand in my room and wait for the next piece of the puzzle to fall into place. The stakes were very high, and the next piece might well land on my head. Clearly I needed to get out of this room as quickly as possible.

On the other hand, I also needed to meet Brian, and he was coming here. But once again, my newly revived brain rose to the challenge, and this time I wasn't even sitting straight. Brian would arrive and, just as I had, he would see the cop car out front and proceed to the rear door.

I left the room, making double sure the door latched securely behind me, and the Do Not Disturb sign was still in place. I walked to the stairway. I went all the way down to the ground floor and stood to one side of the door, so I could see out into the parking area without being too easily seen myself.

Ten minutes passed. A woman in a business suit walked by outside and climbed into her car —or at any rate, I assumed it was her car. If not, she was a very smooth car thief.

Five more minutes went by. Two teenage kids came clattering down the stairs from the second floor and slammed out the door to the lobby without paying me any attention.

I looked out the window in the back door. I couldn't see very much, but none of it was moving. I wondered whether Brian had met with some kind of accident—or, all things considered, more likely an on-purpose. How long should I wait for him? Sooner or later something unpleasant was almost certain to happen. The cops would decide to come up to my room and push me around, or the maid would come to change the sheets. It was even possible that whoever had sent the two Strangers would send another one. Failing that, they might come around in person to make another corpse out of anyone hanging around in my room—or in the stairwell, for that matter. Where the hell was Brian?

I looked out the window again. No sign of him; nothing but a white van. It rolled slowly closer, until I could see the side of it. In big black letters, it said, ATWATER BROTHERS CARPET.

I blinked. Atwater again? Really?

The van backed up into a position that blocked the door where I stood, and a moment later Brian appeared. He wore a pair of tattered gray coveralls and carried a heavy canvas tool bag, and when he put his hand on the door he saw me, and nodded.

I opened the door and Brian stepped through. "Brother," he said. "We may not have a lot of time."

"That thought had occurred to me," I said. "Along with a few others of a more personal nature."

He showed me his teeth and took my elbow. "Time for recriminations later," he said. "Right now there's work to do."

I nodded and let him hurry me along up the stairs and down the hall to Room 324. I opened the door and we went in, and Brian stepped directly over to look at the body on the bed.

"Octavio," he said. "As I feared."

"You do know him," I said.

He nodded. "He was an ally. Perhaps even a friend."

"Friendship is such a fragile thing," I said.

"Like life itself," Brian said, looking down at Octavio with an expression that might almost have been regret, if I hadn't known Brian so well.

"I don't want to intrude on your grief," I said. "But—"

His head snapped up and he looked at me, all traces of expression completely gone. "Yes," he said briskly. "You said there were two?"

"I did," I said. I motioned him over to the closet, and he pushed the door open and knelt beside Stranger Two for no more than three seconds. Then he stood and said, "I don't know him."

"Well," I said. "Even so . . ."

"Right," Brian said. "Let's get them out of here." He reached into his canvas bag and took out a rolled-up gray cloth something. "Put this on," he said, tossing it to me.

I unrolled coveralls that matched his own, and pulled them on over my clothes. By the time I had them buttoned up, Brian had rolled up the bed-spread, with Octavio snugly inside. "If you would, brother?" he said politely. "Take that end, please."

I picked up the near end of the bundle. It felt like the feet. Brian picked up the other end, nodding toward the door, and together we clumsied Octavio out, into the hall, and down the stairs.

For some reason dead bodies always seem to be heavier than live ones, and Octavio was no exception. He was surprisingly heavy for such a small corpse, and by the time we had him down the stairs to the back door I was thoroughly winded, and had acquired a brand-new cramp in my back muscles.

Brian bumped the door open with his backside, and we carried Octavio the short distance to the back of the van. Showing surprising strength, Brian held the bundle with one hand while he opened the van's rear door, and then lifted the body up and in while I came forward with my end. I looked casually around as Brian pulled the bedspread out and slammed the doors shut. I saw nothing at all except a few dozen parked cars.

"All right," Brian said. "Next?"

We went back up the stairs and repeated the process with Stranger Two. Luck was with us, and we saw no one—and hopefully no one saw us, either. In any case, it was only a few more minutes before we had the second body in the van. I stretched and wondered whether I would ever again have feeling in my back that wasn't pain.

Brian slammed the van's back doors, locked them, and nodded at me. "One more trip," he said.

"Really?" I said. "I only counted two bodies."

"Your things," he said, moving past me to the

hotel door. "It might be best if you check out now?" He turned and showed me a small and knowing smirk. "Even better if you do it by phone," he said.

"You may be right," I said.

He nodded. "It had to happen someday."

We went up together, pausing cautiously on the third-floor landing, and again at the door to my room—or ex-room, to be more precise. There was no sign of anything or anyone, and I went on in. It took me less than a minute to gather my meager possessions, and we trudged back down the stairs and out to the parking lot. I walked past the van and threw my suitcase into the trunk of my rental car while Brian climbed into the driver's seat of the van.

"Follow me," he said, and then added, "Not too far."

"All right," I said. I got into the rental car and followed Brian as he nosed slowly out of the lot.

The police car was still parked by the front door, and there was no sign of its occupants. We crawled by and out onto U.S. 1, and a few blocks up, Brian made a U-turn and drove south. I followed along, wondering what he had gotten himself into, and why it should be my problem.

A few minutes south, Brian pulled into a strip mall that held, among other things, an all-night doughnut shop, and I nodded. Nobody would notice my rental car here. I parked it in a spot close enough to the doughnut shop that some of the bright fluorescent lights spilled onto the car, and walked to the far corner of the lot, where Brian sat in the van, engine idling. I climbed into the passenger seat, and he drove back out onto U.S. 1 again, heading south.

Neither of us spoke for several minutes, until finally, as we passed Sunset Drive, I couldn't take it anymore.

"I'm very sorry about your friend," I said.

Brian sighed. "Yes," he said.

I stared at him expectantly, but he said no more, and I was miffed enough to feel that I shouldn't have to drag it out of him, so I was silent, too. We drove still farther south, almost all the way down to Homestead. Then Brian turned off U.S. 1 and headed west, inland, turning several times. We straightened out at last on a long stretch of badly maintained pavement that led due west. The sun was going down, and it shone directly in my eyes, so I turned sideways and looked out the window. There wasn't a lot to see in this old residential area. The houses gradually got older and smaller and farther apart, and then finally they disappeared altogether and we were driving along a dirt road through a landscape of scrub, canals, and saw grass. We had come to the very edge of the Everglades. I looked at Brian, hoping he might be ready to explain all, but he looked straight ahead at the road and the setting sun.

After another ten minutes of awkward silence, Brian finally turned off the dusty road and drove us through a gate in an old and sagging chain-link fence. The gate itself hung forlornly from one rusty hinge. There was an ancient faded sign on it, but I couldn't see what it said.

A hundred yards or so past the gate we came to the lip of a large old quarry filled with milky water, and Brian put the van into park. He turned the engine off, and we continued our silence for a moment. The engine ticked a few times as it cooled, and not too far away an entire symphonic chorus of insects began their evening concert.

And then Brian shook his head, took a deep breath, and turned to me.

"And now, brother," he said, in a dead and very serious voice, "I'm afraid I have to tell you that you have placed us both in grave danger." He leaned closer. "I need to know who you told about your hotel room."

TEN

FOR JUST A MOMENT, I COULD DO nothing but stare at Brian and blink my eyes. I seemed to be doing that a lot lately. Was it a sign that I was really losing it, sliding off the edge into permanent stupidity? Or was it merely an indication that I had never been quite as clever as I'd thought I was?

In any case, I stared, and I blinked. Brian's question caught me completely off guard; *Who had I told?* It was an absurd question on so many levels that I didn't know where to start. I had already concluded that someone had traced Brian, not me, because of his credit card. That seemed so obvious to me that it didn't even bear mention—how could he fail to figure that out? On top of that, Octavio was *his* friend, not mine, so his death meant nothing to me—it was clearly aimed at Brian.

But most basic of all, there was absolutely nobody left for me to tell, not about hotel rooms or anything else. Aside from Brian himself, nobody would talk to me.

After a long pause that was just right for conveying dramatically my sense of dumbfounded surprise at his question, I finally managed to yank my powers of speech out of the ditch and back onto the conversational highway. "Brian," I said, "did you truly think somebody killed Octavio to get at me?"

Almost as if he was working hard to make me feel better, Brian responded with a gratifying gape-and-blink of his own. I thought it lasted much longer than mine had, but it may be that such things seem longer to watch than to perform. But I gave him all the time he needed, and he finally closed his jaw and slumped over just a little. "I did," he said. "I actually thought that. Silly me." He looked at me and shook his head. "I seem to be doing some very stupid things lately."

"There's a lot of that going around," I said.

"But then how did they find me so quickly?" he said, with truly puzzled dismay.

It began to occur to me that, in spite of his many other fine qualities, Brian was not quite as adept as I was at life in the cyberworld. "It's just a guess," I said. "But I think they traced your credit card."

He looked at me with such blank astonishment that I revised my opinion: Brian didn't have a *clue* about life in the cyberworld. "Can they really do that?" he said. "That card was clean— I've had it for only a few weeks."

"Throw it away," I said. "Put it in the quarry here, with Octavio and—Oh. Are we putting them in the quarry? I just assumed—"

"We are," Brian said. "The water has a very high

lime content. Nothing left in a couple of months."
I didn't ask him how he knew that—but I did file
it away for future reference. Assuming I actually
had a future, which seemed to be somewhat in
doubt at the moment. Brian frowned, and looked
very puzzled. "But seriously, I thought a credit
card was . . . well, you know. Don't the banks
guard the data pretty carefully?"

"Absolutely," I said. "It would take me almost
a full ten minutes to hack in and trace somebody."

"Oh, dear," he said, and he shook his head again,
very slowly. "I can see that there are some rather
glaring holes in my education." He leaned back
in the seat and furrowed his brow, looking like
he was trying to remember if he'd done anything
else that might come back and bite him. "Perhaps
I spent too much time learning to get rid of
bodies, and not enough on the more pedestrian
side of things."

"So it seems," I said. "Let me suggest that for
the time being, cash is probably safest? Um—
you do have plenty of cash, don't you?"

"Oh, yes, not a problem," he said absently,
apparently still cataloging the sins of his recent
past.

"Perhaps this would be a good time to tell me
where it came from," I said. "And who is trying to
kill you to get it back. Did you take their drugs,
too? Or just the money?"

Brian jerked upright and looked at me, and then nodded. "Sometimes I forget that you're a trained investigator," he said. "Of course you would figure that out."

"Elementary, dear brother," I said.

"I'm not sure how much to tell you," he said slowly, obviously stalling while he thought about it.

"Tell me enough to keep me alive," I said.

"Yes. That much, at least." He inhaled deeply, then blew the breath out again noisily. "Well," he said. "As you have guessed, I took a little jaunt into the drug trade. Nothing really out of the way, just a new venue for my well-practiced talents." He smiled modestly. "But at a much higher pay grade."

"All right," I said encouragingly.

Brian shrugged. "It's an old and tawdry story," he said. "I was doing very well out of it, financially speaking, and rather enjoying my work." He gave me his terrible smile, but this time there seemed to be real pleasure behind it. "Lots and *lots* of little jobs. A surplus of . . . encounters?"

I nodded. Brian shared my sense that actually speaking aloud about what we did was somehow indelicate, but we both knew what he meant. He had been permanently and painfully removing people who his employers considered obstacles. It seemed like a wonderful job, and apparently quite lucrative. "Freelance?" I asked. "Or working for one particular outfit?"

"Just one. Just Raul." He smiled again. "Rather melodramatic, but they called him 'El Carnicero.' The Butcher."

"Yes," I said. "It is a bit over-the-top."

"That's their world," Brian said with a shrug. "They seem to enjoy histrionics."

"So what happened?" I said. "Did you piss off the Butcher?"

"Oh, no, not at all," he said emphatically. "I was very good at my job, and he appreciated that. But unfortunately for all concerned, the Butcher pissed off Santo Rojo." He showed me his teeth. "More histrionics, I'm afraid. It means the Red Saint?"

"Yes, I know."

"Apparently Raul overstepped his proper boundaries," Brian said, trying very hard to sound regretful. He wasn't nearly as good as I was at that kind of thing. "Santo resented it. And soon we were in a full-scale war." He paused and cocked his head to one side, as if seeing the things he described. "Santo was a much bigger man—far more powerful, with lots more minions and money and influence. Raul was relatively small-potatoes—an up-and-comer, but definitely not there yet."

He shrugged. "To cut to the chase, it seemed to me that I was on the losing side, and it was only a matter of time until Raul and all of us in his little family were eliminated. I discussed this with a coworker—"

"Octavio," I said.

Brian nodded. "Yes. Because as it happened, Octavio knew where Raul had stashed a rather sizable chunk of money in case he needed to, um, relocate? Quickly?" He twitched his mouth in a brief and unconvincing smile. "One of the hazards of the trade, you know," he said. "Every now and then you really do have to get away in a hurry."

"So I understand," I said. "So you and Octavio took the money and ran."

"Yes, that's right," he said, and he sighed. "All that money. I had no idea there would be so much." He looked at me happily. "So very much, brother. You have no idea."

"I'm sure," I said. "But where's the problem? With Raul and most of his gang dead, who was left to come after you?"

"Ah, well, that's the thing," Brian said ruefully. "You see, we made a very small miscalculation. As it happens, Raul managed to plant a bomb in Santo's headquarters. It went off quite successfully; Santo Rojo and a large number of his minions were killed, and the rest flocked to Raul's banner. The war was over—but unfortunately, Raul was still alive." He smiled at me again, no more convincingly than any other time. "And among the missing were two of his trusted associates and an extremely large piece of untraceable cash. Raul feels very possessive about his cash," he said.

"A common failing," I said.

"And so, to conclude," Brian said, "Raul and all his remaining henchmen are working very hard to find me. Probably *not* with the intention of begging me to return to work."

"Almost certainly not," I said. I frowned and tried to reason out loud. "All right," I said. "So Raul's computer guy tracks your credit card to my hotel room. No doubt he assumes that Dexter Morgan is you, a nom de guerre. He sends someone to conduct your exit interview—"

"Nicely put," Brian murmured.

"And he waits in the closet, thinking your return is imminent," I said, and then I stopped. "But what about Octavio? What was he doing there?"

Brian sighed again—the third time he'd done it. It was getting a little annoying, especially since I knew quite well he felt nothing at all, let alone anything that might induce a sigh. It had to be a new habit he was trying out for some reason, just for the effect. "I can only guess," he said at last. "Octavio was staying at your hotel." I must have looked surprised, because Brian spread his hands in apology. "Mere convenience," he said. "Octavio must have seen this other man and recognized him. He followed him to your room, and . . ." He snapped his fingers. "The rest is tragic history."

We were both silent for a minute. "Is it likely," I said at last, "that Raul would send one mere henchman to dispose of you?"

"Oh, no, certainly not," Brian said cheerfully. "He had great respect for my talents."

"So there would be two? Three?"

"Several of them, without a doubt—five, six, even ten," he said, still quite cheerful. "I think this would be rather a high priority for Raul. And he would almost certainly come along with them."

"Just because of a little money?" I asked.

Brian got even merrier. "Oh, it's not a little, very far from it," he said. "But of course, it's much more than the money. If he lets me rip him off, he loses a great deal of respect." He raised an eye-brow at me. "That's everything to these people, you know. No, Raul will send a good number—and *keep* sending more until it's done." And he nodded with satisfaction.

Somehow I could not bring myself to share his lighthearted joy at being pursued relentlessly by several platoons of dedicated, experienced assassins. "Wonderful," I said.

"They're quite good, too," he said. "And completely relentless, of course."

"Of course," I said. He fell silent and I followed

164

suit, using the time to ponder a little bit. Now I knew how Brian was funding his recent great flow of generosity. That didn't tell me *why* he had been so helpful, but I was starting to get a nasty suspicion. I had already suspected that Brian needed my help for something unpleasant. It was starting to look considerably worse than unpleasant—downright lethal, and I wasn't really sure I wanted any part of it, brother or no. While it was true that I have normally been willing, even eager to help out a family member in need, I had always understood that to apply to moving furniture, or providing a ride to the dentist. I didn't think family ties had ever been intended to cover helping your brother survive the relentless attacks of an enraged drug lord.

But as I thought that, I realized that it was already too late for me to politely bow out. Raul's men had been clever enough to trace Brian's credit card rather quickly. They would certainly know the room was registered to me, and they would soon find that it was not Brian's fake identity, and then they would be onto me. They would assume that I was connected to Brian in some important way, and I would become a target. In fact, I had *already* become a target just by being in that room. Although a mere unknown connection might not seem terribly damning evidence of anything to a rational being, I knew enough about the drug world to know that it has very few rational residents. They didn't need to know a thing about me to decide that I had overstayed my time on planet Earth. I was now on their hit list, as sure as I sat here.

Another thought popped into my head, which was a very good sign that things were working the way they should. This thought whispered to me that if Brian truly wanted my help, he might well have sent Octavio there himself while I was out, knowing that he would run into the hit man. And I, faced with two corpses in my room and the certainty that I had been identified, would feel compelled to join Brian in his struggle. Even more—with Octavio dead, all that lovely money was presumably Brian's now, and he had given me no reason to think that he liked Octavio—or anyone—more than money.

I looked at my brother. He was still frowning, squinting into the last rays of the sun that sank down past the horizon as I watched. He turned to me, shook his head, and said, "I'm afraid I have to ask a very great favor."

"Did you kill Octavio?" I said by way of answering. "Or set him up to be killed?"

To his very great credit, Brian didn't even pretend to be surprised or offended. "No, I did not," he said simply. "Naturally, it had occurred to me that I might want to, sooner or later—but I needed his help to avoid being killed myself. And now . . ." Brian suddenly went shy and turned away from me. "As I said," he said apologetically, "it's a very great favor."

"Yes, it is," I said, and I admit I sounded peevish. "I don't know how I can possibly—I mean, I am being watched, you know. By the police. And I may be dragged back to jail at any moment. What did you think I could do?"

"Nothing strenuous," Brian said, a little sulkily. "Some light and entertaining chores. You know, watch my back while I do the heavy lifting, and then join in for the fun part."

I opened my mouth to speak, to point out that we needed to worry about more than the five or six heavily armed homicidal lunatics who were after us now. Even if we disposed of them, there was a large and ruthless organization behind them. And then I closed my mouth again as I realized that of course Brian knew that, and what that meant he was hinting at. The word *hubris* popped into my head, and just to show that I remembered even more big words, I tacked on *overweening,* because if what I suspected about the nature of his plan was true, overweening hubris was a huge under-statement. It was grandiose conceited flamboyant stupidity on a colossal scale that exceeded all earthly boundaries, and I was sure it was exactly what Brian was contemplating.

I looked out the windshield in front of us at the milky water of the quarry. The surface shone brightly, even though it was completely dark now, which I thought was quite appropriate.

"Brian," I said. "You don't have any intention of trying to get away, do you?"

He showed me a great many of his teeth. They gleamed oddly in the darkness. "Why, no, I don't," he said happily. "What would be the point? They'd find me eventually."

"But that's insane!" I protested. "You can't possibly believe that you can take out an entire cartel!"

"Not by myself," he said sweetly. And he very wisely said no more, and cast no Significant Glances at me.

"Shit," I said, and I meant it.

"Quite possibly," Brian said.

"How in hell could you possibly eliminate dozens of armed, crazed *drogas*?"

Brian smiled modestly. "One at a time," he said. "Raul is the only really hard one to get to. And as I said, he will show up to be in at the finish."

"Shit," I said again, quite aware that I was repeating myself, but unable to think of a better summation.

"I admit it's challenging," Brian said. "But with a little help—I mean, you know, the *right* help . . ." He sighed and shook his head. "Octavio was very handy in some situations, and he had *some* skill with a knife—"

"Apparently," I said.

"But he was basically an accountant. This would have been far beyond him."

"I'm pretty sure it's beyond me, too," I said.

"Oh, no, not at all!" Brian insisted. "It's absolutely made to order! Aside from the gifts we share, you know about the law and cops and how they react. And you know a great deal more that may be important. As you have just demonstrated with my credit card?"

He leaned toward me and lowered his voice, as if afraid that Octavio might overhear us from his snug nest in the back of the van. "And in addition to all that, dear brother," he said, with silky suggestiveness, "we could finally do something *together*. More than one something . . ."

I looked away. I knew that Brian had always wanted to play, him and me together, working in unison on the one thing we both liked and needed to do above all else. And quite honestly, the idea was not totally unattractive to me, either. It seemed like the closest I could ever hope to come to sharing a *human* experience with another living creature. That was a little ironic, of course, considering what that experience would be, but even so . . .

But no, it was madness to think about it. In my present circumstances I couldn't even leave town. I was watched, maybe even tailed occasionally, and Brian wanted me to join him in a full-blown bloodbath. Worse than that, I was now involved whether I wanted to be or not. So if I wanted to stay alive—and I thought I just might—I had no choice but to go along with Brian. And if I wanted to stay out of jail—and I was quite certain I did—I had to help Brian create and dispose of dead bodies. At very best, this would clearly violate Kraunauer's instructions to keep a low profile and stay out of trouble. At worst, it didn't bear thinking about.

"Brian," I said at last.

"I know," he said. "As I said, I ask a great deal." He turned to me, and for the very first time I thought I saw genuine enthusiasm, even warmth on his face. "But *think* of it, brother!" he said. "What a glorious undertaking! You and me against the world, into the fray side by side, guns blazing and hearts singing!" He smiled modestly. "Or if not actual hearts—"

"Yes, I get the picture," I said, and somehow I still failed to catch his enthusiasm. In fact, I was rather sour on the whole thing. "But you have to understand the trouble I'm already in, Brian."

"Well, yes," he said. "But doesn't that just add spice?"

"It does not," I said firmly. "What it adds is lethal uncertainty. I am very likely to be back in jail at some point."

"But surely Frank Kraunauer—"

"Frank Kraunauer is hardly a sure thing," I said.

"He himself has said not to be too optimistic."

"I'm sure he's just being cautious," he said.

"Caution is an excellent choice," I said. "I am pursued, hounded, and even chivied by the mangy curs of justice, and you want me to go with you to wade in rivers of blood?"

"I would hope not actually *in* the blood," he said with distaste.

"It's impossible, Brian," I said. "I can't possibly risk it."

"You can't possibly avoid it," he said.

I looked at him. He was very serious now, no fake smiles, phony sighs, or second-rate histrionics of any kind.

"Quite seriously, brother," he said, "they have shown some skill at locating people, and they have your name." He shook his head. "I'm afraid your choice is rather simple: Go hunting—or be hunted."

I clenched my teeth and looked out through the windshield. In the full darkness of this night, the water of the old quarry still gleamed. But in the greater Darkness that surrounded Dexter, there was not even a single tiny pinpoint patch of brightness. Brian was quite right. Whatever I might wish, I was in this thing with him, and my only choice was exactly what he said it was: hunt or be hunted.

"Shit," I said one last time.

Brian nodded with a nearly convincing show

of sympathy. "I'm sure you're right," he said.

I watched the water of the quarry. It wasn't doing anything. For that matter, neither was I. I was in a hole every bit as deep as the quarry. Only a few hours ago I had been filled with grim optimism at the prospect of being free at last— free to guarantee my continued freedom by building a case for my innocence along with Anderson's and Robert's guilt. I was *doing* something, and it was something I was *good* at: finding things with a computer and sniffing out assorted naughtiness. I had finally managed to move the game back to my table, where I knew the rules and the odds, and I had stupidly allowed myself to see just one tiny glimmer of light at the end of the long dark tunnel. And then with a terrible self-satisfied smirk, Life had come breezing in and blown out all the candles again.

If Raul didn't get me, I'd be back in jail. Death or Durance, it didn't seem to make much difference. And quite honestly, Death looked a little more likely at the moment. I couldn't even hide properly—I was forbidden to leave town, which meant my investigation was hamstrung before I started. I couldn't go to Mexico or L.A. to find evidence against Robert. And Brian just sat there with a stupid smile on his face when *he* had dropped me into this mess, and *he* could stroll out of town at will, even flee the country if he wanted to, leaving me behind to twiddle my thumbs and wait for the ax to fall. *He* could go anywhere, and—

Aha.

"Brian," I said.

He looked at me with polite inquiry. "Yes?" he said.

"You know I need to work on my own problems," I said.

He nodded. "You may have mentioned it."

"If I help you with this," I said, "will you help me?"

"Of course!" he said. Then he frowned. "Ah—what kind of help, brother?"

"I need some answers I can only get in L.A. Maybe Mexico. But I can't leave town," I said. "You can."

Brian nodded. "A trip to L.A.? A delightful town filled with kindred spirits. I'd be happy to go." He frowned and hesitantly added, "Um, Mexico might be a little . . . awkward?"

I sighed. Didn't someone once say that every stumbling block is really a stepping-stone? Whoever had said it, if I had them here right now, I would crack them on the head with their stepping-stone and put them in the quarry with Octavio.

"We'll do what we can," I said.

Brian nodded, cheerful again. "Perhaps even more," he said.

ELEVEN

BRIAN HAD TWO STORM ANCHORS IN the back of his van. We wired Octavio to one and his new friend to the other, and muscled them both into the water of the quarry. They sank quickly, leaving not even a ripple to show where they had been, and I tried very hard not to see that as a metaphor for my life at the moment. It didn't work. All I could see was the sad Detritus of Dexter sinking into the dark abyss, cold and murky water closing over my head, leaving no trace at all of the wonder that had been Me.

All the way back to U.S. 1, Brian kept up a polite stream of inconsequential chatter. I responded with monosyllables, for the most part. There didn't seem to be a single ray of hope for me anywhere. Either I would be yanked off the streets and flung in a cell again or, if I was really lucky, I would merely be chopped and shredded by Raul's men. The odds against my coming out the far end of this long dark tunnel were so monumental that I was more likely to grow wings and learn to grant wishes. Once again, saddest of all, I found that all my bitter thoughts led to the same place, the tragically mundane refrain of *Why Me?* It took away any possibility of finding nobility in my suffering. I was just another poor schlub caught up in something he could not control. Dexter's Dilemma—and the most pathetic part of it all was that it was identical with what is generally known as the Human Condition. Me: reduced to mere Humanity. It wasn't even worth one of my high-quality synthetic mocking laughs, not even to rub Brian's nose in the fact that I did it much better than he did.

We drove back to the doughnut shop where I'd left my car, idling past once on U.S. 1 while we looked for any sign of untoward activity, Legal or Otherwise, around my car. There was no sign of anything: no police cruiser or unmarked car, and as far as we could see, there was no conga line of swarthy killers with machine guns, either.

Just to be safe, Brian drove around the block and approached the parking lot from the rear. He pulled up on the street, in the shadow of a large old banyan tree, and put the van in park. For a moment we both sat silently. I don't know what Brian was thinking, but I was still scrabbling across the rough tundra of my brainscape, looking for a way out of the unfolding unending hopelessness of being Me nowadays. As far as I could see, there wasn't one.

"Well," Brian said eventually.

"Yes," I said. "I suppose so."

"Cheer up, brother," he said. "Keep smiling."

"What on earth for?"

He smiled. "It confuses people?" he said.

I sighed. "I'm afraid it's beyond me at the moment," I said. I opened the door. "I'll find another hotel and let you know where I am."

"By phone?" he said, sounding rather anxious. "I mean—I suppose the business with the credit card has made me overcautious, but—"

"You're right," I said, mentally kicking myself; I should have thought of that. "Let's meet here, at the doughnut shop, for breakfast."

"A wonderful thought," Brian said. "I do like fresh doughnuts."

"Eight o'clock?" I said, and he nodded. "All right, then." I jumped down out of the van and Brian put it into gear.

"Good night," he said as I reached to close the door. It was a wonderful sentiment, but it seemed unlikely, so I just nodded and trudged over to my rental car.

I found a small and anonymous motel just south of Goulds, a little north of Homestead. It was an old-style one-story hotel, clearly built in the fifties to accommodate weary Northerners as they rested from motoring down the old Dixie Highway and exploring the wonders of Florida. The place was run by a mom and pop who really should have retired no later than 1963. They seemed surprised and a little put out that somebody would interrupt their TV viewing by asking for a room, but I showed them cash, and after a certain amount of grumbling, they gave me a key and pointed away toward the left wing.

My room was halfway down a row of identically tatty doors with peeling paint and missing numerals. The inside was no better; it smelled like mothballs and mildew and was nearly as tiny as my cell had been. But I hoped that the place was small enough to be off the grid somewhat. And the proprietors had shown no sign of any technical savvy beyond changing channels on their old TV set—and not even with a remote control—so perhaps they would simply pocket my cash without leaving any trace on the information grid.

I locked the door and secured it with the rusty chain that hung there, and then walked over to the bed and looked it over. A large part of the mothball smell seemed to be coming from the bedspread, and the two pillows were so flat I thought they might just be empty pillowcases. I put one hand on the mattress and felt it. It offered all the firm support of a bag of fresh marshmallows. But it was a bed, and I was suddenly very tired.

I flopped onto the bed—a little too energetically, as it turned out. It was apparently a few years older than my hosts, and it did not merely sag; I actually felt my back touch the floor. Then it moved a few inches upward again, leaving me in a half-folded position that was already starting to give me back pain. The mattress in my other hotel room had been bad enough; this one was far worse, enough to make me nostalgic for the nice hard shelf they'd let me sleep on in jail.

I turned and twisted and finally found a position that was not actually painful, though it was very far from comfy. So much to do, and so many distractions. Was it really only this morning that I woke up in a cell? It seemed impossible—so much had happened since that it seemed like another lifetime. But it was true; mere hours ago I had been blinking in the sunlight, thrilled at my reentry into a world with fewer steel bars. And I spent most of the day convinced that nothing in the world could possibly be worse than going back to jail—until my brother had very thoughtfully provided a couple of new options that were far, far worse.

But I still had to keep myself free. I pushed my brain away from contemplating the hordes of savage drug-crazed assassins who were no doubt sniffing my trail, and I forced myself to think about my real agenda, keeping Dexter out of jail and, if possible, putting Anderson in.

Let's see; I had just decided on independent action. I needed to find some proof that . . . what was it again? I was distracted by an enormous yawn that seemed to take over my entire body. Proof—I needed to show that Robert was a pedophile, and Anderson had played games with evidence. I remembered that I had decided my first step was to talk to Vince, ask him to help me gather some stuff that—Another enormous yawn. Something about Anderson being a bad guy or something, that was it. Good old Vince. Bad old Anderson.

I felt a third yawn coming on, and I could tell that this one would leave the other two far behind in the dust. It felt so powerful, overwhelming, gigantic that I was afraid it might actually crack me in half, and I fought against it for a few valiant seconds, and then . . .

The sun was doing its very best to break through the tattered mildew-smelling curtains when I opened my eyes. Somehow it had turned into morning—and an obnoxiously bright and cheerful one, too, just to rub salt in all my psychic wounds. It's very hard to maintain a properly grumpy perspective when the sun is beaming down from a cloudless sky, and the voice of the turtle is so clearly warming up in the wings. But I tried; I lay there unmoving for a while, wondering if it was even worth getting out of bed. If I did, some new and awful disaster would almost certainly leap out of the closet and wrestle me to the floor. And the floor did not look terribly inviting—yellowed, peeling linoleum that had probably been put down to celebrate Eisenhower's inauguration.

On the other hand, if I just lay here on my marshmallow mattress, all the other wicked and unwarranted beasties pursuing me would eventually catch up. Not really a terribly enticing choice either way.

So I lay on my back on the horribly soft bed and avoided making the choice. It was nearly comfortable, even though my knees were surprisingly close to my head. Sometime in the night, my body had curved into the shape of the letter "U," as the bed yielded around me. It wasn't so bad, almost the same position as lying in a hammock, and I'd never heard a sailor complain about that. Of course, I did not ordinarily hang out with sailors—but surely some word would have trickled out.

I lay there, and I thought grumpy thoughts that were only partly generated by my waking up so recently. I grumbled, and it might even be said that I pouted. But eventually a small but potent voice sounded in the depths of my very being, that tiny nagging whisper that has so often guided me, the righteous glowing arrow that always points my way, lights my footsteps, and sends me down the right path, no matter what. There is no denying this Voice when it speaks, for it is never wrong and never out of order. It spoke to me now, softly but insistently, and what it said was, *I'm hungry*.

And once again, I realized that it spoke the

truth. I was hungry. Very hungry, in fact. I am blessed with a total lack of conscience, but my keen sense of hunger takes its place quite ably and keeps my feet on the proper trail. And with a jolt of guilt that very nearly approached panic, I realized I'd had no dinner. What had I been thinking? There was no excuse for such rash and careless behavior. Shame on Dexter.

With that clarion call of duty ringing in my ears, I remembered that I had said I would meet Brian for breakfast. I glanced at my watch: seven-fifteen. I had plenty of time—but on the other hand, it wouldn't hurt to get there early and get a head start on the doughnuts.

I sat up—or to be accurate, I tried to sit up. The bed had wrapped its soft and spongy tendrils around me and locked me into a kind of death grip and it would not let go. I struggled, I fought, I rolled to one side—and the edge of the bed completely collapsed under me and dumped me onto the floor. I landed badly, hitting my left elbow and right knee. And even as I felt a new pain blooming in my elbow, I could not help noticing that the floor was wonderfully firm. Perhaps I could sleep here tonight.

I pushed myself up carefully into a sitting position. That hurt even more. Between the unaccustomed exercise of the day before and the dreadful clutch of the bed, there was nothing left of my back but a vast area of numbness and pain. I tried stretching, twisting from side to side, and after only a few minutes I was somehow able to stagger to my feet and totter to the bathroom. I was quite sure that if I could only get a nice hot stream of water pouring onto my back, my spine would loosen up and return me to something that approached functioning.

And it may well be that I was right. Sadly, we will never know, because the ancient showerhead in the bathroom put out only a thin trickle of rust-tinted water, none of it warmer than room temperature. Nevertheless, I clenched my teeth and stood under it as long as I could, and if nothing else it did wake me up and put me in a proper mood to face what was certain to be a truly awful day.

I climbed out of the shower and stood there dripping, looking around for a towel. I finally found one—but only one—and it was about the size of a large washcloth. I did my best to dry off anyway, more or less pushing the water off me and onto the floor.

I got dressed in a brand-new set of clothes: underwear and socks right out of the package, jeans still stiff and smelling like . . . well, like new jeans, I suppose. I topped this chic ensemble with one of Walmart's finest and most fashionable guayaberas, and I was ready for anything.

Just to show that things were finally going my way, my little red rental car was right where I'd left it, in the space closest to my room. Even better, the key still fit, and the car started right up with the first try. What a wonderful thing life can be when it puts a little effort into things.

I drove north on U.S. 1, and the morning traffic was already thick enough to make me wonder whether I would get there on time, let alone early. At 216th Street a large truckload of tomatoes had spilled out onto the road. Behind the truck where the load had spilled, a very big man with a shaved head was slugging it out with a shorter man who sported a black ponytail. It looked like the short man was winning. They stood up to their ankles in tomatoes, slinging punches with very bad intentions, and traffic slowed to a crawl, and then even less than a crawl.

I am not made out of stone; I understood full well that the spectacle was worth watching, even if it meant slowing and making several thousand people late for work while you watched and hoped both fighters would fall into the tomatoes before you crawled past. But it was precisely because I am not made of stone, and I felt very urgent hunger pangs clawing at my stomach, that I did something that can only be called a Classic Miami Move. I twisted the steering wheel, fought my way over to the shoulder, and with two wheels completely off the road, I drove the half block to the closest cross street.

Several angry horn blasts followed me, but I

ignored them. It would have been more proper, or at least in keeping with tradition, to extend my middle finger, but I kept to the high ground, maintaining my poise and returning only a lofty sneer. After all, I learned to drive here. I know my rights.

I worked my way a half mile north on side streets and then turned back up onto U.S. 1. The traffic was much lighter now, since the flow had been so thoroughly choked off at the scene of Tomatopalooza. I pulled into the lot and parked at the doughnut shop thirteen minutes early. There was no sign of Brian, so I collected a large coffee, a bear claw, and a cruller, took a booth at the back, and sat facing the door.

I had disposed of the cruller and half of the bear claw when Brian came in. He looked around, careful but nonchalant, and then bought himself a large coffee and two cream-filled doughnuts with brightly colored sprinkles on top. He slid into the booth facing me and took a large bite. "Mmm," he said.

"Yes, but really, Brian," I said. "Sprinkles? Are you already in your second childhood?"

He smiled, revealing a row of teeth bedecked with cream filling and rainbow-colored sprinkles. "Why not?" he said, his voice thick with dough-nut. "I never actually got my first one."

"Well," I said, looking with quiet satisfaction at

the remains of my steady, no-nonsense bear claw, "no accounting for taste."

"Mmp," he said agreeably, and shoved half of the doughnut into his mouth. He washed it down with coffee and started on his second doughnut while I finished my bear claw and wondered whether it would be considered greedy if I topped it off with a couple of Bavarian creams. I decided that no one could possibly criticize me for having only one, and I bought one and used it to help the rest of my coffee go down smoothly.

Brian made one more trip to the counter, too, returning with a cake doughnut smeared with maple frosting, leaving me to ponder once again the vast marvels of heredity versus environment.

"Well," Brian said, as we sipped at the last of our coffees. "Where shall we begin?"

"I suppose with my new address," I said, and I told him the location of my little Shangri-la. He nodded and took a sip of his coffee.

"And on to new business," he said happily. "How should we stay alive today?"

"I have no idea," I said. "But you have to remember that I have my own agenda, too. I want to stay out of jail."

He arched his eyebrows at me. "Yes, of course, but really," he said, "isn't staying alive more important?"

"Give me liberty or give me death," I told him.

"Death is much easier to arrange, I'm afraid," he said, shaking his head.

"Maybe," I said. "But I have to do what I can."

"Well," he said, "I suppose you're not much good if you're in jail."

"Exactly my point," I said.

He waggled a finger at me. "But sooner or later, having two separate agendas is going to cause trouble."

"Well," I told him with my customary light-hearted touch, "perhaps I'll think of a way to merge them." And I thought happily of sending a troop of *drogas* after Anderson. A happy ending for all—he would even get a hero's funeral, which was certainly a great deal more than he deserved. "But, Brian—I don't know how much good I am *out* of jail. I mean—I can't risk carrying a weapon of any kind. And that's . . . Seriously, what's the plan?"

Brian said nothing, just finished off his coffee, and to my mind he looked a little bit shifty, as if he hoped his ostentatious coffee swallowing would distract me and I wouldn't remember what I'd asked him.

It didn't work. He put down the cup, looked vaguely out the window.

"Brian," I said, a little testy, "you do have some kind of plan, don't you?"

He looked back at me, hesitated, and then

shrugged. "To be perfectly honest," he said, "I was hoping something might occur to us."

I noticed that he said *us,* and that was almost as irritating as his notion of winging it when pursued by a horde of assassins. "All this time, nothing has occurred to *you?*" I said.

"One thing did," he said, trying hard for a tone of injured righteousness. "I got you out."

I felt myself grinding my teeth together at the realization that, just like Deborah, Brian had decided that when the going gets tough, the tough get Dexter—and then they make him do all the work. "This is *my* problem?" I said with some heat. "I'm supposed to figure out how to keep us both alive?"

"Well," he said. "I mean, you had a much better education."

"Yes, but he's your drug lord," I said, and I realized that he'd succeeded in knocking away my cool control and I was speaking much too loudly. I lowered my voice. "I don't know the first thing about these people, Brian," I said. "Not what they're likely to do, or how they'll do it, or—Nothing at all. How am I even supposed to find them?"

"Oh, that shouldn't be a problem," Brian said soothingly. "I'm quite sure they'll find *us.*"

For some reason, I could not find any comfort in that. "Wonderful," I said. "And I can assume they know what they're doing, of course."

"Of course," he said happily. "Some of them are very good, too." He smiled, and even though it was the closest to a real smile I'd ever seen from Brian, the effect was spoiled somewhat by the bright pink, blue, and green sprinkles stuck to his teeth. "Let's just hope we're a little better," he said.

I ground my teeth some more. It didn't actually do any good, but it was probably better than leaping across the tabletop and sinking my canines into Brian's neck. "All right," I said. "So your wonderful plan is to wait until they come after us, and then be better than them."

"A little oversimplified," he said. "But accurate."

I closed my eyes, took a deep breath, and let it out slowly. When I opened my eyes again, Brian was looking at me with a happy little smirk on his face. "How will they do it?" I asked him. "I mean, if it won't spoil your plan to tell me."

"Oh, not at all," he said. "I know how Raul thinks—I mean, I ran so many of these little errands for him, and he got very specific most of the time." He nodded, and at least he lost the smirk. "He hasn't found me yet, and he is not a patient man. So his first move will be to try to frighten me so I'll do something silly and become visible."

"Frighten you with something like killing Octavio, and dumping him in a room you got with that credit card?" I asked.

"Mmmm, maybe," Brian said thoughtfully. "Of course, he wanted to kill Octavio anyway, and . . . You know, I was really looking for something a little splashier."

"And if we survive the splash?" I asked.

"Then we watch for his men," he said. "Whatever they do, they'll be very close, watching for *us*. We find them first."

I sighed again, wondering whether Brian really believed it would be that simple. "All right, fine, we wait," I said. At least I could do that without too much effort. And in the meantime . . . "I can use the time to try to stay out of jail."

"Oh, certainly," he said. "You do what you must. When something happens, I'll call you." He hesitated slightly, and then, looking a little uneasy, he added, "But do watch your back, brother."

"I plan to," I said.

He nodded. "What are you going to do?" he asked.

"The whole case against me is pure fiction, made up by Anderson," I said. "If I can find something to show he tampered with evidence—"

"He did tamper, didn't he?" Brian asked.

"Only when he didn't just invent it," I said. "So I thought I would have a quiet chat with Vince Masuoka."

Brian nodded. "That would certainly be a good place to start," he said. "He seemed very . . . indignant?"

"Perhaps he still is," I said.

He still was. I called him from my car after Brian left me with a promise to get in touch this evening, and Vince answered right away, speaking in a kind of shocked and reverent whisper. "Dexter, my God," he said. "I can't believe—I mean, I really tried to—Shit. I can't talk now. I'm in the lab, and there's—"

"Can you meet me for lunch?" I said.

"I think so, if I—Yes. I mean, I'll do what I can to—I can get away around noon?"

"Good," I said. "Meet me at Lunar Sushi."

"I will," he said in an eager whisper. "I mean, I'll try. And if—Oh! Somebody's coming . . . !"

"See you at noon, Vince," I said, and broke the connection.

I had three hours to fill before then, and not a great deal to fill them with. I thought about going back to my hotel room, and firmly rejected the idea on humanitarian grounds. If I wasn't going to rest, then the most natural thing would be to eat. But I had just eaten, and I would be eating more when I met with Vince, so it really seemed like a bit much to kill time between meals by eating. I thought about it anyway. After all, doughnuts are not really *substantial,* are they? Very little protein in the average bear claw, in spite of the name. And since I hadn't partaken of the garish sprinkles my brother gorged himself on, I'd had nothing green to eat, either.

I remembered a map I'd drawn in my cell, after days of unspeakable swill they laughingly referred to as "food" at the TGK. The map traced a route that wound its way through South Miami, into the Grove, and then over to Miami Beach. At every point along the route where there was a restaurant I liked, I had placed an ornate little star and a small icon of the appropriate kind of food: tiny pizzas, sushi rolls, stone crabs, and so on. It had been my whimsical thought that if I ever saw the clear light of freedom again, I would trace the whole course, stopping at each star to sample their icon.

I could start my trip now, work my way through the first four or five, and end up close to Lunar Sushi just in time for my lunch with Vince. The idea had its charms—but on the whole, I couldn't make myself believe that gorging myself was the best way to spend my time when both Life and Liberty hung so tenuously in the balance, presumably to be joined at any moment by Pursuit of Happiness. I put the thought away.

What I really needed to do was to keep a low profile, avoid any chance of discovery by either the Good Guys, as played by Anderson, or the Bad Guys, starring Raul and a cast of thousands. Since I had already ruled out returning to my miserable, bone-breaking hotel room, there were very few options left to me. I could always take out my boat; I'd be relatively safe in the middle of Biscayne Bay, and I would see anyone approaching. But the odds were fifty-fifty that Anderson at the least, and maybe Raul's team as well, knew about the boat, and had it watched. It wasn't worth the risk.

That didn't leave too many places—to be perfectly honest, it left exactly none that actually sprang to mind. So I drove north, since that was the direction I was pointed in when I left the doughnut shop. At least it led me farther away from the torture equipment laughingly referred to as a bed that crouched in my hotel room awaiting its prey.

The morning rush hour was dying down at last, and the traffic moved easily enough all the way up to Le Jeune Road. Still with no definite goal in mind, I turned left and headed toward Coconut Grove.

As I drove along through the center of the Grove, I marveled yet again at how much had changed since I grew up here. Most of the shops I had known then were gone, replaced by different, new shops filled with totally different overpriced and pointless items. Of course, there were a few landmarks that hadn't changed since the dawn of time. The park was still pretty much as it had been, and across from it the library was still there, though it was now partially hidden by the newer buildings that had sprung up around it. I had spent many happy hours in the library, trying to find a book that would explain to me once and for all how to act human—and when I was a little older, a book that might tell me why I should bother.

As I turned onto McFarlane Road and headed down the hill toward the library, I wondered whether it might not be a good place to lay low for a few hours. It was cool, quiet, and had both Internet and reading matter aplenty. And then, right in front of the building, I saw that there was a parking space open. In the memory of living man, this had never happened before, so I took it as a sign from God and made an immediate U-turn. I slid into the spot and parked, and thinking that I might do a little bit of diligent low-profile digging while I waited, I grabbed up the folder of legal papers I had been given at the jail when they returned my stuff.

I locked the car, put an enormous amount of money into the meter, and went into the library. I found a nice, quiet spot over by the back window and sat down to go through my folder. What with finding corpses and so on, I'd been far too busy to open the folder; I hadn't even glanced at it yet. I'd assumed that it was copies of the great heap of paperwork that is required to do absolutely anything nowadays, especially within the bureau-cratic hell that is Official Miami. I knew from experience that the Department of Corrections demanded many pages of mind-numbing trivia even for something as simple as getting a box of paper clips, and I expected that the actual release of a prisoner would generate several reams of stilted prose.

But when I opened the folder, the first clump of papers I saw on top of the heap did not carry the imprint of Corrections. Instead, the letterhead said, *Department of Children and Families.*

For a long moment I just stared, and then my very first thought was a rather plaintive, *But I'm an adult!* And then luckily, a couple of gray cells floated up to the surface and suggested that some overworked and underbrained bureaucrat had obviously stuffed somebody else's papers in my folder by mistake. It was a simple, laughable error, and no doubt I would even laugh at it someday, if I lived. I picked up the offending paperwork, intending to fling it in the nearest receptacle—and my eye caught a single word: *Astor.*

I paused, long enough to see that this word was joined to another, *Morgan,* and right next to it there were more: *Cody Morgan,* and *Lily Anne Morgan.* Since these were the names of my three children, it seemed far too much to write it off as coincidence, so I put the paper back down on the table in front of me and looked it over.

After a quick examination of several pages of baroque legal language, I concluded that the party of the first part, one Dexter Morgan, having acted *contra bonos mores* as well as *cum gladiis et fustubus* was now de facto and de jure a persona non grata in his role as legal guardian of said minor children. Further deponent sayeth that the party of the second part, *hight* Deborah Morgan, acting as *amicus paterna* in *uberrima fides*, did solemnly swear and affirm *cum hoc ergo propter hoc* that she would therefore ipso facto assume completely and totally the role of guardian *ad litem, in loco parentis*. The party of the first part hereby confirms that this *ad idem* agreement shall supersede all others and in witness thereof affixes his signature, *quod erat demonstrandum, et pedicabo te*.

Or words to that effect; there was an awful lot, and not all of it was in such nice Latin, but the gist of it was that I was signing over all my rights and privileges as sole surviving parent of Cody, Astor, and Lily Anne, and naming Deborah as their new mommy, which was probably in the document somewhere as *materfamilias*.

In my humble opinion, it is a very great credit to me that this time I did not blink or gape, as I had done so much lately. I remembered right away that when Deborah had finally come to see me in jail, she had asked me to sign over custody of the kids. It had been the sole reason that she finally made herself overcome her complete, violent, and totally understandable nausea caused by looking at me.

Of course, things were a little different now—I was no longer in jail. It was true that I would probably return there, unless I was chopped into bits by savage cartel assassins before then. Even so, did I really want to do this? Completely abandon all my paternal rights and privileges?

My first thought was a mean-spirited, *No!* The kids were *mine,* and no one was going to take them away from me, not Deborah or anyone else. But when I reflected on that for just a few moments, I realized that this was not a well-thought-out response.

How did I really feel about my kids? Of course, only Lily Anne was truly *my* child, biologically speaking. But Cody and Astor were Children of Darkness, just like me. I was their spiritual father, as well as legal, and I had promised to set their feet safely onto the Dark Path. I had failed miserably so far—just never got around to it, what with the frantic pace of school and homework and dentist and pediatrician and new sneakers. It was always, *Yes, of course, later,* and later never came. Why is it that there's never enough time to do anything, unless it's so immediate that not doing it results in instant catastrophe?

It was hard to feel guilty about failing to train them to be successful predators, but I did manage a little regret, at least. And Lily Anne—she was untouched by Shadow, a near-perfect creature of burbling pink light. Quite impossible to believe that she carried my DNA, but she did; Lily Anne, alone in all the world, would take the entire genetic wonder that was Dexter and carry it into the future, so that fabulous *me* would not be lost from the gene pool, and that was a very nice thought.

But she would do that just as well without me— perhaps better. In truth, didn't she deserve something better than a father like me? Deborah would provide a positive role model, something I could never hope to do. And Cody and Astor would be who they were, who they had to be, whether I was there or not. So the only real question was, Did I really want to be there? Enough to fight it out with Deborah and the courts? Was I really that protective of my rights and privileges?

I thought about that for a good two minutes, and to be perfectly honest, I only thought of one or two rights, and I couldn't think of any privileges at all. It had been my experience that fatherhood was mostly a matter of suffering the insufferable, tolerating the intolerable, and changing diapers. Where was the joy in the endless screeching, door slamming, and name-calling? Was it a privilege to sacrifice time, money, and sanity to a snarling horde of sticky ingrates?

I tried very hard to come up with a few fondly

remembered moments of joy. There didn't seem to be any. There was once when I got home late and I was just in time to keep Cody from eating the last piece of Rita's Orange Chicken. I'd been happy then, or at least relieved. And another time Astor threw her shoes at me, and one of them missed. That had been good, too.

But joy? Actual parental ecstasy? I couldn't recall any.

If I was truly honest with myself, which is not as easy as it sounds, I had to admit that I didn't really enjoy fatherhood. I simply endured it, because it was part of the disguise that hid Dexter the Wolf from the world of sheep I lived in. And as far as I could tell, the kids merely endured *me,* too. I was not a good father. I tried, but it was strictly pro forma. My heart was never in it, and I was just no good at it.

So if I didn't really want to be Dear Old Dad, and if the kids were truly better off without me —why was I waffling?

No real reason. I signed.

TWELVE

I CALLED DEBORAH TO TELL HER I HAD signed the custody papers. She was at work, of course, and may have had a very good reason for declining to answer my call. Perhaps she was busy shooting someone, or maybe wading through viscera at a crime scene. Whatever the truth, she did not answer, and I could not help thinking that she just didn't want to taint her righteous ears with the dreadful pollution of my voice. I left a message, and headed for my lunch appointment with Vince Masuoka.

Lunar Sushi was a newish place in North Bay Village. It sat in a strip mall, in between a grocery store and a sports bar. It really should have been a little bit tacky, considering this less than ideal location. But they'd put quite a bit of money into the decor, making it look like the kind of chic, upscale place where you expect to see movie stars drop in for some *kajiki* and a Kirin.

At this time of day, in midweek, there was no problem finding a good parking spot, and I was tucked in at the bar with a pot of very hot green tea when Vince came stumbling in at twelve minutes past noon. He stood in the doorway for a moment, blinking away the effects of the bright sunlight outside and goggling around the cool dark of the interior. It was kind of fun to watch him stand there and gawp, but it was just a little cruel, too— perhaps that was part of what made it fun in the first place. Still, he was here, after all, to do me a good turn, so I took pity on him and waved.

"Over here, Vince," I called.

He actually flinched when I said his name, and raised his hands to make a shushing gesture. But he apparently realized that was a bit much, and he dropped his hands again and came wobble-stepping rapidly across the floor. "Dexter," he said in the same hushed tone he'd used on the phone. He put his hands on my shoulders and, to my complete astonishment, he leaned forward, putting his head down on my chest and giving me a hug. "Oh, my God, I'm so glad you're okay." He took his head off my chest and looked at me. "You are okay, aren't you?"

"Too soon to tell," I said, wondering how I could pry myself out of his strange and unchar-acteristic embrace. Vince was no more a touchy-feely-huggy guy than I was. In fact, one of the reasons I liked him was that I could tell he was faking most of his Human Behavior, too, just like I was. I was merely a little better at it. But as far as I could remember, we'd never even shaken hands—and here he was locking me in a stifling and very awkward clinch.

But happily for me, he gave me one last quick squeeze and then stepped back. "Well, you're out of jail," he said. "That's the important thing." He stood only about two feet away and looked at me with a weird expression, kind of a yearning, searching gaze, as if he was trying to find some hidden pain in my face, and he might cry when he found it.

"I am out," I said. "At least for now."

Vince blinked. "Is there some—I mean, they can't just . . . uh . . ." he said, stumbling to a halt and looking over my shoulder.

I turned. The sushi chef had appeared noiselessly on the far side of the bar and stood there regarding us with solemn expectation. I looked back at Vince. "Let's put in an order and move to a booth," I said. "So we can talk."

Vince nodded and stepped up to the bar. And then, to my utter astonishment, he began to make a series of harsh and sibilant sounds in the direction of the chef. Even more surprisingly, the chef stood a little straighter, smiled, and made some very similar sounds back at Vince. They both laughed—and then actually *bowed* at each other—and the chef scurried away, a wicked-looking blade already raised in his hand. He began slapping great chunks of raw fish onto his chopping block and attacking them with his knife.

I looked at Vince, and it occurred to me again that I really didn't know anything at all about him. "Was that Japanese?" I asked him.

He turned and looked at me as if I was the one speaking a foreign language. "Huh?" he said.

"Those noises you just made," I said. "You were speaking Japanese with the sushi chef?"

He looked a little puzzled. "You did know that Masuoka is a Japanese name, right?" He shrugged. "What did you expect?"

I might have pointed out that Morgan is a Welsh name and I didn't speak a word of that language, but it seemed like a rather low-priority observation. "Let's get a booth," I said.

"Oh, right," he said, looking startled and furtive again, and I led him to a booth in the back, sliding in so I faced the front door. Vince climbed in across from me, and glanced all around the restaurant with a wide-eyed, paranoid glare. If anyone actually was looking for suspicious behavior, they would definitely know that they should start with Vince. But maybe he had a real reason, other than a fevered imagination.

"Vince," I said, "you weren't followed, were you?"

He snapped his head back around and looked at me. "What?" he said. "Why would you—Did you *see* somebody?"

"No, no," I said, trying to sound confident and soothing at the same time. "You're just acting like you expect to be shot at any moment."

He shook his head. "You don't know," he said. "I mean, the things that have been going on since you—" He leaned toward me and lowered his voice. "Dexter, I've never seen anything like this. It's gotten so—Anderson is completely off the reservation. He's gone rogue, and nobody seems to—It's like they all *want* him to do it, because they want *you* to be convicted!"

"What was Anderson doing?"

Vince looked around again. A bead of sweat formed on his forehead and began to roll slowly down his face. "He's falsifying records," he said in a strangled whisper. "Putting in fake evidence and forging the signatures and—" He fluttered his hands in dismay. They looked like two spastic birds who'd forgotten how to fly. "Dexter, Jesus, it's *illegal*. Like a *felony,* and he's just doing it and nobody does anything about it. It's like—"

He stopped abruptly as a young Japanese girl in tight black pants and a loose white shirt came smiling out of the kitchen, put two glasses of cold water and a pot of tea on our table, and then vanished again. Vince watched her go, swallowed, and then picked up his glass and gulped down about half of it.

"Anderson hates me," I said. "He'll do anything to see me burn."

"But that's just it!" Vince said. He put down his water glass with a thump so hard it scared him. He flinched, and then pushed the glass nervously to one side. "It's not just Anderson," he said, back to a near-whisper again. "It's the whole *department,* and even—" He shook his head and sighed. "When I saw the first report Anderson turned in, I thought, Okay, he's got a hard-on for Dexter." He looked startled by what he'd said and stammered out, "Ah, I mean, you know, metaphorically . . . ?"

"Yeah, I got that," I said reassuringly.

He nodded, relieved. "Right. So I thought, No way he'll get away with this. And I reported it." He leaned toward me as far as he could go without climbing onto the table. "I was told to mind my own business."

"But you didn't," I said.

"What? No, how could I? I mean, it's my *name* on the forensic report, and it's not what I wrote!" He rubbed his hands together, hard enough that I could hear a kind of whispery-raspy sound coming from them. "I can't let him do that—not my *name*." He frowned. "Um, and, you know— when they're framing *you*, too?"

"Unthinkable," I said, thinking it was a nice sentiment, even if my life and liberty got second billing to Vince's good name.

"So, I kept at it," he said. "I mean, I tried to tell somebody, anybody, and everybody told me to mind my own business." He gave a one-syllable not-funny laugh and spread his hands. "Mind my own—I just, I always thought it was *everybody's* business when somebody does that sort of thing." He shook his head in wonder. "I even told the captain, and it was the same thing. 'Stay out of it.

Mind your own business. Don't make waves, Masuko.'" He blinked at me, looking like he had reached a new and deeper level of despair and degradation. "He calls me 'Mah-*soo*-ko,'" he said.

"Some people's ignorance knows no bounds," I said.

"Ignorance and . . . and . . ." He picked up his water glass and chugged the rest of the contents. "So I went to the state attorney."

"And *he* told you to mind your own business," I said, hoping I could urge him to the finish line. After all, I'd heard a recap of all this from Brian, and I was really hoping to move on to some sort of understanding on the future agenda.

"He told me . . ." Vince started to say. He sounded like he was choking on something, and he turned his head and coughed violently for a few seconds. Then he looked back at me, took a deep breath, and in a soft and raspy voice he said, "He told me that these were very serious allegations involving an ongoing case, and was I aware that I was bringing them against a distinguished officer?" He gave that one-syllable not-laugh again. "Distinguished. Anderson is distinguished now." He coughed again, just once. "I told him they weren't allegations; I had *proof,* and when I tried to show it to him, he said no, he would have to recuse himself, and I should just stay out of it and let justice take its course. Otherwise, he would speak to the commissioner and see that I lost my job." He blinked and looked away. "And then it got even worse. The next day at work, Anderson grabbed me from behind, lifted me up, and slammed me against a wall." He turned to me. "He's very strong," he said unnecessarily.

"Yes, I'm sure," I said.

"He told me if I tried anything like that again, he'd break my neck." He made a limp-wristed gesture of despair, raising both hands and then letting them flop back down onto the table again. "He *knew*, Dexter. Somebody at the state attorney's office must have told him."

"Probably the state attorney," I said.

He looked at me with his mouth open, moving it like a grouper struggling to breathe. Then he sagged over, looking defeated and helpless. "Well, shit," he said with a very nice mix of hopelessness and despair. "If the state attorney is in this . . ." He shook his head, and he made it look like his skull weighed fifty pounds. "What the fuck can *we* do?" he said, and I looked at him with mild surprise. I couldn't remember hearing Vince use dirty language, except sexual, in the course of one of his awful jokes. Here he had just done it twice in ten seconds. The poor fellow really was on the ropes.

"This is crazy," he went on. "I'm trying to do the right thing, and the people who are supposed to *help* me, supposed to be *grateful* . . . I mean . . ."

He shook his head. "Dexter, my whole life, I couldn't—"

I didn't get to find out what he couldn't, because our food arrived. And if I showed more than my normal enthusiasm in attacking it, it's only fair to point out that I had quite nobly abstained from following my restaurant map in a pilgrimage of gluttony, and I therefore truly deserved to enjoy my lunch now, since there was only one of it. And I did—all the more because Vince just picked at his food. Waste is a terrible thing, so I helped him finish the hand rolls. One of them was quite good—spicy, with a little crunchy something in it, and a burst of *umami* at the finish.

When I was happily full, and somewhat tired of watching Vince mope and push sushi around the platter with a chopstick, I leaned back and decided to get down to the real business at hand.

"I appreciate what you've done, Vince," I said. It's always nice to start with kind words, especially when you want something.

"That's . . . But I didn't do anything," he said. "Not really." His eyes got very moist, and there was even a little quaver in his voice. "I wanted to help you," he said.

"You still can," I said with firmness and an optimism I didn't feel.

For some reason, he didn't look any more optimistic. "You don't know," he said. "They're watching me now, and it's . . . I know it's stupid, but . . ." He leaned across the table again and lowered his voice. "I actually started to think, like, my *life* might be in jeopardy. From *cops*."

"It might be," I said, and he goggled at me, and then nodded, took a deep breath, and leaned back again.

"This is completely insane," he whispered. "I mean, the whole *system* is against us, the captain and the state attorney and . . . They might *kill* me and there's nothing I can do about it?"

The smile I gave him was not quite a shark's smile, but I did feel like I could taste red meat as I did it. "Actually," I said, "there's one really good way to guarantee your safety."

He looked at me dubiously, as if he couldn't believe there was any way out. "That's not . . . I mean, you can't do any, because . . . What?" he said, and the way he said it was so fragmented that for just a half second, I thought of Rita, my dear dead wife. That was the way she had talked.

But of course, nostalgia for run-on sentences in a female voice would not get the job at hand done, so I pushed her memory away. "Do you still have all those doctored reports?" I asked Vince.

"Yes," he said. "I kept the originals and filed copies."

I looked at Vince with surprise. His behavior is usually so eccentric and even goofy that every now and then I forget that he's actually very smart, too. "Well done," I said. "Where are they?"

"They're safe," he said. "In my locker at work."

I sighed. We were back to goofy again. "Vince, that's not actually safe."

"But it's my *locker*," he said. "I mean, you know. It's *locked*."

"They've falsified official documents and threatened your life," I said. "Did you really think they would hesitate to pick a lock?"

He looked very startled. "Oh," he said. "I guess I . . . Oh, right." He shook his head. "Oh, boy. What should I do, Dexter?"

"Bring them to me," I said. "The whole file, all of it."

He actually looked offended, as if I was suggesting something indecent. "I can't do that," he said. "It's a misdemeanor to take that stuff out of the building."

I stared at him, and I admit I was a little shocked at the depths of his naive and loony rectitude. "Vince," I said, "if they get the stuff out of your locker, there's nothing to stop them from killing you, and that will be your fault. And suicide is a *felony*."

"But you—Oh," he said. "That's a joke, right?"

"Almost," I said. "But it's true, too. Vince— your only hope here is to let them all know you have that stuff, and you've put it someplace safe. And in the meantime," I said, with a very small return to the shark smile, "I show it to my attorney."

"Your attorney?!" he said. "But he might . . . I mean that—" He stopped himself mid-dither and said, "Is Frank Kraunauer really representing you?"

"He is," I said. "And they can't ignore him, can they?"

"No, not Frank Kraunauer, they'd *have* to . . ." he said. "But what will he—I mean, even so . . . What will he *do* with that stuff?"

"He'll take it to a judge," I said.

"No," Vince said, the first forceful and undithering thing he'd said so far. "No, they would know it came from me. I could lose my job."

For just a moment I was speechless. Lose his *job?* With his life on the line? And mine, of course, which was considerably more to the point. "Vince, you're not thinking clearly," I said. "They're going to kill you. And then you'll be *permanently* unemployed." But he still looked stubborn.

"No, Dexter," he said. "It's wrong. I can't let you make that stuff public. Think how it would look."

"What do we care how it looks if we're both dead?" I said. "And it might not go public anyway. Once the judge sees it, he'll probably just throw my case out and issue bench warrants."

"But he might not," Vince said, and I really wanted to slap him. "It might get out and then—No, Dexter. There has to be a better way."

"This *is* the better way; don't you see?" I said.

210

"This is perfect. For *both* of us." And now I gave him my best imitation kindly smile. "It's so simple. Kraunauer uses that stuff to prove that I was framed; I am free, and you are exonerated, probably even promoted." I nodded at him to show that I regarded it as a sure thing. "I get out of jail for good, and Anderson gets my old cell. Happy ending all around."

I could see he was wavering a little, so I leaned across the table to make my point. "Of course, there is an alternative." He looked hopeful, so I went for the jugular. "You let them kill you, and they plant all sorts of incriminating stuff in your house—drugs, kiddie porn, dirty money from the evidence room. So you're dead *and* disgraced. And I go to trial and spend twenty years on death row, wondering why I ever tried to help poor old Vince Masuoka, the bribe-taking pedophile junkie." I spread my hands, and then leaned back to show I was all done. "Your choice, Vince. It's up to you. Life or death. Shame or praise. All—or nothing."

He goggled at me again, clearly not quite there yet despite my magnificent oration. I poured a cup of tea and didn't look at him.

"I can picture Anderson standing over your cold dead body with that stupid smile of his and then, just because nobody can stop him, *zzziipp!* He opens his fly and pees all over your cold, dead—"

"All right, all right! Jesus, Dexter," he said, his face twisted into a mask of disgusted anguish.

"Just sayin'," I said. "You know he will."

"All right, fine," he said. He blew out a huge loud breath. It sounded like a radiator bursting. "I'll do it!"

He looked relieved—and, it must be said, a little guilty, too. I didn't care. I had worked so hard on him for something that was, to my mind, so simple and obvious, that it was hard to think of him as an intelligent creature anymore. I felt like I should scratch him behind the ear, say, "Good boy!" and toss him a cookie.

Instead I just nodded and said, "Smart choice. When can you get it to me?"

He shook his head, looking numb, and said, "Jesus, I can't believe I'm doing this."

"Doing what, Vince?" I said sweetly. "Saving your own life?"

"I can't . . . I, uh," he said. He sighed. "I can bring it home with me tonight. After work."

I nodded. But if there is a wicked thought to be had, we must assume that Dexter will have it first. So I said, "Can I suggest that you leave work early?"

"What? No," he said. "I have a ton of work—I mean, we are shorthanded, you know." He looked at me like it was my fault—and of course it was, in a way.

"Yes, I do know," I said mildly. "But if you stay

late, you're giving Anderson a shot at you. And even if you leave on time, he'll be expecting it, and . . ." I turned my hands palm up and shook my head. "We don't know what he might do. Or when."

"Oh . . ." he said, very faint and looking shocked again.

"So the best move is to do the unexpected, right?"

"Yes. Uh-huh, of course, okay," he said, staring down at the table and clearly thinking very hard. He snapped his head up and looked at me, clear-eyed and determined. "I can leave at around three-thirty, dentist appointment or something," he said.

"Perfect. Where should I meet you?"

He blinked. "Um," he said. "My house? Like, a little after four?"

I tried to think of a reason that would be a bad idea. I didn't come up with anything. No one would look for him to be at his house at four o'clock on a workday, and it would make him feel more secure, so I nodded. "All right," I said. "I'll come by to collect it a little after four."

He looked away, staring out the front window of the restaurant as if he could see his childhood out there in the parking lot. "I can't believe I'm doing this," he said again.

THIRTEEN

VINCE MANAGED TO GET ALL THE WAY back to his car without collapsing into a puddle of warm and spineless goo, and I got into my little rental vehicle with a full stomach and the added satisfaction of a job well done. Of course, there were still several hours before Vince actually brought the file home, and after seeing his performance at lunch I was sure he would spend the whole time in a cold sweat, changing his mind, wringing his hands, hopping nervously on one foot, and flinching at shadows. But in the end, he would see that this really was the only way, and I had every confidence that he would come through and bring the file. Well, perhaps not *every* confidence.

I started my car to get the air-conditioning going, and thought about my next move. It was nearly one-thirty, plenty of time left in the day for absolutely everything I needed to do—which, on sober reflection, was not really a great deal. Getting Vince to help had been my Main Event for the day, and everything else that remained was somewhat vague—important, yes, but still vague. The most imperative remaining item was keeping me alive, and although I do not minimize its importance, its parameters were, as I said, somewhat unformed. For no reason at all a synonym for *unformed* popped into my head: *inchoate.* I don't know why I thought of that word right now. I didn't need a synonym. What I needed was a sea change, a paradigm shift, an evolution in the zeitgeist, something to make the entire world get off my back and pick on somebody else for a while.

But if that happened as I sat in my car in a strip mall parking lot in North Bay Village, I saw no sign of it: No young man in bellhop's uniform came to the car window with a telegram on a tray bearing a full pardon from the pope, there was no spontaneous parade in my honor, and no suddenly appearing billboards or mysterious skywriting with a simple but clear message, like, *You Win, Dexter.* Nothing but the traffic, and the sun, and the afternoon heat that somehow worked its way through the car's air-conditioning and made the back of my shirt stick to the seat.

I sighed. This would have to be done the hard way, if it got done at all. By the sweat of my brow shall I something-something. I couldn't remember the rest. I was pretty sure it was from the Bible. If it had been Shakespeare I would have remembered it better. But the meaning was both clear and relevant. Dexter had work to do, a lot of it, and as always, nobody else was going to do it for him.

My eyes fell on the custody agreement, and I

thought, *All right: First, let's clear away the trivia.* I picked up my phone and called Deborah again. Once again, she let it go unanswered. This time I left a message. "Very thoughtful of you not to answer. I don't think I could stand to hear your voice now that I am free, dear sister," I said, just to show that I could play the game, too. "However, I have the custody form for you. I will drop it at your house this evening, shall we say seven-thirty? If you're not home, you can come get it from me tomorrow."

I broke the connection and felt I had been too snarky and yet at the same time not nearly cutting enough. Are relationships with family members always so complex?

Next I called Frank Kraunauer's office. I got through two layers merely by saying that I was a client. The third person I was transferred to was clearly the Ice Goddess at the massive desk who guarded the Inner Sanctum. I told her I had something important for Mr. Kraunauer and she said, in a voice filled with polite scorn and skepticism, "I'll see if he's available." There was a small and refined *click* and soothing music filled my ear. After only a few minutes, the music stopped abruptly and Kraunauer himself came on the line. "This is Frank Kraunauer," he said, quite unnecessarily.

"This is Dexter Morgan," I said, and I realized I had unconsciously copied his stentorian tone. I cleared my throat to show that I didn't know I'd done it, and said, "I have some very important information to give you," I said. "Um, about my case."

"Yes, that would have been my first guess," he said dryly. "What sort of information?"

"Ah, actually, it's in the form of a file," I said. "On paper?"

"I see," he said. "Where did this file come from?"

"If you don't mind," I said, "I'd rather not say on the phone."

Kraunauer chuckled. "I can assure you the NSA is not monitoring my calls," he said. "They wouldn't dare."

"Even so," I said. "It's a little bit, um . . . sensitive?"

He was silent for a few seconds, and I heard a rhythmic clacking sound—drumming his fingers on the desk, no doubt. "Mr. Morgan," he said, "you haven't been doing any amateur sleuthing, have you?"

"Oh, no, not at all," I said. After all, Vince had done all the legwork.

"All right," he said abruptly. "Can you bring it to me at the office? I'll be here until about six."

"I should be there around five," I said.

"See you then," he said, and hung up. No peaceful music this time, just a dead line.

I looked at my watch. I had killed an entire

seventeen minutes, and accomplished just about everything definite I could think of. On the one hand, I was filled with a hard-earned pride at my industry and efficiency. On the other hand, I still had several blank hours before I met Vince, and no place to go other than a lethal hotel room at the far end of town. I sighed heavily and shook my head. For the first time I understood and appreciated the true joy of having a job—it gave you someplace to go! And when you were done there, you could go to a home, however squalid. Suddenly I had neither, and I truly felt it. This whole homeless-and-unemployed thing was becoming a true burden.

Still, I couldn't just sit here in the parking lot with the engine running. Eventually I would die of exhaust fumes, or perhaps boredom. And with the price of gas what it is, I couldn't afford it, either.

I thought about going back to the library, but that seemed almost as bad. I wondered about trying a few stops on my Food Pilgrimage. True, I'd just eaten lunch, but it was only sushi. Wasn't I supposed to get hungry again in half an hour? Or was that only true of Chinese food? It could be both, if the recurring hunger was caused by rice. But it was probably MSG, and I was pretty sure Japanese food didn't have any. In any case, I wasn't hungry, and I was quite sure that a pro forma eating binge would be frowned on in the best circles.

I looked out the side window. The scenery hadn't changed. I was still in a strip mall parking lot.

Was it really the library or nothing? In the time I spent languishing in jail, I had formed an ideal picture of freedom as something worth having, even striving for. As with all idealistic notions, the reality was proving to be quite different. I had a choice of doing nothing in a parking lot, or doing it in the library. I tried to revive my flagging enthusiasm for Sacred Liberty by reminding myself that I could also go back to my hotel room, or even drive pointlessly around the city. It didn't work. My enthusiasm stayed flagged.

With one last heavy sigh to show that I was acting under protest, I put the car in gear and headed back to the library.

It took about twenty minutes to drive over the causeway, down U.S. 1, and back to the Grove. Nothing had changed when I got there, except that the parking spot in front of the library was taken now. So were all the other parking spaces. I drove around for a few minutes until I finally found a place down at the foot of the hill by the sailing club. I tried to put money in the meter, but it was jammed. It still had five minutes on it, though, and it didn't seem to be ticking off the time. A meter that perpetually showed five minutes was a marvelous thing, a real stroke of luck. Perhaps my fortunes were changing after all.

I trudged up the hill to the library and went in. My seat by the back window was still available. I was literally being showered with good fortune. What a wonderful world we live in.

I sat and flipped through magazines I didn't care about and scanned stories that bored me to tears. When I finally glanced at my watch and saw that only fifteen minutes had passed, I was stunned. It had seemed like an eternity. I flung down the magazines and went looking for something more substantial to read.

I found something better: books with lots of pictures. I settled on an art-history book that bragged about having over twenty-five hundred pictures, from cave to contemporary. Even on a day as slow-paced as this one, I could make twenty-five hundred pictures last awhile.

I sat back down with the book. I took my time with the pictures—and not merely because I wanted to while away a few hours. I have always liked art. In the first place, some of it is quite pretty. And even if you don't always understand the picture, or the emotions it tries to convey, there is usually some nice, colorful something to look at somewhere in the picture. There were a lot of religious pictures in this book, many of them quite cheerfully gory. I particularly liked the pictures of saints with holes in them. The blood pouring from the wounds was presented in a very restrained and dignified manner, which is unusual for blood. Nasty stuff, and unpredictable. And the expressions on their faces, which could only be called Justified Anguish, were wonderful fun.

Altogether, it gave me a new appreciation for religion. Although to be truthful, I had always wondered at the blind and unfailing insistence on combining violent and gooey death with human worship. It almost made me wish I could join a church of some kind. What fun they had, especially with their saints! I would fit right in! Dexter the Saint Maker!

But of course, it wouldn't do. I could never sit through an entire service without giggling. Seriously, how can people actually believe such things? And in any case, the altar would almost certainly burst into flames when I entered.

Ah, well. At least religion was responsible for some nice pictures, and that should count for something. If nothing else, the pictures whiled away the time for me until around three-forty-five, when I left for my rendezvous—if not with destiny, then at least with some very nice drapes.

Vince Masuoka had a small house in North Miami, at the end of a dead-end street off 125th Street. It was painted pale yellow with pastel purple trim, which really made me question my taste in associates. There were a few very well-barbered bushes in the front yard and a cactus garden lining the cobblestone walkway up to his front door. His car was in the driveway when I arrived, so at least he hadn't decided he would rather work late than save my life and his.

I rang the bell and he opened the door immediately. He was so pale and sweaty that for a moment I wondered whether he had food poisoning, and I felt a brief surge of near-panic because I had eaten the same things at lunch that he had. But he grabbed my arm with a very strong grip and pulled me inside so powerfully that I ruled it out and settled on mere nervous collapse.

Sure enough, the first words out of his mouth revealed that he was teetering on the brink of total disintegration. "Dexter, Jesus, you wouldn't believe—Oh, my God, I don't even know how— I mean I nearly . . . Holy Christ I gotta sit down." And he collapsed onto a very stylish Deco chaise longue, patting at his brow with a paper towel.

"Fine, thanks," I said cheerfully. "Do you have the file?"

He blinked at me with reproach, as if I hadn't appreciated his suffering enough. "Anderson was right *there*—I mean, he nearly *saw* me! With the *file!*"

"Nearly?" I said. "But he didn't, did he?"

He sighed, long and painfully. "No, he didn't," he admitted. "But, my God. He was . . . I hid behind the, you know the closet by the coffee room?"

"Vince," I said. "Do you have the file?"

He shook his head. "Of course I do. What have I been saying?"

"I don't know," I said.

"Well, I have it right here," he said, waving a limp and sweaty arm at a strange yellow-painted end table. The legs were giraffe necks and the handle of the one small drawer was an elephant's trunk, and the whole was so distracting that I had to squint to see that, as advertised, a manila folder lay neatly on top of the table. I managed to show quite commendable restraint, by stepping calmly over to pick up the file, rather than leaping through the air and snatching it with both hands, as seemed more appropriate.

I opened the folder and leafed quickly through it, page by page. I paused after only the first few pages: Vince had been wonderfully thorough. The file started with the initial incident report, and went on step by step through the long and many-faceted paper pathway that our wonderful System of Justice demands. It was all here, every step, and even to the casual eye it was clear that most of the scribbled signatures were done by the same messy hand, though the names were different. And by a remarkable coincidence, that ubiquitous sloppy handwriting looked an awful lot like Detective Anderson's. I looked at Vince with a raised eyebrow. "How on earth did they get away with this?" I asked.

He nodded vigorously. "I know, right?" he said.

"I mean, anybody can tell—and, Dexter, that's not even the worst of it!" He jumped up off the chaise and leaped to my side, eagerly snatching away the folder and flipping to a page near the bottom of the stack. "Hear—lookit *this!*" he said with a kind of triumphant shock.

I looked. The page in question was the lab report, submitted by V. Masuoka, who signed his name in the same hand as the officer who had signed the incident report. Even better, "Masuoka" was spelled wrong: M-A-S-S-O-K-A.

"Shame on you, Vince," I said. "At your age, you really should know how to spell your own name."

"That's not the half of it!" he said. "Look—he has me using luminol. We haven't used that stuff in years, we use Bluestar now. *And,*" he finished triumphantly, "he spelled *that* wrong, too—with an 'A' instead of an 'I.'"

It was true. And as I gently pried the folder out of Vince's sweaty grip and examined it with a little more care, I saw that the whole thing was almost as shoddy. I found myself sharing Vince's shock; to frame me was one thing, but to do such a terrible job at it was unforgivable. Really, a child could do better work. Either Anderson was truly an overgrown case of arrested mental development, or he was such an arrogant and dim-witted buffoon that he thought he'd done it well enough to get away with it. A moment's serious reflection led me to conclude that the second explanation was correct. Anderson was so completely brainless that he didn't realize just how stupid he really was.

I closed the folder and gave Vince a reassuring pat on the shoulder. "This is wonderful, Vince," I said. "You have truly saved the day." And I wondered whether I'd laid it on too thick, because he seemed to swell a few sizes, and he actually blushed.

"Well, I, you know," he said. "I wanted to help, and . . . I mean, this just isn't right, and everything I ever worked for, you know." He paused and rubbed at the corner of his eye, and I realized with horror that he was on the verge of tears, and who knows what other terrifying manifestations of emotional excess. Sure enough, he sniffed, and said, "What else could I—"

"And it absolutely is," I said, cutting him off before he could burst into a chorus of *I Pagliacci*, followed by grabbing my hands and leading us in a rousing fit of tears and a communal singing of "Kumbaya." "This is just what the doctor ordered."

"That's . . . that's . . . I mean, because . . ." he said, pausing as he visibly filled up with even more emotion.

I took the pause as an opening for my getaway, and began to move toward the door. "Thanks, Vince," I said. "You have saved us both. Bye!"

And I was out the door before he could say more than two more confused syllables.

As I started up my car and drove away I saw him standing in the doorway, gazing mournfully after me, and I was filled with immense relief that I had escaped an episode of naked sentiment that could only have been humiliating for both of us. I did wonder why I should feel so strongly about it, and because I have studied the endlessly fascinating subject of Me for such a long time, I came to a simple conclusion. One of the things I liked about Vince was that he generally faked all the human rituals and expressions. He had a terrible phony laugh, and a habit of making suggestive remarks that were so clearly synthetically generated I marveled that he got away with it. In other words, as far as simple person-to-person interaction went, he was an awful lot like me.

And to see him like this, floundering helplessly in the savage grip of genuine feelings, was very disturbing, because on some deep level I had been thinking, *If it can happen to Vince, it might happen to Me!* and that thought was nearly unbearable.

Still, Vince had brought home the bacon when the chips were down and my fat was truly in the fire. I tried to think of more food metaphors, and wondered whether that meant I was already hungry again. I looked at the dashboard clock; it was nearly five, which was bad news all around.

In the first place, it meant I probably *was* hungry again, and in the second it meant rush hour was already in full swing.

I went up onto I-95 South anyway, hoping for the best. As usual, I didn't get it. Traffic was crawling along at a pace a snail would have laughed at. I had hoped to drive straight down to the MacArthur Causeway and then over to Kraunauer's office to deliver the file. After ten minutes and only about half a mile, I got down onto surface streets and headed over to Biscayne Boulevard instead. The traffic was moving better there, and I got to the causeway and all the way to Kraunauer's office in only about forty minutes.

It was eight minutes of six when I stepped off the elevator and began the elaborate ritual of getting myself passed through the layers of insulation around the Great Man, and the Ice Queen herself nudged me through the door and into the Presence just as the clock began to tick through the last minute before six o'clock. Kraunauer was at his desk, packing things into a gorgeous leather briefcase with one hand and speaking on a cell phone with the other. He looked up at me and blinked, as if surprised. Then he nodded, placing a heap of paper into the case and holding up one finger to me to indicate, *Just a minute.*

"*Sí. Sí, comprendo,*" he said into the phone, and to show that I am no slouch as an investigator, I immediately concluded that he was speaking Spanish, which meant that the person he was speaking with probably was, too. I patted myself on the back for my burst of acumen; if I was this sharp, I would lick this thing yet. "*Sí, seguro, no hay problema*," he said. "*¿Quince? ¿Es suficiente? Bueno, te doy quince*," he said, and he broke the connection and put the phone down. He put both hands on his desk and turned his full focus on me. "Well, Mr. Morgan," he said, with a truly brilliant imitation smile. For the first time in my life, I had met somebody who could fake it better than I could, and it made me feel almost dizzy, like a young boy facing a famous quarterback. "Sit down. Tell me what you've brought me."

I didn't really need to sit down; I'd imagined I would just drop the folder, give a brief explanation of its provenance, and dash away into the evening without taking up too much of Kraunauer's valuable—and therefore *expensive*—time. And I wondered whether I was generating billable hours that would be added to a fee I was quite sure was already astronomical. But I was just a bit intimidated by his awesome faux sincerity, and felt I should do what he told me. On top of everything else, Brian was paying, and to be honest, I was not pleased with him for dropping me so carelessly into a firing range with a bull's-eye on my forehead and a bevy of drug-crazed Mexican assassins on the other end. So I eased carefully into the unquestionably pricey chair across from Kraunauer.

"Well," I said, "this is a folder of documents from the police file on my case. Um," I added, "they're all originals."

"Really," he said, raising one carefully barbered eyebrow. "How did they come into your possession?"

"One of my friends in forensics," I said, conscious of a slight exaggeration. Vince was my *only* friend left in forensics—maybe my only friend left anywhere. It made me truly grateful that I didn't actually need friends. But telling all this to Kraunauer wasn't necessary. Aside from painting an unflattering picture of Dexter, it was also not something Kraunauer really needed to know. So I skipped to the chase and held up the file. "The documents are all filled with deliberate falsifications, forgeries, and fiction. They altered my friend's report—um, rather clumsily, too," I said. He didn't seem to feel the sting of that insult the way I did, so I shrugged. "And when my friend complained about it, they threatened him."

Kraunauer leaned back in his chair and put his fingertips together, the picture of an erudite man deep in thought. "Threatened him how?" he said.

"At first with losing his job," I said. "Then with violence. At the end, he says he was afraid they might even kill him."

"Exactly who made these threats?"

"Mostly Detective Anderson," I said.

"Uh-huh," Kraunauer said. He frowned as if remembering something. "That's the name of the officer who arrested you."

"No coincidence," I said. "It's the same guy."

"Hmm," Kraunauer said. He tapped his fingertips together rhythmically and looked very thoughtful. "He's obviously willing to go pretty far over the line to keep you in jail."

"At this point," I said, "I don't think he can even *see* the line anymore."

Kraunauer thought for just a second, and then he sat up straight and leaned over his desk. He took a business card from a small pile of them nestling in a little silver stand, plucked a fountain pen from the desk beside him, and scribbled on the back of the card. "My cell phone," he said. He handed me the card. A phone number was on it, in still-drying vermilion ink. "You can reach me here twenty-four/seven."

"Oh," I said, somewhat surprised. "Thank you, but, um—"

He smiled again, this time a "gotcha" smile. "If he tries to intimidate you, arrest you without cause, rough you up, whatever. Call me." He leaned back in his chair again and the smile changed to one of simple satisfaction. "We want to keep you on the outside."

"Yes, we do," I said. I put the card carefully—

reverently—into my pocket. Twenty-four/seven; I was surely one of the Blessed.

"Back to this friend of yours," he said, serious again. "The one who Anderson threatened. What did he do about that?"

"He took the file to the state attorney," I said, and Kraunauer sat up straight.

"Did he?" he said softly.

"Yes. And he was once again told to back off, mind his own business, or he would lose his job."

"Well, well, well," Kraunauer said. He drummed the fingers of one hand on the desk, and then leaned back again. "Tell me about this friend."

I told him as much as I could about Vince. It was not as easy as you might think, since as far as I could tell, there wasn't all that much to tell about him. I tried to make him sound competent, trustworthy, and righteous, but I did not have a whole lot to work with. At least I could leave out any reference to the Carmen Miranda costumes, and I did.

But Kraunauer seemed fascinated, and asked several questions about his character, motivation, and job history. When we had parsed Vince more thoroughly than I would have thought necessary—or even possible—Kraunauer nodded and held out a hand. "Let me take a look at this file," he said.

I placed it on the desk in front of him and settled onto the edge of my chair, surprisingly anxious.

It was very odd, but I wanted to impress Frank Kraunauer, wanted him to think this folder was important and relevant and Dexter was a very good boy for finding it and bringing it to his attention. Even so, at least I managed to keep myself from leaping up and pointing out the good parts, and I just watched for several minutes as he frowned at each page in turn, nodding from time to time and making notes—on a legal pad, of all things.

When he was only a few pages from the end, the office door opened, and Her Royal Highness stuck her haughty and perfect head into the office. "It's twenty past, Mr. Kraunauer," she said with immense dignity.

He looked up with a surprised expression. "Is it? Already? Well," he said. He closed the folder and dropped it onto his desk, watching as Herself smiled, at him only, and withdrew. Then he looked at me and let me have his small but charming smile of apology. "I'm afraid I have an appointment I can't miss," he said. "But I want to assure you, this stuff is going to help a lot."

He stood up and came around the desk, and I stood up to meet him. "This is just terrific, Dexter," he said, shaking my hand, and I was ready to believe him, because his handshake was firm, dry, and manly, and this was the first time he'd used my first name. "Absolutely great stuff," he said.

And then he slipped his hand out of mine and put it on my shoulder, easing me out the door while continuing to assure me that everything was coming up roses and life was a wonderful thing. Moments later, I was standing in the elevator, still blinking from the magical experience, and glancing at my watch. Twenty-two past six. I'd been in Kraunauer's Presence for twenty-two minutes. From what I knew of lawyers, that would be at least three billable hours. How much money had that cost me? Or cost Brian, perhaps. Ah, well. How can you put a price on that kind of overwhelmingly competent and focused expertise? It occurred to me that Kraunauer would know exactly how to put a price on it, and he would. But why worry? Being permanently in debt was still better than being permanently dead or in jail.

It cheered me up, and I was actually whistling as I climbed into my rental car. I'd told Deborah I'd drop off the custody papers around seven. Her little house in Coral Gables was about fifteen miles away, and there were no shortcuts. My best guess, based on years of experience with Miami traffic, was that at this time of day there was no possible way I could make it to her house in under forty-five minutes. Surprising or not, that lifted my cheerfulness one more full notch. And why not? She had done nothing to earn my considerate punctuality. She didn't even answer my phone calls—and I wouldn't put it past her to show up late just to irk me.

So fine—I would take my time, enjoy the drive. I might even stop for coffee. Let her wait.

I started the car, nosed out onto Ocean Drive, and began my long, slow drive to Deborah's house.

FOURTEEN

IT SEEMS TERRIBLY ODD, CONSIDERING the general tone of recent events, but I actually felt somewhat chipper as I fought my way into the sludge that is Miami traffic. I had a brief moment of uneasiness as I drove away from Kraunauer's office and headed for the MacArthur Parkway, a small and anxious hiss from the Dark Passenger that said things were not at all what they should be. And sure enough, a moment later, a car right behind me slammed on its brakes and leaned on the horn. I stepped reflexively on my own brakes and looked back, senses on high alert.

But it was no real threat, just an eager idiot, overanxious to get home after a hard day on the job. I watched the car in the mirror, a newish dark blue SUV, as it pulled out into traffic and joined the rest of us in the long, never-ending stream of cars headed for the causeway and home.

Aside from that, I saw no suspicious cars on my tail, and no one on the sidewalk seemed to be pointing a bazooka. I decided that the Passenger was just responding uneasily to our newfound freedom, no doubt simply picking up on tiny things, the perfectly normal universal hostility of the rush-hour drivers all around us, so I dismissed it and settled back to enjoy my own rare and unwarranted high spirits.

There was absolutely no reason for me to feel anything but angst, and yet there was an unquestioned spring of good cheer welling up from some rarely used spot inside. It wasn't just my excellent prospects for making Debs wait for me, juggling children and gnashing her teeth. A larger part of this unwarranted and uncharacteristic brightness came from the general sense of belonging I got from the savage, merciless ferocity of driving in My City at rush hour. In the past I'd always gotten a sort of My-Country-My-People affinity from being up to my neck in a sea of drivers with a total lack of empathy and a naked lust to kill. It was nice to feel this sense of happy belonging settle over me once more; it meant that some tiny, deeply buried part of Dexter had decided that the world was restored to its natural state and Things were going to be all right.

And another cause of my lunkheaded happiness was certainly born of my sense of accomplishment. I had delivered a vital chunk of evidence into the hands of my powerful and supremely effective lawyer, and thereby put the first nail into Detective Anderson's coffin, while removing one from my own. But yet another piece of my stupidly good mood, I realized, was because of the effects of being in the company of Kraunauer himself. His aura was almost tangible. There was something about him that impressed me, which all by itself was impressive enough. I had always considered myself the Master of Duplicity, the Paradigm of Synthetic Behavior. No one else had ever come close—until now. Kraunauer left me in the dust. He was the most highly polished faker I had ever met, and I could do nothing but watch and admire every time he favored me with one of his completely artificial smiles. And he had not merely *one* fake grin; I'd already seen at least *seven,* each with its own very specific application, each so perfect as to leave me breathless with admiration.

Aside from my appreciation for someone who was better than me at something I held dear, there was an unspoken assumption of command in his bearing. And it worked. Just being near him made me want to please him. It should have been deeply unsettling, but somehow it wasn't.

I have no real feelings. And I am certainly not capable of love, or even hero worship. There was no one in this world I cared more for than Dexter. But in our short time together, Frank Kraunauer had impressed me in a way no one else ever had, with the possible exception of Harry, my adoptive father. On the face of it, that was beyond absurd, and I wondered about it. Harry had saved me, created me, taught me how to use my gifts, and consequently made my life into something that, until recently at least, I rather enjoyed in my own quiet way. Harry was the All-Father, the Fount of Wisdom, Maker of the only Map of the Dark Path, and I had known him for many years.

But I had only met Kraunauer recently, spent less than an hour in his company, and I didn't really know him at all, except to know that he was, in his own way, as completely without feelings as I was. I knew this from his reputation, of course. But from being in his company I had also sensed that somewhere behind his eyes there lurked that familiar Dark Emptiness. He was a predator, totally without mercy, the kind of dedicated and enthusiastic shark who didn't even need the smell of blood in the water to strike. He ripped out chunks of flesh because that's what he was made to do, and he liked it that way. Naturally enough, that kind of inborn enthusiasm struck a chord in me.

Beyond all that, he was on my side, and it was universally acknowledged that he did not fail. Drug kingpins, brutal dictators, mass murderers—he always came through for his clients, no matter how heinous the crimes they had committed. Because of him, some truly awful, wicked, dreadful monsters roamed free. And if all went as it should, I would soon be one of them. All hail Kraunauer.

So I settled into my seat and relaxed, enjoying the drive. I made it over the causeway in under fifteen minutes, which was disappointing, since I really did want to keep Deborah waiting. But once I turned south onto I-95, things slowed down again to a very satisfying crawl. I inched along, making only a block or two every five minutes, and taking pleasure from traveling so slowly that for the most part, the speed wasn't even enough to register on the speedometer. With any luck at all, I would make Debs wait for a good half hour or more.

Of course, not everyone was keeping their so-called sister waiting, and very few of the other drivers shared my newfound enthusiasm for creeping along like this. Most of them, in fact, seemed to take against it somewhat, and very few were hesitant about sharing their feelings with the other drivers who were clearly making them go so slow simply by being in front of them. There was a great deal of horn blasting, middle finger raising, and even good old-fashioned fist shaking. All standard fare, but done with real enthusiasm and passion, and therefore a pleasure to behold. I didn't join in; I simply observed, taking a quiet civic pride in watching my fellow citizens interact with each other in such a genuine and meaningful way.

Just before NW 10th, we slowed even more, which was very gratifying. When I had inched forward enough, I could see that a Jaguar convertible had plowed into a van loaded with seafood. There was an impressive array of dents, broken glass, and twisted bumpers, considering that they couldn't have been moving very fast when they collided. But the impact had caused the van's back doors to spring open, and a wonderful variety of fresh and succulent seafood had slid across the Jaguar's hood and filled the car's beautiful leather interior. Luckily for all concerned, it looked like most of the fish would stay fresh, since a massive amount of ice had gone with it.

A nicely coiffed woman still sat in the Jaguar's passenger seat, screaming hysterically, up to her shoulders in fish and ice. The driver was nose-to-nose with two men from the van, and the words they were exchanging did not seem to be the kind that lead to lasting friendship. And because this was, after all, Miami, three young men and one woman, from three different cars, had left their vehicles to gather up the spilled fish and take it home for dinner.

This delightful accident delayed me quite nicely, and it was nearly eight o'clock when I arrived at Deborah's little house in Coral Gables. It was a modest home, and since my ex-sister had neither the interest nor the patience for gardening, it was somewhat overgrown. There was an assortment of fruit trees that had spilled their crop all over the yard unnoticed, and a crumbling coral rock wall around the place. Her car was in the short driveway, and I parked behind it and got out.

And strangely . . . I hesitated. I found that I was a little reluctant to face her, to have my nose rubbed one more time in her dislike and contempt for me, which, it should be repeated, was totally undeserved. But it stung anyway. I didn't like seeing her look at me the way she had when she visited me in jail. Like I was some kind of loathsome contagious affliction, something smeared onto her shoes, perhaps a great and disgusting glob of raccoon feces.

Standing beside my car, I stared at her front door. I knew it didn't matter what she thought of me—and yet, somehow, it did. It was astonishing, but apparently I still wanted her to like me. She never would, ever again, if she ever had in the first place. She'd made that quite clear, and feelings as strong as she'd shown do not change. So why didn't I simply saunter up to the door and get this unpleasant business over with? Why should I dither and mope because I didn't want to face her sneers?

No reason at all. I would do it, and get on with my life—get on with *saving* my life, in fact, which was enormously more important than any of Deborah's mean-spirited snits.

So I leaned against the car and did nothing. A car drove by slowly, a dark blue SUV of some kind, probably a Jeep. Hard to be sure—it was one of the new kind, the ones that look like station wagons, and they all look the same. It didn't matter. I looked up at the sky. Most of it still seemed to be there. That didn't matter much, either. I looked at the front door of the house again. If Debs peeked out, she would see me here, loitering indecisively, and she might think I was hesitating because of timidity. She might think I actually gave a rodent's rectum what she thought of me, which was silly. I didn't care. Not at all. I could go knock on the door anytime I wanted to.

Once again, as seemed to be the case so often in my life, my stomach finally settled things; it growled, reminding me that life goes on, and even more so with a good dinner. And so, rather than risking the wrath of my digestive system, which was much more relevant than the wrath of my nonsister, I straightened up, clutched the custody papers firmly in my left hand, and moseyed up to the door.

Deborah answered in person on the first knock. She looked at me with such a hard, stony face that she must have set the expression in place well before now, so it would be properly congealed when I saw it. She said nothing at all, letting her face do all the talking. Behind her, I could see a dim purple glow from her living room, and hear the sounds of a cartoon show. I recognized one of the voices—it was the only show Cody and Astor could agree on watching, and it involved a platypus, as I recalled.

The kids must be in there, all four of them

together, Deb's son, Nicholas, and my very own Lily Anne, as well as Cody and Astor. I craned my neck slightly to see if I could catch a glimpse, and Deborah immediately pulled the door shut around her, so only her neck and head stuck out and I could no longer see in at all.

I shrugged. If she was that determined to be unpleasant, so be it. And so I saw no need for pleasantries. "I assume you got my message," I said curtly.

She stared a moment longer, and then without any change in expression, she simply held out her hand.

It took me a moment to realize that she was not offering to shake my hand, but I figured it out at last and gave her the custody papers. She took them, stared at me a few seconds longer, and then, before I could even frame a properly scathing farewell, she shut the door firmly in my face.

Well, if nothing else, the papers were delivered. At least I could scratch one thing off my to-do list. And I supposed I could cross the entire bunch of them off my Christmas card list, as well. I doubted that I would ever again really wish Debs a merry anything, and she would certainly make sure that all four kids remained uncontaminated by my toxic presence. I had watched how she behaved with her boy, Nicholas, and although I would not quite call her a helicopter mom, she would certainly be very aggressive about protecting them from all dreadful forms of mental and psychic pollution, like drugs, violence, and Dexter.

Well, she was in for a little bit of a surprise, at least as far as Cody and Astor were concerned. She thought of them as battered waifs, poor little orphans of the storm, sweet and innocent children who had suffered a series of terrible shocks. She would discover soon enough that they were nothing of the kind; Cody and Astor were undeveloped Dexters. The terrible physical, mental, and psychic abuse they had taken from their bio dad had left them just as empty of empathy and human feeling as I was. And they had not had the Harry Course of Miracles to properly channel the impulses that were already slipping up behind them from the Dark Backseat and gently but firmly trying to take the controls and drive them down the Dark Highway. When these impulses began to take over, as they absolutely *must* from time to time, Deborah would begin to realize that she was nurturing a viper in her bosom. I almost wished I could be there to see her face when she found out she had changelings in her nest. I had a feeling that the discovery might alter her perspective just a wee little bit.

It brought me a small glow of much-needed comfort, even when I realized that she would blame the whole thing on me. That didn't matter at all; I was already dead to her, and I could not conceivably get any deader.

So be it. I was never meant to be a father. Another chapter in the Great Book of Me was finished. Time to close the book and move on. No kids, no sister, and no regrets.

I turned away and went back to my rental car.

In Miami, many people eat rather late each night. It is part of the city's cultural heritage, a proud Old World tradition, brought to our shores by our Hispanic brethren. It is not unheard-of to eat dinner at ten o'clock, and certainly nine o'clock is common. But tonight, at a mere eight o'clock, Dexter was simply not in touch with his Cuban side, and he was becoming ever so slightly rapacious. I drove away from Deborah's crumbling, child-infested cottage and began my search for something appropriate to eat.

There were so many choices, even within a two- or three-mile radius. The possibilities were nearly overwhelming; Chinese or Chinese nouveau; Cuban, of course; Spanish classical or tapas; Thai; at least three varieties of French; ribs and barbecue—truly, that was only scratching the surface. And the beauty of it was that I could go to any of them and eat my fill of My City's Great Bounty, delectable viands from every land and every body of water on the globe. My mouth began to water. Freedom is truly a wonderful thing.

I very nearly chose Thai—there was a very good

place not too far away, just off Miracle Mile. But at the last minute, I had the thought—and I am quite sure it is Politically Incorrect—that Thailand was much too close to Japan, and I'd had sushi for lunch. I turned left instead of right, and headed over to Pepino's, a cozy Mexican place in Coconut Grove.

Coconut Grove has always moved at a slower pace than the rest of Miami, and so it was no surprise to me that it was apparently still rush hour on Main Highway. The only difference was that most of the rush was centered around finding a parking place. Unfortunately, all the legal spaces were taken. But I was sure I could find one that was *nearly* legal. I grew up here, and I had a few tricks that latecomers to the Grove didn't know.

I drove down a side street about half a mile from the restaurant. Fifty yards down, I turned into a dark alley that cut between two boutiques. There was a large Dumpster, overflowing with trash, and just beyond it, unlit and invisible to any meter maids with prying eyes, I parked my car.

But apparently there was at least one other Grove native having a night on the town, because as I walked out of the alley feeling just a little smug, another car turned down the alley and went past me, no doubt looking for a place to park. It was another one of those station wagon–style SUVs, dark blue. There were certainly a lot of them on the roads lately. I wondered why. After all, real station wagons were available, and cheaper. Why buy something nearly identical that costs more, just to get the all-wheel drive? There were no muddy mountain roads here, and no treacherous icy highways. What did that leave? Did all these people really spend their weekends racing through mud in the Everglades?

By the time I had hiked back to the restaurant, I was nearly hallucinating enchiladas. The last two blocks had been true torture, as the scent of cumin, hot sauce, and tacos seemed to be everywhere. But I made it safely, without collapsing into a puddle of drool.

Pepino's was a small place, but it had a little bar with four plush stools, and the one at the end was empty. I sat and quickly found out why the seat was available; every time anyone went into or out of the kitchen, or the restroom, I had to move, and for a large tray filled with steaming food, I actually had to stand up and skitter along the wall like a cockroach when the lights come on. But my food arrived quickly, and it was good, and in a very short time I was full and happy once more.

The walk back to my car after dinner was far more of a contented saunter than the famished stagger my hunger had forced me into on the way in. And the car was right where I'd left it, too. Life can be so easy when the Universe is feeling cooperative, can't it?

I drove south to my little torture chamber of a motel, through traffic that was a great deal lighter than rush hour had been. Of course, as a native Miami driver I knew very well that this only meant there were new dangers to watch for. Because there was more room to maneuver, there were more drivers weaving in and out of the lanes at two or three times the speed limit. The motorcycles were bad enough, but they were far from the most numerous. Sports cars, of course, and sedans, SUVs, delivery vans, and even a mammoth flatbed tow truck with a minivan on its bed.

Escalades seemed popular tonight. At least three of them roared by me in the first five miles. Maybe there is some special psychotic wrinkle in everyone who decides to buy a Cadillac. It was an intriguing thought; perhaps I should shop for an Escalade. I didn't really mind the reckless speed seekers. I was used to it. And it's no real burden at all; all you have to do is maintain a steady speed and keep to your lane and let them move around you freely. And if they get a little overeager and actually crash into someone, move carefully around the wreckage with a wave and a smile and a feeling of satisfaction that it wasn't you this time.

So I drove south, and as I did my Mexican banquet began to catch up to me—not in any unspeakably rude digestive way. I just began to get sleepy, as I always did after a large dinner. In fact, I started to feel so entirely drowsy that I was actually looking forward to my horribly misshapen, agony-inducing "bed." I sped up a little—not enough to make the Escalades think I was competing, of course. That would probably have made them kick it up to warp speed and drive the interloper off the road.

But I did go just fast enough to cut a few minutes from the journey, and just when my drowsy eyes beheld the ancient, half-dead neon sign that marked my hotel, my phone began to chirp. I glanced at the screen—not that I needed to. Only one person would be calling me, and that's who it was.

"Hello, Brian," I said into the phone.

"Hello, brother," he said in his favorite fraudulently happy greeting. "Where are you now?"

"I am just pulling into the parking lot of my hotel," I said. And as I did so, I noticed that the lot was nearly full, which seemed absurd enough to be nearly surreal.

"Can you manage a little face time?" he said. "I have one or two nuggets of importance for you."

I sighed, looking around for a place to park. Every slot close to my room had a car in it. "I can barely keep my eyes open," I said. "Can it wait until morning?"

Brian paused, long enough to make me wonder

why. "I *suppose* so," he said at last, a little bit hesitantly. "But . . . Do be a little extra watchful till then?"

"If I was any more watchful I would need at least four eyes," I said. I saw an open parking spot at last, all the way down at the far end of the lot, easily forty feet from my room.

"All righty then," Brian said, back to his synthetic good cheer. "Shall we say eight o'clock tomorrow morning, same place?"

"Fine," I said, pulling into the very last slot in the parking lot. "See you then."

" 'Tis devoutly to be wished," Brian said, and hung up.

I sat there in astonishment for a moment; had my brother really just quoted *Hamlet*? Perhaps it shouldn't surprise me, but he'd never done anything of the kind before—nothing at all, in fact, that gave even the tiniest hint that he was familiar with Shakespeare, or any other classic work. But Brian was always full of surprises, and this one, at least, was not overtly unpleasant.

I turned the key and shut down my rental car, taking one last moment to reflect with weariness on my long and busy day. But before I got much further than, *You done good, kid,* I felt my eyes begin to flutter shut. I snapped them open; this was no place to fall asleep, even though it was probably more comfy than my bed. I took a deep breath and climbed out of the car, fumbling the keys and my phone until I got both safely into pockets, closing the car door with a hip, and stumbling wearily down the cracked sidewalk toward my room.

Music was blasting out of two adjacent rooms a few doors from mine. They probably had the door between them open to give the party more space. It was loud enough to rattle the windows, and not loud enough to mask the gleeful and drunken shouting, singing, and cries of *Whoo!* coming from within. Probably a bachelor party or some such thing. On the one hand, it was nice to have the crowded parking lot mystery explained. On the other hand, it was going to make sleeping a slightly more difficult problem.

I sighed. Where did it stop? When did all the petty persecutions of Poor Deserving Dexter finally trickle to a halt? Impending death or imprisonment wasn't bad enough. Now I would be hearing a sound track of drunken revelry all night long, too. I was doing fine with protecting Life and Liberty, but apparently someone else's Pursuit of Happiness would finally do me in. It's the little things, after all, that finally break us.

Blow, wind, crack your cheeks, I thought. Brian wasn't the only one who could quote Shakespeare.

I made it to my room without thinking of any other suitably apocalyptic line from *Lear*, and I was too tired to start in on *Othello*. I flopped onto the bed facedown—and immediately I was bent into a bow shape, with the soles of my feet facing the back of my head.

I struggled up to my feet and sat on the edge of the bed to remove my shoes. The car keys fell out of my pocket and onto the floor. And as they did, I remembered getting out of the car and fumbling with my phone and the keys, and I couldn't remember whether I'd locked the car. It didn't matter; it was easy enough to step to the window, point the car's clicker down the line, and push the lock button.

I sighed again, more heavily this time. It really is always the little things. Sooner or later, there would be one last niggling little torture flung at my head, something so insignificant that it couldn't possibly matter to anyone, and it would be the one tiny saddle sore too many that finally sent me screaming and drooling over the edge into red-eyed raving insanity.

But this wasn't it, not quite. I fought my way up to my feet and trudged over to a spot two feet from the window. I was tired and cranky and didn't really feel like spending all my precious remaining energy opening the door, stepping outside, and leaning out to watch. And the ancient curtains looked so vile and crusty that I really didn't want to touch them. But they were also worn thin enough that I could probably see the reflection of the blinking brake lights to show me it had worked. I pointed the clicker and pushed the lock button, watching for the flash of lights.

The flash came right away, but it was far too bright for brake lights, and it was followed by a blast so loud and strong that even as it nearly deafened me, it hurled me back from the window, splinters of glass showering all around me, flinging Dexter together with all that was left of the window into a tattered heap on the floor behind the door.

For a moment I just blinked around me, listening to the sudden cacophony of car alarms from outside. I could feel little spots of sharp pain starting to bloom on my face, and a few more on my chest. I blinked some more; at least my eyes were okay. I looked at my right hand; it had fallen into my lap, bleeding from a couple of cuts. I was still holding the car keys. What I could see of the rest of me seemed fine, but my shirt was torn and spotted with a dozen small blotches of blood. On top of everything else, a brand-new shirt ruined.

I closed my eyes in weary resignation and slid to the floor, completely indifferent to anything that might possibly happen now. Let them take me. And when they did, it would be in a terribly torn shirt, which was the final, crushing indignity.

It really is always the little things.

FIFTEEN

EVERY NOW AND THEN YOU HAVE TO give the cops credit. Even if you don't like them, and they don't like you—even if your relationship with them has become strained to a point that approaches open warfare—even so, they some-times earn a small nod. Every now and then a cop does something that, in all fairness, requires you to pause, incline your head, and say, "Well done." Certainly not all cops—maybe not even most of them. But one or two of them, every now and then, come through in a way that really makes you want to give them a hearty handshake and a free doughnut.

Oddly enough, this turned out to be one of those times.

The first squad car was on the scene in less than five minutes. I heard the approaching siren, and a dutiful citizen would certainly have ignored his total weariness and the dozens of tiny puncture wounds that covered the front of his body, and leaped to his feet to greet them. Not Dexter. Not tonight. I had Had Enough.

So I lay on the floor with my eyes closed and listened to the inhuman caterwauling from the partiers. Of course, they had been much closer to the blast, and so presumably might have more serious injuries. But in fairness, they had also clearly consumed a great deal of alcohol, which should have deadened the pain. Instead, it had only loosened their inhibitions, especially those dealing with making truly stupid noises. No injury I could imagine would justify the repulsive clamor coming from the revelers. They sounded like sheep who had been lobotomized and then beaten with heavy clubs festooned with fish-hooks.

But I didn't care; let them bleat. It had nothing to do with me. It didn't even touch me, not in any way. I was all done. I was so completely Finished with It All that nothing could affect me. I was the New Age guru who had attained a perfect state of Enough Already, and if the world wanted any more from me they could damn well come and get it.

So I just lay there as the siren got close enough to drown out the moaning and wordless mindless hollering, and I didn't move as the squad car screeched to a halt and the two officers in it jumped out and began to catalog the chaos. I didn't even sit up when the ER techs arrived in their ambulance and began to treat the blathering ninnies from the party rooms.

It wasn't until I heard the authoritative pounding on my door, accompanied by a hard-edged woman's voice calling, "Sir? Sir!" that I managed to stir myself. Opening my eyes was the hard part.

After that, it was mere unendurable burdensome drudgery to climb to my feet and open the door.

An African American woman in a blue Miami-Dade police uniform gave me a once-over that was as hard-edged as her voice. "Are you all right, sir?" she said. She sounded concerned but completely without compassion, which I thought was a nice trick, and probably much harder to do than it sounds.

"Some cuts," I said, holding up my hands and then waving at my shirtfront. "Other than that . . ." I let my arms drop. The weariness was returning, fed by my realization that whatever else happened here tonight, they were almost certainly going to take me downtown when they found out who I was.

"Right," the cop said. "Why don't you come with me, sir," she said. She put a firm hand on my arm and led me out the door.

My first weary glance at what was left of the little hotel was enough to open my eyes to their widest, and I stumbled and might have fallen if not for the cop's steadying hand. Of course, I knew a bomb had gone off—but knowing that and seeing what that really meant were two entirely different things.

Down at the far end, where I had parked my poor, ill-fated rental car, the devastation was most impressive. Nothing at all remained of my car, except a plume of smoke and some blackened, twisted metal. A trio of firemen was putting out the last few flickers of flame.

The cars on either side of mine were demolished, almost as totally evaporated as mine. And the front of the hotel where they had been parked was blackened, paint burned off, windows blown out, doors off the hinges, and several more firemen were rushing in and out.

All along the walkway, from the firemen to where I stood, there was destruction, ranging from blistered walls to shattered windows and doors. I had seen bomb damage before in the course of my work, but this was something rather special. And all to get little old me? Somebody obviously thought I was rather special, too. "Wow," I said.

The cop just nodded. "Come on," she said, and pushed me gently the other way, toward the hotel's office. The ER guys had set up a little triage station in front, where the driveway curved under an overhanging roof by the office door.

Like most of their ilk, the emergency medics were cheerful, brisk, and efficient. They saved me a trip to the Dumpster by removing my ruined shirt and tossing it into a large plastic bag. Then one of them, a small and wiry woman with short dark hair, probed all the cuts quickly and thoroughly. She took out three or four small pieces of glass, and then swabbed out all my cuts with antiseptic. "We're a little short on the tiny Band-

Aids tonight, sport," she told me. "So you might want to keep the shirt off till the cuts scab over." She smiled. "Lucky for me, you can get away with it. You look like a fireman." She slapped my shoulder, as if I'd done well, and urged me up and onto my feet. "You'll be fine," she said, and she moved away to the next victim of the evening's tragedy.

The same cop was waiting for me when I turned away from the aid station. "Can you answer a few questions, sir?" she asked me.

Nothing that had happened in the last twenty minutes had made me less tired, and each one of the two dozen small perforations that covered the front of my body was now stinging. But neither of those reasons was an acceptable excuse for dodging a police inquiry, as I well knew. So I just nodded wearily and said, "Yes, of course."

She went through a standard set of questions, the ones that are always the same. They're designed for two important purposes: first, so that when the detectives eventually get involved they can be certain that the correct questions, and the same ones, have been asked. The second vital purpose is to make sure that the first-responder cops, usually in a patrol car, don't come across as vacuous idiots. This is important, because most detectives seem to think that the beat cops actually *are* vacuous idiots. And quite honestly, sometimes

258

they are—but then, the same can be said of the detectives, as my recent experience had so thoroughly proved.

My questioner—her name tag said POUX, but offered no suggestions on how to say it—seemed very far from vacuous or idiotic. Possibly having a name that was impossible to pronounce correctly had made her smart. She went through the standard questions, recording my answers on a little steno pad, and she did it very briskly and impersonally, until I finally let it slip that it had been my car that exploded. At that point, she glanced around her in a way that I have to call furtive. I assumed she was looking for a superior officer—but none had arrived on the scene yet.

Officer Poux nearly smiled. She licked her lips and returned her attention to me with a look of feverish concentration taking over her face. She was still in charge, and she had a hot one. There were no standard questions for this, and if she screwed up she'd get a tongue-lashing at the very least. But if she did well, it might mean advancement, and clearly Officer Poux did not intend to remain in a plain blue uniform forever. Among other things, it did nothing at all for her figure. So she began to improvise questions.

"You're certain it was your car?" she demanded.

"Yes," I said. "Um, rented, actually."

"You *rented* the car?" she said. "How long ago?"

I tried to think how long ago it had been. Aside from the fact that I was exhausted, too much had happened too fast, and I found it almost impossible to separate the recent past into coherent chunks of days and nights. It all seemed to be wadded up together into a lump and frozen into a bubble of simultaneous time, more like one of those insects captured in a glob of amber than a well-ordered history. But I puzzled through it and found what I thought was the right answer, as impossible as it seemed. "Yesterday?" I said at last. "I think."

She asked where I had rented the car, who had rented it to me, whether I had left it unattended, where I had been when I did. I answered truthfully, and she wrote it all down. And then she hesitated, licked her lips, and perhaps she thought to herself, *This could help me make detective.* "Is there anybody that, in your opinion, might want to kill you?" she said.

And there it was, the last straw, the final brick in the wall, the one tiny nudge over the line. Was there anybody who wanted to kill me? In all this violent, wicked, sinful world, was there anybody left who *didn't?* I could think of no way to begin, no possible starting point, and the thought of even attempting a complete list was so ludicrous that I looked at her for just a moment—and I started to laugh.

I do not actually feel real emotions, so laughing

was not something that came naturally, or easily, to me. In fact, I had spent a good chunk of my youth learning when and how to laugh properly. I prided myself on the final result, which sounded dignified, restrained, and natural, and it was nothing at all like the sound that came out of me now—a crackly, high-pitched, gasping kind of noise that sounded like an endless cough by a second-rate tenor. Even if you could find somebody who liked me, they would not have said it was an attractive sound.

But it came pouring out, an interminable wheezing cackle, and I couldn't stop it. Officer Poux just watched, and waited patiently for me to stop laughing for perhaps half a minute, and just as I began to slow down, she hardened her face into a near-perfect imitation of Deborah's Stone-faced Cop look, and I had to laugh some more.

Officer Poux waited it out only a little longer, and then she turned away. I thought I had offended her, which seemed funny, but she came right back with one of the med techs, not the one who had treated me. This one was an African American man, about thirty-five, who looked like he should be playing linebacker for the Pittsburgh Steelers. He walked right up to me, peered into my eyes, grabbed my wrist and felt my pulse, and then turned to Officer Poux. "I don't know," he said. "Not really a psych expert." He shrugged. "Probably just shock. Let him laugh it out." And he went back to the victims with more interesting injuries.

Officer Poux watched him go, then turned back to me and just stared. She didn't seem to blink, and she looked like she could wait as long as she had to. That turned out to be not very long, since I was already winding down. After only a few more seconds, I managed to grab the reins away from whatever strange spirit had driven me into paroxysms of cackling glee. I took a deep breath, smiled reassuringly at Officer Poux, and said, "I'm sorry. It's just . . . It's a little hard to explain."

She kept staring for a few more seconds, and then said, like nothing at all had happened, "Can you think of anyone that, in your opinion, might want to kill you?"

"Yes, I can," I said, fighting back a tiny tickle of resurgent hilarity. "In fact, it's a very long list."

"Can you give me a couple of names, sir?"

"Well, well, well" came a voice from behind me. It was unfortunately a very familiar voice, with a tone that held a perpetual sneer and quite clearly said *brainless bully* to those who know about such things, and it was a voice that I really did not want to hear behind me under any circumstance, much less when my car had just blown up.

"Actually," I told her, "here comes one of them now."

Officer Poux glanced over my shoulder and came to a sort of stiff, half-at-attention pose, and the owner of the aforementioned voice stepped into view.

"Detective Anderson," I said. "Wonderful to see you again. But isn't it past your bedtime?"

"Oh, I wouldn't miss this for anything," he said. He looked at me with an expression that can only be described as a gloating glare, and without taking his eyes off mine, he said to Poux, "Cuff him. And it doesn't have to be gentle."

"On what charge, sir?" Officer Poux said.

Anderson spun on her. "On a charge of Because I Say So," he sneered at her. "Do it."

Poux stood motionless for just a moment longer, and it may be that she would have done what Anderson said eventually, but he didn't give her the chance. "Fuck it," he snarled. He leaned over and grabbed her handcuffs. "This goes in my report," he told her, already turning on me.

"Yes, sir," she said. "Mine too."

He didn't hesitate for a second. He just grabbed me by the shoulders, spun me around, and yanked my hands halfway up my back. "I knew you'd pull something," he growled as he put the cuffs on me, much too tight. "Never should've let you back on the street." He gave a final, brutal tug, and then stepped back to sneer at me where I could see it. "You just can't keep away from trouble, can you, asshole?"

"Why bother?" I said. "You'd just make something up and tag me with it anyway." I smiled. "Like now. How many reports will you have to forge to make this stick, Detective? And when are you going to learn to disguise your handwriting?"

He just glared at me for a moment. And then he stepped forward and gave me an openhanded slap to the face, hard. It hurt. It was hard enough to turn the world dim and make me stagger back a step, and I'm pretty sure it loosened a molar, too. But I just straightened up, smiled again, and said, "I notice you didn't hit me until after the cuffs were on."

His face turned darker and he clenched his fists and his teeth and I thought I might have gone too far. But before he could do anything more Officer Poux stepped between us. "Sir! That's enough!" she said.

"It's not half enough," Anderson said. "Get outa my way."

"No, sir," she said. And then she turned to face him. "And *this* goes in my report, too." She glared at him for several seconds and then added, "Sir." It didn't sound respectful in the least.

"You put this in your report," Anderson said through clenched teeth, "and you'll be a meter maid by morning."

"Better than this," she said. "Meter maids got too much *balls* to whup on a man in cuffs."

They stood toe-to-toe and glared for a moment, and then, just as Anderson opened his mouth—probably to threaten her some more—one of the other uniforms called out, "Hey, Detective? Bomb guys are here." Anderson twitched a couple of times, as if he was being tugged in two directions by two equally rotten impulses. But he just told Poux, "Put him in my car," spun around, and walked off to talk to the bomb guys.

Officer Poux watched him go, and when he was at a safe distance, with his back turned to us, she unlocked the cuffs, took them off my wrists, and said, "Your hands are blue. Shake 'em around; get the circulation going."

The hands in question were kind of blue, which was no surprise, since they'd already gone numb. I shook them, flexed them, and then raised an eyebrow at Officer Poux.

She shook her head. "Hold 'em out," she said. I did, and she snapped the cuffs back on again—but in front of me this time, and a great deal looser.

"Thank you," I said politely.

"Just doing my job," she said, and since that was quite true I said no more. But just before she put me carefully into the backseat of Anderson's motor-pool car, she leaned close to my ear. "When it's a bomb, like this?" she said softly, "it's also my job to call the feds."

I looked at her with some surprise. "Did you?" I asked.

She gave me a very brief, nearly invisible smile. "I did," she whispered. And then resuming her role as a tough-as-nails, hypereffective cop, she returned to her normal voice and said, "Duck your head, sir," and she pushed me into the car and shut the door.

I watched her go with a certain amount of admiration. In today's paranoid post-9/11 world, it was indeed part of the job to alert as many federal authorities as possible when something happened that had even the faintest whiff of terrorism— and of course, a bomb always qualifies. But I had seen cases where Homeland Security, the FBI, and ATF were all fighting for jurisdiction with Miami-Dade, FDLE, and representatives of other government organizations so important they didn't even have a name.

And normally, since the local cops really want to be in charge of something that happens on their turf, the first responders would probably wait for a superior officer to arrive before calling the feds. Of course, this can waste precious time and even allow a suspect to get away, but at least it does preserve our local rights, possibly preventing another civil war.

Officer Poux had not waited. She had taken initiative and done the smart thing. And just incidentally, it was the thing that was going to save me from another stretch of sitting in the pokey with no paperwork and no hope of getting out. When the feds arrived, any suspect taken into custody—in this case, Me—would be turned over to them. And since the feds were generally a little more careful about forging documents merely because they didn't like somebody, and since they did not, as yet, actually dislike me, I would almost certainly be turned loose, and rather quickly.

And all because Officer Poux did the right thing. It was a wonder, a rare marvel, and I decided on the spot that if I was ever police commissioner I would promote her first thing. She had gone far beyond the call of duty and actually done her job.

I watched Officer Poux as she walked away and went back to work, thinking kindly thoughts about her. As I said, every now and then, you really do have to give the cops credit for a job well done.

I sat there unmolested for quite a while—nearly an hour and a half, according to my watch, which I could now see quite easily, thanks to Officer Poux. The whole time no one beat me, or threatened me, or called me unpleasant names. On the other hand, nobody brought me coffee and a cruller either. I was left entirely alone, free to do absolutely anything I wanted to do, as long as it could be done wearing handcuffs while locked in the backseat of a car. It's not a long list of activities. Happily for me, though, the list included something I wanted to do very much: sleep.

So I did. I dropped off almost immediately into a deep and dreamless sleep, and didn't wake up at all until I heard somebody opening the door of the car I was in.

I opened my eyes, expecting to see Officer Poux again, and I was not disappointed. But standing directly behind her were two new faces. I did not know either one of them, but when the door opened and Poux helped me out, turning me to face the strangers, it took only a glance to know exactly who they were.

They were a matched set, one man and one woman, in their thirties, fit-looking, and wearing expressions that were as serious as their nearly matching suits, and so it was kind of anticlimactic when the woman held up a badge and said, "FBI. Special Agent Revis." She nodded at her male clone. "This is Special Agent Blanton. We'd like to ask you a couple of questions."

I smiled at them pleasantly. "Pleased to meet you. But I'm afraid I can't answer any questions while my rights are being violated." Just to make sure my point got across, I held up my manacled wrists.

The feds glanced at each other, and then the man—Special Agent Blanton—looked quizzically at Poux. "Officer, is this man under arrest?"

"No, sir, not to my knowledge," Poux said.

"Is he a danger to himself or others?" Revis asked.

"I don't believe he is," Poux said very carefully. "He has shown no sign of it."

The two feds glanced at each other again, and Blanton frowned and looked back at Poux. "Then why is he cuffed?"

With one of the straightest faces I have ever seen, Poux said, "Sir. The detective in charge ordered me to cuff this man. I asked him the charge, and he told me it was a charge of"—she cleared her throat, and made a very clear effort to keep her face blank—"a charge of 'Because I Said So.'"

"He said that?" Blanton said mildly.

"And then you cuffed him?" Revis said.

"No, ma'am," Poux said. "Then the detective in charge grabbed my handcuffs and did it himself." She hesitated, and then added, "I recuffed him later."

"Why?" Revis said.

"The detective in charge had done it in a manner I deemed to be injurious, with this man's hands behind his back, and much too tight, with a resulting loss of circulation."

They all turned and looked at me, and Blanton frowned. He stepped forward and looked hard at my face where Anderson had slapped me. "Did the loss of circulation result in a contusion to this man's face?" he said.

Poux went absolutely rigid in face and body and looked straight ahead. "No, sir," she said.

"Do you have certain knowledge of what *did* cause this contusion?" Revis demanded.

"Yes, ma'am."

Blanton sighed and faced Poux. "Are you inclined to share that information, Officer—" He frowned and looked at Poux's name tag. "Officer . . . Powks?"

"Pronounced 'Pooh,' sir," she said, unmoving.

"Your first name isn't Winnie, is it?" Revis said wryly.

"Melanie," she said.

"Too bad," Revis muttered.

"Officer *Pooh*," Blanton said sharply. "How did this man get this mark on his face?"

"The detective in charge struck him, sir," Poux said. "After he put on the cuffs." She looked so absolutely upright and military I had to stop myself from whistling "The Stars and Stripes Forever."

Blanton closed his eyes and sighed. Revis merely said, "I think you can take the cuffs off him, Poux."

Poux stepped smartly over to me and I held up my wrists. She unlocked them and, just before she turned away, I winked at her. She didn't wink back.

"Thank you, Officer Poux," Revis said. "You can return to your duties."

Poux marched off, and I stepped forward into

the space she'd been in. "Pleased to meet you," I said to Revis as she turned to look at me. "My name is Dexter Morgan."

"Would you be willing to answer a few questions, Mr. Morgan?" she said.

"Of course," I said.

They led me into the hotel's dingy little lobby. It was far enough from the blast that it hadn't been damaged. Considering the state of the rotting old furniture, that was neither believable nor fortunate. The old couple who ran the place had turned off the television. He sat in a moldering overstuffed chair with an expression on his face he must have learned from Edvard Munch, while she bustled back and forth with a pot of coffee and a stack of Styrofoam cups.

There was a small couch that wasn't totally repugnant, and Revis motioned me to sit. She sat facing me in a straight-backed wooden chair. Her partner, Blanton, stood behind her, to her left, clearly giving her the lead. "That was your car that blew up, Mr. Morgan?" she said.

"Rented," I told her with a charming, self-effacing smile.

As good as it was, the smile may not have worked, judging by her next question. "Did you blow up the rental car, Mr. Morgan?"

"No," I said.

She just nodded. "The detective thinks you did it."

"Yes, he would," I said.

"That was a pretty big bomb, Mr. Morgan," she said. "Who put it there?"

"I don't know," I said. And in all honesty I didn't really *know*. I had a couple of very good guesses, but that was really none of the FBI's business. Of course, they thought it was.

"If you had to guess, who do you *think* did it?" she asked.

"Well," I said, "it is a rented car. It could be aimed at the last person who drove it. Or even, you know. Some kind of mistake."

"A mistake," Blanton said, with sharp skepticism. "Somebody put a bomb like that in the wrong car?"

I shrugged. "It could happen. This is Miami."

"Mr. Morgan," Revis said, "that's a little hard to believe, isn't it?" She raised one eyebrow. "Even in Miami?"

"A couple of years ago, only a few miles from here," I said, "a man was killed when a chunk of frozen sewage fell from a passing airplane and crashed through his roof."

"Why did the detective hit you?" Blanton said abruptly.

"He doesn't like me," I said.

Blanton just looked at me, but Revis snorted and said, "That was *my* first guess."

"Do you know *why* he doesn't like you?" Blanton said. "Or is that more frozen sewage?"

I hesitated. I suppose a real human being would have plunged right into the long and twisty tale, full of confidence in the forthright integrity of two upstanding federal agents and the noble system they represented. Unfortunately, I knew better. Everyone has a hidden agenda, and it is never, never, *never* what it looks like on the surface—which is, of course, why it is a *hidden* agenda. Revis and Blanton might decide to help Anderson in order to secure better local cooperation, which would show up on the monthly report and cause a budget increase, resulting in longer coffee breaks for the entire Bureau. There was no way to know. And so there was also no way to know whether telling them all was a good thing.

"Mr. Morgan?" Revis prompted.

I looked at her, and then at Blanton, her partner. They certainly *looked* forthright and upstanding. Of course, so did I, and we all know how much that means. But every now and then, you run out of logical and reasonable options, and you just have to swallow hard, cross your fingers, and tell the truth.

So I did. I told the whole sad story of deceit, treachery, malice, and heinous ineptitude. Believe it or not, I actually told it pretty much as it happened, with only one or two minor changes in emphasis, and a couple of well-timed pauses, mostly when I was talking about Rita's death, in which I cleared my throat. I had learned from watching daytime TV that throat clearing is something Manly Guys do to show that they are fighting back emotions. I thought it was a wonderful shortcut, since clearing my throat was a great deal easier than making all those tragic faces.

Revis and Blanton just watched me, apparently listening intently. When I finished, they looked at each other, and held the stare for an embarrassingly long time. Neither of them said a word, but they apparently had a whole conversation, because eventually she turned back to me and said, "We will probably want to ask you a few more questions later on. Where will you be staying?"

Believe it or not, this was the first time it had occurred to me that I had no place to go. That wasn't entirely a bad thing, since I also had no way to get there. "Um," I said. "I don't know. Can I call you when I find another hotel?"

Revis handed me her business card. It was very nice, embossed with an FBI logo and everything. She wrote down my cell phone number, had one more quick silent chat with Blanton, and then nodded at me. "You're free to go."

SIXTEEN

FOR SEVERAL MINUTES AFTER THE TWO FBI agents left, I just sat on the moldering old sofa in the hotel's lobby, too bone-weary to do anything more demanding than blink my eyes. Only a few hours ago I had felt battered and exhausted because so much had happened—and since that time, I had found out what "so much happening" *really* meant. But with the bomb blast and the consequent utter destruction of my transportation, and then the savage slapping and cuffing from Anderson, I thought I could safely say, *Now "so much" has* really *happened.*

And all of it aimed at my nearly innocent head. It was almost enough to make me believe in a god—since it would have to be a petty, vengeful, mean-spirited god who spent so much time and effort picking on someone who really didn't deserve it. That kind of god I could believe in. At least it would explain the recent history of Dexter, which was starting to seem supernaturally unpleasant.

I thought about this latest blatantly unfair incident. A bomb. In spite of what I had told the feds about coincidence, of course I was sure it wasn't. I had too many real enemies to give coincidence a chance to break into the lineup.

Which one was it this time? It was not terribly mysterious. I ruled out Debs right away; she was much too fussy about the little things, like legality and collateral damage. Anderson would certainly have done it if he could figure out which end of the bomb to hold, but I didn't believe for a second that he had. He was having too much fun whipping me with his custom-modified legal system. And after eliminating him, there really wasn't any doubt that it was Brian's former playmates, Raul and associates, who had put the bomb in my car. The only question was how they'd found me.

The more I thought about that, the more important it seemed. I really and truly didn't want them to find me again. They would almost certainly do a more thorough job next time.

More immediately, though, I had to let Brian know what had happened. It was quite possible that they would find him, too, and I thought it would be best if he knew about the possibility. After all, he was the last person who still seemed to be on my side—unless I counted Officer Poux, which was probably a little bit of a stretch.

So I reached into my pocket for my phone—and of course I didn't have it. Somehow it had been magically replaced by a small piece of cardboard with vermilion ink on it—Kraunauer's card, and his personal cell number, of which I could avail myself twenty-four/seven. A bomb in my car and subsequent police brutality certainly seemed like something he would want to know about, and I knew I should call him—except that I didn't have a phone.

Come to think of it, I still didn't even have a shirt. Both items could be had in abundant quantity if I could somehow manage to travel all those weary feet from the lobby to my room. It seemed like much farther away than it had been before, but there really wasn't much choice.

So I dragged my exhausted, battered, punctured, and slapped self up off the ancient couch and staggered manfully out the lobby door and down the walk toward what had recently been my room. Alas, it was mine no longer. A different uniformed officer informed me politely but firmly that I could not enter until after forensics had finished, not even to retrieve my phone. I was too tired to do more than blink at him resentfully a few times, and that seemed to have no effect. You just can't put good, hard-edged resentment into a blink.

And now what? I could think of nowhere else to go, unless I returned to the backseat of Anderson's car, or to the dreadful little sofa in the lobby. Believe it or not, the sofa was so uncomfortable, old and repellent, that I had to think about it for a minute. But no matter how far beyond the established norms of civilized furniture it might be, at least the couch was not in any way connected to Anderson. I trudged back to it.

As I trudged, I tried to think of a way to call Brian without my phone. It seems stupid in retrospect, but it must be admitted that the cell phone, that personal ubiquitous all-encompassing nearly everything device, has become so important to every one of us that we cannot imagine life without it, and most of us cannot complete the simplest tasks unless we are holding our techno BFF in our hand. Without it we can't write anyone, check the weather or stocks, find out where we are and how not to be there, pay bills, keep an appointment, make a flight—nothing at all. It has taken over nearly every aspect of our lives. And every now and then, when we actually want to make a phone call, our phones can even do that. They have replaced an entire suitcase full of other devices, and it is no longer possible even to think of life without one.

And so it was not until I walked all the way into the lobby and sat, allowing the ancient couch cushions to suck me down into their vile grasp, that I thought of a novel and ingenious way to get in touch with Brian. In the interest of full disclosure, I must admit that I did not actually *think* of it; the truth is, the ancient, battered landline telephone on the hotel's front desk rang. I turned to follow the sound, saw the archaic device, and thought, *Aha. I remember what those things are for.*

The ancient phone rang for nearly a minute

and no one answered it. The old man had disappeared, and the old woman was just visible in the back room moving back and forth much too energetically in a rocking chair. She made no move to get the phone, and so when the thing had stopped ringing, I got up and went to it.

My memory is a wonderful thing, and I was quite sure that I knew Brian's number, so I dialed with calm confidence. It rang several times, and then a soft and husky voice I did not recognize said, "Yes?"

"I'm sorry," I said, thinking as quickly as I could in my current state of collapse. "Is this Atwater Brothers Carpet?"

After only a slight hesitation, the answer came—but in a completely different voice. "Brother," Brian said. "I didn't recognize the number. Where are you calling from?"

"Hotel lobby," I said. "My phone is being examined by forensics at the moment."

"Really," he said. "May one ask why?"

I told him in short and simple terms. He hissed out a long breath. "I was afraid of this," he said.

For a moment I was speechless. *Afraid* of it? Meaning he thought it might happen and had decided not to warn me? "Were you?" I said at last.

"Remember I called?" he said, and of course there was not even a tiny trace of guilt in his voice. "I meant to tell you, but you pleaded fatigue."

It was just barely true, but even so I was so upset that I didn't even correct him for saying *pleaded* instead of *pled*. "All right," I said wearily. "What did you mean to tell me?"

"I received a warning," he said, "that a certain associate of Raul's had arrived in town."

"An associate," I said. I thought back on what Brian had told me of the epic struggle between Raul and his rival, Santo. "Would this perhaps be the associate who blew up the Red Saint?"

"The very same," he said, sounding quite happy that I had remembered.

"And when were you going to tell me this exciting news?"

"In truth, I thought it would keep until breakfast," Brian said. "I assumed that I was the target."

"Apparently you were wrong," I said.

"So it seems," he said with great and completely unwarranted good cheer.

For just a moment I stood with my eyes closed, letting the waves of fatigue wash over me. "I need to get out of here," I said. "And my car is not going anywhere. Can you come get me?"

"Weeeeeell," he said. "That might not be the wisest course right now. I have to believe they're watching you and hoping I do just that."

It was true; no matter how selfish I thought it was, and how very contrary to all that was Decent for Dexter, I could not deny that it would be just a tiny bit stupid for him to come get me. Raul's men were almost certainly watching. "I suppose you're right," I said.

"Yes," Brian said. "But this is troubling. Somehow they found you first. Any idea how?"

"Brian," I said. "I have just been bombed, perforated with glass slivers, slapped—and I was already exhausted. I'm not having ideas right now."

"Of course not, you poor thing," he said, oozing fake sympathy that still sounded much too happy. "Get some sleep. We'll talk in the morning." And he disconnected without waiting for me to say good-bye. Possibly he thought I would want to say a few other things first, of a more personal and antagonistic nature. After all, any reasonable person would have to say that this was all his fault. And possibly I would have said more—but he hung up, and even that small comfort was denied me.

I replaced the old phone in its antiquated cradle, marveling at how well it fit. Say what you will about modern technology; people back then knew how to build things that *worked*. And then, still looking at the phone, I thought, *Kraunauer.* I pulled his card from my pocket, carefully smoothing a small wrinkle. I picked up the phone again and dialed.

Kraunauer answered on the second ring, which was nice. But the way he answered took me by surprise. "*¿Se hace?*" he said in his wonderful Mexican-Spanish accent.

For just a second I wondered if this old telephone had made some kind of mistake and given him the wrong caller ID. But then I remembered that it was, after all, an antique—and Brian, too, had not known who was calling. "It's Dexter Morgan," I said. "I'm calling from a hotel lobby."

For a moment he was speechless, which was a first in my dealings with him. "Oh, that's . . . ah," he said at last. "Well, then, I—And are you all right?"

"I'm a little rumpled," I said. "Someone put a very large bomb in my car."

"What?!" he said. "I take it you were not actually in the car when it went off?"

"I was not," I said. "Or I would be considerably *more* rumpled."

"Of course you would," he said. For some reason he did not seem to be showing his usual eloquence. Perhaps it was the lateness of the hour. "Well, then, um, the police are there?"

"They are," I told him. "And the FBI. Um—the police are represented by Detective Anderson?"

"Ah," he said. "That's the same officer who has been troubling you?"

"It is," I said. "He accused me of bombing my own car, and he slapped me. Kind of hard, too."

"Was there a witness?" he said, and his voice seemed suddenly sharper, more alert.

"Another cop," I said. "A uniform. Officer Poux—Melanie Poux."

"Well, crap," he said. "We'll never get her to testify against another cop."

"She might," I said. "She let the feds drag it out of her."

"Did she!" he exclaimed. He sounded delighted. "Well, then. We may have something here. An FBI agent's testimony is as good as it gets. We just might have something. Oh—they don't think you blew up your own rental car, do they?"

"I don't think so," I said.

Kraunauer chuckled. "Good, good," he said. "Well, believe it or not, this is actually a real break."

"It doesn't seem like it at the moment," I said.

"No, but it will," he said. "The bomb story will be all over the news tomorrow, and when they find out that *you* are the intended victim—no, no, this is excellent. We can use it to get some sympathy going—it could be a real turning point."

"Really," I said.

"Absolutely. Don't kid yourself, Mr. Morgan. Nine out of ten cases are won in the media before you even meet the judge. And if we roll into it with something like this—I hate to repeat myself, but this really is a big break."

"Oh, well, good," I said. And in spite of being well aware that I needed to maintain my sense of awe when speaking with Kraunauer, I was suddenly overcome with fatigue—and I yawned. "Excuse me," I said.

"Perfectly all right, you must be exhausted," he said briskly. "You go get some sleep, and we'll talk in the morning. Ah . . ." His voice slowed down and he sounded suddenly very casual. "Where are you staying?"

"I don't know yet," I said. "I'll find another hotel somewhere."

"Of course. All right," he said, all business again. "Get some sleep, and call me tomorrow."

"All right," I said.

"Good night," he said cheerfully, and broke the connection.

I thought about his excellent advice: sleep. The whole concept was starting to take on mythical proportions. It had begun to seem like something only epic heroes could do; I certainly couldn't manage it. I wasn't yet so tired that I would take the risk of sleeping here, in the lobby, surrounded by Anderson and mad bombers and horrible tattered curtains.

Mere rest was no longer enough, and I didn't think I could face the couch again anyway. So I did the only thing I could, the last pitiful choice left to me in this world of pain and dwindling options. I left the lobby and stood outside beside what had once been my room, standing in a miserable bovine stupor until forensics finally finished. Then I went in and put on a shirt, grabbed my few sad belongings, and used my phone to call a cab.

SEVENTEEN

BY THE TIME MY CAB ARRIVED I HAD used my phone to find another hotel, only a few miles from this one. But at the last second, just as I opened my mouth to give the address to the driver, one final tendril of consciousness waved the little red flag of caution and instead I told him to take me to the airport. It would mean an extra hour or more of being painfully awake, but it might also make it a little harder for the bad guys to find me.

At the airport I decided to play the game a little longer. I went in and wandered for a few minutes, and failed to spot anybody following me. I rode the Skytrain around the whole circuit twice, getting off and on suddenly and randomly, until I was quite sure I wasn't being tailed. I picked up a shuttle to a hotel in Coral Gables, got another cab there, and ended up at a small hotel in Homestead with barely enough strength left to stagger up to my third-floor room and flop onto the bed, still fully dressed.

I remember thinking that this bed, at last, seemed very firm, and then I was blinking at the bedside clock that told me it was eleven-fifty-three. That didn't seem possible. It had been well after midnight when I fell onto the bed. How could it be seven minutes *before* now? I closed my eyes again and tried to think, which was even harder than it had been lately. For just a moment I thought I must have slept backward through time, finally arriving here in bed before I actually got here. I spent a few pleasant moments thinking of what I should say to myself when I saw me walk in the door. But then I opened my eyes again, and noticed a bright edge of light showing around the bottom of the heavy curtains, and I thought, *Aha. It's daytime. I slept through the night, and lo! The sun has riz. That explains everything.* Still, a little disappointing. I'd been hoping for a really interesting conversation with someone I knew to be a brilliant conversationalist—Me.

I rolled over and sat up. Everything hurt. My entire body was as sore as if I had just gone ten rounds with the heavyweight champ. Or one of them, anyway—there seemed to be quite a few lately. Perhaps they'd taken turns working me over. On top of all that, each one of the two dozen perforations from the glass splinters was stinging, my head throbbed, my jaw ached where Anderson had hit me, and I had a cramp in the arch of my left foot. I tried very hard for some positive spin: I was alive! It was the best I could do, but at the moment that didn't seem like any real cause for celebration.

I looked at the clock again: eleven-fifty-seven. At least time was behaving properly and moving *forward*. I got slowly and gingerly off the bed. It was such a painful experience that I just stood there for a minute, hoping that returning circulation would begin to take away a few of the aches and pains. My left foot gradually felt a little better, but that was about it.

Still, I was, in fact, alive, and that had taken some doing. I thought about patting myself on the back, but decided I was too sore. I looked around the room, wondering what other miracle I could perform next. There was a small one-cup coffeemaker on the desk. That seemed like a good place to start.

The coffee began to brew, and as the first tendril of fresh coffee aroma steamed up and tickled my nose, it must have jump-started a synapse or two, because I remembered what Kraunauer had said: *The bomb story will be all over the news.* I looked at the clock again. It was now twelve-oh-one. Miami is blessed—or cursed, depending on your attitude—with several very active TV news departments that broadcast a *News at Noon* program. I clicked on the TV that sat next to the coffeemaker and turned to the station whose reporters had the best hair.

The last person to occupy this room was clearly hard of hearing, because the TV began to blast at a life-threatening volume. I hurriedly turned it down, just in time to hear the breathy blonde at the desk saying,

". . . that authorities are now calling a deliberate attempt to murder this man—"

A terribly unflattering picture of Me appeared behind the blonde.

"Dexter Morgan," she said, "who was recently arrested for multiple murder and molesting his stepdaughter." And of course she had to say it in a rather accusing tone of voice, since pedophilia was involved. Even so, it was a wonderfully surreal moment to see Me on TV like that, in spite of the fact that I was really not at my best in that picture. But if you don't love yourself, no one else will, so I admired my features for just a moment, and missed what was being said, until I tuned back in at, ". . . well-known criminal attorney Frank Kraunauer, who told our Matt Laredo his client was completely innocent and still being harassed by the police."

The picture cut to a head shot of Frank Kraunauer. He looked much better than the picture of me. In fact, he looked magnificent: angry, yet composed, intelligent, formidable, and every hair in perfect place, which is very important to all major news outlets nowadays.

"There's no longer any question that Mr. Morgan is being railroaded," he said. "From the very beginning the evidence has been manipulated or even manufactured. My client has been falsely accused, unjustly and improperly jailed, and even physically assaulted by a member of the Miami-Dade police force."

An earnest tenor voice cut in and the camera swung to the reporter, Matt Laredo, a young guy with wonderful brown hair and a very serious look. "Mr. Kraunauer, you want us to believe your client was assaulted by a *cop?*"

Back to Kraunauer. "He went into police custody last night unmarked, and came out of custody with a huge bruise on his face." He favored the reporter with a sardonic smile, one I hadn't seen before, bringing his total to eight separate great fake smiles. I was overcome with admiration and almost missed him saying, "No doubt the police will tell you he hit himself. But I have a witness who saw the officer hit my client. This is the same rogue cop who threatened my client's life."

Matt Laredo jumped in. "Where is your client now? Can we talk to him?"

Kraunauer gave him a pitying look. "No, of course not. Mr. Morgan feels that it isn't safe to show his face, and I agree." Kraunauer paused, a perfect two-second interval for maximum dramatic effect. "Mr. Morgan's life was threatened. By a *cop*. And then *somebody* . . . put a bomb in his car."

Matt Laredo's face filled the screen, wearing a wonderfully crafted expression of dubious amazement and shock. Great hair *and* acting ability—the kid had network potential. "Mr. Kraunauer," Laredo said, "are you asking us to believe that a *police* officer planted this bomb?"

Back to Kraunauer, who left Laredo in the dust, facially speaking, with a superb expression of cynical amusement, combined with disgust and angry outrage. "Draw your own conclusions," he said grimly. "I make no accusations. But the threats were made, and then the bomb happened —and it would be very convenient for certain members of the police department if Dexter Morgan was no longer able to testify against them."

The camera jumped to Matt Laredo, standing at my previous hotel, with the blasted ruins of my car behind him. "Anita, it seems like a clear-cut story of a multiple murder is morphing into an epic case of police corruption and cover-up, and it begs the question: How high does this go? And just how much can we trust our cops to do their job fairly and honestly? With or without Frank Kraunauer, we suddenly have some huge questions . . . and very few answers."

Three full seconds of Matt Laredo looking nobly serious, and then back to the breathless blonde in the studio. "Thanks, Matt. And federal authorities have now intervened in the case, although terrorism is not suspected at this time.

And that sure makes it look like the FBI doesn't trust the Miami-Dade police, either."

The picture behind her changed to an aerial shot of a pod of whales, and the blonde went right on without skipping a beat. "Another tragedy on the beaches of South Florida, as eleven pilot whales have been stranded near Everglades City. Debbie Schultz is on the scene."

Even with Debbie Schultz on the scene, it was hard to get worked up about the tragic plight of a few whales, when poor Disheveled Dexter was in such terrible straits. I turned off the TV. Of course, it meant that I would never get to admire Debbie's hair. It might even be riffled by a light breeze, and that was always a marvelous news moment. But perhaps I could comb my own hair instead. Besides, the coffee was ready. As I sipped it, I tried very hard not to gloat, but I admit a few sly smirks snuck out anyway. Kraunauer had done a wonderful job. He was worth every penny I wasn't paying him. He even made *me* believe I was a poor innocent victim of an evil corrupt police force. And of course I was, at least in this one case, but I would never have dared to suggest it if not for Kraunauer.

The coffee did its job, too, and I was almost up to normal speed when my phone began to chirp. I glanced at it; the call was from Vince Masuoka. I picked up the phone and answered. "Hi, Vince," I said.

"Dexter, my God! Are you all right?" he said in a voice that was near hysteria. "I mean, I know you must be, because—But holy shit! A *bomb!* The news said? And you were—I mean, are you? Okay, I mean?"

Vince's outburst had been so frantic it was near the legal definition of assault, but I gathered he had seen something in the news similar to what I had just watched. "I'm fine, Vince, really," I said. "Just a couple of scratches."

"Oh, my *God,* but you could have been *killed!*" he said.

"I think that was the idea," I said, but he was already rushing on.

"Jesus, Dexter—a *bomb?!* And they just . . . I mean, who would do that? To you, I mean?"

"I don't know," I said. "But the FBI is handling it now. They took it away from Anderson."

"Anderson?" he said, sounding even more alarmed. "But that's—Anderson is . . ." He lowered his voice to a near whisper and added, "Dexter, you think *Anderson* might have—I mean," he said, dropping to a full whisper, "I found out he's reading my e-mail."

It's always wonderful to witness the emotional agility that some people with actual feelings can manage, and Vince had just performed a truly acrobatic feat, from concern for my life right to a petty problem he was having at work, all without losing a step. But beyond that, it was interesting in another way. Anderson? *Hacking?* "Vince, that's not possible," I said. "Anderson can barely work his phone."

"I'm positive, Dexter," Vince said. "I wrote a note to my mother? Just, you know, about going to see her at Easter. And then Anderson comes up to me and he says, 'What makes you think you'll still be *alive* at Easter, Masookoh?' He calls me Masookoh," he added, in case I wanted to remind him that wasn't really his name.

"Oh," I said. It certainly sounded like Anderson was, in fact, reading Vince's e-mail. "He must have some technical help."

"I know, but it could be anybody," Vince said. "Dexter, this thing is just crazy—it's like *everybody* is in on it all of a sudden, and I—I mean, it's so totally *overwhelming. . . .*"

Vince sounded like he was about to cry, which would have been a bit much for me, so I tried to calm him down. "It's almost over, Vince," I said. "It's all coming to a head now. You just hang on for a couple of days."

"Days, but Dexter," he said. "I mean, it's just *crazy* here."

There was more, but I got him calmed down eventually. I told him he was a good boy who had done a good thing and only good things could happen to him, and oddly enough, he began to believe it. So I said I had to go, and promised to call him and let him know what was going on, and put the phone down with a cramp in my neck and a sore ear. Anderson was growing into an even bigger problem, which hardly seemed possible— or fair, for that matter. If this truly was a rational and well-ordered Universe, wouldn't it be enough that somebody was being chased by a posse of hired killers, and nearly blown up by an enormous bomb? I mean, what was the point of adding Anderson's persecution on top of that? It really seemed kind of small-minded of the Universe, like cutting off somebody's legs and then saying, "And you're ugly, too!"

I thought briefly about doing Something about Anderson, but I quickly realized I was fantasizing rather than planning. He was a problem, yes—but not as immediate as my other ones. I could worry about Anderson if I managed to stay alive for a few more days.

I reached for my phone and called Brian. He answered right away, but instead of hello, he said, "Front page of the *Herald*, lead story on TV, and now me? So glad you haven't forgotten the little people now that you're famous."

"Fame has its price," I said. "That was a terrible picture of me."

"It was," he said agreeably. "But unfortunately, it's good enough to help my former friends identify you."

"I don't think they need help," I said.

"Perhaps not," he said. "And perhaps the phone

is not the place to speak of it. Can we meet somewhere?"

"As it happens, I'm hungry," I said.

"What a surprise," Brian said.

"It might be wise to pick a new place, though,"
I said. "And not because I'm tired of doughnuts."

"Where would you suggest?" he said.

"Well," I started—and then stopped as a relatively relevant thought hit me. "Brian, I am
carless. Can you come get me?"

"Where are you?"

I told him, and he promised to arrive within a
half hour. I spent the next twenty minutes
showering, and then looking at my multiple
punctures in the mirror. None of them actually
seemed life-threatening. In fact, they seemed to
be healing up nicely already. I remembered what
the paramedic had said, that I looked like a
fireman, and I tried out a calendar pose in the
mirror. It was not terribly convincing; aside from
the fact that I'd never actually seen a fireman
calendar, I still had an unhealthy jail pallor to
my skin, and it must be admitted that there was a
slight roll of nonessential material beginning to
form around my waist. I frowned at it, and then
realized what I was doing. Oh, Vanity, thy name is
Dexter.

I brushed my teeth, combed my hair, and
dressed in a clean set of brand-new Walmart
clothes, and made it down to a place outside the

hotel's front door with five minutes left in Brian's half-hour interval. I stood beside a large cement urn with a dead-looking tree in it. It also had quite a few cigarette butts squished down into the potting soil. I tried to look casual, but I was anything but as I looked around the parking area and out onto the street. There was no sign of anything living anywhere, aside from two birds on the power line.

I walked nonchalantly down to each end of the building, as if I was just a bored man waiting for a ride, and glanced to the sides. Still nothing. A handful of empty cars. We were past the hotel's checkout time, and still a few hours before check-in, and the whole place was as lifeless as it could be, which was all to the good.

I stood beside the urn for another two minutes before Brian arrived. Today he was driving his green Jeep, and he stopped it right beside me and I climbed in. "Good morning, brother," I told him.

"Hardly morning, and not quite good," he said. "But thank you for the thought." He drove slowly out onto the street, turned left, and as soon as he got up to speed he made an abrupt U-turn.

"Nicely done," I said. "All clear?"

"So it would seem," he said, peering into each of the three mirrors. He turned down a side street, then another, and finally, after several quick detours, out onto U.S. 1. "Well, then," he said, relaxing visibly. "What shall we eat?"

"Something nice, not too expensive," I said, and even as I spoke a franchise restaurant hove into view, one that specialized in pie. "There!" I said.

"Pie! How wonderful!" Brian said. "I do like pie."

He pulled into the parking lot and drove slowly around the whole thing one time, and I did not think it was an excess of caution. He found a parking spot right in front, where the car would be visible from inside, and we went in and found a booth where we could watch it. I ordered a large breakfast, in spite of the small roll at the waist I had seen in the mirror. Time to improve later; today we live. At least, that was the plan.

Brian ordered something called French Silk Pie, and a cup of coffee, and as we waited for the food to arrive, he lifted one eyebrow at me and said, "Have you given any thought to how they found you?"

"Not a great deal," I admitted. "But my best guess is, they traced the rental car, just like the hotel room. From my credit card."

Brian looked doubtful. "Maybe," he said. "But I used a different credit card at the hotel, with a fake name, totally different. So that would mean they already knew your name well in advance. And they didn't learn it from me."

"You're sure?" I said.

"Positive."

I thought about it, and from Brian's expression, he was doing the same. A small and vague thought stirred, deep down on the floor of my brain, but as I reached for it a cheerful clamor from my cell phone interrupted me. I picked it up and looked at the screen. I didn't recognize the number immediately, but it seemed familiar, and just before I pushed the button to decline the call I knew it—Kraunauer. "My lawyer," I said to Brian.

He waved his permission. "By all means," he said.

"Mr. Morgan," Kraunauer said. "The FBI would like to ask you a few more questions."

"Oh," I said. Not a truly brilliant response, but he had reminded me that I had not checked in with the feds as I'd said I would. "Um, in your opinion," I asked, "will these be *hostile* questions?"

"Not at all," Kraunauer said. "Apparently just a few loose ends, some bureaucratic stuff. Shouldn't take more than half an hour. And," he added in a casually reassuring tone, "I will be there to hold your hand."

"That's very thoughtful," I said.

"All part of the service," he said. "Can you meet me there in, oh, say, forty-five minutes?"

"Yes, I can," I told him. "And, Mr. Kraunauer?"

"Mm?"

"That was a wonderful performance on the

news," I said, fighting to keep the naked admiration out of my voice.

Kraunauer chuckled. "I played that kid reporter like a violin," he said. "It was really much too easy." There was some background noise, papers rustling and a few whispered words. "Ah—I'm sorry, I have to get going. See you in forty-five minutes," he said, and hung up.

Brian looked at me with raised eyebrows. "The feds want to ask me a few questions," I said.

"Oh, dear," he said. "That sounds a little chancy."

"I don't think so," I said. "They seemed reasonable last night—and Kraunauer will be there with me."

"Well, then," Brian said. "I guess it will be all right—if there's still time for some pie?"

"There's always time for pie," I said.

EIGHTEEN

IN SPITE OF MY GRAND CLAIM, IT WAS closer to fifty-five minutes before Brian dropped me at the corner of NW 2nd Avenue and 165th Street, across the street from the FBI's Miami Field Office. I didn't mind the short extra walk across the street and a half block down. Brian was certainly not going to put himself any closer than necessary to such a hornets' nest of law enforcement.

Kraunauer was waiting for me in the lobby. "There you are," he said in greeting.

"Yes, sorry to keep you waiting," I said. "Travel is a little iffy without a car."

He nodded. "Miami is a big city with a small-town infrastructure," he said. "They're waiting for us." He nodded toward reception, where a young woman in a severe blue business suit stood beside the desk. She was looking at us with a very serious expression, which told me even more certainly than the suit that she was an agent and not a secretary or file clerk.

She led us to a conference room on the second floor, where Revis and Blanton, my two new friends from last night, were waiting. And alas for all that is right and decent in the world, they were not alone. Sitting at the foot of the table, leaning back in his chair and displaying his well-polished sneer, was Detective Anderson.

"Oh, wonderful," I said. "You've arrested him already."

Kraunauer gave a short snort of amusement, but nobody else thought it was terribly funny—especially not Anderson, who scowled at me, which at least meant he understood me. "Mr. Morgan," Agent Revis said, taking the lead again. "In the interest of interagency cooperation, we have agreed to allow a representative of the Miami-Dade police to be present at your questioning."

"You are aware, are you not," said Kraunauer smoothly, "that this officer has a history of animosity toward my client? As well as a great deal of questionable behavior?"

"Detective Anderson will not take any active part here," Blanton said. "He's here as an observer only."

Kraunauer looked at me and raised one perfectly groomed eyebrow. I shrugged, and he turned back to the feds. "As long as that is clearly under-stood," he said. Revis and Blanton nodded in unison. Kraunauer turned to Anderson, but he merely looked away, so Kraunauer shrugged. "Then I have no objections," he said to Revis. "Let's get started."

Blanton pulled out a chair and nodded me

toward it; I sat, Kraunauer sat next to me, and the two feds sat side by side across the table from us. Blanton opened a manila folder and frowned into it, but it was Revis who began. "Mr. Morgan, have you ever been arrested for possession of a controlled substance?"

She said it very seriously, as if she was asking whether I had a driver's license, but it was such a totally loony question I was speechless for several long seconds, and my sad state was not helped by the fact that Anderson had leaned forward with glittering eyes and a new improved version of his sneer. I found my tongue again, but all I managed was a pathetic, "Have I—What, what?"

"Just yes or no, Mr. Morgan," Blanton said.

"No, of course not," I said. Anderson shook his head, as if to point out how sad it was when somebody tells blatant fibs.

But Revis just nodded, very calm and reassuring. "How long have you been using illegal drugs?" she said, with a slight emphasis on *using*.

"Is this really relevant?" Kraunauer said, a slight twist of dry irony in his voice. "That was a *bomb* in Mr. Morgan's car. Not a *bong*."

Two pairs of Official Federal Eyeballs clicked to Kraunauer, but he just looked back at them with an easy amusement that was contagious, at least to me. I felt like putting my feet up on the table and lighting a cigar.

"We think it might be relevant," Blanton said.

"Really," Kraunauer said with mild disbelief. "How so?"

"Counselor," Revis said. "We have some reason to believe the bomb was built by a known narcoterrorist. And"—she nodded seriously—"we have received information that Mr. Morgan has a well-established pattern of drug use."

Kraunauer looked at Anderson. So did I. But Revis and Blanton were far too polished. They looked straight ahead, as if they'd forgotten that Anderson existed. I wished I could forget, too. "Received . . . information," Kraunauer drawled, caressing the words and still looking straight at Anderson. "May I ask *where* you received it from?"

Anderson had begun to squirm just a little in his seat, and as Kraunauer's accusing stare went on he actually started to blush. It was very gratifying to see, worth the entire field trip to the Field Office.

"Our source is confidential," Blanton said.

Kraunauer slowly turned his head back to the feds. "Really," he said. "Confidential."

Blanton looked uncomfortable, and he and Revis had one of their wordless conferences. "We can't reveal the source," Revis said at last. "But I'll show you the file."

Kraunauer nodded. "Good enough."

Blanton pushed the manila folder across the top

of the conference table and Kraunauer picked it up. I leaned over and looked, too.

The top page was a copy of the log from the evidence room. Whenever anyone accesses the evidence room, cop or forensics geek, they are required to sign the log. On this page, picked out in bright yellow highlighter, was an entry that said Dexter Morgan had been there, and it was signed with a childish scrawl that looked as much like my signature as Egyptian cuneiform writing does.

Kraunauer flipped the page: The second page was a copy of an interdepartmental memo stating that someone had removed two kilos of confiscated cocaine from the evidence room, at a date and time that was amazingly similar to the time "Dexter Morgan" had been there.

"Well, it does prove one thing," I said. "I have superpowers." Kraunauer looked at me and raised an eyebrow. I tapped the line with the date. "I was in a cell at Turner Guilford Knight on this date."

Kraunauer looked at me blandly for a moment, then turned to Revis. "Easy enough to check," he said.

"What about the signature?" Blanton asked.

"It's not even a good forgery," I said. "It looks like a third grader's handwriting. Tell me, Detective," I said, facing Anderson, "as the only third grader here, do you always have trouble making your letters?"

Kraunauer cleared his throat, whether from amusement or postnasal drip I couldn't tell. "Agent Revis," he said. "My client seems to think that's not his signature."

Revis nodded. "May I see your driver's license, Mr. Morgan?" she said, holding out a hand.

I looked at Kraunauer, who nodded. "Of course," I said. I pulled out my wallet and placed the license in Revis's hand. Kraunauer slid the folder back across the table and Blanton picked it up. He and Revis huddled together for a moment, comparing the signature on my license to the cheesy scrawl on the evidence log.

It didn't take long. I have always prided myself on my penmanship. I like to make neat, regular letters, and write words that are legible to anyone who can read. The forged signature was so obviously by a different hand that even a total clot like Anderson should have known better. And the two feds were by no means total clots, nor even partial. After just a few seconds Revis flipped my license back to me.

"Not the same signature?" Kraunauer said to her.

"Probably not," Revis said.

"He changed it!" Anderson said.

"Detective," Revis said warningly.

"He disguised his signature; it's obvious!" Anderson went on.

Blanton stood up. He took the two steps along

the table to Anderson and stood over him, looking down at him with an expression of ice-cold annoyance. Anderson looked back, and for a moment he thought he might bluster on. But Blanton leaned down, until his face was only an inch from Anderson's.

"The understanding was," Blanton said softly, "that you would observe." He held up a finger, making Anderson flinch. "Not talk. Observe."

Anderson opened his mouth, but thought better of it, and Blanton nodded and returned to his own chair. He sat, looked briefly at Revis, and then both agents looked at me. "Thank you for your cooperation, Mr. Morgan, Mr. Kraunauer," Revis said. "You can go now."

Kraunauer stood up and said politely, "Thank *you,* Agent Revis. Agent Blanton." He looked at me, said, "Mr. Morgan?" and then turned away and headed out the door.

I stood up, too. I felt like I should say something polite to the two feds, but nothing came to me that didn't make me sound like a puerile lickspittle, so I just nodded and turned for the door.

Anderson was there ahead of me. He stood right in the doorway, filling it with his bulk and making it impossible for me to pass. "This ain't over yet, fuckwad," he said softly.

"Not while you're still at liberty," I said. "I mean, really, Detective. Drugs? That's the best you can do?"

He stared at me some more, perhaps hoping I would melt. But I didn't, and after a long and dull pause, he just nodded. "It ain't over yet," he repeated, and stepped aside. I went gratefully through the unblocked door, and closed it behind me.

Kraunauer was waiting for me, standing next to the same young and serious agent who had brought us up. "I'm beginning to believe," Kraunauer said, "that Detective Anderson may not like you."

"Whatever gave you that idea?" I said. He just chuckled briefly, and said to the young woman, "Agent?"

She had clearly been waiting with some impatience to take us down to the lobby, and now, given her freedom, she did so very briskly, without wasting any expensive Bureau time on idle chitchat. She set such a vigorous pace, in fact, that it was not until we arrived at the reception area that I remembered I had no way to get back to my hotel. "Oh," I said to her, "um, Ms. Agent?"

She looked at me without any trace of expression. "Yes?" she said.

"Is it possible to get a cab in this area? I don't have a car."

"Oh!" Kraunauer said, before the agent could speak. "My God, of course you don't! Well, hell, I can certainly run you back to your hotel."

"That's very kind," I said. "If you really don't mind?"

"Not at all, of course not, come on," Kraunauer said, sounding oddly eager. He put a hand on my elbow and propelled me toward the front door, leaving in his wake the serious young agent, who looked rather relieved to be rid of both of us.

"My car is right over here," Kraunauer said, steering me toward a modest-looking gray sedan with a stylized letter "B" on each hubcap. And in spite of that, it wasn't until I opened the door and saw the walnut-lined instrument panel and soft glove-leather seats that I realized the "B" stood for "Bentley." I slid onto the sweet-smelling seat and tried not to soil it by sweating or thinking impure thoughts.

Kraunauer jumped in behind the wheel and started the car. It started right up, with a purr like a large cat with a throat full of honey. "All right," he said. "Where are you staying?"

I gave him the hotel's name and address, and he took us up onto I-95 and headed south. His car was so quiet I was afraid even to clear my throat, so we rode in silence for a few minutes, and then Kraunauer finally spoke.

"I hope you understand that this is all positive," he said. "Extremely positive."

"I know," I said. "Except for the bomb."

"Oh, no, that was the best part," he said quite

seriously. "That bomb is buying you a lot of sympathy, Mr. Morgan. The newshounds are already starting to wonder out loud if you might be innocent."

"I actually am innocent, you know," I said. He just nodded, poker-faced, and kept his eyes on the road. "I suppose all your clients say that," I said.

"No, not all of them," he said, and added a small chuckle. "One or two of them have been quite proud of their accomplishments."

"That must make it a lot harder for you," I said.

"Not at all," Kraunauer said. "It doesn't matter at all what I know, or what I believe. All that matters is what I make the court believe. And in your case, that just got a lot easier. And anyway, I'd be very surprised if your case even goes to trial," he said. And then he jerked his head around to give me a quick look, as if I'd startled him somehow. "I mean," he said, "they might, you know. Drop the charges."

"Oh. Great," I said, and he turned his attention back to the road and left me wondering what that strange facial expression had been about. Other than that, it was a quiet and exceptionally smooth trip down to my hotel. The Bentley provided a ride that was supernaturally gentle, and neither one of us had anything else to say, which was a relief, to tell the truth. Most of the time, when you're cooped up in a car with a relative stranger, they want to talk about football or politics or sex. I can't muster much interest in any of those things. Of course, as one small part of my Human Disguise I've learned enough about all of them to keep a polite conversation going, but it really was a relief not to have to try to compare the Dolphins' current offensive line to the one they'd fielded in 2008.

In a little more than twenty minutes Kraunauer was pulling into the driveway of my new hotel. I looked at it out the window as we ghosted up to the door, wondering how long I would be able stay at this place before something forced me to move again. I hoped I could get a couple of nights out

of it; it had the best bed yet, and I was looking forward to spending a little more quality time on it.

"Well," Kraunauer said as he came to a halt at the front door, "this place looks adequate, at least." He smiled at me, a small and polite smile, not really one of his world-beaters. "I hope the room's okay—they didn't put you on the ground floor, I hope?"

"No, the third floor, with a lovely view of the Dumpster," I said.

"Excellent," he said. "Now, uh—I may have to send you some papers for signature. So what's your room number?"

"Three seventeen," I said.

"Good. All right," he said. "Now, I know it's got to be frustrating, but I want you to stay put up there as much as possible. We can't have you showing your face, giving the reporters a chance to find you."

"Yes, I know," I said. It was not technically a promise to stay put, which of course I had no intention of doing.

"Don't talk to anybody in the media; that's vital," he said.

"I won't," I said, and I actually did intend to avoid that.

"All right, then," he said. He pushed a small button and my door unlocked. It was a clear signal for me to go, and I opened the door.

"Thanks, Mr. Kraunauer," I said. "For everything."

"Oh, don't thank me yet," he said with an airy wave. I got out of his luxurious rolling pleasure palace, and he vanished, silently, before I was even in the hotel's door.

NINETEEN

THE CLOCK IN MY HOTEL ROOM SAID IT was only four-thirty-eight, which didn't seem possible. I certainly seemed to be packing an awful lot of excitement into a very little time. It had made me hungry, too, but there was nothing close to the hotel except a franchise fast-food place, and it was even lower on the evolutionary scale than the one that had given me agita the day before.

So I gave a heavy sigh, pushed away hunger and fatigue, and sat instead at the horribly uncomfortable desk chair, and I pondered. The day had not been a total loss so far; it was at least possible that Anderson might be held in check for a while. It was far too much to hope that the feds would investigate or prosecute him, of course, but they were aware that something was not quite right in Smallville—"Small" referring, of course, to Anderson's IQ. That knowledge should restrain him, at least temporarily. Of course, it was almost as likely to prompt him to try something even more outrageous.

His last words to me, *It ain't over,* certainly made preemptive action seem more likely. And the fact that the FBI now had good reason to believe he'd been playing hokeypokey with evidence and forged signatures would probably make him even more desperate to prove I was a True Naughty Boy of epic proportions. It seemed logical to assume that his best stratagem was framing me for drug possession. He already had that on the record, and if he could "prove" he'd been right, that would not only take Me off to jail, but it would also restore his reputation.

The more I thought about it, the more certain I became that this would be Anderson's plan. He would take some of the "missing" drugs and slip them into my meager possessions. It was simple, which was de rigueur for him, and it would probably work. Even if everybody was certain he'd planted the drugs himself, they'd go along with it. I nodded; that's what he would do—*if* he found out where I was. He hadn't so far, and as long as I made sure he never did, his plot couldn't get off the ground.

I slid that worry onto the back burner. Anderson was not on the same level of threat as the bombers. There was no wiggle room with someone who wants to kill you badly enough that they are willing to take out half your hotel as long as they might get you, too. They'd missed once, but there was no doubt that they'd make another try as soon as they could. How? I didn't have enough raw data even to guess their next move. I had no clue at all what they might do, or how many of them there might be—I knew nothing about them except that the size of their bomb revealed a reckless joie de vivre that I might have admired, except that it also indicated an unsettling seriousness about getting rid of me.

Brian, on the other hand, *did* know them. And as a special bonus, he had a car, a vehicle well known for its ability to take people to places where food was available. That sealed it; I called Brian, and he agreed to come get me.

Half an hour later we were sitting together in a nice, quiet diner over in Homestead. "I believe the meat loaf is quite good here," Brian told me. "If you like that sort of thing."

"I do," I said, and in truth, the mere mention of it had made my stomach groan audibly.

A brisk and efficient waitress took our order: two meat loafs, garlic mashed, green beans. Coffee, sweet tea (for Brian). She swished away, and I leaned back in the red plastic booth. "The thing is," I said to Brian, "it all comes down to what we were talking about this morning."

"Early afternoon, actually," Brian said politely.

I waved it off. "The point is," I said, "Raul's little buddies found me. There are two things wrong with that."

My brother was already nodding, proving once again that he was no slouch. "First, it's *you*," he said. "Instead of me."

"And second," I went on, "it happened much

314

too quickly to be coincidence or luck. So the question is—"

"How," Brian said. "And without knowing *that,* it's really much harder to put an end to it, isn't it?"

" 'The most difficult part to invent is the end,' " I said. He blinked at me inquiringly, and I tried to look modest. "De Tocqueville," I said.

Brian just nodded, and looked down at the table. He frowned very thoughtfully, and I realized my face was wearing an exact duplicate of his expression. How odd it was, after all my years of thinking I was alone and unique, finally to find somebody who was so very similar, even down to appearance. Of course, my handwriting was much better. And Shakespeare or not, I was positive Brian couldn't quote de Tocqueville like I could. Even so, it was rather strange—but nice, in truth. Brian was *real* family—not a fair-weather sibling who turned her back at the merest hint of trouble. Brian had instead arrived, unasked, when my problems began, and he was helping me solve them. Except, of course, for the small detail of dropping me into the middle of a lethally violent drug war. But I could forgive that; I had to, because he was family. Permanent, undeniable family, and as much like me as he could be. Not like some I could think of.

And that thought might as well have been a cue in a well-rehearsed theatrical performance, because as the words formed in my brain, my phone rang. I glanced at the screen and saw, to my irritated astonishment, that the call came, by all that is unholy, from a certain fair-weather sibling: It was Deborah, and that made absolutely no sense. Did she need instructions on how to change Lily Anne's diaper? Or perhaps permission for Cody to play with sharp objects? Well, too bad—she was on her own, and it was all her doing. As far as I could tell from our last two conversations, we had nothing at all to say to one another. Not now, not ever again. She'd made it quite clear that our family ties were untied, and she preferred it that way.

I felt a small surge of annoyance bordering on resentment, and decided that Mr. Dexter Morgan was not available. I pushed decline and put the phone back in my pocket.

I turned my powerful brain right back to the problem at hand with not even a small thought of my ex-sister. How *had* they found me so quickly? Because there was really no reason for Deborah to call.

My phone chirruped again. Either I had suddenly become Mr. Popular, or some other unthinkable event had just occurred. I looked at the screen, and unthinkable won. It was Deborah again.

Once more I pushed decline and my irritation ratcheted up a few notches. Would she never give me any peace? Was the woman going to hound me to my grave? Assuming no one else got me there first by more conventional means?

Again: How had Raul's men found me so quickly and easily? They had to have picked me up after I'd already left the first hotel, the one where I found Octavio dead on my bed. Otherwise, they would have been onto Brian first, not me. But they could easily have gotten my name from that hotel room. So they knew that something called a "Dexter Morgan" was somehow connected to Brian. Had I used my credit card since my precipitous departure from that hotel? I didn't think so.

So how had they found me? I couldn't believe that they had simply roamed around the city looking for a Dexter until they found the right one. If nothing else, you didn't waste a lovely big bomb like that one on an uncertain target. They had *known* it was me when they planted the bomb. But how? Where had I been that they could latch onto me like that? It could not have been at any time or place when Brian and I were together, either, for the same reason—that they would have hit Brian first.

So: I had been to several restaurants—and that sent one quick bright surge of adrenaline up my spine, because I remembered that one of those restaurants had been *Mexican*—just like Raul! But of course, it didn't hold up. Aside from the fact that it was politically terribly incorrect, it made no real sense. Pepino's restaurant had no more connection to a drug lord than the sushi place where I'd had lunch with Vince had with bombing Pearl Harbor. And that sushi place was just as certainly ruled out—I had sat there in my car for half an hour, a perfect and stationary target. Even a mad bomber would have said, *What the hell,* and taken a whack at me by some more direct method.

Not the restaurants. Where else? I had been out of jail a very short time, and I hadn't been very many places, and was my phone really ringing *again?!*

It was. And once again it was Deborah calling. A great number of things ran lightly across the surface of my brain. Most of them were biting things I could say to her. Unfortunately, the best of them would involve raising my voice and saying things that might even affect the service of my meat loaf.

But one other thing slowly worked its way to the front of the line, gently shoving aside all the salty, profane, and entertaining words and phrases. Deborah, after making it quite clear that she never wanted even to say my name again, had just called me *three times* in two minutes.

Why?

It would be fun to think that after such a short time with my children she wanted to give them back—and more fun still if she'd had an incredibly illuminating insight into the error of her ways and she wanted to beg my forgiveness and make up. But as stubborn as I knew her to be, it would have to be an epiphany on the order of Saul on the road to Damascus—and Debs in the fast lane of I-95 didn't sound like it even belonged in the same league. So ruling out the ridiculous, that she had suddenly forgiven me, I could think of absolutely no reason in the world why she would call. And therefore no reason I should answer.

Except . . .

Curiosity, as the saying goes, killed the cat. And it has frequently proved lethal to nonfelines as well. And yet a tiny but powerful tendril of curiosity was tugging relentlessly at my concentration, demanding all my attention. On top of that, it may even be that some small shred of family loyalty as instilled by Harry might still be lodged in a crack somewhere. Whatever the reason, I did the unthinkable, the unwise, the unresistible.

I answered.

"Yes?" I said smoothly, so she could see that her call—and, by extension, she herself—meant nothing.

"I need your help," Deborah said between her teeth.

"Reeealllllyyy," I said, and I think I sounded as surprised as I felt. The possibility that she would even dare to ask such a thing had never occurred to me. "What on earth could you believe I would ever help *you* with?" And I put as much dry scorn into it as I could, knowing there was absolutely no possible satisfactory answer she could make.

"The children are gone," she said. "They've been kidnapped."

Except that, of course.

TWENTY

BRIAN VERY AGREEABLY DROVE ME north on U.S. 1 and then turned left into the Gables, over to Deborah's little house. He said nothing, except to ask for directions, and I was grateful. Nearly anyone else in the world would have chattered away the entire time, filling the silence with sentimental expressions of sympathy and compassion—or worse, declarations of total support for me in my hour of need.

Brian did no such thing, proving once again that he knew me better than anyone else in the world. He understood that the very first dewy-eyed gasp of empathetic blather from him, the very first manly compassionate *I'm here for you, buddy,* would result in my leaning over and clawing his eyes out. Of course, it could also be that he knew I was aware that any such thing he might utter was completely artificial and meaningless, since he could not feel sympathy any more than he could feel anything else.

And I was supposed to be just the same— vacant, unoccupied, null and void in terms of inner content. No emotions, no feelings, no compassion or empathy or any of the other gooey human shortcomings. So it must have been hunger, caused by missing breakfast, that made my stomach churn and roil and my pulse thump at my temples like two small pointy fists.

Kidnapped.

My kids.

The more I thought about it, the less I could actually *think* about. A powerful rising tide of anger mixed with anxiety flooded through me and I could only grit my teeth, clench my fists, and fantasize about what I would do to whoever had taken them. It was counterproductive, even debilitating, since the only result was a return of this morning's headache, and a couple of new cuts in the palms of my hands, where I had unconsciously shoved a fingernail in too far while clenching my fists.

Stupid, useless, sickening anger—and yet it did pass the time, and before I knew it Brian was pulling up on the street outside Deborah's house. "If you don't mind," he said with great polite reserve, "I don't think I'll go in."

"No, of course not," I said. It was obviously unthinkable for him to go in, or to go anywhere near Deborah, and he was wasting my time even mentioning it. I reached for the door handle and his voice stopped me.

"Dexter," he said.

I turned and looked at him, angry at the delay.

"I will help all I can," he said, without artifice of any kind, just a clean simplicity that said he really would. It meant more to me than all the crocodile tears in the world, and I unclenched my jaw for the first time since Deborah's call.

"Thank you," I said. "I'll call you when I know more. When I can."

He just nodded, and I opened the door and climbed out of his car.

Brian's car was well out of sight before I even got to Deborah's front door. That was just as well, because she opened it when I was still on the front walk, ten feet away. She stood there, framed by the doorway, her fists clenched tightly at her sides, and as I looked at her face I saw with utter astonishment that she had been crying. Deborah did not cry. Ever. The last time I had seen her tears was when she was eight years old and fell from a tree, breaking her wrist. Since then she had been icy control, tougher than nails, practically bionic. I knew she *felt* things—she just never, ever *showed* them. I had often thought it was funny; she felt everything and showed nothing, and I was just the opposite. The Legacy of Harry.

I stopped on the stoop, several feet away, unsure what happened next. Clearly she was just as unsure, because she looked at me, looked away, looked at me again, and then simply turned away and went inside, leaving the door open as an unspoken invitation to follow. I did, locking the door behind me.

Deborah was already seated at her rickety kitchen table when I joined her. She slumped over a cup half-filled with coffee, staring down into the mug like she thought she could find an answer in it. I stood watching her for a moment, but she didn't look up, so I pulled out a chair and sat opposite her. Some paperwork sat in the middle of the table, and I recognized it—the custody agreement I had signed.

Yesterday's news—what mattered now was the kids. "How did it happen," I said. Even to me, it sounded like, *How could you* let *it happen.*

But Debs just nodded like she deserved it. "I dropped them at day care, like always," she said. "I went to work. Half hour later they came. Three men with guns. They said, 'Bring us the Morgan kids.' And nobody did anything, so they shot one of the teachers." She looked up quickly, and then down again. "They got the kids. All four of them. Threw them into a car and drove away." She slumped down even farther. "They have our kids."

She sounded half-dead, nearly empty, like she'd already surrendered. I'd never heard her like this, and it made me very uncomfortable. "Who were they?" I said. She frowned, but kept staring down. "The men with the guns," I said. "Who were they? Any hint at all?"

She shrugged. "Hispanic," she said. "Thick accent. Two of 'em short and dark, one taller, lighter hair. That's all I got."

"Wonderful," I said. "Hispanic accent. Shouldn't be hard to find in Miami."

"The car was an SUV, dark blue. Nobody saw the plates," she added in the same dull voice.

I opened my mouth to say something sarcastic, and then snapped it shut again as a gigantic alarm gong began to ring in the back of my brain. Something Debs had said had raised the hairs on my neck and sent the troops to the parapet. I didn't get it at first. I rewound her last few sentences. Three men with guns—check. Hispanic—check. Two short, one taller—check. Dark blue SUV—

Ding-ding-ding-ding-ding.

I had naturally assumed that Raul's men had taken the kids. The only question had been, as it was with everything else at the moment, How? How had they found me? Having found me, how did they make the connection and find the children?

Suddenly a very large part of the answer had come clear.

A dark blue SUV. I had seen one recently—in fact, I had seen it more than once. When I parked my car in the alley at Pepino's—and then later right here, outside Deborah's house, a dark blue SUV had gone crawling by. And hadn't there been one other time recently?

"Dexter," Deborah said, interrupting my train of thought. "I can't do this. I have to . . . They put me on administrative leave. And I'm supposed to sit here and let *them* find *my* kids?!" She looked up at me with a pleading expression, something else I had never seen from her. "I can't do that. Jesus fuck, we have to do something!"

"What do you suggest?" I said.

For a second it looked like she was going to lose her temper and snarl at me. But then she wilted, just slumped back over the coffee again. "I don't know," she said, barely over a whisper. "They won't let me near it. I can't even . . . They sent me home, and I just . . ." She shook her head slowly, as if she barely had the energy.

"So you called me?" I said. "Because you think I can find these guys?"

"No," she said. And then she raised her head and looked at me and she was Debs again. More—she was Über-Deb, the Dragon Slayer. The fire that showed in her eyes would have melted a Buick's fender. "I called you because when I find them I want them dead."

I nodded as if that was the most natural thing in the world, for her to ask me to tag along and do the finish work. And actually, for a moment or two, it really did seem quite natural. She would find them, and I would take it from there. Each of us doing what we did best, working together in harmony, world without end. A proper display of Harry's *real* legacy.

But on a moment's reflection, it didn't seem that natural at all. Mere hours ago I was as good as dead in Deborah's eyes, lower than pond scum—

and for the very same reason that she now found my company desirable. It was such a cold and utilitarian about-face, so completely reptilian, that I should have admired it. I didn't. I needed more.

Because I have no real human feelings, Harry had molded me to look on family bonds as *rules*. I've always been quite good with rules. They help keep things neat and orderly, and it would be a much better world if everybody paid more attention to them—or even if we all agreed on the same set.

Deborah had broken a very important rule, one that Harry had pounded into me over and over again: *Family comes first.* Everything else in life will come and go, and things that seem important now will melt away like snowflakes in a summer rain. Not this. Family is forever. I had believed it, even relied on it. And Deborah had violated it. I had needed her as I'd never needed anyone else in my life—needed her help and comfort and support, the things only family can really provide. And she had swept me out of her life like a dust bunny on the living room rug. The only reason she was letting me back in now was because suddenly *she* needed *me*.

Of course, it's always nice to have your talents appreciated, especially by a family member, but at this point in our present nonrelationship, I thought she should give me just a little bit more than a temporary come-kill-things-for-me pass.

So I met her gaze with a steely one of my own. "I think that's absolutely wonderful," I said. "But why should I do that for you? Why," I went on as she gaped angrily at me, "should I do anything at all for you? And don't," I cautioned her, showing her the palm of one hand, "*please* don't say because I'm your brother and they're my kids. You burned those bridges, and very thoroughly, too."

"For fuck's sake, Dexter," she said, and it was nice to see some color returning to her cheeks, "don't you care about anything but yourself?!"

"I've got nothing else left to care about," I said. "You let Anderson take away my job, my reputation, and my freedom—and then *you* took away my family." I nudged the custody papers toward her and raised an eyebrow. "Remember? It wasn't that long ago."

"I did what I thought was best for the kids," she said, and it may be that now she had just a little too much color in her cheeks. "That's what I always do." She tapped the tabletop with a finger, hard, once for each word. "It's What I'm Doing Now."

"Really? It's best for them if I stay in jail until I come sneaking in to kill a few bad guys for you? And then I disappear conveniently again, is that the plan?" I shook my head. "That's something only my sister could ask for—and I no longer have one."

"Well, *fuck,*" she snarled. "What do you want, an apology? Fine, I'm sorry, okay?"

"Nope. Not okay. Not enough."

Debs leaned across the table as far as she could go and still stay seated. "You miserable shit," she said. "They're your kids, too!"

"Not anymore," I said, and I glanced meaningfully at the custody papers.

For a second she just showed me her teeth, anger building up in her eyes and looking for somewhere to go and something to burn. And then she lashed out with a hand—I flinched, but it wasn't my face she was going for. Instead, she snatched up the custody papers, ripped them in half, and flung the pieces at my head. Since I had already used up my flinch, most of the pieces hit me. Considering what I'd already been through in the last few hours it didn't hurt that much. In fact, in an odd way, it felt kind of good.

Apparently I had a family again.

"Apology accepted," I said. "How do we find them?"

She glared a few seconds longer; after all, she had to go from rage back to plotting revenge, and it's much harder to shift gears that quickly when you have emotions. Debs leaned back into a more normal sitting posture and shook her head. "I don't know," she said. "I told you everything I've got."

"Three Hispanic males," I said. "And one dark blue SUV."

"That's it," she said, and she slumped back over her coffee cup again. "That's all of it." She picked up her coffee cup, looked at the contents, and put it back down again without drinking. "I don't even know *why* they snatched the kids. Revenge, somebody I busted?" She shook her head. "If only I knew why . . ."

Deborah has always had a fairly healthy ego, and I was glad that the present crisis had not beaten it down; she believed that someone had taken the kids to get at *her*. I hadn't even considered that idea; I had just naturally assumed that it was Raul's men getting leverage on me. But I thought about the possibility that it was an attack on Debs instead, and right off the bat the notion had several very appealing elements. For starters, it let me off the hook—I didn't have to tell her that it was my fault, which might have put a damper on what was turning into a rather heartwarming reunion. I also didn't have to tell her about Brian, which would almost certainly dampen his life even more severely.

But it wouldn't do, of course. I had seen the blue SUV, and was now certain it had trailed me to Deb's house. From there, it was a simple matter for them to watch her, see the kids, follow to day care, and grab them. The only real question remained the same: How had they found *me* in the first place? I had seen them at dinner, and so they had picked me up before that—and if I could remember where I had seen the blue SUV earlier—

"Are you out for good now?" Deborah said abruptly.

"Out?" I said, still with one foot in my thoughts. "You mean out of jail?" She nodded. "Well, it's not certain. The state attorney really wants me for this."

She snorted. "Well, shit," she said. "If Frank Kraunauer can't get you out—Jesus, Dex, what's the matter?"

The matter was simple: My head was spinning like a carousel. Or possibly I was motionless and the room itself was spinning—maybe even the entire Universe, suddenly whirling around like an enormous insane dervish. It must have shown on my face, because the whole natural order as I knew it had suddenly flipped over on its axis. East was now up, and West was tomorrow, and nothing was what it should be, and yet because of that everything suddenly made sense. It was sickening, maddening, dreadful, gut-lurching sense, but it added up perfectly.

I knew where I had seen the blue SUV earlier.

I recalled clearly where I had been and what I had been doing and suddenly all the nickels were dropping into every available slot, and every single light, bell, gong, and siren in the big pin-ball game of Dexter's Universe was going off at once. I knew. And with one abrupt, reality-shifting moment of recall, everything fell into place.

And not in a good way. Not at all.

"Dex?" Deborah said uncertainly, as if she wasn't sure whether our relationship had healed to the point where she could show concern. "Are you all right?"

"I am a dolt," I said. "A naive, trusting, gullible dolt. Blind in one eye, deaf in both ears, and dumber than a fence post."

"Maybe," she said, "but what made you realize it?"

"I know how to find them," I said.

The look of concern dropped off her face, instantly replaced by a very wicked hunger. "How," she said.

I looked at her and started to tell her—and stopped. Could I really tell her? That the kidnappers had followed *me* to her and the kids?

"Dexter, goddamn it, how?" she demanded. "Where are they?"

I couldn't decide. I temporized. "I don't know where they are," I said. "But," I went on, overriding a stream of very professional curses from Deborah, "I think I can get them to come to me."

"To you? Why would they come to you?"

I took a deep breath—and I paused.

I am not a trusting person. From my own hard experience and my unclouded observations of people in general, I have always regarded non-trust as a very wise stance. And I had also made an exception for family, for the most part—especially Deborah.

But at the moment, when our new relationship was still defining itself, it did not look like a very good idea. For all I knew, telling her about Brian and Raul and that whole mess—and admitting that the children's abduction was my fault—might have some very unpleasant consequences.

Trust is such a fragile thing, isn't it? Once it's broken, there is no superglue in the world that can put it back together again. Perhaps with time I would come to trust my neo-ex-sister. Not yet.

"Goddamn it, Dexter!" Debs said. "Why the fuck will they come to you?"

I fought down the impulse to smile reassuringly, since it might easily turn into a leer at this point, and instead gave her my very best stout and loyal manly stare.

"You'll have to trust me," I said.

TWENTY-ONE

D EBORAH WANTED TO COME ALONG, OF course. It wasn't that she didn't trust me, though of course she didn't. It was merely that she was, and always has been, what is known as a Control Freak. She could not stand the thought of letting something she cared about slip out of her sight and into less competent hands—and of course, all hands were less competent, as far as she was concerned.

But it just wouldn't do. There were far too many variables, and she might grab at any one of them and use it to upset an applecart or two. So in the end, after she had tried blasphemy, bullying, wheedling, blackmail, extortion, and the threat of enormous and violent physical force, she gave in. She even supplied me with a Cold Piece.

In case you don't know the term, or worse, if you know it but believe only crooked cops have them, let me explain. A Cold Piece is a gun with no history. It's unregistered, and quite often the serial numbers are filed off. This means that if it is used in the course of a casual felony or two, it cannot be traced back to any past or present user. As you can see, this makes it quite a handy thing to have around.

And if you cherish the notion that no true-blue

righteous cop would ever entertain the thought of owning such a vile object, let me just say this: Ha. Even more, Ha, ha.

Cops won't talk about it, of course. But every now and then, in the course of doing a job that is routinely life-threatening, demeaning, and contradictory—every now and then a situation arises in which even the Good Cop faces a Bad Situation, and the Greater Good demands just a tiny little bending of the absolute standards entrusted to their care.

And so, the Cold Piece. Deborah had one, a very nice Ruger nine-millimeter with a fifteen-round clip, and she assured me it was absolutely untraceable. She put it in my hands, even supplying a full second clip, and although she did not actually tear up and whisper, "Godspeed," she did actually look into my eyes for a full two seconds before saying, "Fuck," and turning away. For Deborah, it was very close to, "Godspeed."

I do not like guns. They are cold, impersonal, nasty things with no beauty at all. They have no real *soul,* and they take all the fun out of things. But they are also quite effective at evening the odds, and as the adopted son of a man who was an ex-Marine combat vet as well as a cop, I knew how to use them quite well. And since I had no real idea what might be lying in wait for me, the weight of the Ruger in my pocket was reassuring.

Deborah very grumpily drove me over to

Dadeland, an old mall in South Miami, and dropped me there at the main entrance, still with a complete lack of good cheer. She glared at me long and hard before she let me go, but all she said was, "Call me, goddamn it."

I wandered through the mall for a half hour or so, just to give Debs a chance to give up lurking hopefully in the parking lot, and then I went straight to the food court and took care of some very important unresolved issues. I had, after all, never gotten my meat loaf. It may be that I should have been so focused on getting my kids back safely that I forgot how hungry I was. But the mighty machine that is Dexter does not work that way. In order to perform at the highest possible level, it needs fuel on a regular schedule. And since I was facing a very daunting task or two in the near future, I needed it now.

The food court offered a wide array of choices, as they often do. I settled on two slices of pizza, for very good reasons. First, it was the first place I came to. Second, and almost as important, it was lying right there under a red spotlight all ready to go. I wolfed it down fast, so I wouldn't notice that I didn't like it.

After I'd eaten I found a Starbucks and got a Double Super Reverse Mega Ultra Extra Wonder Something-or-Other that tasted surprisingly like coffee. I took it to a table in a quiet corner, sat, and called Brian.

He answered right away. "Brother," he said with his usual fake bonhomie.

"I have something of great importance," I said. "Can you come get me?"

"*Great* importance?" he said.

"Practically immense," I assured him. "A problem solved."

"Oh, well, then," he said. "On my way."

I sat and sipped my Ultimo Ridiculoso Stupenda blend while I waited for Brian to arrive. I went through my reasoning again, checking it carefully, looking for any indications that I had added things up wrong, and found none. I was as sure as I could be, and that's always a nice feeling. If I lived through all this, I must remember to have that feeling more often.

And why couldn't I have it more often right *now?* Why couldn't I think of something feeling-forming to solve the absurd bumbling malice of Anderson? It really was too bad; for the first time since this whole thing started I'd just begun to think there might be a way out. But if my new theory was right, I still had to deal with Detective Dolt.

I remembered something my adoptive mother, Doris, had been fond of saying: "Two little problems make for one big solution." It had been her version of turning stumbling blocks into stepping-stones, I suppose, and I'd never really found it to be true. But if it ever *could* be true, this would be a wonderful time.

Every now and then, I think my thoughts are fixed on one thing, and in fact they are not. When this happens, they will quite often clear their throat politely to get my attention, and then let me know what I was *really* thinking. And as I sat there in Dadeland Mall remembering Dear Doris, I heard a soft but very distinct *ahem* coming from an unused corner of my brain. I politely turned my focus there, expecting to hear a request for one more slice of the awful pizza. But what I found instead was much, much tastier.

So much better, in fact, that I had That Feeling again.

Once more I picked up my phone, and this time I had only good feelings about the device. In fact, I regretted ever disliking it—what a marvelous piece of equipment it was! It can take pictures, send text messages, access the Internet, become a GPS or a dictating machine or a hundred other things—and even make phone calls! And on top of all that wonderful possibility, it can send e-mails!

Working quickly, I began to use a few of those splendid features. I went online and found a site that allows you to book hotel rooms; I booked one at the Galleon in South Miami under the name of Brian Murphy, the name that had been on my brother's fake credit card. The site allowed me to pick a room and I chose Room 1221 for no particular reason, pressed confirm, and clicked off.

Next, I used my beloved phone to send an e-mail

to Vince Masuoka. "Hi, Vince," I wrote. "Thot u shd know—I am @ Galleon Hotel, room 1221. Don't tell anybody!!!" And then I added, "PS—I am out of the room for about 2 hrs, so don't come right now."

And finally, just to keep things in proper perspective, I used the delightful device to make an actual phone call. "Vince," I said when he answered. "I just sent you an e-mail—"

"What?! No!" he wailed. "Dexter, I told you—Anderson is reading my mail!"

"Yes, I know," I said soothingly. "I'm counting on it."

"You're—what?"

"Just make sure you ignore it," I said. "Okay?"

"Ignore—But it's my e-mail."

"Vince, please, it's very simple," I said. "Pay no attention to e-mails from me. Understand?"

"I—I guess so," he said. "But, Dexter—"

"Gotta go, Vince," I said quickly, before he could take off again. "Bye!" and I hung up.

Have you ever noticed what a wonderful place the world can be sometimes, on those very rare occasions when Things behave properly and fall into place the way they should? This was just such a time, and to celebrate it with all due ceremony I got up and bought another Mighty Superbo Magnum Yum-Yum. Once again, it tasted a lot like coffee, but that was all good, too. I sipped and waited for my brother.

And mere minutes later Brian was sitting across from me and sipping a Gigundo Fantastica Triple Colossal Cosmic Miracle of his own. "You're quite sure about this?" he asked me, wiping some whipped cream from his upper lip.

"I am," I said. "But if I'm wrong, the worst that happens is that nobody shows up."

He nodded, sipped again. "Well, then," he said. "Let's do it."

I reached into my pocket and pulled out my phone, as well as the business card that I'd kept in the same pocket. I dialed, waited three rings, and then heard, "Frank Kraunauer."

"Dexter Morgan, Mr. Kraunauer," I said. "I think a reporter saw me in the lobby? So I moved to a different hotel, and I wanted to let you know where I am. You know, just in case."

"I'm sure that's wise," Kraunauer said. "Better safe than sorry, after all. Where are you?"

"The Galleon Hotel in South Miami, Room 1221," I said, thinking that this was the very first time I'd heard him use any phrase as stale as that. Clearly his mind was occupied with other more important matters—like giving Dexter's new location to his pet killers. Using a cliché wasn't truly airtight proof of guilt in any legal sense, but it was enough for me.

"All right," he said. "Be patient, and stay put as much as you can, right there in the room."

"I rented a movie," I said. "I'm not going anywhere for two hours, and then I'm going out for something to eat."

"Terrific," he said. "I think we'll have some good news very soon."

"Wonderful," I said. "Thanks, Mr. Kraunauer."

"You're entirely welcome," he said, and broke the connection.

Brian was looking at me inquisitively, so I shrugged and said, "He didn't actually confess."

"No, he wouldn't."

"But I think I'm right," I said. "And I think it will be soon. Now if only the timing works out."

"It's still a bit hard to believe," Brian said. "He has a very good reputation in certain circles." He flashed me a quick smile. "You know, the circles I recently left behind." He frowned at his coffee. "Why would he do this to you? A client?"

"Simple economics," I said. "I am one case, and with a limited fee. Raul, on the other hand, represents a limitless wellspring of high-cash clients. And," I said, "Raul would probably kill Kraunauer if he didn't do this."

"That can be persuasive," Brian said.

"And since you learned about Kraunauer from your work with Raul?" I said, and Brian nodded a yes. "We know that there is already a connection. I think it's pretty close to conclusive."

"I suppose it is," he said thoughtfully. He was

silent for a moment. Then he sighed and shook his head. "What a world," he said. "I guess nothing is sacred after all."

"Only two things," I said. "Lawyers and money."

"Amen," he said. "Well. What do we do next?" he asked.

"We wait," I said. "Somewhere near the hotel, where we can see without being seen, would be best."

"Yes," Brian said. "With an emphasis on Not Being Seen, I think."

The Galleon was only about a mile from the mall, and we were in place in under a half hour. We found a perfect spot half a block away, in a parking lot that was surrounded by a chain-link fence. A scraggly hedge had been planted right up against the mesh of the fence for extra privacy. It was twilight, and rush hour was starting to die down a little, and we had a clear view of the hotel's front door through small breaks in the hedge. But no one over there could see us, not through the hedge and our windshield.

We waited, and I had a disturbing thought. "What if they use a bomb again?" I asked.

"Oh, I don't think so," Brian said. He smiled a happy little smile. "Raul is very impatient with failure. They'll want face-to-face confirmation this time."

"How many of them?"

"This will be the first team," Brian said. "Raul's

best shooters. At least two of them, and maybe a driver."

"I hope so," I said. "The driver would be easiest to take alive."

"If we really have to," Brian said.

"We do," I said firmly. "We need at least one of them to talk to us."

Brian actually pouted. "It seems a shame," he said.

"Yes, but, Brian," I said, "we need somebody to tell us where the children are."

"Oh, I know that," he said. And then he brightened visibly. "But that means we'll have to *persuade* him to talk! I hadn't thought of that! Oh, what fun." He began to hum softly, and somewhat off-key. And almost immediately I found his nonmusic irritating, almost beyond endurance.

It may be that I was just a little nervous—but who had better right? I finally had a way to hit back at all the pain, persecution, and perfidy that had taken over my life, but it was a risky move, and an exceedingly delicate one. If the timing was just a little off, or if one of my pawns did not react properly, the whole thing could collapse. There were far too many variables, and I couldn't control any of them, and after three minutes of waiting and hearing Brian's horrible humming I wanted to strangle him.

But only a few minutes later a Ford Taurus slid up to the front of the hotel and parked at a sloppy angle. The Taurus was the Miami-Dade motor-pool car, and the parking was vintage I'm-a-cop-whatcha-gonna-do, and sure enough, Anderson climbed out. "Bingo," I said.

"Party of the first part?" Brian said.

"Yup." We watched as he moved quickly up the short walk and into the hotel, a shoe box under one arm. Now it all came down to the timing. I wished for just a second that there really was a god, and that he would listen to a prayer from something like me. It would have been nice to say a little prayer and actually believe it would work. But as far as I could tell, there was no god, and I didn't know any prayer except, "Now I lay me down to sleep," which didn't really fit the occasion.

But happily for me, no prayer was needed. Two minutes after Anderson disappeared into the hotel, a blue SUV cruised slowly past our hiding place and into a spot in front of the hotel. "Party of the second part," I said. "Life is good."

Brian nodded, already staring intently at the other car. Two men climbed out: stocky, swarthy, one of them carrying a small suitcase. "The one with the baggage is Cesar," Brian said softly. "A very bad man. I don't recognize the other one."

The two men slammed the car's doors and towed their suitcase into the hotel.

"No driver," I said, feeling a stomach lurch of anxiety.

Brian shook his head. "I don't see one," he said.

"Damn." This made things a bit harder—but there was nothing to do but let it play out and hope for the best.

We waited two more minutes, and then Brian looked at me. "Shall we?"

"We shall," I said.

We got out of the car and crossed the street at the corner to the far right of the hotel. And then, moving quickly, but with every sense on high alert, we went up the sidewalk to the front door. "Let me go first," Brian said, and I nodded.

He strode in the door, and I waited for thirty seconds that seemed much longer, before he stuck his head out and said, "Clear," and I followed him in.

It was a very nice lobby, if you like old terrazzo floors and golden wallpaper, peeling slightly at the edges. A bored clerk at the desk was tapping at an iPad. He didn't even look up as we went past to the elevators, and I found to my delight that one of them was right there on the ground floor, waiting for us.

We rode up to the twelfth floor. Soft and flaccid music played, and Brian hummed along to a tune I didn't recognize. I no longer felt like strangling him. I was too busy wondering what would go wrong next.

When the doors slid open on the twelfth floor, Brian held up a hand and once again went ahead of me, his pistol held at the ready. But this time he was back in mere seconds. "Quickly, brother," he hissed, beckoning frantically.

I stepped out of the elevator and right away I saw what had alarmed him.

Room 1221 was the second room to the right from the elevators, and the door was wedged open about three inches. Even from fifteen feet away I could smell gunpowder, and I could see that the thing jamming the door open was a human hand. It wasn't moving.

I looked down the hall in both directions; surely somebody had heard something? But there was no sign of life, and no cries of, "Police!" or, "Help!" or even, "What ho!" Every other door along the hall was securely closed. It seemed impossible that nobody had heard a thing—and in all likelihood, it *was* impossible. But this was Miami in the twenty-first century, and when one hears gunshots, piteous cries for help, and multiple bodies hitting the floor, one simply double-locks the door and turns up the sound on the TV. Once more I felt a quiet swelling of civic pride; this is Dexter's city.

But even love of my hometown would not protect me if somebody in Room 1221 was still breathing. I drew my Ruger and followed Brian across the tatty carpet to the partially open door. Gently, carefully, gun raised in front of him, Brian pushed the door open with his foot. His body blocked my sight of the room; he was really being quite protective. I could only watch his back as he swept the pistol from left to right, and then abruptly dropped it to his side. "Your plan worked a little too well, brother," he said, and he moved aside.

I leaned into the room. The body blocking the door was the second of Raul's gunmen, the one Brian didn't know. The large raw hole where his left eye had been was a pretty good sign that he was no longer among the living. And beyond him, over beside the bed, was the rest of our little party.

Cesar, the Very Bad Man, had turned out to be Not Quite Bad Enough. He lay on his back, or most of him did. Several small parts of him were actually displayed on the wall behind him, decorating the two holes in the plasterboard made by the two shots that put them there. There was enough gore lying around him on the floor that there was no need to make sure that Cesar was dead.

Both of Raul's gunmen. Dead and gone and far beyond the reach of any questioning technique I knew of, unless we got a Ouija board. I was no closer to finding my kids than I'd been two hours ago. Some plan. Nothing to show for it but more dead bodies.

I suppose I should have felt some kind of guilt, but of course, I never have and I hope I never will. And in this case, it would have been the height of hypocrisy, since I had arranged for this to happen. My only regret was that we didn't have a live gunman. Without that, without someone to tell us where the children were, the whole thing had been pointless.

Or nearly pointless: One very large point had been made.

Directly in front of Cesar was Detective Anderson.

Anderson as I knew him was many things, and most of them were unpleasant, but one thing he was as well was, apparently, a better shot than I would have thought. Two head shots, two kills. And he was also quite a bit tougher than I'd have guessed.

He sat on the floor, his back against the foot of the bed, his legs splayed straight out in front of him. His hands had fallen by his sides, one of them still clutching a Glock pistol.

Beside the other hand the shoe box he'd carried in had fallen to the floor and spilled open, revealing several large plastic baggies filled with some white powdery substance.

Anderson himself wasn't moving. There were three bright red circles on the front of his cheap white shirt. Any one of them might have killed him. Three of them absolutely had. But as stupid as he was, Anderson apparently didn't know that he was dead. As I stepped toward him to be certain, I could see that his chest was moving, very faintly, and one eyelid flickered open and slowly, dizzily focused on me.

For one long moment he stared, and I stared back. His lips parted and moved a little; he tried to say, "Help," and nothing happened, except that one of the chest wounds spouted a tiny bit more blood.

I squatted down beside him. Here was the relentless dumb ass who had tried to ruin my life, and come very close to succeeding, and for once I really wished I had emotions, so I could enjoy this a little more.

"I'm sorry," I said to him. "Did you say *help?* You're really asking *me* for help?"

He just looked at me out of the one bloodshot eye he could open and moved his lips again, like a fish that had been out of water far too long. The eyelid fluttered and then opened wide, as if he finally realized who he was talking to.

"Yes, it's me," I said happily. "Remember you said it isn't over?" I leaned in as close to his ear as I could get without actually touching him. "Now," I said to him, "it is over. At least for you."

I was just in time; Anderson's eye got wider and wider, still fixed on me, and I saw the old familiar beauty of That Moment, the final second when you realize it *is* the final second and there will never be any more of them, not for you, not ever again, and all the simple and wonderful things you took for granted, like breathing and sunshine and everything else in the world aboveground, all that starts to recede, pulling away from you slowly as you try to hang on to it, and then whirling away faster and faster and spinning you down into the endless darkness—and then you are gone and it is all over forever.

I watched all this in Anderson's eye, the awareness that this was *It* and I was watching It and I followed it, as always, feeling this time like all the others that special sense of quiet bliss that comes from witnessing that moment, and if this time it felt just a little better, I had earned it.

I watched as that last awareness faded away to no awareness. And then Anderson's legs twitched, and the slow movement of his chest stopped, and he seemed to grow just a little smaller and a little dirtier and then he was all gone, ripped away forever from the world of puppies, rainbows, and torturing Dexter.

It should have been a wonderful moment for me, in at the last minute, in time to see my tormentor yanked out of his mortal coil. But the glow didn't last. Even in dying Anderson had made himself a nuisance. By fatally shooting both gunmen, he'd made absolutely certain that no one could tell me how to find my kids. My plan had gone perfectly, and he'd still spoiled it.

"Bastard," I told Anderson. I stood up, and I

would have kicked him, except that I'd get blood on my shoes.

"It's best we go quickly," Brian said softly.

I turned to go, and then paused. There was no reason to waste an opportunity like this, when the addition of one small touch could make this scene an even more memorable one—one that might even make Anderson look bad enough to cast a large load of doubt on my guilt.

"Brian," I called, and he looked back to me. "Can you spare some cash?" I asked.

"Dexter, why on earth—Oh, of course," he said. He reached into a pocket and pulled out a large wad of what seemed to be mostly hundreds. "This will have to do," he said, and he flung the money through the door.

I took a last look, and liked what I saw. The scene could not have been more obvious with subtitles. A dirty cop tried to sell drugs stolen from the evidence room. An argument over money had resulted in a shoot-out. A quick ID check would certainly reveal that the other two men had ties to organized crime. And Anderson was clearly as guilty as a dead man could be. Good riddance to all three. Case closed.

I followed Brian back to the elevator. We rode it down to the third floor, got out, and took the stairs the rest of the way. I followed my brother out the hotel's back door, the long way around the block, and to our car.

"Well," Brian said as he drove slowly away from the Galleon Hotel, "I suppose it's back to square one."

"Not quite," I said. "At least we know for sure about Kraunauer."

"Yes," Brian said, and he sighed. "But I wish we'd managed to save Cesar."

"Really?" I said, somewhat surprised. "He was a friend of yours?"

"Oh, no, far from a friend," Brian said. "In fact, we had a few very bitter differences." He looked at me with a somewhat shy smile and said, "So I was kind of looking forward to getting him to a quiet place for a little chat."

"Next time," I said. And again I wished I could pray, just a little. Because there was no guarantee of a next time.

And without it, my kids were as good as dead.

TWENTY-TWO

BRIAN DROVE US TO A COFFEE SHOP over in Coconut Grove. It was full dark when we got out of the car and went inside to a booth at the back. Neither of us had a great deal to say. Brian fiddled absentmindedly with the laminated menu, and I was trying to think of a logical next step, now that plan A had flushed itself away. Even more immediately, I was quite sure that Deborah would be sitting at home chewing through the furniture until I called, and I did not want to jeopardize our still-fragile reconciliation by keeping her hanging too long. And because My Plan had resulted in what Harry would have called a Total FUBAR, I also had to find some truly magical combination of words to explain things to her.

And Debs would unquestionably have heard about Anderson, and she could put things together as well as anybody. The short math here would quite clearly add up to Dexter Did It. Whatever else Debs was willing to do at this point, authorizing a hit on a cop—even a dirty cop—was not in the picture. Add that to her panicked worry over the kids, and she would no doubt be on the verge of insanity at this point. I was so certain of that I hadn't even switched my phone back on.

Coffee arrived, in chipped porcelain mugs, and it was hot and very welcome. Brian ordered strawberry pie, and I settled on a tuna melt. Time was lurching past at a ridiculous pace. I even thought I could hear my watch ticking, and I still didn't have any wonderful speech for Deborah. But I didn't see how I could put it off any longer, so I pulled out my phone and turned it on.

Almost immediately it began to ping with missed calls, and all of them were from Debs. I waited another minute, but no inspiration came. I called her anyway.

"Where the hell have you been," she said in a voice halfway between grating and snarling. "What the fuck is—Did you find the kids? And, Jesus, *Anderson?* Was that you? Because—"

"Deborah," I said, much louder than I liked, and Brian cocked an eyebrow at me. But it got her attention, and with only a few more muttered bad words—none of them terribly original—she slid back down to a less hysterical grumpiness.

"Jesus fuck, Dexter," she said. "You go trotting away with a pistol and Anderson turns up shot dead and . . . How does that get our kids back? Can you tell me that?"

"Not while you're talking, I can't," I said, and I could hear her teeth click shut—but at least she was quiet, which allowed me to lower my voice. "As sad as it seems to me, I didn't shoot Anderson," I said softly. And at that moment, happily for me, I thought of the perfect explanation to let me off the hook. "But, Deborah—Anderson shot the men who could tell us where the kids are."

Deborah made a remarkable sound, a moan that seemed to be hissed out through clenched teeth. "Fuck," she said. "Oh, fuck."

"But there are more of them," I said.

"More of the kidnappers?" she said. "Can you get to them?"

"I . . . *think* so," I said carefully, because it was an obvious question and I didn't have an answer yet.

Debs was silent, and then suddenly blurted out, "I have to come with you this time. I have to, Dex."

"No, Debs, not yet," I said.

"I *have* to, goddamn it!" she said. "I can't just fucking sit here and do nothing while you fuck around and my kids are still . . . where, Dexter? Where the fuck are my kids?!"

"I'll find them, Debs," I said.

"Goddamn it, I want to find them with you!"

"I'll find them," I said again. "And I'll call you later."

"Dexter, you miserable piece of shit!"

I already knew I was a miserable piece of shit, so I hung up.

"Well," Brian said with his brightest smile, "and how is your sister?"

"As well as can be expected," I said. "Brian, do you think we can work the same trick again?"

"You mean getting Raul's men to come after you?" he said, and I nodded. He frowned thoughtfully. "Weeellllll . . . If I know Raul, he's somewhere close by. He'll have your children with him. But they aren't bringing you to him on your knees, and he's missed *twice*. So I'm quite sure he's starting to get just a teeny bit, um —upset? Angry, frustrated, perhaps even approaching apoplectic." He shook his head sorrowfully. "The man simply has no self-control. And he absolutely *hates* not to get what he wants, when he wants it."

"I suppose that goes with being a drug lord," I said. "Will he take it out on the kids?"

"Mmmm, noooo," Brian said, not very convincingly. "Not just *yet* . . ."

"What will he do?"

"He'll want to kill something, of course," he said. "Preferably you and me." He shrugged, as if that was the first rational thing Raul had thought about. "But he'll be way past being patient. Or subtle."

"So you think he'll bite on the same bait?"

"At this point," Brian said, "I think Raul would bite on bare hooks if it might get him to us."

"All right," I said. "And you did say he'd have more shooters?"

"Oh, absolutely," Brian said. "Manpower is never a problem. Not for a successful man like Raul."

"Good. So what's the best way to do this?"

We both thought about it for a moment. Then Brian said, somewhat hesitantly, "Um . . . perhaps through Kraunauer?"

"Will Kraunauer go for it? I mean, he has to suspect something by now, doesn't he?"

"I don't think so," Brian said. He raised a finger and wagged it like he was lecturing me. "Raul when angry has a way of making everybody around him very jumpy. Very anxious to please. Even Frank Kraunauer."

I frowned and I pondered and I didn't see any other way. "All right," I said, reaching for my phone. "But, Brian—we absolutely *have* to get one of them to talk this time."

"Oh, yes, absolutely," Brian said.

I dialed.

Kraunauer answered right away. "Mr. Morgan, what the—Are you all right?"

"I'm fine," I said.

"I just . . . I heard—I mean, there was some kind of shooting at your hotel, wasn't there? And that detective—that was the same one that, ah—"

"Yes, that was him," I said. "But I wasn't there when it happened."

"Oh," he said, and even he heard the disappointment in his voice. He cleared his throat hurriedly and rushed on. "I mean, that's good, absolutely, but how—and what . . . what . . . where are you now?"

"Actually, I'm hiding out," I said. "I'm up in North Miami." Which was in reality quite far from where I was, since for some reason, I just didn't trust him.

"Good, good, okay," he said. "But that's . . . How did you . . . with that detective. I mean, what happened?"

"He called me on my cell phone," I said, letting my imagination run. "He, um, he said he had documents. That he said would prove I was innocent. And I would never get them—that he was going to burn them in front of me and I couldn't stop him."

"All right," Kraunauer said. "And then?"

And then? Nothing—my mind went completely blank. "Then . . . then," I stammered, waiting for something to occur; it didn't. "I have the documents, Mr. Kraunauer. And they really do prove I'm innocent," I blurted out. I could only hope that Brian was right and had Kraunauer so anxious he wouldn't notice the rather large gap in the story line.

"Wonderful," Kraunauer said with no hesitation at all. "Where are you now?"

I said a silent thank-you to Raul and sprinted for the finish line. "The thing is, I don't think I can keep them safe," I said, lowering my voice for sheer theatrical effect. "I want to get them to you as soon as possible."

"Great!" he said, with very believable enthusiasm. "I'm having dinner at Tick Tock at ten o'clock; do you know it?"

"Um, South Beach?" I said.

"Right." He gave me the address, and said, "Can you be there a few minutes before ten?"

"It'll take me forty-five minutes," I said. "But I need to be careful, make sure I'm not followed, so—maybe a little longer?"

"Perfect," he said. "I'll be there about a quarter of. Can you meet me out back then? There's a parking lot."

"Behind Tick Tock. Quarter of ten," I said. "I'll be there."

I broke the connection and returned the phone to my pocket. Brian looked at me quizzically. "Tick Tock?" he said. "It's a clock store?"

"A restaurant," I said. "Supposed to be very good."

"Would he really do this at a good restaurant?" Brian asked doubtfully.

"I know the area a little," I said. "There's an empty lot next door, and the parking lot behind is pretty well screened. It's actually a perfect place."

"If you say so, brother," he said.

"I do," I told him.

He nodded. "It might be wise to get there first?"

"Agreed," I said, and I stood up. "Shall we?"

We dropped some cash on the table and went out to his car, and Brian rolled out onto U.S. 1. "I'm not sure what we do next if this doesn't work," Brian said as he drove us north and then up onto I-95.

"Then let's make sure it works," I said.

We crossed over to South Beach on the MacArthur Causeway, and drove straight up 5th. Brian cruised right past Tick Tock without slowing, and I looked carefully as we went by. Of course there was nothing to see but a small crowd waiting to get in. None of them seemed to be carrying assault rifles. A block past, Brian turned right and then into a parking lot with a concealing row of trees around the perimeter. He parked in a spot with a view of the restaurant, and left the engine running.

"How would you like to proceed?" he said.

"It would be nice to know the odds," I said. "How many of them should we expect?"

"They think there's only one of us—you," he said. "There were two of them last time, but this time it's public. So probably three," he said. "The extra man will be the driver. He'll wait with the motor running. And he'll provide backup, of course, but the shooters won't want to use him. Pride, you know," he said, shaking his head. "They really take their work seriously. So I think three men. Any more would seem like overkill."

He gave me a large and very bad smile. "If you don't mind me saying so."

"Better you than them," I said. "Three men, then—the two shooters, and the driver."

"Probably," he said, nodding.

"If they split up, it gets very difficult," I said. "Three targets in three different places."

"And probably a cross fire on us," he said. "That's what they'll do."

"But they have to get there first for that," I said, thinking out loud.

"They won't," Brian said happily.

"So for just a minute or so, we'll have all three of them together, in their vehicle."

"And *we* will have a cross fire on *them*."

"Right," I said. "We have to assume that they will have assault rifles, at the least."

"Almost certainly," he said.

"But if we surprise *them,* an automatic weapon takes a bit longer to bring up and fire. And I would guess that the driver will probably not be as much of a shooter."

"That's why he's driving."

"Yes," I said. "And his hands will be on the wheel. So, we each take one of the other two. One each."

"The one nearest to me is mine," he said.

"Likewise. And we take the driver alive."

He made a pouty face. "For your so-called sister?"

"Because he will know where the children are,

Brian," I said. "That's what this is all about, you know. Saving the kids."

He sighed heavily and shook his head. "Easy to forget when we're having such fun."

"So I absolutely *must* take him alive. Okay? Alive, Brian."

"Just for now," he said agreeably.

I patted him on the shoulder. "Just for now," I said. I looked at my watch. It was still only a bit more than twenty minutes since I'd talked to Kraunauer. But merely to be on the safe side, we needed to get in position as soon as possible. I looked at Brian and nodded. "Shall we?"

"We shall," he said with undisguised glee. "Oh, I *do* love surprises."

The car was another SUV, gold this time. It drove into the back parking lot about fifteen minutes after we got in position, and there could be no doubt at all about who they were. They came nosing in slowly, checking the area out carefully in a way that was completely unlike a trendy late-night diner looking for a parking spot, and just exactly like a crew of professional killers looking over a kill zone. From where I waited I could just make out one man in the passenger seat, turning slowly around and putting his eyes everywhere. Just visible, as the car crawled under one of the streetlights that lit up the parking lot, was another man on the far side, behind the driver. And the driver himself made three, just as Brian had said—unless someone was crouched down on the car's floor, hiding. It didn't seem likely. The two faces I saw seemed quite confident, relaxed. And why not? They were heavily armed, and they were here first. And they were professionals, setting up one frightened amateur who didn't have the faintest suspicion that he was walking into a trap.

The car paused at the end of the lot farthest away from the restaurant and facing down a bordering alley. It was exactly where Brian and I had hoped they would stop, since it put the getaway car where they would want it, positioned for a quick departure, and also allowed the two shooters to see all around the area as they worked into position for their ambush.

It was also right where I was waiting, crouched in the darkness between the last car in the lot and the adjacent building.

And so, as the driver put the SUV into park and the two shooters reached down for their weapons, I stepped out of my hiding place and tapped on the passenger window with my left hand. An annoyed face looked up at me. He had an enormous mustache, three little teardrop tattoos at the corner of his eye, and a scar on his forehead. I smiled at him, and it took him almost two full seconds to recognize my face—far too much time, alas for him. Just as his eyes went wide and he opened his mouth to shout a warning, Brian stepped out from behind a parked car on the other side and shot the gunman behind the driver. As the one I was smiling at jerked around to see his partner die, I shot him in the back of the head, twice.

The car's window exploded from my shots and Mr. Mustache pitched sideways into the driver. I reached in through the shattered glass and opened the car's door. The driver gaped at me in horror, and then began to scrabble at the seat beside him for a pistol. I leaned in and shoved the barrel of my Ruger roughly into his ear hole. "Don't," I said.

Very obligingly, the driver froze. "Hands on the wheel," I told him. He hesitated, and I twisted the pistol vigorously in his ear.

"Ayah!" he said.

"*Manos*," I told him, nodding at the wheel. "¡*Los dos*!"

He put his hands on the wheel, and a moment later Brian opened the back door of the car. I heard a heavy thud as the gunman on Brian's side fell out onto the pavement. "Oops," Brian said, followed by, "Oh, Ee-bahng! Is it really you?" He leaned in and patted the driver on the head. "That's how he says his name, 'Ivan,' " Brian said. "Cuban pronunciation. *Ee*-bahng is Cuban."

"Wonderful," I said.

"Ee-bahng is Raul's mad bomber," Brian said

happily, ruffling Ivan's hair playfully. "I bet he brought some toys!"

"I'm sure he did," I said. "Can we get moving, please?"

"One more second," Brian said. He leaned in and looked into the back. "Thought so!" he said, and came up with a heavy canvas gym bag. "I've always wanted to play with these," he said. "And it might come in handy."

He put the bag down gingerly and then yanked open the driver's door of the SUV, shoving his pistol in Ivan's face, smushing the man's nose roughly to one side. "Ee-bahng! *¡Afuera!*" and for emphasis he rapped Ivan on the forehead with the barrel of his pistol. "*¡Ahora!*"

Ivan hissed in pain. A small rill of blood started down his face from where Brian had hit him, and he fumbled himself out of the seat, stumbled out of the car and into Brian's grasp.

I heard a door slam, and glanced toward the restaurant. Frank Kraunauer was hurrying across the lot toward us. I hissed, "Brian!" and ducked reflexively back into darkness. My brother glanced up, and he actually smiled, very close to a believable smile, too. "How perfect," Brian said. He slid down to a crouch directly behind Ivan and jammed his pistol into the base of the bomber's spine. "*Sonrisa*," he hissed. "*No dice nada, ¿comprendes?*" *Smile. Say nothing.* Ivan nodded numbly.

And then Kraunauer was there, moving quickly around to face Ivan. "Is it done?" he said. "Where's the—Urk!" He jumped back as Brian straightened and faced him and then, as I stepped out of the shadows and came into view, too, Kraunauer stumbled back one more step. "How—" he said. And then, just as I was preparing a sharp, withering riposte that would settle Frank Kraunauer's hash once and for all with great wit as well as with perfect justice, he moved his hand—moved it so fast that I didn't really see the gun he was holding until a half second later, when Brian's gun went off: once, twice, three shots.

Frank Kraunauer took a jerky half step back with each shot. And then, for a long moment, he stood there looking surprised. He frowned at the little pistol in his hand, as if it was all the weapon's fault. And then he took a last slow step backward and collapsed as if his leg bones had been removed.

Brian watched him fall, still smiling, and then looked at me. "Oh," he said. His smile vanished. "I'm sorry, brother. I'm afraid you're going to need a new attorney."

I was sorry, too, but I was more concerned with getting out of here before someone else came running out and saw us.

"I'll find somebody online later," I said, glancing around us anxiously. "We need to go.

Sooner or later somebody will report that they heard shots."

"Even in Miami," Brian agreed.

In a few more seconds we got Ivan into the backseat of Brian's Jeep, which was waiting for us in the nearby alley. I got in back next to the bomber, but he kept his eyes fixed on my brother the whole time. From the look on his face, he knew very well who Brian was and what he might do, and he was ready to do anything at all to keep Brian from doing it. He was so fixated on Brian he made no resistance at all as I secured him with a roll of duct tape I'd brought along. Brian drove away down the alley and out onto 6th Street as I taped Ivan's hands, feet, and mouth. No matter what I did to him, though, Ivan kept his eyes on Brian.

"Well," Brian said at last, "I thought that went quite well, on the whole."

"We're alive; they're not," I said. "And we have a new playmate, too."

"Oh, yes, and I just *know* he's going to be a real chatterbox for us," Brian said. "Life is so good."

Brian drove straight back to the MacArthur, which I thought was wise. On surface streets, too many things can happen that might result in an awkward conversation with an overdiligent officer of the law. Sometimes the nosy cops want to know trivial things, things that are clearly none of their business—like, "Why is your friend all bound up with duct tape?" In expressway situations, you are much safer from that kind of meddlesome interference, as long as you keep to the speed limit and don't have an accident.

But once we were over the causeway and onto the mainland, Brian turned north on I-95. It shouldn't really have surprised me, since I hadn't thought at all about where we would go if we were triumphant. Clearly my brother had given it some reflection, but he had so far failed to share his thoughts with me. "Where are we going?" I asked him.

"A little place I rented, a storage locker," he said. "Up near Opa-locka airport." He caught my eye in the rearview mirror and showed a few teeth. "A modest retreat. It has come in handy in the past."

"A very good choice," I said, and it was. Opa-locka airport is a truly strange place, a kind of neutral zone in time and space and, more important, in law enforcement, too. So many different spies and spooks and smugglers and transients of uncertain origin and loyalty go in and out that over the years an unspoken agreement has evolved: Law enforcement, at every level, stays away. It is much simpler that way; it avoids the awkwardness of arresting a vile, drooling, tattooed monster who is clearly smuggling heroin, as well as every sort of weapon from pistols to Titan missiles—and then finding out that he is, in fact, a fully sanctioned, ex-Marine, former Eagle Scout, crew-cut and shoe-shined-in-his-heart federal agent working in deep cover on a project so secret it doesn't even exist.

So the area around the Opa-locka airport is mostly unpoliced, which has many small side advantages—such as making it a perfect place for Brian and me to relax, unwind, and have a leisurely conversation with Ee-bahng. I looked fondly at my brand-new friend on the seat beside me, and I thought of all the fun that lay ahead. It had been far too long since I'd had a chance to relax, kick back, and encourage someone to really open up. And this nice man, quivering so quietly next to me, was an absolutely perfect candidate for some leisurely exploration. He had certainly earned some very careful attention; bombs are such nasty things, aren't they? It would be pleasant to make him understand that society at large disapproves of blowing things up, especially when there are people inside. I thought we might find a way to show him the error of his ways. And oh, yes, as Brian had said, Ee-bahng would be a real chatterbox, no doubt about that. I just hoped he wouldn't start talking *too* soon and cut short the fun.

So I was feeling quite chipper as we drove north, and really looking forward to having a chat with Ivan—and having Brian beside me, chatting with him at the same time. I'd been looking forward to that for a good long time. We both had; we had so much to learn from each other, so many technical and procedural techniques to compare and demonstrate. This could well be a truly exemplary combination of recreation, education, and sibling bonding, and I was happy as can be about what was just ahead.

Ivan . . . ? Not so much. He had not taken his eyes off Brian, and he'd begun to shiver, though it was a very warm evening. His color was not good, either, and his teeth were audibly clicking together. I began to worry that he might have some awful medical condition that would kill him before we had our talk. That would be a very distressing development. Aside from the real disappointment of losing a new friend before I really got to know him, we would also lose our best shot at finding out where the kids were being held.

And so, because showing kindness to a stranger puts a little plus mark by your name in the karmic registry, I leaned over and patted his cheek. He jerked upright like he'd been slapped, and for the first time his eyes left Brian and snapped over to me.

"Are you all right, Ivan?" I asked with gentle faux concern. He said nothing, just stared at me with bulging, bloodshot eyes.

"*¿Estás bien, Ee-bahng?*" I repeated in Spanish.

Ivan blinked three times, but made no attempt to answer. Of course, his mouth was fastened shut with duct tape, but still, he might have tried to mime a reply, or waggle his eyebrows affirmatively. He did not; he just stared, and when he was done blinking, he looked back at Brian again, as if afraid my brother would punish him for looking away.

I shook my head sadly, thinking that he must be a very good bomb maker. Clearly he would never get a job based on conversational skills.

My brother had just as little to say, but the trip was short and uneventful, and soon we were at the gate of a sprawling storage facility a half mile south of the Opa-locka airport. Brian punched in a code, the gate lifted, and we rolled in. The area was illuminated by a battery of those ugly so-called anticrime lights, but I was not terribly worried that they would prevent anything. Naturally enough, storage lockers near a neutral zone like the Opa-locka airport are routinely used by the assorted spooks and spies that use the airport, and so they are also exempt from unwanted police scrutiny. And if there were any neighbors in a nearby locker, they would almost certainly avoid asking questions about the unusual noises Ivan was about to make. Many of them, in fact, would be far too busy creating similar sounds of their own.

A good storage unit is a wonderfully flexible

space. It has lights, power, and even air-conditioning if desired. The walls and floor are generally of industrial strength and utilitarian design, so there is no need to fret about scratching the paint or leaving unsightly blood-stains on the floor. In truth, a unit is such a terrific place for mischief that it's a real wonder that anyone ever uses them to store things.

Brian parked right in front of a large unit, with Ivan's side of the car facing the heavy steel entrance. "All righty, then," he said. He turned and beamed at Ivan. "It's playtime!" He said it quite happily, and even Ivan could tell that his happiness was very real, and the knowledge of *why* Brian was happy made the poor nervous bomber tremble in all his limbs.

But when Brian opened the car door and reached in to help Ivan get out, the poor fellow began to buck and twist frantically, enough so that even when I tried to hold him steady, he jerked away. It was a true waste of time and energy, since his only way out of the car was through the door Brian held open, but he seemed quite committed to his display—until Brian leaned in and said, "Stop it, Ivan." He said it quietly, even gently, but the effect on Ivan was electric. The bomber froze completely—and then he slumped forward, began to shake all over, and, to my amazement, started to sob and snivel. It's never an attractive routine, even in the best of times. But when your hands and mouth are secured with duct tape it's even more distasteful, and Ivan began to dribble moisture and mucus from every opening but his ears.

Still, at least it was much easier to get him out of the car than when he'd been bucking. We did, and I held him as Brian rolled up the door of the storage unit, turned back to us, and bowed us in.

Ivan walked as if he had no tendons in his lower body; his legs hung loose from his hips and his feet flopped forward with each step, which made it necessary for me to keep a strong grip on his arms from behind. And since I was busy with that, I didn't really get a good look at Brian's little playground until he had rolled down the steel door and flipped on a strip of fluorescent lights that hung from the ceiling. But when Brian came and guided Ivan from my grasp and over to a waiting chair, I looked around me—and what I saw was enough to bring a full portion of quiet joy to my heart, if only I'd had a heart.

Brian had decorated the space in an understated but very tasteful style that I can only call Industrial Nazi Dentist. On the walls in neat and careful clamped rows was a full range of saws, drills, and other interesting power tools whose use I could only guess at—at least, their use in this context. I know very well how trees are trimmed, and I have seen commercial grinding equipment before. But seeing these things here was a pleasant surprise, and I had to give my brother new props for a creativity I hadn't known he possessed.

I watched as Brian led Ivan to a dental chair, which was bolted to the floor and apparently complete with the hydraulic lifting function. It had also been slightly modified with a set of metal-mesh restraints for hands, feet, chest, and head, and these my brother fastened carefully onto our guest, whistling tunelessly the while, not quite loud enough to cover the sound of Ivan's nasty wet whimpering.

I stepped over beside the chair, where a large rolling toolbox stood just behind Brian. "May I peek?" I asked him.

Brian looked up briefly and smiled. "Of course, brother," he said. "Perhaps you could even ponder a few opening gambits?"

"With pleasure," I said, and I turned to open up the top tray of the toolbox. I lifted the lid, and although I did not actually gasp with pleasure, I did pause for several seconds, speechless with delight. And then I leaned into it eagerly and began to open all the drawers, bubbling over with the joy of discovery.

I have always been very neat and well organized. It makes everything proceed a little smoother in this messy chaos we call life. My workspace at the lab and my little office at home were always clean, well ordered, and logical. But because of the dual nature of my life until recently, I had never been able to be as thorough as I would have liked with acquiring and organizing tools I might have used for my hobby. My space and my privacy were so very limited that my choice of apparatus, too, was far more constrained than I would have liked. Nearly every day I would see some intriguing item intended for a more pedestrian use, and think to myself that it had some wonderful untried possibilities.

Untried no more, for Brian had collected—and clearly *used*—all of these things, and many more I hadn't even thought of. There were rows and rows of surgical instruments, of course, scalpels and saws of every possible size and shape. And then there were the kitchen implements—cutters and grinders and mashers and corkscrews and sharp little things for more delicate work. There were rows and rows of bright, gleaming, top-quality knives ranging in size from the tiniest little blade to some the size of machetes. There were straight blades and curved, needle thin, wide, and saw-toothed. It was truly a tool kit for a great artist, and I felt a quiet pride in being related to someone who was so thorough, creative, and well prepared.

"Brian . . ." I said, when I had finished my first quick inspection. "It's breathtaking."

"And finger, toe, and nose taking," he said

happily, his beaming face hanging over Ivan's terrified and sweaty one like a pale and wicked moon. "Where shall we begin?"

"So hard to choose," I said thoughtfully. I looked at the toolbox, thinking over all the wonderful choices I had seen, picturing a few of them, how they might unfold with a squirming squealing Ivan so snugly secured and my brother and I so wonderfully together above him—

—and as I paused a rising tide of anticipation rolled through me and seeped into all the nooks and crannies of Castle Dexter, flowing slowly down the dank and windy staircase from the ramparts to the cellars and down still more until it came at last to the very deepest sub-basement of Me, the place where Forbidden Things slumber and dream. And for the first time in far too many months I felt a quick stir of leathery wings and a dark uncoiling joy hissing its glee in the shadowy basement where the real Dexter waits in restless naptime. *Yes,* I heard it sing, and then it stretched in languorous glee and began to bat-wing its way up the shadowed twisty stairs, and in spite of the bright glare of the fluorescent lights It touched everything with perfect Darkness as it rolled up out of the basement and began *at last* to stretch its lovely wicked tendrils into every corner of daytime Dexter and out, into the wicked weary world around us until the temperature in the room began to drop just like the colors of the spectrum, and reality slid down into the cool shadows of Nighttime Truth and everything was once again bathed in a cool and dreadful twilight of so-very-soon delight that finally, at last, was about to unfold into utter long-awaited bliss. It would not solve the many problems my mundane self faced, and it would not make anything truly right outside the walls of this small chamber of glee, but that mattered less than the smallest drop of sweat now rolling from Ivan's pale and trembling face. All that mattered, all that had any weight or reality in this world or any other was that at last, *at last,* we were free to be what we must and do what we must and we were now going to be it and do it.

"So hard to choose," we said again, and even to our ears the voice was different: lower, darker, cooler, alive with the reptilian tones of the Passenger when it has taken the wheel, and Ivan's eyes jerked sideways to see what new and terrible thing was lurking. "But certainly," we said, "we should start with something small and refined—"

"And yet completely *permanent,*" Brian added. "If only for the effect."

"Oh, yes, clearly *permanent,*" we said with a slow deliberate relish of a word that would come to mean so much to the contemptible wriggling mucus-producing thing in the chair. We opened the third tray down, where there was a delightful array of items for snipping and clipping, everything from manicure scissors to a small bolt cutter. With chilly glee we picked up a garden clipper, the kind used for trimming rosebushes. "Perhaps a finger or two?" we said, holding up the clipper.

"Mm, yeeesss," Brian said reflectively. "Just the little one, I think. For now," he added in a soothing tone.

"Of course," we said. "For now." And we took the instrument over to him and held it out. He reached to take it and our hands touched and our eyes met.

And for a wonderful long moment we looked at Brian and he looked back and as he did the shadowy *something* flickered to life in his eyes and uncoiled in its dark and potent glory and it reared up and roared at the Dark Passenger—which roared back a greeting of its own, and although we had many times encountered another Passenger in someone else and heard that challenge and given back one of our own, this was different. This was my brother, my same-self twin in twisty glee, and for the first time ever the two Passengers sent out their black fog of recognition and met in the middle, coming together in greeting and then flowing into a joining of brotherly equals, rearing up as one, with one blended voice, calling out joyfully in a sibilant chord of perfect harmony. *Together . . .*

It was Ivan who interrupted us, yanking fruit-lessly at the metal bonds securing his hands and making a quick sharp *clack* that made us turn and look at him. He froze and looked back and he saw the two identical smiles aimed at him and he saw too what those smiles meant and another small and necessarily disposable piece of Ivan the Bomber withered and died.

"Shall we begin, brother?" we said, holding out the clippers.

"After you, brother," Brian said with a tiny polite bow. We felt the joy of need-ending delight about to bloom and we turned to the chair and flexed the clippers once, twice, *snick-snick,* and Ivan watched and squirmed and made a nasty wet mucusy mewling sound that made us more eager than ever to begin, if only to wipe away the awful damp noise of his disgusting helpless flaccid weakness, and so we did it once more, *snick-snick,* closer, and watched his eyes bulge and his tendons stand out and his veins vibrate and it was a perfect siren symphony of pain-to-be calling us forward, onward, downward, into the chilly pain-filled promise of our mutual delight.

And so we began.

TWENTY-THREE

I HAD TURNED MY PHONE OFF BEFORE
our little meet-and-greet with Ivan and his
friends in the parking lot. Naturally enough, I
didn't want any unexpected noises giving me
away. And I had left it off during the tête-à-tête
with Ivan, because quite frankly, an artist needs to
focus to perform at his very best, and any sudden
chirps or tweets from the infernal omnipresent
machine might have broken our very beautiful
concentration.

And as I stepped out of the storage unit and into
the fresh air of the early hours, I was very glad I
had done so. Because when I turned it on again,
out of mere reflex, I saw that Deborah had called
me seven times—and even as I counted, call
number eight began to ring: Deborah again.
Really, it seemed a bit much—I mean, persistence
can be a good thing, and in her professional life
it has always been a positive virtue. But in this
case, it seemed very close to presumptuous and
perhaps even annoying. After all, we had barely
resumed speaking to one another. She had no real
right to intrude on my glow.

Still, I had to remember that she had not just
enjoyed a long and leisurely session of relaxing,
tension-releasing playtime, as I had. And as

dreamily drained and delighted as I was, I reminded myself that there had been an actual *purpose* to what I had done, beyond even the achievement of such a satisfying warm blush of accomplishment. I had been trying to find out where my kidnapped children were being held, and Debs was quite interested in hearing what I had learned. And I understand very well the importance of compassion and thinking of other people's feelings—after all, I'd been faking these things my whole life, and quite well, too. Deborah was naturally very anxious—eight calls' worth—for me to share my newfound, delightfully obtained information with her.

So in spite of feeling like I wanted to sit in relaxed contemplation and enjoy my mellow mood, I answered the phone. "Hello, Debs," I said, and before I could add even a single syllable more, she snapped out, "What the fuck do you know about Kraunauer? It's all over the fucking news!"

I blinked stupidly for just a second. I should have known that something like this would create a local sensation—perhaps even a national one. "Prominent defense attorney gunned down in plain sight! Film at eleven!" And I should also have anticipated Debs putting two and two together and once again reaching a sum of Dexter. But I had selfishly thought of nothing but the pleasant task at hand, and I was momentarily unprepared. There were many things I could have said, most of them falling somewhere between temporizing and tall-tale spinning, and I thought up a couple of quite good whoppers in those few little blinks of hesitation.

But if we were going to save the children from what sounded like a very hairy situation, we would need her help. Additionally, if Debs and I were truly going to reconcile, she should almost certainly hear some version of relative truth. She'd probably figure it out anyway—she was, after all, a detective. So instead of dancing around it, I decided I would very bluntly tell her the truth—or at least a very close first cousin of the truth. "Kraunauer told us where to find the children," I said.

I heard a sharp intake of breath on the other end of the line, followed by what can only be called a stunned silence. "Jesus *fuck,*" she said at last.

"Yes, isn't it?" I said.

"And then you *shot* him?" she said incredulously.

"He pulled a gun," I said. "He had a very fast draw."

"What about the two Mexican tourists who tried to help?" she demanded. "What, you shot them because they saw you?"

I very nearly laughed at that—"tourists" indeed. "Is that what they're saying? Tourists?" I said. "I think if you pull rap sheets on the 'tourists,' you'll get a more interesting picture."

"The fuck does *that* mean?" she snapped.

"It means," I said, "that they were assassins, *drogas*, that Kraunauer called in to kill us, but we killed them first."

"Who's *we?*" she snapped at me, and I realized that in my eagerness to be honest I had just made a very grave error. Whoever claimed honesty is the best policy, or even a *good* one, clearly had very limited experience with the real world.

I had always been very careful to keep all knowledge of Brian from Deborah. Quite natural, since the one time they'd met Brian had abducted her and taped her to a worktable for slow and careful dissection. And my brother, being no fool, had worked even harder to avoid running into Debs, since he reasoned, rather soundly, I think, that the kind of first encounter they'd had is usually quite memorable, and she was, after all, a cop. So Debs did not know Brian was even alive, let alone working with me. I was on the very edge of letting an extremely slippery cat out of the bag, and there was no way to predict which way the thing would run if I let it out the rest of the way. Deborah might fly into a violent and possibly justified rage, and decide to arrest Brian. And that, of course, might nudge Brian in the direction of even more serious action, something a little more permanent than anger. That would be very awkward for everyone involved, and especially me, since I would be jammed squarely in the middle, pushing the two of them apart and chanting, *Why can't we all just get along?* I certainly didn't want to be forced to choose between the two of them. And in all honesty, I had no idea which way that choice would go.

On top of everything else, I needed all the help I could get if I was to have any chance at all of retrieving my kids. The odds were already formidable, and one more steady hand with a motivated gun in it would make a very big difference. Somehow, some way, Debs had to accept Brian, and vice versa. They had to work together, with me, or there was simply no hope for any of us, especially the children.

And it had to be done quickly, too. I looked at my watch: a little after two a.m. If we started right now, we could hit Raul just before dawn, the ideal time for it. If we delayed, arguing about who did what to whom so many years ago, it would be daylight before we got there, and they would see us coming from three miles away.

"There's no time for this, Debs," I said firmly. "Stay put. We're on our way to get you."

"Goddamn it, who's *we?!*" she was yelling when I hung up.

I put my phone away and turned back to the storage unit, and I paused as I realized the job I had in front of me now. It was a daunting task, right enough, and if I had thought Debs was going to be difficult to convince, Brian would be twice as hard. If I had any hope of persuading him to accept her I would need all the tongues of men and angels. At the moment I only had one.

I sighed heavily, and not merely because I realized I was wishing for more tongues. Somehow, a relatively simple and logical proposition—*let's do this together*—had begun to seem like it would be harder and more dangerous than the real task at hand, rescuing the kids from a bevy of heavily armed *drogas*. Still, it is usually best to take care of the hard jobs first. So I strode manfully back into the storage unit to face my brother.

Brian was standing beside his work chair, looking fondly down at the ruin that was Ivan. The bomber was still alive, since we had to be sure he'd told us everything. Alive—but he didn't look like he was completely sure that this was a good thing at this point. There were so many little parts of him that he would never see again—insignificant parts, perhaps, if taken one at a time. And actually, they *had* been taken one at a time, and very carefully, too. But there were a great many of them, and they were gone forever, and at some point the dear boy would have to add them up and ask himself if it was really worth going on without them.

It would have been very pleasant just to stand next to my brother and enjoy what we had done together—or perhaps *un*done is more accurate, considering the state of Ee-bahng as he lay in fragmented repose. But there was too much to do, and most of it was very time-sensitive, as well as unpleasant. So I girded my loins, stepped over to Brian with a firm stride, and said, "Brian. We have to go meet somebody. Now."

"Really?" he said, in a voice so unhurried and even mellow that it was nearly indecent. "Who, pray tell?"

"Deborah," I said.

Brian snapped to attention as if he was dangling from puppet strings and somebody had yanked them tight. All traces of mellow afterglow were gone as if they'd never been. "What? No, of course not," he said, shaking his head vigorously. "Completely out of the question."

"We need her help," I said.

He hadn't stopped shaking his head. "No, ridiculous, she'd arrest me or something," he said. "And we didn't need her help with Ivan."

"This is very different."

"What is? What is different? I mean, different how?" he said, piling word on word with a brittle and worried energy I'd never seen from him before. "There is no reason to . . . to—She's a *cop,* Dexter, and she has no reason to like me, you know. And she would completely . . . I mean, why on earth do we need *her?* She's not actually one of *us,* you know."

"Brian," I said, cutting off his manic monologue.

"You do remember why we're here? With Ivan?"

"But that has nothing to—Oh, yes, I know, but . . . really, brother," he said. "Even so, what can *she* possibly do? That you and I can't do better without her?"

"We will need every gun we can get," I said. "And we are not likely to pick up any other volunteers."

"But she's a *cop,*" he repeated, and in the interest of full disclosure I have to say he sounded just a little whiny. "And if we do this, we are breaking all kinds of laws."

"She's also a very good shot," I said. "And these are her kids, too. She'll do whatever it takes to get them back. Including shooting a couple of illegal immigrants who grabbed them."

"But . . . but, Dexter," he said, completely whiny now. "She'll remember me."

"Almost certainly," I said.

"And when she finds out that this whole thing was because of me, I mean—"

"She doesn't have to know that," I said. And then I waved a fond farewell to my recent resolution to stick close to the truth with Debs. "We'll tell her it was all Kraunauer."

"She'll believe that?" he asked dubiously.

"If I know Debs, she'll be so anxious to get going and rescue the kids, she won't question it until much later." I shrugged reassuringly. "And by then you can be long gone, if you want."

"Or dead," he muttered.

"I will prepare her first," I said. "You can wait in the car, and if it goes against me, you don't even have to come in."

He shook his head again, but slower this time. "It can't possibly work, Dexter," he said.

"It can," I said. "It has to."

Twenty minutes later Brian parked his Jeep facing out on the street in front of Deborah's house. He drummed his fingers on the steering wheel and made no move to turn off the engine. I reached for the door handle, and he said, "Dexter," and looked at me quite nervously.

"Please, Brian," I said. "This gives us our best chance."

He licked his lips. "I suppose so," he said, very unconvincingly. "If she doesn't just shoot me."

"She carries an old Thirty-eight Special," I said. "You won't even notice it."

He didn't appear to appreciate my light wit. He just looked straight ahead through the windshield and shook his head. "I'll wait here," he said. "But I don't see how—"

"I'll call you either way," I said, and I got out of the car and walked to Deborah's front door.

Once again Deborah opened the door when I was only halfway up the walkway. But this time she just flung it open and spun away, and I closed it behind me as I came in and followed her back to the kitchen.

She had apparently been there for several hours, because she had shredded the old wicker place mat in front of her and started on the one to her right. Three cups stood beside her on the table, one of them still half-full of coffee, one of them empty, with the handle snapped off, and one of them lying on its side, half-shattered.

"Where are they," she snapped at me before I could even settle into the chair opposite. "Goddamn it, what the fuck is Kraunauer—and who is *we,* for fuck's sake?!"

"Please, Deborah," I said, as soothing as I could be. "One question at a time."

Deborah lifted her hands off the table and flexed them as if she was thinking she might strangle me. She bared her teeth and locked them together, hissing out a long breath between them. "Dexter, so fucking help me—" she said. Then she dropped her hands to the tabletop and made a visibly huge effort to control what seemed like an urgent need to kill. "All right," she said. She picked up the battered stainless-steel spoon beside her tattered place mat and began to tap it rapidly on the table. "Where are the kids?"

"It isn't wonderful," I said.

"Where, goddamn it!"

"They're on a drug lord's yacht."

Some people might have turned pale and faint at the news that their children were in the murderous clutches of a true archfiend. And others might have pounded the table and roared with impotent rage. Deborah simply narrowed her eyes, and you would have thought she was completely calm—except for the fact that the spoon she held in her hand was now bent neatly in half. "Where," she said softly.

"It's anchored off Toro Key."

Deborah dropped the ruined spoon onto the table and flexed her fingers. "How many men will he have?" she said.

"I don't know," I said. "But he has three less now."

"Three?" she snapped. "They only found *two* with Kraunauer."

"We took one alive, for questioning," I said.

Deborah was completely still for a moment, her eyes locked on mine. "Who is *we?*" she said, back to her dangerously soft voice. "And why did a *drug lord* take the children?" she said, still quiet, but obviously it was the very dangerous kind of quiet.

It really is stunning how a simple question like that can knock you right over. I had been trundling along, convinced that my brain was operating at a truly high level, prepared for all the bizarre and unlikely possibilities. And I was sure I had all of them covered, too—but then one completely *obvious* question—"why?"—comes along, and I realized I hadn't even thought about it. *Why* did a drug lord have our kids?

Why, because my brother pissed him off, of course!

. . . And if I said that to Deborah, the operation was over before it even began. I had to tell her something, and it had to be convincing, but all I could think of was how totally stupid I had been not to be ready for that most obvious question.

"Why, Dexter?" Debs repeated, and there was a dangerous edge to her voice that went far behind frustrated anger.

"It's kind of complicated," I said, stalling in the hope that either a brilliant idea would occur to me or, if not, the house might be hit by lightning.

"Make it *simple,*" she snapped.

"Well," I said, still waiting, "it all starts with Kraunauer."

A good start: Debs nodded. "Okay," she said.

"One of his clients is this Mexican drug lord. Raul," I said.

"I don't give a shit what his name is," she snapped.

"Well, ah—Raul found out that Kraunauer was representing me. And, um . . ." I paused, and not for dramatic effect. This was where the whole thing would fall to the ground—unless I had a sudden flash of inspiration. I waited for it. Deborah waited, too, but not quite as patiently. She began tapping the mangled spoon again, faster and faster. "Raul is very paranoid," I said. "And, um, he felt that, you know . . ."

"I *don't* know, goddamn it," she said. "And you're not telling me, either!"

I closed my eyes and thought once again about the relative merits of honesty. It seemed to me that the only thing you could say about it, as far as its being a good thing, was that if you didn't tell the truth, sooner or later your made-up story would whirl around and bite you in the crotch. The only other thing I could say about honesty was that whatever else you try first, it never works and honesty ends up as your last resort anyway. And then you're standing there with a crotch wound, and you have to tell the truth just the same, but now you have to drop it into an atmosphere of anger and resentment. Life is a rigged game; there's really no way to win.

Here I stood, bitten to the bone by my feeble fictions. And there was Debs, more than ready and willing to bite, too, and quite probably add a few kicks to the injured area.

I took a very deep breath and opened my eyes. Debs was looking at me, and she was not wearing an expression of calm patience. "Well?" she said. A very large tendril of ice spread out from her voice and sent a slow and jagged spear of frigid malice across the table at me. She flung down the mangled spoon. It bounced twice on the table and then slid onto the floor. "Why, goddamn it?"

All righty, then, I thought. *Here goes nothing.*

"Do you remember my brother, Brian, Deborah?" I said, putting as much nonchalant charm into the words as possible.

It wasn't quite enough. Debs hissed at me and half rose out of her seat. "The psycho son of a bitch that tried to *kill* me?" she said. "*That* Brian?" There was not a single vestige of soft or quiet left in her voice. "Why isn't he *dead?*"

"Sit down, Debs, please," I said.

She stayed in her half crouch a second longer, glaring and panting with rage, and then she lowered herself back down into her seat. "You miserable shit," she grated at me through a still-locked jaw. "You hooked up with *him?*"

"I needed *help,* Deborah," I said. "There was no one else."

I hadn't really intended that as any sort of shot against Deborah, but she clearly took it that way. She turned bright red and lowered her voice to a dangerous rasp. "You needed *help* because you expected me to put my entire fucking life and career in the dumper for you! And you're nothing but a fucking psychopath who finally got what he deserves—and your *brother* is even *worse!*"

It really was a shame that Deborah chose to retreat into saying the same hurtful things, just when we'd been on the verge of getting along again, and the mere fact that they were mostly true things did not take away the sting. *Mostly* true—after all, what fair-minded person could possibly call me "nothing but" a psychopath? I'm very good at board games, too.

"He helped me, Deborah," I said. "When I was all alone with no hope left, he helped me." I spread my hands. "He didn't have to, but . . . I'm not saying he's Mother Teresa. But he helped me. And he hired Kraunauer to defend me."

"He's a psycho fucking killer," she said in a voice that could grind granite.

"Of course he is," I said, a little peevishly. "But he's my *brother*. And he *helped* me."

She glared. I could see her jaw moving in a half circle and I thought I could even hear her teeth grinding away. "What does he have to do with this?" she said. "With this Raul taking my kids?"

"Brian thought Raul was dead," I said. "He took a large chunk of money and ran with it."

"And Raul wasn't dead."

"No, he wasn't," I said. "And he came after Brian."

"And Kraunauer put Raul onto you?"

I nodded. The story still had a few holes in it, but I hoped we were done; it already sounded bad enough. "And so Brian and I lured Raul's shooters into a trap and captured one, so we could learn where the kids are," I said. "And now we know."

I watched Deborah work her jaw again. It might be that I was seeing only what I hoped to see, but she looked like she was actually thinking it over and deciding to accept things as they were. In any case, she didn't seem to be grinding quite as hard.

"Deborah," I said. "We need to get going." She looked up at me and there was still anger in her face, but not as much—and it was mixed with something else, too—determination? Acceptance? I didn't know, but I pushed it anyway. "Whatever you think of Brian is beside the point," I said. "What matters is that we need him." Debs opened her mouth and began to rise up from her seat again, but I overrode her with, "The *kids* need him, Deborah."

She goggled for a second, her mouth half-open, and then she thumped back onto the seat. "What the fuck does that mean?" she hissed.

"Do the math, Debs," I said. "We have no idea how many guns will be against us when we get on that boat—but I promise it's more than two. Maybe as many as a dozen." I leaned forward and tapped the table for emphasis, a dramatic technique I'd seen used effectively many times on TV. "We need everybody we can get," I said.

"Even your fucking psycho killer so-called brother," she snarled.

I shook my head impatiently. "Debs, come on. We're not going out there to arrest these people."

"I'm still a cop! I can't just let you—"

"You can—you *have* to," I insisted. "You don't

want blood on your hands, fine, that's your choice—but we can't leave Raul alive."

"For shit's sake, Dexter—you want to *execute* him!"

"Oh, grow up!" I snapped. "He's a drug lord—and as long as he's alive we're not safe—the *kids* are not safe!"

"Goddamn it . . ."

"Deborah, you know it's true. We need Brian for this," I said. "Any of your buddies on the force likely to help us? Want to ask one of the other detectives? Maybe Captain Matthews? Think they'll want to tag along for a completely illegal raid and firefight, followed by an execution? And we have to execute him, Debs." And then I pointed my finger right at her, another technique culled from TV, and I said very forcibly, "If Raul lives—the kids die."

It was a wonderful point, forceful and logical at the same time, and Debs knew it. She bit down on her lips and hissed and growled, but she didn't say anything else, so I said again, "We need Brian, Debs."

I glanced significantly at my watch. "And we need to do this *now*."

She glared at me, but it was a slightly more human glare. Then she looked away, swallowed visibly, and finally looked back at me. She nodded once, very briskly. "All right," she said. "For the kids." She leaned over the table toward me as far as she could go. "But when we get this done—"

"*If* we get it done, Debs," I said, suddenly weary of wading through so much of what Harry had always called Bullshit Soup. "It's still a very long shot. But *if* we do it . . . Shit. We'll worry about it then."

She looked at me, then nodded. "Where is he?" she said.

"He's parked out front," I said.

She bit down hard, took a deep breath, and said, "Get him."

"Your word, Deborah—"

"For fuck's sake, get him!" she snarled. "We're in a hurry, remember?" I looked at her for a second longer, and she glared back, but she nodded one time. "Get him," she said. "I'll behave."

It was as good as I was going to get, and better than I'd really expected. I pushed back from her rickety table and headed out the front door.

Brian was waiting where I'd left him, which was a relief. His engine was still running, of course, but he'd stayed, which was wonderful. I'd half expected to find him gone, racing away in a lather of panic. And when I opened the door, he certainly looked at me with something very close to alarm. I heard the engine rev one time as his foot stomped down reflexively, but he didn't put it in gear.

"All is well," I said as soothingly as possible.

"The Maginot Line is secured, the truce is agreed, and I have her promise not to invade Poland."

Brian blinked at me with owl-large eyes. "That's even worse than de Tocqueville," he said. "Sometimes, brother, you try too hard."

I was quite sure that his snappishness was no more than jealousy; he hadn't managed anything clever for hours. But the important thing was that he took me at my word, turned off the ignition, and climbed out of his car. He walked around and stood uncertainly beside me for a moment. Then he shook himself, squared his shoulders, and said, " 'Twere best done quickly." He gave me a glance to make sure I'd noticed the Shakespeare, and then he stepped through the gate onto Deborah's front walk.

I followed along right behind, but even so Brian was quicker. Perhaps he really did want to get it over with. By the time I got back inside, he and Debs were standing face-to-face in the kitchen, only a few feet apart. Deborah wore her working scowl, but at least her clenched fists were empty of weapons. Brian just gazed at her neutrally, arms crossed. Under the circumstances, and con-sidering why we were joining together, it would have been wildly inappropriate to call it a Mexican Standoff. But it did look like they were each waiting for the other to attack with a knife so they could open fire with an Uzi. Still, it was probably the best family get-together I could hope for.

It was also quite clear that it was up to me to keep things moving at a lively pace, and along the way try to prevent these two from killing each other, so I made a modest and optimistic start. "Deborah, Brian. Brian, Deborah. Okay? Now," I said, dragging out one of the rickety kitchen chairs and sitting. "I think you'll both agree that we should get there quickly, and try to take them in the dark, by surprise?"

"Surprise," Debs said bitterly, still staring at Brian. "He's got our kids, and he knows you two are killing his men. How will this be a surprise?"

"He doesn't know we're coming," I said. "He doesn't even know that we found out where he is."

"People don't usually come after *him,*" Brian said helpfully, still watching Deborah. "I really don't think he'll expect it."

"And what if he guesses?" she demanded. "Then what the fuck are we supposed to do?"

"We could stay here and have coffee instead," Brian said.

I wouldn't have thought it possible, but Deborah's glare got meaner and angrier. She opened her mouth to say something back, and I'm sure it would have been a real doozy.

But I was actually more interested in *preventing* doozies and promoting an atmosphere of willing cooperation. So I jumped in before she could say something that might collapse our alliance before it even started. "It doesn't matter," I said. "We still have to try, right? Now, what can you tell us about this yacht, Brian?"

Brian sat in an equally flimsy chair, without taking his eyes off Deborah. "I have seen it," he said. "I've even been on board once." He glanced at me, then quickly back to Debs. "The *Nuestra Señorita*. It's a very nice boat," he said. "*Very* nice."

Deborah snorted. "*Nice*. Thanks, that's really helpful."

As I said, it was all up to me. "Could you sketch out a floor plan, Brian?" I said. "Debs, maybe you could get paper and pencil?"

She clearly didn't want to look at anything but Brian, but she took a step back and turned quickly to a drawer in the counter behind her. Brian tensed as she reached into the drawer, but Debs turned back around holding only a notebook and a badly chewed ballpoint pen. Still watching Brian, she dropped them on the table in front of him and then, at last, she sat down right across from him.

"Good, thank you," I said in my best bright and cheerful Mr. Rogers voice. "Brian?"

My brother picked up the pen, flipped open the notebook, and then, slowly and reluctantly, dropped his eyes from Debs and onto the paper.

"Well," he said, beginning to sketch quick lines, "as I said, it was only once. But what I remember is this." The lines became the back end of a large boat, superstructure looming above. "The rear end . . ." He looked up at me. "The *stern,*" he said happily. He made a few quick lines. "Like this. I think they call it *stepped?*" He glanced up for confirmation. I nodded. "You know," he said, turning to Debs, "it's much lower to the water than the sides. So you can get on and off to go swimming. And onto the launch—there's a beautiful launch that hangs on these hooks on the back." He tapped the drawing with the pen. "That's the easy way to get on board."

"No good," Debs said, spitting the words like they tasted bad. "If there are guards, that's where they'll be."

"Oh, there are guards," Brian said, just a little too cheerfully. "Lots of them."

"About how many, do you think, Brian?" I said.

"Why, I don't really know," he said.

"Terrific," Deborah muttered.

"But I think we can count on ten or twelve," he said. "Plus Raul, his captain, probably a few *mujeres* from his harem." He smiled again, and it was inappropriate as well as being poorly executed. "Raul is really quite the ladies' man."

"They won't all be on deck," I said. "Not if we get there before first light."

"Mmm, nooo," Brian said thoughtfully. "I'm

sure most of them will be asleep. I mean, I hope so."

"Great," Deborah snapped. "You can't tell us how many or where they are or anything except that we should hope they're taking a siesta?"

"I would guess two on deck, probably at the back," I said, as if we were having a reasonable chat. "And maybe one up on the bridge. What do you think, Debs?"

She looked at me and chewed on her lower lip for a second. Then she nodded. "That makes sense," she said. "That's how I'd do it."

"Of course, technically," Brian said thoughtfully, "*you* aren't actually a Mexican drug lord."

I suppose Brian wanted to prove he could snark, too, and it worked. Debs whipped back around to face him, and once again I had to leap in and keep things moving in a positive direction.

"How high off the water is the bow, Brian?" I said.

"Oh, well, I don't really know, much higher than the *stern*," Brian said. "But I was mostly downstairs."

"Okay," I said, and nodded at the pen and paper. "Give us an idea of what that's like."

"Hmm," he said, picking up the pen and frowning. "I seem to remember . . . a really big lounge area, like a living room." He flipped to a new page and drew a wide space, with sofalike benches along the sides. "A big flat-screen TV. Wet bar, kitchenette—just for snacks. The main kitchen is downstairs." He smiled at me conspiratorially. "The *galley*."

"What else?" I prompted.

Brian tapped the paper thoughtfully. "Well," he said, "at the far end, toward the front of the boat . . ." I waited for the terrible smile and the word *bow,* but apparently he didn't think of it, and I was spared. "The stairs go down to the cabins," he said.

"How many stairs?" Deborah snapped.

"Oh, not that many," Brian said. "Five or six? Not many."

"And how many cabins?" I asked him.

Brian shrugged. "You have to understand, I didn't go down there," he said. "I just glanced down when Raul came up. His cabin—the main one—it's all the way up at the front." He frowned. "I saw four or five doors along the hall. One's the kitchen. . . . I'd guess three more cabins."

"The kids will be together in one of the cabins," Deborah said.

"You'd better hope so," I said. Personally, I would have put kids in the bilge—especially mine.

"They will be in a cabin," Debs said positively. "But as far from Raul as possible."

I thought that part made sense, and I glanced at Brian. He nodded. "That's probably right," he said. "Raul does like children. But he also likes his privacy, especially when he's with his *mujeres*."

"Good," I said, trying to sound dynamic, forceful, and optimistic, as if we'd actually accomplished something. "So how do we do this?"

The two of them looked up at me, and I had to suppress a snort, because their faces wore identical expressions of blank befuddlement. They were both equally surprised at the question; neither of them had a clue how to go about our little quest, and it was the only thing they'd agreed on yet. Once again, the one thing that can always be relied upon to unite absolutely anybody and everybody is Ignorance.

Deborah broke the spell by standing up abruptly. "We got about four hours until dawn," she said. "Let's just go, and take it as it comes. Whatever it takes."

I opened my mouth to object and point out that careful planning is the mother of success—but Brian was already nodding his head and standing up. "We'll take my car," he said, looking at me. "Over to your boat? After that, we'll just have to wing it." He turned and walked out of the room, and with no more than a nod at me, Deborah followed, and I could only shrug and trail along behind.

As I said, Ignorance unites us all.

TWENTY-FOUR

BISCAYNE BAY AT NIGHT CAN BE A VERY beautiful place. A warm wind usually blows across the surface, and the water glows with a slight luminescence, and if there is some moonlight and the waves are behaving, it can remind you that every now and then, being alive and on a boat here on the bay is a very good thing.

I steered my boat south from my rented dock in Coconut Grove, and I was reminded of exactly that: I was glad to be alive and on the water on a beautiful moonlit night. And I really did appreciate the charms of a predawn boat trip on the waters of my beloved home. But I also thought I would like to *stay* alive, and I would have a much better chance of that if the moon was not quite so bright.

There was no way in the world we could hope to approach Raul's yacht unseen, not with this three-quarter moon beaming down in rancid glee. I had always felt a cool and welcome comfort from the moonlight. It had been my friend and ally, my strength and my refuge. Tonight it was no such thing. Like everything else I held dear it had turned against me. The cold light of this traitorous moon would get me killed, and I took no joy from the sight of it. And it shone mercilessly down from a sky that was almost completely clear. Far off on the horizon, over toward Bimini, there was a dark line of clouds scudding along, low and fast, but where we were there was only a lethally bright sky above.

Because of a very light chop, we traveled at a good speed, just over twenty-five knots. Even south of Cape Florida, where the swells can pick up from the roll of the open ocean, the water was calm enough to let us maintain the pace. We would be there in about half an hour—and perhaps that made me enjoy the ride even more. Because if the visibility was this good when we arrived, I was quite sure that this would be the last boat ride I ever took. Raul would have sentries, and they could not avoid seeing us, and that would be just about the end of it. And of us.

We had talked about this, of course. The car ride from Deborah's house to my boat had been full of talk. I had listed what might happen, what we might do about it, and how to maximize what was truly a very slim chance of success. And even though Debs and Brian remained united in shrugging off all the certain dangers I could think of, I have to admit that at least things were going much better than I could have hoped in the personal relations department. Debs had some-how kept herself from shooting Brian, and he had not slashed her throat and bounded away for the high ground.

Before climbing into Brian's car we had maximized our firepower—Debs took a pump-action shotgun from the trunk of her car, as well as her first-aid kit, which I thought was rather pessimistic. And she brought her Glock pistol, which made me glad. She had a sentimental attachment to Harry's old .38 revolver and I'd been afraid she'd bring it, even though it had half the number of shots and half the firepower of the Glock. Brian and I had our pistols, reloaded and ready to go, each of us with a spare clip.

It was only a ten-minute drive from Deb's house to my rented dock space in a quiet residential area of the Grove. The house was owned by an elderly couple who lived in New Jersey most of the year, for some reason. They were very glad to have someone stopping by their Southern manse from time to time, which might discourage burglars, and they gave me a very good rate. And my boat, in spite of sitting unused for several months, was in excellent shape and needed only a few moments of chug and spew from the bilge pump before it was ready to go.

As we motored out the short canal to the bay I opened the dry locker on my boat, and grabbed some very good fillet knives, which were a lot quieter than guns, and might preserve our element of surprise a few extra minutes. The fact that they were also a great deal more fun than guns was not really a factor. Brian was delighted with the one I gave him, of course. Debs refused to take one and that, too, really wasn't much of a surprise.

In addition to all that lethal hardware, my brother had insisted on bringing along the canvas bag he'd taken from Ivan. It was full of sinister-looking things Brian insisted on calling "toys" and which he was convinced we might need. "If nothing else," he'd said brightly, "it can cover our tracks afterward." And again, astonishingly, Debs had agreed.

"If one of those things can destroy the evidence," she said, "we bring it."

So we were lugging along a couple of very ugly bombs, unknown and probably unstable explosive devices, merely because we *might* get a chance to use them. And maybe we would. But first we had to get on board Raul's yacht silently and alive, and to do that we had to approach it without being seen. So far, we had come up with no way to do that, other than go-take-a-look-and-see-what's-what. If it had been up to me, this casual plan of attack would not have been plan B—not even C. I don't like to improvise. When I slide out into the night for the purpose of making Mischief, I need to have a plan, and I need to stick with it. Beginning, middle, and end, all thought out ahead of time, and all executed in good order. Far too much could go wrong, even when it's just me and one carefully selected playmate, one who suspects nothing until it is too late for suspicions to do any good.

In this case we were approaching perhaps a dozen men who were expecting trouble and were paid handsomely to prevent surprises—and we were improvising. I hated it, and I hated having no choice but to go through with it, and even on a beautiful night like this one I could not shake the feeling that things could not possibly go well. There was only one likely outcome, and that was a violent finish to the Saga of Dexter—and just when things were looking up for me, too. With Anderson killed in such a toxic setting, I was reasonably sure the case against me would go away, even without Kraunauer, and I would be free once more to live a happy life of perfectly balanced wage slavery and Wicked Fun. But unless a true miracle occurred, all that was about to end.

I was left alone with my dark thoughts—there was no point in trying to have an encouraging conversation over the noise of the engine and wind—but from what I could see of Debs and Brian, they were not thinking of sunlit rose gardens full of kittens and ice cream either. Deborah simply sat and scowled at her feet, and Brian stood in the bow, holding the bowline and staring anxiously ahead. It did not cheer me up at all to see them; none of us looked like something a dozen well-armed mercenaries would find terribly threatening.

My thoughts, left to themselves, turned even darker. This was a hopeless errand, doomed to failure, and failure meant certain death, and death was something I have always tried to avoid—at least, my own. And why, after all, did we really need to go to all this bother? To save the children? Why? When you come right down to it, who really needs children? And especially *these* children. The only thing special about them was that Lily Anne and Nicholas carried DNA from me and Debs—and if either of us truly felt the need to replicate that, there was a lot more where that came from. As for Cody and Astor, they were Dark Yearlings, waiting to grow into something like me. Surely no reasonable person could want more Passenger-infested night stalkers in the world.

And in any case, didn't all the child-rearing experts agree that it was actually a *bad* thing to do too much for your kids? It was well known that if you hover protectively around them, they never learn to fend for themselves. They would grow up to be wards of the state, permanently on food stamps and welfare, knocking over gas stations on the weekends. Weren't we really just *enabling* these kids, shoving them into a life of crime and servile dependency on others?

And if we went home now and the worst happened to the children—so what? They were easily replaced—if not by breeding, then why not by adoption? There are millions of homeless children in the world—which proved again that kids were a low-value commodity, didn't it? I mean, there are very few homeless *Bentleys* in the world. Probably near to zero, except for Kraunauer's, and it wouldn't be homeless for very long. People would line up around the block to claim it—but on that same block there might be a dozen children nobody wanted, and no one would lift a finger for them. Didn't that prove something? Wouldn't a reasonable being conclude that the only logical, fair, and healthy thing to do was turn around, head for home, and give the children a chance to develop by taking care of themselves?

It was pure and unassailable logic. But, of course, there was no point in trying to get anybody else to see it. Human beings have never really been influenced by logic, whatever they tell themselves. And I was fairly sure that Deborah, at least, would not see things in this rational and sensible light. And Brian, for all his laudable lack of emotion, seemed quite determined to put an end to Raul. If he had to rescue a few kids to do that, he didn't appear to mind very much, as long as taking out Raul was part of the deal.

As if he had heard me think about him, Brian turned around and met my eye. He nodded once and flashed his truly terrible fake smile, and then turned back around to face front again. There was no help there. I was almost certainly the only one of us with his head screwed on properly and wanting to turn around and go home. And I couldn't help thinking that by a wonderful coincidence, I was steering the boat—*my* boat. I could do it—just a slow invisible nudge of the wheel to put us into a big circular loop, back to home and sanity. I really *should* do it—and someday Debs and Brian would realize I had saved their lives, and they'd thank me for it.

Something touched my elbow; startled, I turned and saw that Deborah was standing there. She didn't look like she was ready to thank me for anything. She just leaned close to my ear and said, "How soon?"

I glanced down at my GPS Chartplotter. We were only a couple of miles out from Toro Key. Too close to turn around; I had dithered too long.

"We should see it in a few minutes," I said to Debs. She nodded, and for a moment she just stood there, silent. And then surprisingly, perhaps more surprisingly than anything else that had happened lately, she put her hand on my arm, squeezed hard for a moment, and then went up to stand beside Brian.

It was a very touching moment, in both the physical and sentimental sense of the word. My sister, symbolically reaching across the great gaping space that had grown between us, and saying, *We are in this together. You and me,*

Dex, side by side, all the way to the rapidly approaching final curtain. If we go down, we go down together. Very warm, very human, and it really should have made me buck up. I'm sure that's what it usually does, at least to those of us who have emotions. I don't, so it didn't. And I did not want to go down at all, together or alone.

Ahead of me I could see the bright flash from Fowey Rocks Light, which was due east of Soldier Key, a small island a few miles north of Toro. We had to be getting closer, but I just kept steering the boat onward, feeling more and more certain that I was aiming us directly at our doom.

Debs saw the yacht first. I watched her lean over to Brian and say something, pointing at a spot just ahead and to the left. Brian looked where she pointed, nodded, and came back to me.

"That has to be it," he said, leaning in next to my ear.

I throttled back immediately, bringing us down to a slow and, I hoped, mostly silent glide across the water. I nudged the boat left a few points, and soon I could see it too. At first it was no more than a spot of muted brightness high above the water, the anchor light required by law. This one was a little dimmer than it should have been, probably on purpose, but it passed muster.

Brian went back up to the bow and stared intently at the spot. We moved slowly closer and

413

a vague silhouette appeared under the light and began to take on the shape of a large and expensive boat. And as that shape got closer and clearer, I had to wonder whether I had chosen the wrong profession, because what we were looking at was no mere yacht. This was a *superyacht,* the kind that sheikhs and Greek arms dealers buy for their summer vacations on the Mediterranean, the kind that can leave Athens while a gourmet meal is served and race all the way to Venice in time for dessert. This yacht was only about sixty feet long, but the lines screamed out speed, class, and megabucks. Whatever else he might be—and mostly really *was*—no one would ever accuse Raul of being cheap. I began to wonder just how much cash Brian had taken from him. It had to be an awful lot for Raul even to notice it was gone.

They had dropped anchor on the bay side, just north of the key, in the only hole deep enough for a boat that size, as far as I knew. But it was protected from the bigger ocean waves and the prevailing winds this time of year, and if the little launch was in the same class as the yacht, Raul could make it from here to Miami in about twenty minutes. And if he needed a sudden getaway, he was pointed straight out at the Atlantic, and it would be a quick hop back to Mexico in a yacht as fast as this one.

Two hundred yards away, I turned south and

sped up a little, running parallel now to the yacht, and hoping they would think we were no more than a passing boat filled with early morning anglers. It made sense; there was a reef just south of Toro that offered good fishing. But it made no sense at all to Brian and Debs; they turned and looked back at me in perfect unison. "What are you doing?" Debs said in a savage whisper.

"We can't see enough," Brian said in the same tone.

I shook my head. "We can't see," I said, "so *they* can't see *us,* either. That's a *good* thing," I added, since neither of them seemed to understand that.

Debs came back to my side again. "Dexter, we have to know about the guards," she said. "How many, where they are—we can't go in blind."

"If they spot us getting close we aren't going in at all," I said.

Brian joined us, standing at my other elbow. "Brother, it would be nice to know—"

"Are you both out of your fucking heads?" I snapped. They looked at me with equal surprise, and I admit I was feeling it, too. I almost never use bad words—there are so many *good* ones that sting more. But seriously, I seemed to be the only one of us interested in staying alive. Brian and Debs were treating this like a snipe hunt. "We go past like we're headed to the reef to fish. Then we approach from the bow," I said firmly. "Quietly.

415

That's our best chance of staying unseen." And I think I sounded quite commanding.

"It's too high," Debs said petulantly. "I'm not a fucking chimp—we can't climb up the anchor line."

"There's a boarding ladder in the locker back there," I said, nodding toward the rear of my boat. "Go get it." And the first confirmation of my new authority came when Debs turned quickly away and got the ladder from the locker. She returned just as quickly and held it out to me.

The ladder had six wooden steps and two hooks at the top end. I needed it because my boat has high gunwales for offshore use, and if ever I wanted to swim or snorkel, I hooked the ladder on.

"You have a plan, brother?" Brian asked.

"I do," I said, still sounding very much in charge. "We glide up from the front. You"—I nodded at Brian—"climb onto the gunwale of this boat, and hook the ladder to the yacht's rail."

"It's still too high," Deborah said.

"Then you and I, Brian," I said, ignoring Debs and her negativity, "climb up the ladder onto the deck. Debs, you wait with the boat and—"

"Fuck you—I'm not waiting in the boat like some fucking cheerleader!" she said.

I skipped over the obvious fact that neither boats nor execution squads are generally equipped with cheerleaders, and instead just told her, "Deborah, we have to take the kids off at the stern. So you have to bring the boat around after Brian and I take out the deck watch, okay?" She set her face in a fierce, dark pout, and so even though it wasn't quite playing fair, I added, "It's got to be done quietly—it's *knife* work, Debs."

She glared a little more, but then she nodded. "Fine," she said. "But you call me up there right away or so help me—"

"Good, that's settled," I said. For the next few minutes nobody had anything to say. I had to think that was a good thing, considering the blather they'd been spouting so far. I didn't need the distraction and arguments, and I didn't need anybody objecting that it was *still* an insane, suicidal plan. Because it was; I was sure there would be somebody on the bridge, and he would certainly be looking out over the bow from time to time. It was just barely possible that we could get ridiculously lucky and time it so that he was looking away when we climbed on board—but I didn't feel lucky. Nothing about this whole absurd expedition felt lucky. I had only a heavy sick feeling of dread and a cold lump in my stomach and a totally unshakable conviction that we were all about to die—or at least that I was, which is just as bad, as far as I'm concerned.

Still, I was here, and I had to go through with it. So I steered south until the yacht was only a very dim anchor light again, and then I turned around, cut the throttle to idle, and headed straight back at the little light. And back, I was sure, to a very nasty death.

Just at the point where I could barely make out the yacht's bow and I had started to screw myself up to the point of being ready to commit suicide by leaping on board, I felt a small, chill drop of water on my cheek. I ignored it at first, thinking that it was just more proof that this whole trip was stupid and doomed. I'm as good as dead; why not make me wet, too? I pushed it away; killing yourself is serious business and one really should concentrate fully. But I felt another drop, and then two more, then five, and it was really much too cool to be salt spray, and finally, in my first bright moment all evening, I realized what it might be, and I looked up.

Racing straight at us a few hundred feet overhead was a low dark line of clouds—the squall I had seen out over the ocean toward Bimini. As these little stormlets often do, this one had sprinted across the water and come down on us, and I don't think I have ever been quite so happy about anything to do with weather as I was when I saw the thick sheet of rain hurrying across the water at my boat.

In another few seconds it was on us, a furious icy deluge of water. And even as I was applauding the fact that we were now invisible from the yacht, it occurred to me that the yacht was just as invisible to us, and if I didn't want to ram our target I had to be careful.

I turned to Brian, who was still standing next to me, anxiously clutching the boarding ladder. "Get up in the bow," I told him. "Don't let us bump the yacht." He nodded, put the ladder down carefully, and went forward.

Just as I was beginning to think we'd missed our mark, Brian waved at me urgently. I cut the engine, letting us drift forward, and a moment later, looming up out of the heavy shower of rain, I saw the bow of the yacht towering over us.

"Take the wheel," I said to Debs. She just nodded and grabbed the steering wheel, and I picked up the ladder and went forward to join Brian. He said something I couldn't hear over the thumping of the rain. He leaned close to my ear and repeated it: "Hold my belt." I nodded and, as he stepped up onto the gunwale of my boat, I grabbed his belt and held him steady.

When he got his balance Brian stuck his hand out to me and wiggled his fingers. It took me a moment to understand: the ladder, of course. I passed it to him and he stretched up on tiptoes with the ladder held above him. He wobbled, teetered, and shot down to a crouch to recover his balance, but then slowly and carefully he stretched back up again. I couldn't see much, standing more or less under him, but I could feel him moving around up there. After a few moments, he squatted down again. "Got it," he said.

I nodded and started to climb up onto the gunwale. Brian put a hand out to stop me. "If you don't mind, brother," he said. "I'll go first." He cocked his head at me, as if waiting for an objection. I didn't give him one. He smiled, the same awful fake display of teeth without emotion, and straightened up. He gave a little hop, and then disappeared up the boarding ladder onto the deck of the yacht. I followed as quickly as I could, waving a hand at Debs and pushing the boat away with my feet as I climbed.

I didn't hear anything at all as I clambered up onto the deck, and that seemed like a very good thing. I crouched down; there was a kind of gently curved upward slope in the deck here at the bow, a sort of half cone painted a dark blue so it stood out from the white deck around it. It was probably intended to make headroom for Raul's cabin. I climbed up onto the blue strip and crouched low, hoping my dark clothing would blend in. Raul would be directly below me now, in his cabin. I wondered if he had his *mujeres* with him. I hoped they were keeping him busy.

The rain was starting to slacken. I looked up toward where Brian had disappeared. At first I didn't see him. I looked farther up to where the easy slope stopped and jagged upward at a sharper angle to the bridge. There was a darker blotch right in the middle of it, more than halfway up to the windscreen that marked the bridge. It was Brian, crawling upward carefully but rapidly. As I watched, he glanced back to me. He had his fillet knife clenched in his teeth like a pirate. It was a very sharp knife, and if he wasn't careful, he'd get a new smile, probably better than the one he had now. Brian motioned me to wait, and then slowly lifted his head up to peer over the windscreen.

For a moment he froze like that, no more than half his head showing above the windscreen. Then he gathered himself and half pulled, half jumped upward and out of sight.

And I was all alone, crouched in the rain, on a boat filled with well-armed men who wanted to kill me.

TWENTY-FIVE

I WAITED. IT'S A LOT HARDER THAN IT sounds. I could imagine a thousand things happening up on the bridge, and only one of them was good. What was taking so much time? Was there a guard up there? There must have been or Brian wouldn't have jumped over like that. Did Brian surprise him? If so, why was it taking so long? Maybe he was enjoying himself, making it last a little longer than necessary. Maybe the guard had surprised Brian. It could be that the boat was about to explode with shouts and shots, and here I was crouching at the bow like an idiot.

And if that did happen, I wasn't ready to offer even token resistance. I'd left my fillet knife in its sheath, so I wouldn't cut myself climbing up. It was still there. I pulled it out and held it ready. It didn't seem very dangerous, not compared to six or seven men with assault rifles. And why did the grip feel so slippery? Almost as if my hands were sweating, which was silly. I was Dark Dexter, Cold Killer. My hands didn't sweat, even now, when Brian was really taking far too long and it was almost certain that something had gone drastically wrong.

Just when I had persuaded myself to follow Brian and take a look, he appeared again, waving happily, the fillet knife in his hand still dripping red. He motioned me up; clutching my knife anxiously, I crawled up the slope and onto the bridge as quickly as I could, grumbling the whole way. He didn't have to look so pleased with himself. One guard, big deal—and he had clearly taken his time and had a little fun, while I huddled abjectly below.

I pulled myself up and over the bridge windscreen. It really wouldn't screen out much wind; it was only around a foot high. But at least that made it easier to climb over, and I did. Brian stood a few feet away, looking fondly down at a crumpled body. It had fallen onto a cushioned area about knee-high off the deck that was, astonishingly, right next to an actual honest-to-god hot tub, big enough for four people at a time. I was still gaping at it when Brian leaned over and took my elbow.

"There's only one guard outside below us," he whispered, nodding toward the stern of the yacht. "He's standing right at the foot of the stairs." He dropped to his knees and motioned me down with him, and together we crawled to the edge of the bridge, where a flight of molded steps led to the main deck ten feet below.

I dropped to my belly and peeked over. At first I didn't see anything. Maybe he'd gone inside to pee or something. Then he coughed, shuffled his feet, and I saw him—right below me, hugging the shadows and looking around vigilantly.

I pulled back and put my head next to Brian's. "I thought there'd be *two*," I whispered.

Brian shrugged, very difficult when you're lying flat on your stomach. "Raul must be very overconfident," he whispered back.

I looked over again. There was still only one guard. I slid back and Brian raised an eyebrow at me. My eyes fell on the padded bench beside the hot tub. I crawled over and stood up, grabbing one of the cushions, a heavy, canvas-covered thing about three feet square. I beckoned to Brian and handed it to him. "Drop this over here, onto the main deck," I whispered, pointing to my left.

He understood right away, taking the cushion and moving silently over to the rail. He looked at me expectantly and I once more dropped to my belly and slid forward to the steps. I held my knife ready, took a deep breath, and waved to Brian.

Right away I heard the cushion thump onto the deck below. It was followed immediately by a muffled, "*Conyo*," from the guard, directly below me—all according to plan. And now the plan said the guard would step around the corner of the cabin to the deck along the rail, and look to see what had made the sound, and I would be down and on him.

But the idiot on the main deck clearly didn't know the script; he leaned forward instead and

424

stared upward, right at me, and I barely pulled back in time to escape being seen. " 'Tonio, *pendejo*," he whispered loudly. "*¿Qué es eso?*"

'Tonio, of course, did not answer, since he was fully occupied with being dead at the moment. I waited, feeling my palms sweat again. Until tonight I'd never had sweaty palms, and now twice. I didn't like it, and I didn't like being the kind of nervous Nellie who had sweaty palms. But I also didn't seem to have a choice. I waited, feeling my hands go slick and disliking myself. At last I heard "*Conyo*" again, and then a light shuffling of feet—moving *away* from me.

I inched forward. The shadowed spot below was empty. I rose to a crouch and slid down the stairs as quickly as possible, stepping into the darkness at the corner of the cabin. A moment later I heard a few more whispered syllables of what was probably profanity, and then the cushion Brian had dropped came marching around the corner.

In a fit of tidy pique, the sentry had picked up the cushion, probably to carry it back up to the hot tub and, in the process, berate 'Tonio for his sloppiness. But alas for Neatness and Tongue-lashing everywhere, he did not make it up the stairs. Because by holding the cushion in front of him like that he had provided the ideal blind spot for Dexter, and before the guard could do more than blink twice I slipped behind him and then I was on him, one arm tight around his throat and my knife diving into him.

He was very strong, and he nearly broke loose, but I held on tight, twisting the blade out and plunging it back in, and he gave out only a single croak, muffled by my forearm on his throat, and then he went limp.

I held him tight until I was very sure he was absolutely no-kidding dead. Then I lowered him carefully to the deck and straightened slowly, quite pleased with myself. I had taken my turn, and I had done it just as well as my brother—a little better, in fact, since I hadn't dawdled to enjoy myself like he had. No, I had been pure lethal efficiency, and a true shining example of how these things should be done.

I was only halfway up to a standing position and still congratulating myself when the cabin door beside me opened outward and I heard a new male voice whisper, "*Ah. Una meada buena es como—¿Qué?*"

A shame I never learned what a good piss was like. But as the new man stepped out from the cabin and closed the door, he saw me, and all thoughts of poetic rhapsody on the subject of piss left him. Luckily for me, he spent a full two seconds gaping, which would have been more than enough time for me to silence him forever—

—except that as I stepped forward to do that I stumbled on the body at my feet and dropped to one knee, and I could only watch as the pisser scrabbled at the assault rifle that hung from his shoulder on a sling.

All the guard had to do was move the rifle into firing position and pull the trigger, and Dexter was as dead as the dodo. But Time slid down into a sludge-muddled crawl and the sentry seemed to be taking forever at this oh-so-simple task. It was like watching an old silent comedy run in slow motion as he fumbled with the strap, broke a fingernail on the stock, and smacked his own forehead with the gun barrel, jittering the whole time with a sluggish but frenzied stiff-fingered anxiety, his tongue stuck out one side of his mouth, and I watched helplessly as he awkwardly but finally brought the gun slowly around and scrabbled for the trigger, and just before he found it a dark shape dropped from above and drove him down to the deck and a moment later he found his voice at last, just in time to give a final gurgle, kick his legs, and go still.

"Well," Brian whispered from his crouch above the newly dead sentry. "Apparently there were three guards after all."

"So it seems," I whispered back crossly. "You sure it isn't four?"

We crouched there like that for a minute, just to be sure no one had heard the *thump* of Brian and the guard hitting the deck. It had seemed awfully loud, even in my slow-motion stupefaction. But apparently Raul and the rest of his crew were sound sleepers. There was no outcry, rush of feet, sound of the trumpet, nothing. So we left the two late members of the night watch where they'd fallen and took a quick and silent tour of the deck, avoiding the windows—they were too big to call them portholes. When we were done I stepped over to the rail and leaned out. The little rainstorm that had made all this possible was fading now, and I could see Deborah quite clearly, a few feet off the bow and hanging on to the anchor line with my boat-hook. I waved to her and she let go of the line, put the boathook down, and pulled herself along the side of the boat, back to the stern.

I stepped down onto the diving platform on the back end of the boat. Brian was just behind me on the deck, watching for signs of unwanted life. The superyacht's launch was already there, tied to a cleat and bobbing gently behind us, and I peeked into the cockpit. It looked like it cost more than a three-bedroom, two-bath house. It had a control panel that Captain Kirk would have felt at home with, plush seats, and even a small step-down cabin. The keys were in it, dangling from the ignition beside the wheel. Maybe Raul really was overconfident. Maybe having a boat filled with heavily armed men did that.

I heard a soft swirl of water and Debs came around the corner. She pulled my boat in beside the launch and I grabbed the bowline from her and tied off so my boat would drift about ten feet back, where it wouldn't bump the yacht and send an unwanted alarm.

Debs grabbed her shotgun and scurried up and onto the yacht's deck like she was famished and late for dinner. "What the fuck took you so long," she whispered fiercely.

"Traffic," I told her.

She didn't seem to think that was funny, and she kept her scowl. But before she could charge up onto the yacht and start shooting everyone, Brian made a *psst!* sound from his spot above us on the deck. I turned to him and he pointed. "The bag," he whispered. I must have looked blank, because he stepped quickly down and pulled my boat back in. He hopped into it and grabbed a heavy canvas bag from the bow, next to where he'd been standing as we approached the yacht. He slung it over a shoulder and brushed past me again, murmuring, "Ee-bahng's toys."

I wasn't sure what he wanted with Ivan's bomb bag at this point. It seemed to me that we should save the explosions for the cleanup, after we'd found the kids. As I now knew quite well, bombs are loud, messy things, and I didn't like them. I also didn't trust them—they might go off at any moment for no rational reason, and it seemed foolish to carry them into a situation where shots might well be fired in anger.

But Brian had made up his mind, and anyway he was already gone, up onto the yacht's deck. So I shrugged it off and climbed up after him, and Debs followed me back to the door that led into the main cabin, where Brian waited impatiently. He pulled open the door and stepped carefully inside, and a moment later I followed.

The room was lit with only a couple of very dim lights, but even so, I had a very strange moment in which I thought I'd gone through a wormhole instead of a door, and ended up miles away in the penthouse of a luxury hotel. The room seemed too big to fit on the boat, and it was impossibly opulent. Except for the long heavily tinted window along the sides, the walls were lined with gilded mirrors. As Brian had said, there was a kitchenette in the corner at the far end of the room and the stairs down to the cabins beside it. But there was also a formal dining area, with low-hanging candelabra and a heavy golden table and chairs, and an absurd number of overstuffed glove-leather couches and chairs, and a huge flat-screen TV.

There was more rich furnishing than I could possibly take in at one glance, and I turned slowly to see it all, but Brian saw me gawking and grabbed my arm, shaking his head at me with disappointment. We cat-footed toward the stairs, Brian in the lead, Debs jostling me for second place.

At the head of the stairs Brian paused, peering downward intently. He motioned with one hand for us to wait and carefully put the canvas bag of Toys to one side. Then he drew his pistol and slunk silently down the steps. There were only five or six stairs and I could see my brother's head and shoulders quite clearly as he edged forward a few feet, paused, and then backed up again. He glanced up and beckoned, and before I could move Deborah bolted past me and onto the stairs with her gun out and pointed up.

As I joined them in the hallway at the foot of the stairs, Debs and Brian were having an animated mime argument. Debs was pointing to the door on the right, and Brian was making slow-down gestures and apparently urging caution. Debs screwed her face into a determined frown, lowered her head, and stepped to the right-side door, hand out to open it. I stepped over quickly and grabbed her arm and she looked up at me with fierce resentment. But I just held up one finger, then used it to tap my ear. She stared at me with blank hostility, until I leaned forward and placed my ear on the door.

As I listened intently for some kind of telltale sound, Debs put her own ear on the door beside me. As if that had been the cue, we were rewarded by the sound of a thunderous snore from the other side of the door, followed almost immediately by another, softer and higher-pitched.

Debs jerked her head back from the door, and I straightened, too, in time to see her crossing the hall and putting her ear on the door opposite. She listened for only a second and then jerked upright so suddenly that I thought someone had poked her through the keyhole with a knife. But her face, even more frighteningly, was covered with a huge smile. She pointed excitedly at the door and mouthed, *Nicholas!* And then, without waiting to explain what she'd heard that made her think her son was in the room, she shoved her shotgun into my hands, grabbed the doorknob, and pushed the door open.

Brian looked at me with a face full of panic and jumped forward to stop her, but he was too late. Debs was already in the room and moving rapidly across a thick shag carpet. My brother stepped back from the door, glancing about wildly. I followed Debs into the room.

The kids were there, all of them. Cody and Astor were on the nearest bed, sound asleep and snuggled up together. Lily Anne and Nicholas, the babies, were on the other bed. Nicholas was kicking his feet and gurgling, the sound that had clued his mother in that he was here.

And lying next to the two babies, also asleep, was a stocky young woman. She had dark hair and wore a pink flannel nightgown, which I thought was an odd touch for a drug lord's nanny. But it would be far too much to hope that she would

432

remain asleep for long. I could think of only one sure way to keep her quiet while we took the children and ran for home. So as Deborah carefully scooped up Nicholas, I took my fillet knife from its sheath and stepped forward—and an iron hand clamped onto my arm.

"No!" Debs said in a ferocious whisper. "Not like that!"

I looked at her with exasperation. Of all the times to be saddled with empathy, this was one of the worst. One tiny peep from the sleeping woman and we were all dead—but no, I couldn't make her permanently quiet. "Then how?" I whispered back.

She just shook her head and nodded at Cody and Astor. "Wake them," she said softly.

I stepped around Deborah to the bed where Cody and Astor lay sleeping. I leaned the shotgun against the wall beside the bed and put a hand on Astor's shoulder, shaking her gently. She grumbled, frowned, and then opened her eyes. She blinked at me several times, then shot straight up in bed.

"Dexter!" Astor said excitedly.

I waved frantically for her to be quiet, and she bit her lip and nodded. I shook Cody, only twice, and he sat right up and looked at me, fully awake. "Knew you'd come," Cody said, and it was a mark of his excitement that he actually said it loud enough to hear.

"Quick as you can," I told them, soft but urgent. "And be quiet! Up the stairs and out—my boat is tied to the back. Go!" They blinked at me, then at each other, so I said it again. "Go! Now!" and Astor jumped up, grabbed Cody's hand, and the two of them hurried out.

Deborah was standing impatiently in the middle of the room, her pistol in one hand and Nicholas in the other. I moved around her and back to the other bed, where Lily Anne slumbered on. She lay quietly beside the sleeping nanny, sucking fiercely on a pacifier. I bent over with all the quiet care I could muster and slid a hand under the baby's head, then the other one under her bottom. I lifted her slowly, carefully, and I had her nearly halfway up before she grumbled and spit out the pacifier. I held my breath, but Lily Anne settled right back into sleep. I looked down onto the bed to retrieve the fallen pacifier, and saw right away that it would not be possible.

The pacifier had fallen right onto the nanny.

And the nanny was now awake, staring up at me with very wide-open brown eyes.

And then her eyes went wider and she opened her mouth just as wide. I juggled Lily Anne quickly to my left arm and clamped my right hand tightly on the nanny's throat. "*Silencio*," I whispered, sounding as deadly as I could. "*No un sonido*."

Her mouth slapped shut and she nodded

vigorously. I stepped back, keeping my eyes on the nanny, and handed Lily Anne to Deborah. "Take them to the boat," I said.

Deborah tucked Lily Anne into her other arm, but only took a step backward. I glanced at her and saw that she was preparing to argue about running to the boat. Before either of us could say a word, Brian stuck his head in the door. "What is *keeping* you?" he whispered savagely. And then, "Oh, for shit's sake," as he saw the nanny staring at us with gigantic eyes. "She'll scream any second," Brian said, and he stepped toward her, pulling out his knife.

But he was wrong. The nanny didn't scream. She didn't say a word. She looked at my brother approaching with knife at the ready, and calmly reached under her pillow, drew out a revolver, and fired point-blank at Brian.

I could not see where, but I was sure he was hit. Even so, he leaped forward with incredible quickness. Before the woman could fire again, Brian's left hand was pinning her gun to the bed, and his knife was in her throat. She thrashed briefly; I couldn't see what Brian did, but his shoulders bunched with effort and the thrashing stopped abruptly. Brian stood, much slower than he'd jumped onto her, and there was blood all over his hands, the front of his shirt, his pants. Throat wounds can spray horribly, and most of the mess had to be from the nanny. Most of it, but not all.

As Brian straightened he swayed slightly and put a hand to his abdomen, just above and to the right of his navel.

It's funny how the mind works, isn't it? It might have been because I was stunned by the incredibly loud bang of the gunshot in this small room, but whatever the reason, my head was spinning. And for half a second it flashed through my mind that Raul would need a new nanny, and I pictured what the ad would say. *Nanny wanted. Must be comfortable with Spanish, English, and small arms.* But Brian wobbled again and I shoved the thought away.

"Brian," I said.

That's all I got out. From somewhere outside the room I heard a shout, and then another. A gunshot in close quarters is a remarkably effective alarm clock, and the nanny's shot had been enough to wake the other guards. "Debs, go!" I said, and this time she didn't argue. She spun on her heel, a baby under each arm, and sprinted for my boat.

"Brian," I said, moving to his side. "Are you all right?" It was a stupid question, since I knew he'd been shot, which is not "all right" no matter how you care to define it.

But Brian just gave me a pained look. "I believe we may have lost the element of surprise," he said. He grinned feebly, and I was worried enough not to notice what a terrible job he did.

"Can you make a run for it?" I asked him.

"I don't see very many choices," he said. He dropped his knife to the floor and pulled out his pistol. "I think we're going to want that," he said, nodding at Deborah's shotgun. I grabbed it, racked a shot into the chamber, and we hurried out of the room.

The moment we stepped into the hall I was very glad the shotgun was ready to go, because the door opposite, where we'd heard the snores, was inching cautiously open. Without bothering to aim, I pointed the gun at the door and fired.

The noise was deafening, far beyond the sound the nanny's pistol had made. But the result was truly gratifying. A hole the size of a basketball appeared in the door as it slammed partway open and then bounced shut again. I turned and hurried up the stairs.

Brian was already there, kneeling beside the top of the steps, rummaging in the canvas bag of Ee-bahng's toys. He was moving stiffly, obviously in pain, but other than that he looked like he was enjoying himself. "I knew these would come in handy," he said. He pulled out a chunk of something grayish-brown, about the size and shape of a brick, and held it up happily. "Ivan did very good work," he said. He pointed to what looked like a calculator taped to the side. "Simple to use, and very effective." He poked at the calculator with a finger. "Just set the timer, and—"

I heard more noises below, voices raised and clearly urging each other to get up and get 'er done. "Brian," I said, but he ignored me. I crouched down, half-behind my brother, shotgun ready.

"One, two," Brian said. He threw the brick, hard, down into the hall. He turned his head toward me, almost certainly to say, "Three." And he might have said it. But if so, it was drowned out by the enormous roar of an explosion, a huge bright ball of noise and smoke and flame and debris that lifted Brian up and flung him right at me, and I went over backward and into a dark red-tinted place where there was no light and no sound except a terrible painful too-loud ringing noise that wouldn't stop.

And I lay there. At first I couldn't move, and then I just didn't. I couldn't think at all, not even the simplest thought, and apparently you need to think in order to move.

So I just lay quietly. I don't know how long. It could not have been as long as it seemed. Eventually I became aware of something heavy on top of me. Then I had my first thought, which was: *It shouldn't be on top of me.* I let that ring for a while, and then slowly, syllable by syllable, I added: *I should move it off.*

I did. I shoved at the heavy thing. It slid to one side and I sat up. That made my head hurt a lot. For a few more moments I just sat there and clutched my head. I still couldn't hear anything, but if I opened an eye I could see things now. When my head didn't hurt as much I opened my eyes.

I looked at the heavy thing. It looked a lot like it used to be Brian. It wasn't Brian anymore. It didn't move and it didn't breathe. It just lay where I had pushed it and watched the ceiling with calm, wide-open eyes. His face was frozen into a half smile, that same awful awkward terrible fake grin plastered forever now onto that face that looked so much like mine.

I just stared until the word came into my head. *Dead.* Brian was dead. My brother was gone and I would never have another one. *Dead.*

I felt a small rush of wind on my face and I turned to where the stairs had been a few minutes ago. I still couldn't hear anything but the ringing noise, and I couldn't see the stairs anymore. Instead there was just a lot of smoke. A few tiny flames flickered under it, down very low. They were pretty. I watched them for a while. My head was pounding and it felt like it was full of thick dark mud, and I couldn't think of anything at all, not right now, so I just watched the small twitching flames under the great bloom of smoke.

Then something moved out of the smoke.

At first it was just a dim shape in the hall below, a slightly darker shadow in the surrounding darkness. It moved slowly toward me, gradually taking on the shape of a person. Slowly, one careful big cat step at a time, the shape came out of the smoke until I could see what it was.

It was a man. He was average height and build. He had dark black hair and a smooth olive complexion. It didn't make sense, but he was wearing only a pair of dark green boxer shorts. Why would somebody dress like that? I frowned and shook my head to clear it, but it didn't work, and it didn't change the picture. The man still wore nothing but green boxers, and he still came forward. He had several pounds of gold chain around his neck, some of it with large and gaudy gems attached. He looked at me, and then he smiled. That didn't make sense, either. I didn't know this man. Why would he smile?

But slowly, as he took one more tiger-smooth step toward me, another word formed in my brain: *Raul.*

I thought that over. It was hard to do, but I tried, and I thought of something about *Raul.* That word was a name. I knew something about that name, but I didn't know this man. Was it *his* name?

And then he raised his hand. It had a pistol in it, and I remembered, and I knew why he was smiling. And I was right, because as he aimed the pistol right at me his smile got bigger. I watched him, trying to remember what I was supposed to do. I knew I should do something, but with the pounding in my head I couldn't think of it. Say something? Maybe ask him not to shoot me? Or did it involve movement of some kind? So hard to think . . .

Just before the man pulled the trigger, I remembered something else. *Guns can hurt you. Stay away from them.* And at the very last instant I thought, *Run!*

I couldn't run. I was still sitting down. But I rolled to one side and somewhere very far away I heard a tiny muffled *bang!*

Something hit my shoulder very hard, as hard as if somebody had smashed me with a metal baseball bat. I felt my mouth go open, but if I made a sound I couldn't hear it. But the pain did something. It made my brain start to work just a little. I knew I had to move again, get away from the man with the gun, and I began to crawl away from the stairway.

It was very hard. The shoulder that had been hit didn't work. Neither did the arm hanging from it. I pulled myself along the floor with the other arm, and my brain was working even better, because I remembered that I had guns, too. If I could find one I could shoot Raul. That way he couldn't shoot me again.

I raised my head and looked. The big explosion had flung everything back, away from the stairs. Far away, over by the door that led out onto the deck, I saw the heavy canvas bag that had caused so much trouble, and beside it I saw what had to be the shotgun. If I could get that, I could shoot the man.

I crawled harder, faster. But I hadn't gone very far when something grabbed my ankle and yanked and flipped me onto my back.

The man with the gun stood above me, pointing at me. Raul. He was staring down at me like I was a stain on the carpet. He looked very dangerous for somebody wearing only green boxers and a lot of gold chains. And then he smiled again. He squatted down beside me. I could see his mouth moving, but I couldn't hear anything. He cocked his head, waiting for me to say something. When I didn't, he frowned and poked my hurt shoulder with his gun.

The pain was enormous. I opened my mouth and I heard a strange, animal noise coming from far away that matched the shape of my mouth. It was a horrible, inhuman sound, but the man liked it. He poked me again, much harder, and this time he twisted the gun barrel inside my shoulder and I felt something inside where he touched it give way with a kind of *snip* and I made the noise again.

But Raul must have gotten tired of my noises. He stood and stared down at me with a look of complete contempt. He raised the gun and looked at me like he could make me vanish just by staring at me hard. And then he nodded and pointed the gun directly at a spot between my eyes.

And then *he* vanished.

Dimly and distant I felt a huge roaring percussive bang. It slapped the air in the room into a sharp jerking *bump,* and it was so loud that I could hear it too, just a little. It blasted out once and took Raul away and then it stopped. I lay still for a moment, in case it happened again. Before I could decide to move a new person appeared and knelt beside me and I knew who this was right away.

Deborah.

She was holding the shotgun in the crook of her arm and looking at me and moving her mouth urgently, but I still couldn't hear. She put a hand under my shoulder and helped me sit up, still moving her mouth and looking at me with terrible concern. So I finally said, "I'm fine, Debs." It was a strange sensation, knowing I had said something, and feeling the vibrations of it in my throat and my face, and still not actually hearing my own voice. So I added, "I can't hear anything. The explosion."

Debs looked at me intently a moment longer, but then she nodded. She moved her mouth in an exaggerated way and I am pretty sure she said, "Let's go," because she stood up and helped me stand up, too.

For a few seconds it was almost as bad as when

I sat up right after the explosion. Huge and violent waves of dizzy nausea crashed through me, accompanied by a thundering pain in my head and my shoulder. But it didn't last quite as long this time. Debs led me over to the door and I could walk okay. And oddly enough, even though everything inside me seemed to be much too loose and my legs felt tiny and far away, my brain started to work again. I saw the canvas bag beside the door and I remembered one last important thing. "Evidence," I said. "Get rid of evidence." Deborah shook her head and tugged at my arm, and it was the wrong arm, the one that was attached to the shoulder with the bullet in it. I made a sort of dumb spastic *aaaakkh* sound that I couldn't hear and she jumped back.

The shoulder pain didn't last. It dropped down into a kind of dull background agony. I looked at the wound. I was wearing a black shirt, of course, for nighttime stealth, so there wasn't a lot to see other than a surprisingly small hole. But there seemed to be an awful lot of wet shirt around it. I patted it with a hand, gently, and looked. My hand was very, very wet with blood.

To be expected, of course. Gunshot wounds bleed. And when Raul had poked it the second time, I thought he might have broken a vein or something in there. It did seem like rather a lot of blood, though, and I don't like blood. But that could wait until later, and anyway Debs was tugging at my arm again. I shook her hand off. "We have to blow it up," I said. I felt the words in my mouth without hearing them.

Deborah heard them. She shook her head and tried to pull me out the door, but I lurched away, back into the ruined cabin. "There's too much evidence, Debs," I said. "From the kids, from the guns, Brian's body. It connects to you, Deborah. And to me." She was still shaking her head, looking more scared than angry, but I knew I was right. "Have to blow it up," I said. "Or we both go to jail. Kids all alone." I knew I was speaking much too loud, and the words were taking too much work and they felt sort of wrong, too, as if I wasn't quite shaping them properly.

But she clearly understood me, because she shook her head and tugged me toward the door, moving her mouth rapidly and urgently. It didn't matter. I couldn't hear her. "Have to blow it up," I said in my hollow wrong-sounding unheard voice. "Have to." I bent and picked up the canvas bag. For a moment everything spun in bright red circles. But I straightened at last. "Go," I told her. "With the kids. I'll be right there."

Her mouth was still moving as I took the bag and stumbled back toward the stairs, but when I was halfway there I turned to look. Deborah was gone.

I paused for just a moment. The bomb that killed Brian had made a lot of noise, smoke, fire, but it had not made a hole in the boat big enough to sink it. I had to put this bomb in a better place. Someplace where it would take out the whole superyacht. Maybe next to the fuel tanks? But I didn't know where they were, and I wasn't sure I could move around until I found them. And the bag was much heavier than I remembered and I was very tired. And cold. I was suddenly feeling very cold. Why was that? It was a warm Miami night, and I didn't think the air-conditioning could still be working. But a definite chill settled over me, all of me, and some of that bad red-tinged dizziness came back at me. I closed my eyes. It didn't go away, so I opened my eyes again and looked at the stairway ahead. I could just put the bomb down there. It would probably do the job. And it couldn't really be as far away as it looked. I could probably get there in just a few more steps.

I stepped. It was harder than it had been a moment ago. In fact, it was almost impossibly hard. I was so cold. And I needed to rest, just for a moment. I looked for a place to sit. None of the chairs or sofas had stayed upright in the explosion. There was still a built-in plush bench over at the wall. It seemed very far away. I couldn't really go all that way just to sit, could I? No, of course not. But I did want to sit, and right there at my feet, there was the floor. It was still flat. I could sit there.

I did. I sat and closed my eyes and tried to find the strength to get up and finish it. *It isn't that hard, Dexter.* Just stand up, set the bomb where it will do the job, and go back to my boat. Simple.

Except that it wasn't. Nothing was simple now. Come to think of it, things hadn't been simple for some time. Not for Dumbo Dexter, the Ninja Nerd who gets everybody close to him killed—Rita and Jackie and now Brian and probably Debs and the kids in just a minute or two. And when things are almost all wrapped up nicely he gets himself blown up and shot. And now he doesn't have to do anything at all but put a little bitty bomb in the right place and set the timer and go home . . . and he can't even do that. It just seemed so hard to get up and do anything. I couldn't do even the simplest things anymore—hadn't been able to this whole time, ever since I let Jackie get killed. And Rita, too. Dead because of me, my incompetent empty-headed fumbling dumbness. Dead, along with my whole beautiful simple life . . . dead just like Brian. Killed by my bumbling thumb-brained delusions that I was smart and I could do things. Killed because I actually couldn't do things anymore. Couldn't think at all. And now I couldn't even walk three or four more steps to set the bomb so I could go home. And maybe find somebody to make the gunshot wound stop bleeding so much. Because it really was bleeding too much. I was soaked now, all along the whole front of me, and I didn't like it.

All right, enough. Up and at 'em, Dexter. And if there's no "up" left, then just crawl over there and do it. Set the timer, toss the bomb down the stairs, crawl back to the boat. One, two, three. So simple even a dolt like me could do it. Ready?

One: I reached in the flap of the canvas bag. It was still open from when Brian had used it, so I didn't need to unzip it, which was a very good thing, since I didn't think I could. I felt around and my fingers closed on something that seemed about right. I pulled out a big square shiny thing. It had the same kind of timer that Brian's bomb had, but this brick was much bigger. More than enough to do the job. But the timer was throbbing in and out of focus, and the red numbers kept blending with the red background that was pulsing back over me again. That wasn't good. I frowned and stared at it so it knew I was serious, and it settled down. I punched in zero, zero, five. Five minutes. Plenty of time.

Step two: A deep breath, and then I crawled forward on my one good arm, pushing the bomb ahead of me. No scientific placement needed, not with this great big baby. It wasn't necessary, and it wouldn't happen anyway, not with Dexter the Doofus on the job. Still, several feet away I felt myself running down. Not good. Have to save something for my escape. Escaping very important. I tried to stand up. Very hard—I was so heavy! I would really need to go on a diet when this was over. But I was still holding the entire canvas bag—another stupid blunder. I let go of it and worked my way all the way up to a standing position. I rested for a minute. Just one little minute, just resting—and I remembered the bomb. Now I only had four minutes. *Still have to escape.*

I leaned forward and threw the bomb. It was a very feeble throw. Of course. But it bounced on the top step—and then, happily for us all, tipped over and rolled downstairs. At the bottom it clattered onto something that went *bong*. That didn't seem right. I staggered forward one more step and peeked down.

The fire had picked up a little, but that meant the smoke was not quite as thick. I could see a big hole where the carpeted deck had been. The first bomb had taken out the deck, and below it there was something metal, something that went *bong* when you dropped a big bomb on it. I blinked stupidly for a moment, swaying a little. Then I thought, *Fuel tank . . . ?* Must be. Fuel tanks go bong, and then *boom*. Bingo. *Very good, Dexter. Very, very good.*

I stood there congratulating myself, and then I thought, *Why stand to celebrate? I'll sit here and relax and celebrate at my leisure.*

I sat. Not as gracefully as I would have liked.

Rather too fast and awkward, truth be told. There seemed to be a few control elements offline. Legs all wobbly, vision in and out, one arm just hanging and the other made of cardboard . . . But I sat, feeling pleased. I hadn't hurt myself. And I had put the bomb on the fuel tank. Steps one and two done. *Good work, Dexter. Not bad for an incompetent meathead. Because what about step number three, Oh, King of the Dim?*

Three. That's right. Step three had involved going somewhere, hadn't it? I hoped it would be better lit than this. It was getting awfully dark in here—and even colder, too! Why was that? Why did I have to sit here in a cold place with this icky red all over me? I could feel it under me now, too, sort of a frigid squishiness that I did not like at all. Why did it remind me of something very bad? When had I ever been this cold and this covered with icky-sticky red before? Why did it seem like—

Mommy was just over there. I could see her face over there and she was somehow hiding and peeking up over the . . . things—just her face showing, her unwinking unblinking unmoving face. And even when I called her really loud she didn't answer. . . .

"Mommy," I said. I couldn't hear it, but I felt the word on my lips. Why did I think of Mommy now? Why here on this battered billionaire's boat that was about to go boom? Why think of

Mommy at all, who I had not even known except for seeing her over there unmoving, and she hadn't even answered me even

now that I saw her. Why didn't she even wink? Make some sign that she heard me, that this was all a trick, and soon we would get up and get out of here and go home and be with Biney. But Mommy did nothing at all, like she wasn't even there, and without Mommy I was alone, sitting here in this deep puddle of awful nasty wet sticky horrible red stuff and I didn't want to sit here, didn't want to sit in that, not here on the carpet, not again, not wait and wait in the cold sticky awful until finally the door would open and Harry would come in and lift me out and take me away and the whole thing would begin again in its endless cycle of brainless clueless helpless hope-less Dim and Dark and Dopey Dexter blood blood BLOOD

Not again.

I opened my eyes. I was still sitting on the ruined wet carpet. And I didn't want to be, not just sitting, not here in the deep puddle of sticky wet while silently somewhere close the timer ticked—

Up. Up. I had to get up, get out of this—and this time I would not wait for Harry. I would get up and get out of it by myself. Do everything different, better, *my* way, so maybe this time it wouldn't all turn to shit on me. This time everything would be different, better, smarter, if I could only get myself up and away from the little cold room and go home where things were better, nicer, warmer, brighter—

Somehow I got up. I stood and swayed and everything was very clear somehow and I thought, *How much time is left? How long until the big bang?* It couldn't be much. I had to hurry.

But hurry was not on the menu, not tonight, not in Dexter's Diner for the Dim and Dopey. I tried, but I didn't really seem able to do more than stand and stagger slowly.

I flop-foot my way over to the side of the room and I flounder toward the door, sliding along the walls and windows and furniture and hearing a terrible soft insistent ticking of the timer in my head and finally feeling the doorknob in my hand, the horribly stiff impossible-to-turn door-knob. And somehow, so slowly, so impossibly brick-fingered, I open it and feel the frigid night breeze on my face, like a blast of punishing cold wind, so strong I almost go backward and I have to lean both arms on the wall again and work my way out and then around the corner to the railing, and I lurch over and lean on that and I know I have gone the wrong way, around the side instead of straight back to my boat, but there is nothing to lean on back that way and I need to lean and so I look over, look back, look for my boat and Deborah and I don't see her.

And I try to turn to look back and I can't and my head rolls over instead and I am looking up, into the endless black night above, in its on-and-on forever darkness—

—except no. It isn't darkness, not all of it, not at all. Right there, right above me, floating over me in its cool and welcome glow. There it is. Dexter's last friend, last family, last fond familiar face. Old Mr. Moon, come to watch and whisper soft and silvery songs, the music of Dark Joy, the sound track of Dexter's Life, the beautiful symphony of shadows that follows me into every night of need, that lights me now in its soft and urgent beams as it has forever before, singing sweet nothings to the tune of impending snicker-snee—

—but different now, different tonight. Different notes and a chorus I have never heard, swelling up in the soft and shining light of its distant knowing smile. And not so distant now, not tonight. Closer than ever before. Much closer, and singing a new refrain, not of sly encouraging but of welcome, calling out in sweet and clear harmonies, *Come home, Dear Dexter, come home. . . .*

The beautiful silver song is shattered by an awful noise, a mechanical cow-sounding blat that cuts through the lilt and tease of that welcoming melody, smashes through so loud that even I can hear it, and even in my halfway-home head I know what it is: a boat horn. My boat horn. And with a wonderful rush of insight I realize what this means—Deborah is calling me, pulling me away from the beautiful welcoming silver darkness, trying to bring me away and back to a very different home. . . .

But no. Not home, not now. Not if I don't move. The bomb, the boat—I must not linger and listen to the wrong song, and I try to straighten up and stand and I can't and I hear the horn again and I hear the terrible soft *tick, tick, tick* louder than ever and I know that any second now the fireball will come and lift me up and out of everything into the deep dark forever nothing and I am not ready for that. Not even with the moon crooning its mother's summons. Not yet, not now. Not Dexter. No. And so slowly, far beyond effort and pain and almost everything that has ever been, slowly I straighten up. And slowly, still holding on to the rail, I put one foot over and look.

I can just see my boat bobbing easily over there, at an almost safe distance that seems so very far. I look down. The dark water is there, surface rippled with wind and mocking moonlight, and if I can just get down there, get into the water, I can swim to my boat and everything will be all right, and so slowly, carefully, every movement dragging like it was pulled backward by lead weights, somehow I get both feet over the railing and I wave to Debs so far away over there and I make a huge idiot sound to let her know to come get me and I know she will because family is so important no matter what and she sees that now I am sure of it and then I am over and falling and even as I fall the water seems so impossibly far away—and so dark, so deep and dark—

—and then there is a warped and rippled picture of the moon with its happy savage face that morphs into Me rushing up at Me and I hit Me with a soundless crash and Me breaks apart still soundless into a million bright red shattered shards of moon glow that slowly bend their darkening beams around me as I fall through the flickers of light-dark-light until the last of the cool silver light fades away to welcome shadows and now there is cool and comforting peace and I start up again, up into the blackness that whirls me away to the happy welcome of the moon's dark side and I fall up and in and away and the wonderful chorus of silence swells up as I rise up and up and I feel like I am home again at last as I slide down, down through the beautiful shadowy silence and into the cool and welcoming moon-Mommy Darkness at last and—

ABOUT THE AUTHOR

Jeff Lindsay is the *New York Times*–bestselling author and creator of the Dexter novels, most recently *Dexter's Final Cut*. He lives in South Florida with his wife and three daughters. His novels are the inspiration for the hit Showtime and CBS series *Dexter*.

Center Point Large Print
600 Brooks Road / PO Box 1
Thorndike, ME 04986-0001 USA

(207) 568-3717

US & Canada:
1 800 929-9108
www.centerpointlargeprint.com